Praise for *The Florabama Ladies'*
Auxiliary & Sewing Circle

"Lois Battle is one of those fearless novelists who can take on any subject and make it distinctly her own. *The Florabama Ladies' Auxiliary & Sewing Circle* is a magical and surprising tour of a Deep South I had no idea existed. It's the best novel she's ever written."
—Pat Conroy

"*The Florabama Ladies' Auxiliary & Sewing Circle* is full of warmth, humor, and atmosphere, with characters you'd like to hijack off the page so you can hang around with them."
—Lorna Landvik, author of *Patty Jane's House of Curl*

"*The Florabama Ladies' Auxiliary & Sewing Circle* is stitched together flawlessly with humor and depth. Lois Battle wraps you in the rich fabric of women's lives."
—Lynne Hinton, author of *Friendship Cake*

"If there's a woman over forty who can't recognize herself in at least one of the characters of *The Florabama Ladies' Auxiliary & Sewing Circle*, I'll eat a magnolia bud. Lois Battle's new novel covers the Deep South from Atlanta to the Alabama coast, with women you'll love and hate, dealing with circumstances that challenge the best of us."
—*The Dallas Morning News*

"A rich tale of friendship among women, their determination, achievements and mishaps. . . . You may find yourself in it, and it will surely make you laugh."
—*St. Petersburg Times*

"This is just the kind of book you'd like to take onto the porch of a clapboard house, to read curled up in a wicker chair with glass of iced tea at your side."
—*Houston Chronicle*

"This book is so full of good stuff it's hard to know where to start. It has a feel of *Places in the Heart*, a little of *Norma Rae*, and maybe a touch of *Fried Green Tomatoes*. But [it] stands on its own as an intelligent, poignant, funny, wistful novel."
—*Richmond Times-Dispatch*

PENGUIN BOOKS

THE FLORABAMA LADIES'
AUXILIARY & SEWING CIRCLE

Lois Battle is the author of seven other novels including *Bed and Breakfast*, *Storyville*, *War Brides*, *A Habit of the Blood*, and *The Past is Another Country*. She lives in Beaufort, South Carolina.

The
Florabama
Ladies' Auxiliary
&
Sewing Circle

Lois Battle

PENGUIN BOOKS

PENGUIN BOOKS
Published by the Penguin Group
Penguin Putnam Inc., 375 Hudson Street, New York, New York 10014, U.S.A.
Penguin Books Ltd, 80 Strand, London WC2R 0RL, England
Penguin Books Australia Ltd, 250 Camberwell Road, Camberwell, Victoria 3124, Australia
Penguin Books Canada Ltd, 10 Alcorn Avenue, Toronto, Ontario, Canada M4V 3B2
Penguin Books India (P) Ltd, 11 Community Centre,
Panchsheel Park, New Delhi – 110 017, India
Penguin Books (N.Z.) Ltd, Cnr Rosedale and Airborne Roads,
Albany, Auckland, New Zealand
Penguin Books (South Africa) (Pty) Ltd, 24 Sturdee Avenue,
Rosebank, Johannesburg 2196, South Africa

Penguin Books Ltd, Registered Offices: Harmondsworth, Middlesex, England

First published in the United States of America by Viking Penguin,
a member of Penguin Putnam Inc. 2001
Published in Penguin Books 2002

1   3   5   7   9   10   8   6   4   2

Grateful acknowledgement is made for permission to reprint excerpts from the following
copyrighted works:
"It All Depends on You" by B. G. DeSylva, Lew Brown, and Ray Henderson. © 1926
DeSylva, Brown, & Henderson, Inc.; © renewed. Rights for extended renewal term in U.S.
controlled by Chappell & Co., Ray Henderson Music Company, and Stephen Ballentine
Music. All rights reserved. Used by permisssion of Warner Bros. Publications U. S. Inc.,
Miami, Florida.
"Looking at You" by Cole Porter. © 1929 (renewed) Warner Bros. Inc. All rights re-
served. Used by permission of Warner Bros. Publications U. S. Inc., Miami, Florida.

Publisher's Note
This is a work of fiction. Names, characters, places, and incidents either are the product
of the author's imagination or are used fictitiously, and any resemblance to actual persons,
living or dead, business establishments, events, or locales is entirely coincidental.

THE LIBRARY OF CONGRESS HAS CATALOGED
THE HARDCOVER EDITION AS FOLLOWS:
Battle, Lois.
The Florabama Ladies' Auxiliary & Sewing Circle / Lois Battle.
p.   cm.
ISBN 0-670-89469-9 (hc.)
ISBN 0 14 20.0036 1 (pbk.)
I. Title: Florabama Ladies' Auxiliary and Sewing Circle.   II. Title.
PS3552.A8325 F58 2001
813'.54—dc21   00-047740

Printed in the United States of America
Set in Simoncini Garamond / Designed by Francesca Belanger

*D*edication

Shirley M. Carson
1912–1998
"The best and the brightest"

Louis J. Roempke, M.D.
1933–2000
"His life was gentle; and the elements
So mix'd in him that Nature might stand up
And say to all the world, *This was a man!*"

Acknowledgments

To friends who, against the odds, have always backed me up, buoyed me up, and tried to smarten me up: Frank Orbach; Lynn Schwartz; Kenneth L. Geist; the Miscreant Maidens of the Tuesday Night Club; Will Balk; Bethany ("REDNECK HEAVEN") Bultman; Thelma Abrams—and the women, especially Rose-Ann Tuck, whose experiences in the mills of Alabama gave me the seed from which this story grew.

The
Florabama
Ladies' Auxiliary
&
Sewing Circle

Chapter I

*T*he good-bye hugs and kisses were over. As she got into the car, her stepmother, Elice, repeated her injunctions to drive safely, take care, and call as soon as she was settled in, while her daughter, Gervaise, reached in through the window and patted the head of the puppy settled on the backseat. Her father, the Duke, came to the driver's side, bent to whisper, "Don't worry, you'll do fine," then stood back and whacked the hood of the car to send her on her way. Moving slowly down the circular drive, she stopped before turning into the street and looked back to the portico. Elice and Gervaise had already started into the house, but the Duke still stood, one arm raised in farewell. She gave a wave before turning onto the broad-lawned, tree-lined street.

The late-summer sunset was coral and gold, with fiery streaks of red as she gunned the car onto Interstate 65, heading south toward the Gulf. Now she was really on her way. "Florabama, here I come!" she said loud enough to make the puppy bark. But once she was beyond Birmingham's outskirts, clipping along at a brisk seventy, her enthusiasm wilted, and her thoughts reverted to her usual concerns. She added up bills, didn't like the totals, obsessively added them up again, only to reach the same totals. She'd once heard someone say that money was like sex: If you had it, your mind was free for other things, but if you didn't have it, you thought about it all the time. But even when she'd been a nineteen-year-old virgin, sex had never dominated her thoughts the way money did now.

She barely noticed when, more than an hour later, lightning cracked the horizon. Silver pinpricks of rain jumped off the hood of the Volvo that she'd managed to save from the bankruptcy. She rolled up the window as fast as she could but still got spattered. Another flash of lightning, a clap of thunder, then the rain came down as though a hole had been punched in the clouds. The puppy started to whimper. "Don't be a baby," she said, more to herself than to him. "It'll be over in a minute."

Easing into the slow lane, she turned the windshield wipers on high and set the cruise control at forty-five. The driver in front of her, apparently too dumb to realize that driving too slow was as dangerous as driving too fast, was crawling along at thirty. She swung back into the middle lane. First one truck, then another thundered by in the fast lane, honking and sending up spumes of water. Heart pounding, she swerved back into the slow lane. Winds of hurricane strength made the car shudder. Another streak of lightning cracked the sky. Mother Nature was throwing a real hissy fit. "It'll be over in a minute," she said again.

Half an hour later it still hadn't let up. The windshield wipers slapped at the relentless torrents, drowning out the CD. Her hands were cramped from gripping the wheel, the muscles in her neck felt like gristle, and her eyes couldn't seem to adjust to the darkness. Another trucker with a death wish roared past. The Volvo shuddered. The puppy continued to howl. "All right. All right," she said, barely able to hear her voice above the storm. "I give." She would have to stop for the night.

As soon as she made the decision, the exit and motel signs, plentiful until now, seemed to disappear, and it took another fifteen minutes before she saw the golden arches of a McDonald's and a purple neon motel sign up ahead. Flooring the accelerator, she swung off the highway, climbed a steep rise to an overpass, squinted through the downpour at the signs, made a right onto a rutted side road, then bumped and splashed into a desolate parking lot. She turned off the motor. The puppy stopped keening, and even though the rain pounded the roof like the Rockettes dancing on tin, it seemed strangely quiet. She rested her head on the steering wheel and closed her eyes. Here she was, on her way to the first real job of her life, stranded in front of a run-down motel off Interstate 65. What a beginning.

Opening her eyes, she reached for her purse and tilted her head to see the neon sign. One of the letters had been burned out, so it said S EEPYTIME instead of SLEEPYTIME. She'd never stayed in such a seedy place. In fact, she'd never stayed alone in any motel or hotel. With a punch-drunk giggle, she reached for the door handle, said, "Keep calm," in the direction of the backseat, and made a dash for it.

A gust of wind slammed the motel door behind her, and she stood, dripping and breathing in a strong smell of curry. A beaded curtain parted, and a middle-aged woman emerged. She was dressed in a pink and orange sari, bracelets jangling on pudgy wrists, a single long braid draped over her shoulder, and food pouched her cheeks. After swallowing, she said, with inappropriate cheeriness, "Nasty weather. Veddy nasty."

Too tired to mask her surprise, she asked, "Do you have a vacancy?" though the lone truck and single late-model Oldsmobile in the parking lot already answered that question.

The woman studied her with slightly bulging but warmly curious eyes, touched the plastic badge pinned to her left breast that said, MRS. V. PATEL, MANAGER, then asked, "Single?"

She almost said, "Not yet"—the divorce wouldn't be final for another six months—before she got out, "Yes. Just me."

"Smoking or nonsmoking?"

She hadn't smoked for over a decade but, feeling a craving for a Marlboro, said no with quick defensiveness.

"This will be thirty-three fifty plus tax." Picking something from her teeth, Mrs. Patel added, in a *Masterpiece Theatre* accent, "We have also on offer movies in the rooms and"—she waved in the direction of a card table holding a pot of tarlike coffee, a bowl of bananas, and packages of cornflakes—"continental breakfast. Cash or credit card?"

"Credit card." Easy enough to find the MasterCard since she'd cut up all the others. She slid it across the counter. Mrs. Patel pushed a registration form toward her and she began to fill it in. NAME: Bonnie Duke Cullman. Retaining her maiden name, Duke, had been more an expression of family pride than a feminist gesture, but she was glad she'd kept it. Soon she'd be just Bonnie Duke again, which seemed like her real identity. ADDRESS: She put down the address of her Atlanta house though, strictly speaking, she no longer lived there. She hadn't met the Japanese executive who'd leased it and was scheduled to move in later that week, but the real estate lady had assured her that Mr. Hyodo had been charmed by both her decorating and gardening skills. She pictured him moving through her sun room, wife and children following at an appropriate distance, contemplating her plants with Zen serenity. BUSINESS AFFILIATION: None yet, but soon. LICENSE NUMBER OF VEHICLE: She'd been driving the Volvo for four years but was damned if she could remember. Looking through the window at the slashing rain, she said, lamely, "I should know it, but I can't seem to recall . . ."

"This is O.K. Sometimes when we are . . ." Mrs. Patel turned her palms up and rolled her eyes, mimicking confusion. "Just please to show me your driver's license."

Bonnie didn't think it was customary to require a driver's license but she was too tired to argue. Mrs. Patel studied it, grunting softly: That's me, Bonnie Duke Cullman, born in 1950, five feet six inches, 135 pounds (all right, it's more like 150 now), eyes blue (at one time her husband, Devoe, had said they were cornflower blue), hair blond (though not so blond as when I went to the hairdresser every week), and I know I look older than I do in the photo, but it's been a very tough year.

"Have you many belongings in your car?" Mrs. Patel asked.

The car was packed to the gills. Clothes, pots and pans, dishes, the computer her daughter, Gervaise, had insisted she take so they could E-mail each other, a box with "Important Papers" scrawled on the top (who knew what was in that?), framed family photos (Grandma and Grandpa Duke in farm clothes; her parents' wedding photo; one Devoe had taken of her sitting near the pool in their first house, two-year-old Gervaise in her lap, five-year-old Eugene at her side), a scarlet cyclamen plant she couldn't bear to part with, a line drawing of embracing lovers she'd taken from the bedroom, a coffee grinder, five pounds of coffee beans, three boxes of Godiva chocolates (admittedly an extravagance, but who knew if she'd be able to get such things in Florabama?), and boxes and boxes of books. Her well-worn Jane Austens, leather-bound classics she'd bought for the home library but had never had time to read, college sociology texts (probably useless) she'd pulled out of the attic, a clutch of self-help books given by well-meaning friends (how to cope, how to rebuild your life after divorce, how to manage your finances) that she couldn't bear to read but didn't want to throw away, May Sarton's *Journal of a Solitude,* and a blank journal she'd promised herself she'd write in daily. "Yes," she admitted, "I do have rather a lot of things in the car."

Mrs. Patel shouted, "Parvati!" swiped the MasterCard through the machine, then turned her head and called again, "Parvati! Quickly! To help the lady with her bags."

A teenage girl wearing the international costume of youth (jeans, T-shirt, and running shoes), her black hair frizzed in an unbecoming perm, wandered out carrying a plate of rice and curry.

"Sorry to interrupt your supper," Bonnie said.

"Have I not told you that food is not acceptable in reception?"

Mrs. Patel snapped, then, reverting to the *Masterpiece Theatre* accent: "This is my daughter, Parvati."

"My name's Patti," the girl said.

"Parvati," Mrs. Patel insisted, "the lady is having many things in her car. Please to help her bring them to her room."

Parvati sighed. "Ma, there's a hurricane watch on. I mean, who's gonna want to burgle a car in a storm like this?"

"The lady has been driving alone through the storm, and she is most distressed," Mrs. P. explained with murderous calm.

"If you put her in room 101 and she pulls in under the lights, her stuff will be perfectly safe," Parvati reasoned.

Not wanting to be part of a domestic dispute, Bonnie looked past them to see an American flag pinned alongside a Confederate flag and a calendar from Vandu's Ethnic Grocery. The calendar featured a four-armed baby elephant wearing a tiara and garlands of flowers. Next to the calendar was a NO PETS!!! sign with exclamation marks in red Magic Marker to show it meant business.

"She's right," Bonnie said quickly. "There's nothing really valuable in the car. I'm sure it'll be fine," and, gesturing toward the calendar, asked: "Isn't that Ganesha?"

Surprised, Mrs. Patel said, "You know the Hindu gods?"

"Not really. Just a class on comparative religions back in college."

Parvati laughed. "I mean, like, who prays to an elephant?"

"And you, Miss Patti," Mrs. Patel asked with sly sarcasm, "you believe in what? Television and Nike shoes and hip-hop?"

"No need to unload the car," Bonnie insisted. Her desire to escape was almost as strong as her desire to get to a bathroom. "Matter of fact, I want to pop over to McDonald's and get a bite to eat."

Parvati shrugged and said, "Whatever," with Valley Girl indifference and left.

Mrs. Patel took a key from the board behind her. "Room 101. To be located to your right, under the brightest lights. My daughter is probably correct. Your belongings will be safe."

"I'm sure. Thank you."

Bonnie took the key. Mrs. Patel sighed heavily, turned her bracelets, and said, "You send them to school and you hope . . . But these things you know, because you are a mother." Bonnie's mouth opened to ask how she knew that, but Mrs. Patel smiled, saying, "Of course I am aware that Ganesha is a symbol only. But he is a good symbol. He is the remover of obstacles."

"Yes." Bonnie moved to the door. "I can see where, with that trunk—"

"Not just physical obstacles." Mrs. Patel's dark eyes fixed her with a meaningful stare. "Obstacles of the mind. Sometimes when we are in difficulty, old habits of the mind are the worst obstacles." She tapped her forehead, then rested her hand on her heart, bowing her head in what seemed to be a blessing. "May he come to your aid."

Bonnie flipped on the light, slid the safety lock into place, and wiped a strand of wet hair from her face. She hadn't expected the Ritz-Carlton (which was the last place she'd stayed) but this . . . The walls were Pepto-Bismol pink; the floor was carpeted with bright green AstroTurf; a print of a Paris street scene hung, slightly askew, between twin beds covered with shiny plaid spreads. The air conditioner clattered, TV sounds leaked from the adjoining room, and the reek of disinfectant mingled with smells coming from the McDonald's bag she was clutching.

The puppy, zipped into her jacket, nosed the paper bag, squirming so energetically she felt as though she were pregnant with twins. "You get us thrown out, and I swear I'll throttle you," she warned, dropping him onto the floor. "Wasn't it enough that I took you behind McDonald's and got soaked while you nosed around as though you were sniffing flowers before you peed?" The puppy wobbled toward one of the beds and wiggled under it. Bonnie dropped her purse, took off her jacket, tossed the paper bag and a fistful of change on the dresser, and made a beeline for the bathroom, unzipping her jeans as she went.

Ah, what relief. She flushed the toilet and thought she'd better call her friend Cass to tell her she wouldn't be arriving tonight. She'd take a shower, feed the dog. . . . Looking at the pitted tub, paper bath mat, and raggedy towels, she decided to put off the shower until she got to Cass's place.

Passing the dresser, she saw the bills and coins she'd tossed onto it. She smoothed out a dollar and stared at good ol' George, stiff with integrity and wooden teeth, then turned it over, looked at the pyramid with the eye in the sawed-off top, and wondered what ANNUIT COEPTIS and NOVUS ORDO SECLORUM meant. Strange how you handled money every day and never really looked at it. Money was spooky, both real and unreal. As a material substance it could be metal, paper, or plastic, but it was so much more. It was the big green, stash, gelt, wampum, bread, loot. There was hush money, slush money, and dirty money. Money could talk. Money made ends meet. Money made things happen. Until last year she'd rarely thought about it. Because until last year there'd always been enough. More than enough.

When she was in first grade, one of her schoolmates had told her that her daddy, the Duke, was rich, but when she'd asked him, he'd laughed and said no, they were just "comfortable." She'd liked that word. It was how she felt when she snuggled down under the comforter. It was what her mother said about her favorite shoes. Other things the Duke had taught her about money were that it wasn't polite to talk about it, that buying things you didn't really need was just showing off (bad), but giving it to people who didn't have much was called charity (good). These precepts had stayed with her into adult life. Devoe had very different attitudes about money, and this in fact was the source of most of their arguments. Devoe didn't just want to keep up with the Joneses; he wanted to outdistance them. He was, to her mind, extravagant, even ostentatious. He couldn't go shopping without buying something, though she often had to nudge him about charitable contributions. But maintaining marital harmony required a certain detachment, so she'd bitten her tongue when he'd overspent. After all, he earned the money, and he was openhanded with her. So, apart from saying that he was setting a bad example for the children, she usually backed off. Until last year she'd chosen to think of their differences as a matter of style rather than character. Until last year, if someone had said "bankrupt," the first thing that would have come to her mind would have been a game of Monopoly.

She still couldn't believe that Devoe had filed for bankruptcy, still couldn't grasp the fact that they were broke. When the children had gone off to college, she'd thought about getting a job or maybe an advanced degree, but she was busy with the house and the social activities that helped Devoe's business. She enjoyed being a queen bee of Atlanta charities, raising money for everything from string quartets to summer camps for ghetto kids. She'd believed she was doing important work, and she still believed it, but as Cass had so pointedly said, "Volunteer means anything that isn't important enough to get paid for." After what she privately thought of as the Crash, when Devoe had moved out and his lawyers pressured her to put the house up for sale, she'd desperately needed a job. But who would hire her? A photo spread in *Southern Living* and a commendation from the City Council didn't constitute a résumé. What did a middle-aged woman with a sociology degree from Agnes Scott and one job reference (twenty-five years old) for a six-month stint in the Department of Social Services have to offer?

Nikki Parrish, a friend from the country club who owned an upscale children's boutique, had given her a part-time job at eight dollars an hour plus commission, but after a month of selling imported teddy bears and three-hundred-dollar christening gowns to wealthy customers, many of whom she knew, she'd thrown in the towel.

She'd applied for a position as arts program administrator in the schools, but the grant money had fallen through.

She'd gone to the offices of the liberal Republican representative her volunteer work (and Devoe's check) had helped to elect, but when she'd asked the man's aide for a paying job, he'd looked at her as though she'd asked him to donate a kidney for a transplant.

Her friend Cass had come to the rescue. Returning to Alabama after years of working abroad, Cass now taught composition and what she called Dumbbell English at Marion Hawkins Community College in Florabama, a small town in the southern part of the state. Cass had told her that the college was looking to hire a coordinator for a new program for displaced homemakers. She'd laughed at the irony (she was a displaced homemaker herself), and her heart sank when she saw the job requirements (a master's degree, computer skills, recent experience, and references), but at Cass's insistence, she'd applied. She'd been dumbfounded when, six weeks ago, she'd got a call asking her to come to Florabama for an interview. She was so sure she wasn't a serious contender that Cass had to talk her into driving down, saying that at the least they'd have a chance to visit. Then—miracle of miracles!—the college had offered her the job. She'd summoned up her courage and accepted, but now that she was actually on her way she was sick with fear.

The rain was still pelting down. She dropped the dollar bill onto the dresser and, hearing the puppy whimper, unwrapped the Quarter Pounder and sat on the bed. Instantly alert, the puppy lifted the skirt of the bedspread and wiggled, flat-bellied, tail wagging, toward her. Under other circumstances even she, not really a dog lover, would have been charmed. She'd had a dog once, a Lab called Rustler, who'd been hit by a car just weeks after her mother had died of cancer. She was eight at the time and felt secretly guilty because she missed Rustler even more than she missed her mother. The Duke, with that perfidious adult sensibility that believed lost loves could be replaced, had asked if she wanted another dog, but she'd adamantly refused. Less than a year later, without asking if she wanted another mother, he'd married Elice.

She tore off a piece of hamburger, watched the puppy wolf it down, took a bite herself, then sprawled across the bed and reached for the phone. She hated to tell Cass, who, as a Peace Corps volunteer, had survived drought, floods, and famine in obscure African villages, that she couldn't cope with a storm on I-65, but there it was. Ever since they'd been roommates at Agnes Scott, Cass had been the adventurous one. She'd challenged teachers, worn jeans instead of skirts, smoked pot, and ditched classes to go to peace marches in Washington. So it was no surprise when, in their junior year, Cass's adviser had asked, ever so politely, if she might not be happier in another environment. Cass had wholeheartedly agreed, telling Bonnie that she needed intellectual stimulation, challenge, and excitement, none of which was to be found in a southern women's college where "a bunch of DLDs [daddy's little darlings] are working for their MRS. degrees." Knowing that might be an apt, if harsh, description of herself, Bonnie'd wondered why she and Cass were such good friends. Sure, she'd loaned Cass clothes and money and signed her in on the dorm roster when she was gone overnight, but the fact that they were both passionate readers who talked about fictional characters as though they were real people had been their strongest bond.

Saying good-bye when Cass had gone off to the University of Chicago, they'd wept and hugged each other with the delicious emotional indulgence of teenage girls, and as they hefted the suitcases (one of which Bonnie had given to her) into the hallway, Cass had said, "And please, please, don't marry Devoe. He's not nearly good enough for you." If the warning had come from another girl, she'd have put it down to envy. Devoe was good-looking, popular, ambitious, and already had his degree in business, what most other girls, admitting their principal occupation was fishing for a husband, would call a catch. But since it came from Cass, she'd taken it as a sweetly prejudiced compliment, the sort of protective remark one's mother, if she were alive, might make. But there wasn't any question that she'd marry Devoe because though she'd never confessed it, even to Cass, she'd already gone to bed with him.

In the intervening years she and Cass had rarely seen each other, but they'd never lost touch. Cass, to her credit, had never said anything negative about Devoe. Even when things had gone horribly wrong, when Atlanta friends had offered Bonnie unsolicited sympathy of the "All men are bastards" and "Let me know if I can do anything" variety before they stopped calling, Cass had been the only one who'd actually *done* anything. She'd simply announced that she was coming to Atlanta; then she'd come. She'd stayed for a week, fixing meals, fielding phone calls, making countless pots of coffee and more than a few pitchers of Bloody Marys. Usually voluble and opinionated, she'd reined herself in, listening and questioning. When Bonnie'd wondered aloud if she looked as bad as she felt, Cass, perhaps too honestly, had said she could do with some pampering. Over Bonnie's objections, she'd made, and prepaid for, appointments with a hairstylist and a massage therapist, saying Bonnie could consider them her birthday and Christmas gifts.

The phone rang a couple of times before Cass picked up with "Bonnie, is that you? I heard on the news that a major storm was raging across the middle of the state."

"Yeah. One of the worst I've ever seen. Hit 'bout an hour out of Birmingham, and I just had to stop. I wanted to leave yesterday, but Elice pressured me into staying for the Sunday dinner."

"So where are you now?"

"Damned if I know. Some seedy motel just off the highway. It's the strangest place. When I checked in, this Indian woman in a sari came out and looked at me like she was going to tell my fortune."

"Yeah. Lot of Indians in the motel business down here now."

"I hope you don't think I'm a wimp for stopping, but it's really a bad storm."

"Not to worry. I didn't make a soufflé. I forgot you were stopping off in Birmingham."

"The Duke wanted to see me, and I left Gervaise there. The Duke and Elice are going to drive her up to Brown."

"So you couldn't talk her into transferring to a local college?"

"She said she'd rather die first. And Daddy offered to pick up the tuition tab."

"Wouldn't he just."

"He's paying for Eugene's last year too. I don't like it, but I'm not in a position to argue."

"Elice give you a hard time?"

"No mor'n usual. She just pulled me into the pantry and laid a guilt trip on me. Said the Duke couldn't admit it, but he's worried sick about my going off alone, so maybe I should just give up on the idea of working and move in with them. 'Course she'd never make the offer if she thought there was a chance of my taking her up on it."

Cass laughed. "If you moved in with them, you'd pull a Lizzie Borden inside of a week."

"Desperate as I am, I'd never even consider it. I told her, 'I'm not going to Iraq, Elice. I'm going to work at a community college in southern Alabama.' And then she tells me that she's worried about my keeping the job because she knows I'm not really qualified."

"What a piece of work! Of course you'll be able to handle it. It's not like you faked a license in brain surgery."

"I don't know. Closer I get, the more frightened I feel."

"You'll be fine. We'll talk about all this when you get here. Mark fixed linguine with clam sauce, and we're about to eat."

"Sorry to interrupt." Mark, Cass's lover, had only recently moved in with her. Though Cass insisted that having Bonnie stay was "no problem," Bonnie felt edgy about intruding and was determined to find her own place as soon as possible. "I'll hit the road as soon as the sun's up, so I should arrive well before lunch. And Cass"—she watched the puppy nose the Styrofoam container—"I have this puppy with me."

"You what?"

"A puppy. I thought he'd be company, my living alone and all." Liar. "Actually, Gervaise found him near a Porta Potti on a construction site while she was out running. We put an ad in the paper, but no one claimed him. Gervaise can't take him up to Brown, and Elice is too house-proud to have an animal, and—"

"And you couldn't say no. So, what breed is it?"

Mongrel seemed too harsh. "Little bit Scottie, little bit Airedale, little bit spaniel? Seems to have a feisty personality. Very active tail."

"Housebroken? Oh, why did I bother to ask? Well, we'll put him on the back porch so he won't hassle with my cat. But you may have trouble finding an apartment that'll let you have pets."

"Oh, God, I didn't even think about that! Elice is right. I am stupid."

"Hey, you've had a lot on your mind, getting things in storage, leaving your house and all."

"Yeah, it was kind of tough." If she thought about it she might break down in tears. "OK, girlfriend. I'll see you tomorrow. And thanks again. I don't know how I could have gotten through this without you."

"You're not through it yet. And stop thanking me. See you tomorrow. Bye."

When the line went dead, it was as though some vital link, an oxygen tube or an intravenous drip, had been removed. She lay back on the bed, arms behind her head, staring at the ceiling and listening to the pelting rain and the noise of the TV leaking in from the adjoining room. Talk about a sound track for misery! She got up abruptly, threw the hamburger container into the trash can, and punched the button on the TV. The ten o'clock news flickered on, and she listened with half an ear as she took her toiletry bag from her purse, wandered into the bathroom, and brushed her teeth and washed her face without looking into the mirror.

When she came back, the puppy was settled on the floor looking up at the TV as though he were actually interested. A male reporter in a trench coat, standing in front of a factory as a crowd of bedraggled women filed out, was saying, "Over two hundred millworkers were laid off today when Cherished Lady, makers of women's fine underwear"—she rummaged in her toiletry bag, found moisturizer, and patted it on her face as she padded to the door to check the lock—"shut down their Florabama plant." Hearing "Florabama," she glanced back at the screen. "The firm's public relations office denied rumors that the plant will be relocated in Mexico, but—" Sitting on the edge of the bed, she watched as the reporter asked a sweet-faced, weary-looking factory worker if she'd like to comment. The woman opened her mouth but put her hand to it as though she were choking, while a blowsy redhead, her face sharp with anger, pushed forward and said, "You wanna know what this closing is about? It's about greed. It's about—" The sound cut off, but the picture stayed, creating the impression that the redhead was spitting out a stream of tobacco juice. The screen went blank. Amateur night in Dixie, she thought, reaching underneath her T-shirt to unhook her bra. The picture came back on. Another woman, sobbing and wiping tears from under the frames of her glasses, was talking about the importance of prayer. The reporter nodded with unctuous sympathy, then wrapped up the segment with an innocuously hopeful tag line. A commercial for Bubba's New-To-U RVs came on, a salesman's voice bleating over the twang of dueling banjos.

She clicked off the set, thinking, There but for the grace of God go I, and felt, if not comforted, at least relieved. She wasn't a middle-aged redneck factory worker who'd just been laid off. She'd never have to face *real* poverty. Not as long as the Duke was around. He'd kept her afloat in his usual openhanded style, and she knew he wasn't keeping tabs on what he'd given her, but she was. Someday, someway, she'd pay him back. He'd told her that he'd set up trust funds for Eugene and Gervaise, but she wondered if in light of the changes in her circumstances, he'd changed his will to provide for her. He'd bounced back from the bypass he'd had a couple of years ago and looked physically fit, but if he died and left everything to Elice . . .

Ashamed of even thinking about her father's death, she started to undress. She usually slept in the buff, but as she started to shimmy out of her underpants, she heard sounds from the adjoining room (probably one of those truckers who had tried to run her off the road getting off on *Debbie Does Dallas*), and pulled them back on. She tried to turn down the rattling air conditioner, but the dial was stuck. Shivering, she switched off the bedside lamp and got into the bed farthest away from the window, pulling the bedspread up to her chin.

The sheets, a polyester blend smelling of bleach, made her cringe. She remembered the sheets, silky soft, inviting luxuriant sex or pampered sleep, on the king-size bed at the Ritz. When she and Devoe had come back to the room after the party downstairs, the sheets had been turned down, and chocolates wrapped in gold foil had been placed on the big, downy pillows. Though she hadn't been conscious of recording it at the time, she found she could recall the details of that room: the cream brocade curtains draping windows that looked out on the Atlanta skyline, the coffee table with the slick "where to shop" magazines, the thick terry cloth robes, the little card assuring, "If you've forgotten anything you might need, please call the concierge." She could see her clothes laid out on the bed: her navy blue satin bustier with matching panties and stockings, her new off-the-shoulder midnight blue cocktail dress (which, since she'd been dieting, hugged instead of squeezed her waist), the velvet headband studded with pearls (Devoe liked her hair down, so even though she thought it too girlish, she'd brushed out the French twist the hairdresser had fussed over). That night in the Ritz couldn't have been the last time they made love. Life as she knew it had not blown up in her face until a few weeks later, and given their pattern, there must've been a few more times. But that night, or rather morning, at the Ritz was the last time she could remember.

When they'd received the invitation to another couple's twenty-fifth-anniversary party in the Plaza ballroom, Devoe'd suggested, though the Ritz was less than an hour from their home, that they should stay over. The suggestion had delighted her. They'd always talked about all the things they'd do together once they were free from the daily responsibilities of parenting, but in reality life hadn't changed much since Eugene and then Gervaise had gone off to college. In fact, the absence of the kids seemed to drive them both into more solitary pursuits. He continued to travel alone on business, and when he came home, it was mostly to rest up or go out and play golf. She took on more responsibilities with this committee or that fundraiser and devoted even more time to making their home a stylish sanctuary, though she seemed to be the only one who truly enjoyed it. She dutifully asked, "How'd your day go?" when they met over dinner, but she no longer expected a real response, and when, after rattling on about her activities until the sound of her own voice annoyed her, she tried to express deeper thoughts or feelings, Devoe seemed politely detached. She didn't know how to reach him and was somehow afraid to try.

On good days she could look five, maybe seven years younger, but inside, she felt the creeping cautions of age. Yet what was there to be afraid of? What was there to complain about? Aphid infestation? The high cost of college tuition? The fact that Devoe dozed off at concerts and only liked sex-and-action movies? No. All things considered, hers was a charmed life. Devoe was a good husband; she was a good wife. They'd raised two kids who, as far as she knew, had kept away from drugs and hadn't had any brushes with the law (if she didn't count speeding tickets and curfew violations). Dwelling on dissatisfactions was petty, spoiled. Still, her spirits had lifted when he'd proposed the weekend at the Ritz. It promised novelty, sex, and—

dare she hope?—intimacy. Perhaps they'd be able to break free and talk, really talk, about how they'd changed over the years, plan how they might advance through middle age with curiosity and a sense of purpose instead of numbed acceptance.

She'd looked pretty at the party; at least people had told her so. Devoe had told her so too, but in an offhanded way, and uncharacteristically (though she hadn't registered it at the time) he asked how much her new dress had cost. In the elevator after they'd finally left the party, she'd pressed up against him and made a joke about having sex in strange places. He'd kissed her long and hard, but when they reached their suite, he'd gone straight to the bathroom. She'd undressed and gotten into bed nude, but when he joined her, he'd just hugged her and rolled onto his side.

In the morning she'd woken up first and slid over to him, kissing his back and slithering her hand down between his legs. Years ago anytime had been the right time, but now he was more reliable in the mornings, and she wanted to take advantage of that. The bed was drenched with early-morning sun, and she felt warm and damp as she snuggled, whispering and stroking him. She hoped he'd open his eyes and look at her, but she knew he didn't find eye contact as stimulating as she did; in fact, she sometimes wondered if he kept his eyes closed because he was imagining someone else. Still, her eyes were open, and in the act of exciting him she excited herself, mounting him and moving slowly and steadily until she'd brought them both to a sweet climax.

Afterward, moving from him and flopping onto her back, she sighed to show her satisfaction, then curled into him, wanting to prolong the closeness. He moved and muttered. She only heard "I'm . . ." and anticipated what she wanted to hear: I'm happy, I'm satisfied, or better yet, Wow, baby.

"What?" she whispered.

He said, "I'm sweaty," and got up.

She followed him into the bathroom and asked if she could join him under the spray. Playing out her geisha mood, she stood behind him, soaping his chest, scrubbing his back, and massaging his head. His face, neck, hands, and forearms were permanently blotched by too many sunny days on the golf course, his religious application of Rogaine had failed to work the promised miracle with his receding hairline, and despite the fact that, against her wishes, he'd put an exercise machine in their bedroom and toiled with pulleys first thing every morning, he hadn't been able to flatten his little paunch. Poor Devoe. He was even more vain than she. She was strangely fond of his little paunch, but she didn't think he had a similar affection for her softening thighs (he'd given her that workout video titled *Buns of Steel* last Christmas but passed it off as a joke). She toweled him off, even sinking to her knees to dry between his toes. He'd said, "Thank you," in a soft, detached way, as though she really were a geisha, then reached for his razor. She'd gone back to the bed and called room service.

Looking back on it, she wondered why she hadn't trusted her intuition that something important was troubling him and made more of an effort to draw him out. She had tried, when breakfast arrived, to enliven their desultory conversation. She'd kissed his ear as she'd poured the coffee. She'd jabbered about the luxury of having eggs Benedict delivered to the door. But he'd already turned on the TV and was riffling through the *Atlanta Journal* for the business section, and she knew better than to spoil it by asking, "Honey, what's wrong?" Twenty-three years of marriage had taught her that sexual passion might, fleetingly, be restored, but probing conversation, especially at breakfast, was a definite no-no. It would only be met with annoyance and/or denial. So she'd backed off from questions and confrontation. She'd sipped her coffee, read the arts and leisure section of the paper, gotten up, and stretched like a cat in front of the window with the big, harsh, unreal world below, then—because checkout wasn't until three—gone back alone to the big, comfortable bed and told Devoe to "wake me when it's time to do something." It had been another month before disaster struck, changing their lives forever.

She'd been shopping at Neiman Marcus for a wedding present. When the salesgirl had come back from the register and told her that her MasterCard was maxed out, she'd been more annoyed than embarrassed; in fact, she'd calmed the flustered salesgirl by saying it must be a computer glitch, then handed over another card. But driving home, she'd started to worry. Apart from household bills, she knew next to nothing about their overall financial situation. Devoe, as a point of manly pride, had always handled their finances, and she, comfortable to the point of apathy and wanting to avoid confrontation, had let him. When the mail arrived that afternoon, she saw a letter from Brown University, addressed to Mr. and Mrs. D. Cullman, and instead of putting it on his desk, as she usually did, she opened it. Her stomach turned when she saw that it was a notice informing them that unless Gervaise's tuition, now three months in arrears, was promptly remitted, "action" would be taken. When she asked him about it that night, he told her he'd been so busy he'd forgotten to take care of it. But there was an angry defensiveness in his tone that put her on guard, and from that day on, worry about money, or the lack of it, had crept into her thoughts, silent and scary as the smell of escaping gas.

A month later, as she'd been curled up on the couch reading the issue of *House Beautiful* that had arrived in that afternoon's mail, he'd come in from an appointment with their accountant, his face ashen. What was wrong? She'd had to ask twice before he'd told her, sotto voce: The commuter airline in which he'd invested heavily had gone belly up. Another development deal on a strip mall had fallen through. Faking a calm she didn't feel, she'd suggested taking out an equity loan on the house. They'd done that, he told her, over a year ago. Didn't she remember signing the papers? She didn't. Her stupidity? Or had he slipped them by her in a drift of tax and business documents that "just needed her signature"? Incredulity, sharpened by shame at her self-willed ignorance (which he was more than eager to acknowledge), left her numb. The blood didn't seem to be circulating to her hands, let alone her brain. There was nothing they could do about the fifty thousand they were paying in college tuition but—

She babbled a host of suggestions about large and small economies. They could give up their share on the St. Simons vacation cottage, cut back on the cleaning lady and the gardener, entertain at home instead of at the club. That, he told her, wouldn't begin to fix things.

She felt as though she were hearing something she couldn't take in, like a doctor's announcement of a fatal illness. "Well, then. Well . . ." she'd said. "I guess we'll have to ask the Duke for a loan."

But even as he turned away, crossing his arms on the mantelpiece and lowering his head, she understood that he'd already done that. "How much?" she asked simply.

"About three hundred thou."

"Three hundred thousand dollars! And you didn't tell me!"

"I thought I could pay it back. I didn't want to worry you."

"Didn't want to . . . Sweet Jesus!"

"Hey, he can spare it."

"He can what? How dare you take advantage of my father's generosity? How dare you not tell me! What kind of marriage is this?"

"Shit, Bonnie. Have you taken to watching soap operas? 'Cause that's what you sound like."

"But you've withheld information that . . . Sweet Jesus, three hundred thousand dollars!" She couldn't find the words. "You *lied*," she finally got out, more sorrowful than indignant.

"I didn't lie. I just didn't—"

"Not telling something like this is the same as lying. Don't you understand that?" Her voice had risen to a shriek. "You lied. And it's not the first time."

"What the hell are you talking about?"

"That weekend you were supposed to be playing golf at the

Greenbrier. I called, and they said you weren't registered. Do you really think I was dumb enough to believe that you were sharing a room with Hank Pastore? Not when I ran into him at the tennis club that very weekend."

He turned, quickly putting up a defensive shield to cover his bewilderment. "Why can't women stick to the goddamn subject? Why the hell are you talking about the Greenbrier? We've got a big problem here, Bonnie. A BIG money problem. Can we deal with that before the bank forecloses and we're thrown out on our asses?" He sat down heavily and put his head in his hands, his fingers working on his face as though he wanted to remold it.

She stood rigid, breathing through her mouth, trying to calm herself. He was right. The Greenbrier didn't matter. It was another lie, another betrayal, but one she'd thought she had forgotten. There was no point bringing it up. The past was the past. Their immediate problem was definitely more important. She sat down on the love seat across from him. After a time she reached out, shifted the vase of red tulips on the coffee table, and took his hand. But when he squeezed her hand, she couldn't stop herself from saying, "Dear God, Devoe, why didn't you tell me?"

He bounded up, knocking over the vase and with a hurt majesty she found wholly insincere, said, "I don't think I can stay in this house if you're going to be accusatory."

"Accusatory? Accusatory!" she shrieked, rage fueled by his rejection. "Well, big shot, what do you think my reaction should be?"

The rest was a blur. He'd left the house. She'd felt, as she'd gone to the kitchen, found the roll of paper towels, come back to kneel on the carpet and collect the flowers, and sop up the spill, that no matter what she'd said or done he would have left because—she didn't pretend to understand why—that was what he *wanted* to do. She leaned back on her haunches, then reached for a shard of the shattered vase, but even before she tried to fit it into place, she let her hand drop, knowing it was beyond mending.

* * *

The puppy wiggled and whimpered. Making shushing sounds, she reached down, pulled him onto the bed, and settled him near her hip, absently stroking his head. Of course it had hurt her pride when she'd heard that Devoe was living with another woman, but she hadn't really been surprised and hadn't spent much time wondering if the affair had started before or after their breakup. When the children had been growing up, life had been good, full of laughter and purpose. She missed the past, sometimes with gut-churning nostalgia. She missed the idea of a loving husband. But she didn't really miss Devoe.

The wind was still gusting, but the storm seemed to be over. The occupant of the adjoining room had, blessedly, turned off the TV, but she could hear water dripping from a loose drainpipe that banged outside the window. The muscles in her neck still felt stiff, and she remembered what the massage therapist she could no longer afford had told her about deep breathing and imaging. She inhaled and exhaled, kneading her neck and imagining gristle softening to the consistency of Play-Doh. Finally, as she dropped off to sleep, she saw, in her mind's eye, a baby elephant struggling to roll away a giant fallen tree with his little trunk. Ganesha. Mover of obstacles. What was wrong with praying to an elephant?

Chapter II

*E*ver since she'd been a girl, Ruth Elkins's throat had seized up when she was scared. If her father was about to give her a whipping, she couldn't open her mouth to defend herself even when she was innocent; when a teacher called on her, she'd be struck dumb even if she knew the answer, and when she'd stood at the altar of the First Baptist Church to marry Freddie Elkins and the preacher had come to the big "Do you, Ruth Forrest . . ." question, her throat had squeezed so tight she'd thought she'd choke to death. When she'd finally said yes, it had come out as a barely audible squeak. Afterward, at the reception, her father, his mouth still full of wedding cake, had made a joke, saying that Freddie should count himself lucky to be getting a girl who wouldn't answer back.

Over the years she thought she'd mastered this affliction, but it had happened again today. Coming out of Cherished Lady with the other women, she'd seen the TV crew in front of the factory, and she'd known, as clearly and smartly as if she'd written it out, just what she wanted to say. But when the reporter shoved the microphone in front of her, her throat had seized up, and she'd stood, dumb as a post. Then, to make matters worse, she'd started to cry.

The day had started badly, but Mondays were always bad. Mondays made her feel like a hamster that'd been let out of her cage for a little while but was now put back on the wheel where she would paw and scramble, going nowhere fast, until the next Friday.

The alarm went off at six, and her body stiffened and twitched as though she were being tortured with electric shocks. She resisted the impulse to punch the SNOOZE button, groped on the night table for her glasses, crawled out of bed, and pulled aside the curtains, thinking she must find time to launder them next weekend. Looking past her vegetable garden, she saw an overcast sky and a rising sun that already looked like a fried egg. She pulled off her nightgown and headed to the bathroom, careful not to make a noise because she didn't want to wake her grandchildren, six-year-old Kylie and his four-year-old sister, Cheryl (nicknamed Moo because of her baby pronunciation of *milk*). The children had slept over the previous night, and her daughter, Roxy, was supposed to come by and take them to school and day care before she joined Ruth at Cherished Lady for the seven-thirty shift.

After showering to wash off her night sweats, she swiped deodorant under her arms, shook talcum powder onto her chest and feet, and got into fresh white cotton underwear, socks, worn jeans, and the pink WORLD'S BEST GRANDMA T-shirt she'd set on the toilet tank the night before. She didn't like printed T-shirts, but the kids had given her this one for her birthday and got a kick out of seeing her wear it. Toweling her hair as she went, she tiptoed to the kitchen. She put on a pot of coffee, leaning against the sink, trying to come to full consciousness while it dripped; then, cup in hand, she hurried back to her bedroom and made the bed, glancing at the clock (6:20) as she smoothed the coverlet.

Hoping Roxy was on her way, she sipped coffee as she brushed her hair, clipped it behind her ears with a couple of plastic barrettes Moo had left on her dresser, then took off her glasses to lean into the mirror and apply lipstick. The questioning expression that had begun to form a vertical crease in her forehead when she was still a teenager was now a deep furrow. Tiny squint lines fanned out around her eyes, and she noticed a wiry white hair sprouting from her left eyebrow. She pulled open the dresser drawer, rummaging through the mess of buttons, safety pins, aspirin, toenail clippers, hair curlers she never used, arthritis liniment, discount coupons for Burger King, and a mess of Mary Kay cosmetics her co-worker Celia Lusk had pressured her into buying, but couldn't find the tweezers. You don't have time for this, she thought, glancing at the clock as she pushed in the drawer, reached for the telephone, and punched in Roxy's number. Waiting for it to ring, she caught a glimpse of her reflection and turned her back on it.

She'd never believed she was pretty, even when Freddie, while courting/seducing her, had said she was; she'd compared herself with the ideals in magazines and movies and found herself sorely lacking. Only now that she was older did she understand that while she'd never been a glamorous long-stemmed rose, she'd once had a country girl appeal as vibrant as a fistful of wildflowers. It made her sad that she hadn't recognized it at the time. But then, she hadn't entirely gone to seed. Her best friend, Hilly, was always complimenting her on her trim figure, but to her own eyes she just had a stringy look. Her arms, legs, and neck were firm; her belly was slack from three pregnancies and lack of exercise. Her light brown hair was still thick, but the gray was coming in fast as weeds after rain, and the girl at the beauty school had cut it to a manageable but hardly flattering ear length. Hilly had offered to style and dye her hair, but seeing Hilly's own wild mane, she'd begged off. But what did it matter? She didn't have time to launder her curtains, let alone worry about her hairstyle. Besides, her grandchildren thought she was beautiful.

On the fifth ring Roxy's answering machine kicked in. Ruth hung up as soon as she heard it and, still hoping that Roxy was on her way, went into the other bedroom to wake up the kids. Moo was dozy-eyed and whiny, asking where her mother was, and as Ruth lifted her from the bed, she saw that the sheets were wet. Kylie refused help getting dressed, struggling into his jeans while he chattered about McDonald's: Would he order the Egg McMuffin or the Sausage and Eggs? "Maybe I'll fix you something here at home," Ruth said, wanting to ward off disappointment in case Roxy didn't come in time to take them to breakfast. But Kylie was adamant; he'd been promised. Oh, Lord, she thought, how could she teach the boy to honor a promise when promises made to him were always being broken?

At 6:40, after trying to teach Moo how to tie her shoelaces and dipping into the toilet to retrieve the huge wad of toilet paper Kylie had used, she washed her hands, threw some Pop-Tarts into the microwave, and tried to call Roxy again. This time she hung up after the third ring. Shoving Pop-Tarts and paper napkins into the kids' hands, she bundled them into her car, raced back into the house to retrieve her forgotten lunch bag, dashed back to the car, and, after making sure the kids had their seat belts on, backed out of her drive and floored the accelerator. After dropping Kylie off at school, she raced to Moo's day care center. Moo, in tears because she'd smeared raspberry jam from the Pop-Tart on her T-shirt, didn't want to get out of the car, and when Ruth carried her into the playroom and handed her over to the teacher, her face had such a look of abandonment that Ruth's impatience turned to guilt and she felt like crying herself.

She went through two yellow lights on the way to the mill and, since she was late, had to park way in the back of the lot. She'd all but run to the "Employees Only" door, shoving her lunch into her purse instead of putting it into her locker, and was breathing hard as she grabbed her time card—Lord, it was 7:48!—and . . . She froze as though someone had shoved a gun between her shoulder blades. She couldn't hear the sewing machines. Maybe this was it. Maybe this was the day they'd start laying people off.

Rumors that Cherished Lady was moving operations to Mexico had been circulating ever since Ellen McClatchy, a floor supervisor who was always sucking up to management, had taken a sudden "vacation" two months ago. Albertine Chisholm, who sat next to Ruth on the line, had a cousin who worked in the front office, and the cousin had leaked it to Albertine that she'd snooped and found out that McClatchy's round-trip ticket to Mexico was paid for by Cherished Lady. The information had caused a firestorm of conjecture, but Hilly had been the only one who'd had the guts to go to the front office and ask questions. She'd been assured that their jobs were secure, though, with her usual cynicism, Hilly'd said that management could look you in the eye and lie as easy as Little Jack Horner could have pie drooling from his mouth and tell you he wasn't eating it. But Ruth had convinced herself that things were OK. Cherished Lady was coming out with two new lines of underwear, so there was a lot of work. One line, called Jezebel, featured scarlet and black garter belts, waist cinches, and push-up bras that looked as though they belonged in a turn-of-the-century brothel; the other, called John L. Sullivan, was gray, with breast-binding Lycra tops and cotton men's style baggy shorts. When they first saw the styles, the women had joked that New York designers apparently thought that American women wanted to be either prostitutes or prizefighters. But they had big orders, and everyone hoped to make extra money on overtime. Hilly still maintained that their services could easily be replaced by "dumb spics who'll work for a bowl of beans," but Ruth had believed, perhaps because the notion of being without a paycheck was too scary to think about, that everything was OK.

She took her time card out of her name slot and shoved it into the machine. The sound it made when it punched 7:50 seemed loud and ominous. Rigid with anxiety, she pushed open the swinging doors to the factory floor.

It was a huge windowless room, the only natural light seeping from the open doors of the receiving dock on the right and the loading dock to the far left. Two hundred women sat, row after row, in front of their silent machines, their heads—brown, blond, gray, nappy, covered with bandannas or baseball caps—bright but unnatural-looking in the fluorescent light. Her eyes shot to the back of the room, and she spotted Roxy in the row next to the Coke machine. "Thank God she's here," Ruth thought, before realizing that Roxy's punctuality, or lack of it, was probably irrelevant. Making her way to her own place (third row down, two girls in) she was aware of Mrs. McClatchy's eyes on her, and even though she knew it couldn't matter now, she sped up her pace. As she moved behind Albertine Chisholm's chair, Albertine turned her broad walnut brown face to her and whispered, "They told us not to start work. Some guy from Atlanta's coming to talk to us."

Celia Lusk, pale eyes swimming behind her new glasses with the turquoise frames, moaned, "Dear Jesus! Dear Jesus! They're gonna fire us for sure."

Ruth took her place between Celia and Lyda Jane McCracken. Lyda Jane's head was bent, her freckled scalp showing through her wispy white hair. Her hands moved swiftly, crocheting another baby blanket for another grandchild. Without looking up, she cautioned, "Now, Celia, don't jump before you're pushed."

"Oh, we about to be pushed," Albertine muttered. "We 'bout to be pushed right over the cliff."

"Looks like it," Ruth agreed, staring straight ahead. The manager, Mr. Stamford, Mrs. McClatchy, and another floor supervisor were standing near the bins where they dumped the finished garments for inspection. All three had their arms folded and their eyes on the floor. Tyrone, Cephus, and the men who did the heavy work, rolling bolts of fabric onto the cutting tables, packing, loading, and unloading goods, stood off to the side, shifting their feet and whispering like pallbearers waiting for the funeral to begin. The wizened old Jew they all called Saint Jerome, a hermit bachelor who serviced and repaired all the machines and was never seen anywhere except the mill, was hunched against the wall, reading a book through thick-lensed glasses. Her best friend, Hilly Pruwitt, her hair teased wide and high and looking like hot copper under the fluorescent lights, was leaning on one of the long cutting tables, her right hand cupping her chin. Her rear end, squeezed into tight jeans, jutted out in a pose so seemingly nonchalant that she might have been at her favorite bar waiting for a shot of Wild Turkey to be poured. But her left hand, covered with the protective chain mail cutter's glove, hit her hip with a steady rhythm, and when she and Ruth locked glances, Ruth could see she had blood in her eye.

Swiveling around, Ruth looked for her daughter again. Roxy was getting up from her chair and heading for the Coke machine, but her friend Johnette, who sat next to her, grabbed her hand and pulled her back, urging her to stay calm. Sensing Ruth's look, Roxy stared back as she sat down, her glance sullen and resentful. The expression was nothing new. Ruth had seen it flash across the faces of all three of her children, mostly during their adolescence when she'd tightened the parental reins. Her boys had grown out of it, but with Roxy it had become as permanent as a birthmark. Ruth's stomach turned, and sweat broke out on her forehead. Dear God in heaven, with two small children and no husband around, what would Roxy do without a job?

Someone coughed. Someone suppressed a nervous giggle. The faint melody of "Stand by Your Man" strained out of an unseen transistor radio. Celia blew her nose and dabbed at her eyes. Hilly shifted her weight, slapped her hip, and said, "Time is money," out loud. Since this was one of Mr. Stamford's favorite expressions, he glared at her. She smiled back with challenging insouciance, then turned her back to him. Then the door to the office opened, and all attention flew to it like filings to a magnet. A man in his thirties, prematurely bald, walked briskly toward Mr. Stamford, followed by two women in sober dress-for-success suits. Mr. Stamford held out his hand, but the man, busy removing his jacket, either didn't see or chose to ignore it. Stamford smiled nervously and cleared his throat, but when he spoke, his voice still cracked. "This is Mr. Dash from the Atlanta office—"

"Just call me Jack," Mr. Dash insisted, smiling at the women sitting at their machines as though inviting them to be on friendly terms.

"And Ms.—" Stamford was stuck. "From the firm's legal department, Ms.—"

"Shirley Jackson," Mr. Dash offered, touching the shoulder of one woman's gray suit. "And Ms. Dottie Ingram"—he nodded in the direction of the woman in the charcoal—"from Atlanta Personnel Services." He handed his jacket to Stamford, who handed it off to Mrs. McClatchy, then clicked his tongue and rolled up his shirtsleeves as though he were about to tackle some bothersome but necessary task, like changing a tire.

Ruth's skin felt cold but prickly all over. She bowed her head and held her breath. Here it comes, she thought. Here comes the ax.

"Good morning, ladies and gentlemen," Dash began. He smiled again, then passed his hand over his head, raised his eyes above their heads, and fixed his glance on the back wall. "I know you folks appreciate honesty, so I'm going to give it to you straight: Cherished Lady is being forced to shut down all production here at the Florabama mill."

The room went so quiet that Ruth heard herself choke, then exhale. Shock melted into a weird sense of relief. Thank God. A nice quick cut! So please, she thought, don't spoil it by going on about the company's honesty and loyalty. Please don't say you feel our pain when you know you'll have a job tomorrow and we won't. Please just let me sit here and bleed in peace.

"I don't think I need to tell you how much Cherished Lady has always valued its employees. We know our company has achieved its reputation as one of the finest manufacturers of women's personal apparel not only because those of us in management have always tried to be on the cutting edge but because we've maintained a partnership—not just a partnership, but a sense of family—with those of you who are on the line. Unfortunately, in today's global economy . . ."

As he rattled off numbers, statistics, cost analyses, Ruth looked around. Albertine was grunting uh-huh, uh-huh slowly, regularly, and just a bit bored, as though she were at a church service listening to homilies she'd heard too many times. Lyda Jane kept her head down and concentrated on her baby blanket, calm as if she were sitting in her living room. Celia snuffled and wiped her eyes on the tail of her

MY BOSS IS A JEWISH CARPENTER T-shirt. Lyda Jane reached into her purse and handed her a minipack of Kleenex. Ruth gave a barely audible and inappropriate snort as she remembered the first time Celia had worn that T-shirt to work and Hilly had said, "Better do a reality check, Celia. Your boss is Cherished Lady. And never forget that boss spelled backwards is double SOB."

Mr. Call-Me-Jack Dash was droning on in constipated tones about how, out of its heartfelt loyalty, Cherished Lady had kept the Florabama mill open way past the time it had ceased to be cost-effective. But, he appealed to their reasoning, if keeping the plant open just meant greater financial problems further down the line, what was the point? "Therefore"—he drew in a breath, then blew it out in little puffs—"a decision has been made to implement an MIA process and in furtherance of that process—"

Hilly called out, "What's MIA mean?"

Taken aback by the interruption, Dash explained, with pained tolerance, "MIA means 'management-initiated attrition.'"

"Great," Hilly yelled back. "For a minute there I thought it meant 'Missing in Action.'"

There was a smattering of laughter before Dash started again, spewing acronyms like a kid spitting up alphabet soup, regurgitating statistics and figures as though he'd had a double dose of ipecac. To Ruth his voice was no more than background static. She was totaling up figures of her own: her mortgage note, the two hundred dollars still owing to the dentist. Her Chevy needed a new clutch, and the insurance was due next month. She tuned back in when she heard Dash say, "Special educational and social programs have been set up with the help of local and federal government agencies. Marion Hawkins College will be offering a subsidized reeducation program for displaced homemakers that I'm sure many of you can take advantage of. It will be a chance for you to go to college and prepare yourselves to be competitive in today's ever-changing job market. Ms. Ingram"—a nod toward Charcoal Suit—"will be here at the mill all next month to answer your questions and help you to enroll in appropriate programs. As we move into the twenty-first century . . ." and blah, blah, blah.

Finally, when he'd talked so long that even Mr. Stamford's eyes were beginning to glaze, Mr. Dash reached for his jacket with a peremptory "Any questions?"

The room was still deadly quiet—nothing like fear to make people mute—but then Cephus, who'd tried to interest them in a union a couple of years ago, called out, "You be movin' operations to Mexico, right?"

Mr. Dash gave a dismissive "No decision has been made at this time. We're considering all options."

"But you've known you were closin' us down for some time, right?" Cephus persisted.

Saint Jerome peered over his spectacles, saying, "It's a surprise they didn't have the decency to tell us?" with an upward inflection that turned the statement into a question.

"Yeah. How come you didn't have the decency to let us know sooner?" Hilly demanded. "'Cause when I asked about the possibility of a closing a couple of months ago, I was told—"

Dash, passing his hand in front of his face as though waving away a mosquito, raised his voice to say, "As I just told you, you may take the rest of the day off, with pay, to get your affairs in order. Informational notices have now been posted on the employees' bulletin board. Ms. Ingram and her assistants will be here tomorrow morning, seven-thirty sharp, to aid you with your career transition plans. They'll answer your questions about severance pay, unemployment compensation, special educational programs, and . . ." For a split second a look of confusion crossed his face; then he rallied with "On behalf of Cherished Lady I want to thank y'all"—his use of the "y'all" southernism made Ruth want to spit at him—"for your devoted service and wish y'all the best luck in your transition. Thank you again."
He walked toward the office with the speed of someone who'd just

been caught short after taking a large dose of Ex-Lax, his sober-suited handmaidens scurrying after him.

Stamford raised his hands as though he were a policeman stopping traffic, then lowered them in settling gestures, urging everyone to remain in place. "Tomorrow morning, regular shift time, seven-thirty sharp, informational tables will be set up. All employees, taken in alphabetical order, will—"

But all hell had broken loose: a babel of voices, cries of disbelief, whispers, curses, an odd wail. Chairs scraped the floor as most of the women got up, but some stayed seated, arms crossed or heads down on their machines. A few stood motionless, staring straight ahead.

Lyda Jane folded her baby blanket and tucked it into her purse, sighed, and said, "It's just something else to get through. See you tomorrow, gals," and shuffled off. Ruth looked after her, wondering how she could face disaster with such equanimity.

Albertine got up, pushed in her chair, hoisted a bra strap, and shook her head so hard her long gold earrings swayed. "Well, blessed is she who expecteth nothing, for she shall not encounter disappointment." Picking up her purse, she added, "Don't know what y'all are going to do, but I'm going to buy me a gallon of Barber's butter pecan ice cream whiles' I can still afford it, and I'm gonna sit down and eat the whole blessed thing. Any you gals wanna call me to talk, you know the number," then lumbered off.

Hilly, standing a few feet away, bag slung over her shoulder, her face blotched as though she'd crawled through a patch of poison oak, said, "Come on, Ruth. Let's get outa this sorry place." Ruth turned and motioned to Roxy to meet her outside, then picked up her things and followed, struggling to keep up as Hilly strode ahead, overtaking women who were already pushing open the swinging doors. They moved past the time clock and lockers. Hilly slammed open the front doors leading to the parking lot, then stopped so suddenly that Ruth bumped into her. At first she thought Hilly had stopped because it was spitting rain, but then she saw the lights, the cameraman, and a reporter she recognized from the evening news. "Well, ain't this something," Hilly said. "They let the TV people know what was gonna happen before they told us poor slobs." Taking Ruth's hand, she said, "C'mon. Let's give 'em a piece of our minds."

Miserable and angry, Ruth waited while the other women crowded behind them. If that reporter asks me, she decided, I will speak out. I'll say, calmly and clearly, "I've been working here at Cherished Lady since my husband passed away. For sixteen years I've given an honest day's work for my pay. What really hurts is that management didn't have the decency to let us know what was coming down, even though we'd asked." But when the reporter shoved the microphone in front of her face and asked how she felt, her mouth suddenly felt as though it had been stuffed with wool. She tried to swallow, but her throat was closed so tight she couldn't get anything out. Blood rushed to her face, and tears came to her eyes. Hilly put her arm around her, then leaned in close to the microphone, blazing, "You wanna know what this closing is about? It's about greed. Greed and lies. We know Cherished Lady made a good profit last year, but they're so goddamn—"

The reporter pulled back reflexively, saying, *"Please,* ma'am. *No profanity!"*

The reporter told the sound man, who was shaking with laughter, that they'd edit it out, and looked around for a less volatile subject. Celia Lusk was weeping, copiously but quietly, her mouth working in silent prayer. "And you, ma'am," he asked, "how do you feel about the closing?"

"I only pray that the good Lord . . ." she began, but Hilly muscled in with "We've been screwed blue and tattooed. Don't you jerks get it?" She looked around at her co-workers' shocked faces, spit out a disgusted "Aw, fuck it!" and shouldered her way to Ruth, who'd already worked her way to the periphery of the crowd as the reporter barked, "Stop laughing, Jerry. Let's keep going. We'll edit."

They walked in silence to Ruth's car, but as Ruth started to open the door, she suddenly felt weak in the knees. She put her arms on the roof and lowered her head. "I didn't mean to embarrass you," Hilly said so grudgingly that Ruth knew she was full of shame. Ruth shook her head, laughing softly, tears coming to her eyes. She *was* deeply embarrassed, not by Hilly but by herself. What a pair they were. Hilly with a mouth as big as the Grand Canyon; she not able to utter a peep.

"Hey," Hilly said, "why don't you come on out to my place?"

Ruth shook her head. "I'm s'posed to meet Roxy. I'll have to check with her to see which one of us is gonna pick up the kids."

I could answer that question for you, Hilly thought, shoving her hands into her back pockets and looking toward the rear entrance, where she spotted Roxy and her sidekick Johnette, lolling near a Dumpster, smoking and having themselves a pity party. She knew Roxy had seen them too, but Roxy took her sweet time stubbing out her cigarette and saying good-bye to Johnette before she started toward them with a hangdog, hip-swinging slouch that made Hilly's blood boil. The girl was so much like her father that Hilly sometimes thought of her as Freddie's clone.

"So, I guess I got the shaft," Roxy said as she came up to them.

"*You* got the shaft?" Hilly said. "Sure, Roxy, and when it rains, only you get wet." Damned girl thought she was the world's belly button.

Ignoring her, Roxy turned to Ruth. "Well, Mama, guess there's nothing for it but to go on welfare."

Ruth snapped, "Don't even think it. We never did, and we never will. Let's go pick up the kids."

Roxy shook her head. "No can do, Mama. I told Johnette I'd go to her place so we can look over the want ads."

In a pig's eye, Hilly thought. More likely you and Johnette will go to the Tailgate to look over the lounge lizards and hope one of 'em will buy you a beer to cry in. "Well, you gals sort out what you're doing. No point standing around licking our wounds in this drizzle. I'm heading home. Like I said, Ruthie, you're welcome for supper, an' you can bring the kids if you like. This ain't no time to be alone." As she walked off, she thought maybe she was lucky not to have kids. Motherhood seemed to make women stupid. Ruth was smarter than she was in lots of ways, but when it came to being exploited by that daughter of hers, Ruth was purblind. Celia Lusk said Roxy was Ruth's cross to bear, and for once Celia's religious imagery was right on target: Ruth's back would break before she'd lay down that cross, and though she was Ruth's best friend, Hilly knew better than to remind her that she was carrying it.

Her new red Saturn had a bumper sticker with DON'T TREAD ON ME and LIVE FREE OR DIE printed on a background of a coiled snake and a Confederate flag. She unlocked the door, slid in, punched on the air conditioning, and sat, breathing deeply. Nothing as good as the smell of a new car. It was damn near aphrodisiac. This was the first new car she'd ever driven in her life, unless she counted her first husband J.K.'s white Thunderbird. Looking back on it, she could see that she'd wanted his car more than she'd ever wanted J.K. Why else would a seventeen-year-old girl marry a forty-year-old man with bad teeth and a worse temper? But the title for the Thunderbird had always stayed in J.K.'s name, and he'd taken it back after he'd found her in bed with Rich. Forget a divorce settlement; she'd been lucky to escape with her life. After Rich she'd had almost as many cars as men, but the cars, like the men, were always secondhand and always had something wrong with them. This was the first time in her life she'd put down her own money on a new car. And before she'd signed the loan agreement, she'd gone to those bastards in the front office and they'd told her her job was safe. And now, after just three payments, she was out of work.

She switched on the ignition and put the car into reverse, turning her head to look back and seeing the women still flocking around the factory door, bleating and baaing for TV's Good Shepherd. "Damned sheep!" she cursed, punching up the volume of a Patsy Cline CD and laying rubber as she peeled out of the parking lot. Hot damn, but she was mad! She hadn't been this pissed off since she'd got fired from the Pork Barrel for throwing a platter of barbecue at that cook who'd grabbed her ass in front of a customer. What a job that'd been! She'd noticed her first varicose vein while she was working at the Pork Barrel. She hadn't had a washing machine at the time, so she'd had to take her uniform into the shower with her and wash it, and her hair, twice to get out the cooking smells. Before that it'd been the battery factory—lucky she hadn't got cancer or some lung disease—before that it had been the convenience store where she'd been held up at gunpoint, before that . . . well, the jobs were pretty much like the men and the cars. "Dammit to hell!" She banged the steering wheel. The worst part was that she liked her job at Cherished Lady. It was steady, it paid good, she had friends there, and when she left at four o'clock, she had some daylight to herself. And she had pride in her work. OK, being a lace cutter wasn't like being a brain surgeon, but she was one of the best lace cutters in the business. Trouble was, there wasn't going to be a business anymore. Business was going south, to one of those border shantytowns that had grown up around a factory—*maquilladoro* they called it—where they could get girls to work an eight-hour shift for a cup of water and a cold tortilla. Well, she thought bitterly, life's like a dogsled: If you ain't the lead dog, the scenery never changes.

Chapter III

*D*riving to Hilly's place, Ruth passed the cement factory, recycling shed, and automobile graveyard clustered behind the sign that said INDUSTRIAL PARK and shook her head. Some park. What was that word that meant you'd substituted a pleasant word for one that was distasteful? Miss Bradshaw had taught it to her in high school. It was on the tip of her tongue. It was—

Kylie leaned from the backseat and draped his arms around her neck. "Kylie, if I've told you once, I've told you ten times. Buckle up that seat belt right now, or I'm gonna pull over to the side of the road and—"

"And what?" Kylie asked, testing the limits.

"Just do it NOW." She shrugged off his arms and downshifted onto the rutted dirt road. "I swear I don't know what's the matter with you today." But of course she did know. He'd overheard the argument she'd had with Roxy when Roxy'd come back from Johnette's, even though she'd dragged Roxy into the bedroom and made her shut the door. Roxy had howled, "What am I going to do with no job?" over and over until Ruth'd wanted to smack her, and when she tried to turn the conversation to practicalities like totaling up their bills, Roxy'd thrown herself on the bed and beaten the pillows and cried that she'd never had a chance in life and Ruth didn't know what it was like to be young and have to live like you were old, with nothing but kids and trouble. Ruth did know, and it liked to break her heart to see her daughter in the same fix she'd been in. The only way she could think to help was to take the kids for the night. They'd be better off with her. She'd smelled liquor on Roxy's breath.

When she and Roxy had come out of the bedroom, the kids had been sitting in front of the TV, and she'd told them she'd be taking them to Hilly's. Kylie had whooped and jumped, and Moo said with quiet satisfaction, "Then I'll get to see Garbage," meaning Hilly's pet goat. Neither of them had wanted to kiss their mother good-bye, but as soon as Roxy shut the door behind her, Kylie'd turned wild and Moo curled up in the corner of the couch, one hand between her legs and her thumb in her mouth. Of course they'd sensed something out of the ordinary, something really bad, was going on. Kids always sensed things. Hadn't she, when she was a kid, felt the heat and violence of arguments behind closed doors, even if she hadn't been able to make out the actual words? Hadn't she always known who loved whom and who hated whom even though she didn't know why? Hadn't she always known when her mama was getting one of her migraine headaches or when her daddy was about to reach for the strap? You knew it all when you were little. Sometimes you knew it better than when you were grown; you just didn't have words for it. Maybe only poets had words for it. Words couldn't cure it, but sometimes they were like ointment rubbed on a sore place, with a kiss-it-better magic.

"Cows. See the moo-cows, Cheryl?" she asked, pointing to a small herd standing in a pasture made golden by the sunset.

Moo, buckled so tightly into the seat that her legs stuck out, craned her head, whining, "Grandma, I can't see."

Kylie leaned into her, pulling down the flesh under his eyes and braying, "Moo. Moo. You're a big fat cow. A big fat cow with big fat titties."

"Kylie, don't you dare talk to your sister like that. I swear you're testing my patience. If you don't stop that . . ." Ruth thought, as she did almost daily, that she was too old for this. But what good did it do to complain, even to herself? Kylie's teacher had told Roxy that the boy was hyperactive and should be put on Ritalin, but Ruth had talked Roxy out of it, arguing that it just didn't make sense. Kids couldn't have changed so much, just in a couple of decades, that so many had to be put on mind drugs. What the boy needed was less TV and more chores, more outdoor activities to tire him out. Also, the presence of a father would have made the world of difference. It wasn't Roxy's fault that Big Kylie had gone off, almost four years ago, just before Moo was born. His jobs in trucking and construction (all part-time) had dried up, and when a buddy who was recruiting cleanup crews for Middle Eastern oil fields had offered him a job, it seemed like a golden opportunity, even though it meant leaving home for six months.

Neither she nor Roxy had expected him to write home often, but for the first few months his checks had been regular and large enough to allow Roxy to stay home with the kids. Then the checks had stopped coming. Roxy had gone into a rage, then drifted into such a fog of depression that Ruth had to make sure there were Pampers and food in her house. Finally they'd got in touch with Globe-Op, the firm that had hired him, and been told that he'd gone for a weekend of R&R in Italy—and had dropped off the face of the earth.

"Kylie, I'm warning you. We're almost to Miss Hilly's, so stop that damned bouncing 'fore I lose all patience." They were in the woods now, and it calmed her some to see trees, small fields of cotton and peanuts, and hand-painted mailboxes along the roadside, but her mind was still working. Roxy wouldn't be able to put Kylie on drugs now even if she wanted to because now they wouldn't have health insurance. They'd have to have insurance, at least for the kids. How much would that cost, and where would they get the money? But Kylie would be all right, she told herself. She knew about boys. Boys had a rougher time growing up these days than girls. But Kylie wasn't what that teacher said; he was just wild. Because he had a mother who didn't know how to be one, and a long-gone daddy and . . . *hyperac-*

tive was just a euphemism. Euphemism! That was the word she'd
been searching for. "That's it," she said out loud.

"Grandma, you talking to yourself again?" Kylie asked in perfect
imitation of his mother's sarcasm.

"Stop sassing me, Kylie. We're almost there."

Moo asked, "Grandma, if you don't have to go to work, can we
stay home with you all the times?"

"No, precious. And why would you want to stay home when you
can go to play school with your friends?"

Moo put her thumb in her mouth, removed it to say, "Because,"
then put it back in, sucking away on her thoughts.

Ruth pulled off the road and drove past a stand of trees and into
a clearing where Hilly's double-wide trailer was set up on concrete
blocks and her shiny new car was parked alongside the chicken coop.
Hilly, who must've heard the car, opened the screen door and planted
herself on the top step, one hand on her hip, the other splayed next
to the sign that said IF THE TRAILER'S ROCKIN', DON'T COME KNOCKIN',
though as far as Ruth knew, Hilly hadn't brought a man back to her
place since a couple of years ago, when an overnight guest had turned
squatter and settled in. Hilly had been determined to chase him off
herself, but on Ruth's advice, she'd finally called the sheriff to evict
him. Hilly still went to the Tailgate because there were line-dancing
contests, which she often won, but she told Ruth she'd changed her
style: If she met a guy, she went to his place; that way she knew right
off if he was lying about being married, plus she could leave when she
wanted.

"Miss Hilly, we come to have supper with you," Kylie shouted,
crawling out of the backseat and slamming the door.

"Well, get yourself on in here." Hilly scanned the thunderclouds
above the treetops. "'Cause it looks like it's gonna rain some more."

"Where's Garbage?"

"He's tethered up 'round back. If you help your little sister out of
the car, I'll give you a carrot so you can go feed him," Hilly called

back, holding open the screen door. Kylie brought Moo to the steps, then raced into the trailer. Hilly swooped Moo up and nuzzled her neck, telling her, "Why, look at you! You're so cute we oughta make a key chain out of you," while Ruth opened the trunk to collect the casserole and the bag of groceries.

Hilly was rummaging in the refrigerator as Ruth came in the door. "I know it's like a furnace in here," Hilly said, breaking a carrot in half and handing the pieces to Moo and Kylie. "That damned thing"—she waved in the direction of the air conditioner fastened into the single kitchen window—"snorts like it's got sinus trouble. I was gonna replace it but . . ." She and Ruth exchanged a look and started to unpack the groceries.

Ruth said, "I was going to fry some chicken and make biscuits, but it's just too hot, so I bought some salad fixings, and there's this broccoli-cheese casserole we can heat in the microwave."

"Oh, girl, sit down and take a load off." Without asking, Hilly poured her a glass of iced tea.

Kylie danced from foot to foot. "Don't be sittin' and drinkin', Miss Hilly. Let's go feed Garbage."

"Get on out there. And take Moo with you. I'll be right out." She sipped her tea as she watched them go, then turned to Ruth. "You know who called and blessed me out for a heathen."

"Celia Lusk?"

"Who else? She said she'd forgiven me and was gonna pray for me, so I said, 'Celia, is it true that Baptists never have sex standing up 'cause they're afraid someone will think they're dancing?' Then I told her I was busy gettin' drunk, and she hung up real quick." Hilly winked, drained the glass, and moved to the back door. "Come on out to the yard when you're finished putting things away; it's cooler out there."

Ruth put the gallon of milk she'd brought for the kids into the refrigerator and sipped her tea, shaking her head. Celia had told her that she couldn't understand how a "good woman" like her could be tight with someone like Hilly, who was "on a bullet train to hell." Celia wasn't the only one who didn't understand the friendship. True, she and Hilly were as different as chalk and cheese. Ruth was a churchgoer, more for the children than for herself, and still entertained a vague hope that life's struggles would be rewarded on the other side; Hilly said flat out that she was a broad-based heathen. Ruth tended her grandkids and her garden and, in her few leisure moments, read books; Hilly drank hard, danced harder, drove like a demon, and didn't care where she lived as long as it was "away from civilization." Ruth'd had but one man and, if she didn't dwell on it too much, was mainly relieved "that part" of her life was over. Hilly'd had more boyfriends than Madonna had hit records. Sure, she confessed, she looked for love in all the wrong places, but "In a few years I'll need bifocals to *see* the sheets, let alone muss 'em up, so I'm gonna pitch hay while the sun's still shining." But Fate had thrown them together when they were both young and full of hope, and they'd been through things together that made them closer than blood.

Ruth leaned against the sink and looked out at Hilly and the kids feeding the goat. Seemed as though half her life had been spent looking out of kitchen windows. She'd been looking out the kitchen window of the house she and Freddie had rented right after Curtis was born when she saw Hilly for the first time. In point of fact, she'd heard her before she'd seen her; a vibrant Texas twang yelling orders to "come on slow an' don't mash them sorry-looking flowers" had caused her to pull aside the curtains and peek out. A young strawberry blonde with a dynamite figure was directing a pickup loaded with furniture into the adjoining driveway. It backed up, avoiding the geraniums (which Ruth had planted), and a tall young man in a cowboy hat got out. They played around as though he were chasing her; then he caught her, bent her back over the hood of the car, and kissed her so long and hard that his hat fell off, revealing a lion's mane of dirty blond hair. It was the wildest kiss Ruth'd ever seen except in the movies. Gasping and laughing, the young woman drew back, sensed that they were being watched, spotted Ruth, and called, "Hi, there! I'm Hilly, and this is my man, Rich. We're movin' in next door." Later in the day, after they'd unloaded the truck, she had gone over with a plate of oatmeal cookies. It sounded as though they were moving furniture, but when she raised her hand to knock on the door, she'd heard laughter so intimate that she'd left the cookies on the doorstep.

Hilly'd come over the next day to thank her. Ruth had liked her from the first. Soon they were shopping together, going to the Laundromat together, sitting in each other's kitchens drinking gallons of iced tea. Initially they tried to include their husbands, but Freddie's competitiveness with Rich and barely concealed attraction to Hilly doomed that to a failure both women accepted but never discussed. About all other subjects they were easy and open. "I'm not much given to Envy," Hilly said one day while playing with Curtis. "Lust, Pride, and Anger would top my list of the Seven Deadlies. But I do envy your fertility. I used to think makin' love with Rich couldn't get any better, but now we're trying to make a baby it's like the center of the world, know what I mean?" Ruth admitted that she didn't. It was difficult to imagine what it would be like with a man who wanted her to conceive. Freddie still referred to Curtis as "the shotgun kid" and, though he didn't want her to use birth control, was none too happy that she was pregnant for the second time. "Well"—Hilly rallied—"I won't keep comin' up empty forever. We'll just keep workin' and savin' so that when the chick does hatch, it'll have a nice feathery nest."

About six months later, right after Ruth delivered Freddie Jr., Rich was drafted. At that stage they'd all known that Vietnam was a useless, dirty war, but Rich—a "my country right or wrong" Texan—never considered trying to get out of it. After basic training, when he was about to be shipped out of the country, Hilly dipped into their savings and flew to San Francisco to be with him one last time, saying, "Cross your fingers for us," as she hugged Ruth good-bye. "If I get

pregnant, it'll be like part of him is still here with me." Ruth knew it
would be pointless to talk about the hardships of being pregnant
alone, let alone suggest that Rich might not come back, so she was relieved when Hilly returned home "empty." Hilly took a second job to
keep herself busy. She wrote to Rich daily. His letters, some of which
she shared with Ruth, were, despite misspellings, painfully poetic
about his love for her. When they stopped coming, Hilly went wild.
"I pray he's wounded," she told Ruth. "Whatever it is we'll cope with
it. At least he'd be home." A few weeks later he was shipped to the
VA hospital in Montgomery. The entire left side of his body had been
crushed in a helicopter crash.

Amazingly, Hilly conceived the first time she was alone with Rich.
"When his roommate left for blood tests, I pushed a chair against the
door because it wouldn't lock and climbed into bed with him. Took
some weird maneuvering what with the cast and tubes an' all, but
where there's a will there's a way. Then this nurse shoved the door
open and interrupted us," Hilly confided, her expression roguish and
her eyes shining. "But she had the good manners to say, 'Scuse me,'
and shut the door. We laughed so hard! Maybe it was the laughin'
jarred somethin' loose, 'cause we got us a baby."

But Hilly's joy was short-lived. A few weeks later she turned up at
Ruth's kitchen door, shaking with fright and anger. The hospital had
called to say there had been "an altercation." Rich had been moved
to the psychiatric ward. No, they couldn't give any details over the
phone, but she should come up as soon as possible. "I know he's been
acting strange," she wailed. "He's irritable, and he gets the shakes
and has these weird mood swings, but he's on all those painkillers.
The man's not crazy." For once she accepted Ruth's offer of help, and
after Ruth had called her mother to come take care of the children,
they set out for Montgomery. Ruth drove while Hilly sat very still,
staring straight ahead, eating Saltines and sipping 7-Up to quell her
nausea. At the hospital they waited for over an hour while the con-

sulting physician, a Dr. Erickson, completed his rounds. Hilly asked if Ruth could come in with her. When Erickson hesitated, Ruth said, "She's pregnant, and she's all shaken up." His look of surprise was overcome by one of dismay, but he nodded and ushered them into his office. As soon as the door was closed, Hilly said, with insistence, "My husband is not crazy."

"No, ma'am," Erickson agreed gently, "your husband is not crazy. But"—his tone changed to one of brusque and indisputable candor—"he is addicted. To heroin." And then he told them. Rich had been caught trying to make a drug deal with one of the janitors. There had been a scuffle with an orderly. No charges were being pressed, but Rich was being held in the psychiatric ward for observation. Arrangements would be made to send him to a facility that specialized in drug treatment, but that wasn't the whole story. Rich had also been exposed to a jungle exfoliant called Agent Orange. Studies so far were inconclusive, but there was a chance that his exposure might damage the fetus. "In view of all this, you may decide that your pregnancy . . . Well, I'll be here to talk with you about that later."

Hilly's body convulsed as though she were about to retch. Head lowered, voice quivering, she said, "Can I see him?"

Ruth stood at the door of the psych ward as Hilly went in. After reaching Rich's bed, she put her head on his chest and said, "I know all about it. It's OK. We'll beat it."

Hilly quit her jobs and went to live in a hotel near the hospital while they waited for Rich's transfer. Three weeks later he broke out of the ward. His body was found in an alleyway of one of Montgomery's back streets. A week later Ruth went with her when Hilly terminated the pregnancy.

Ruth heard a whoop and went to the back door. Kylie, much to Moo's delight, was being chased around the yard by one of the chickens. Hilly lunged, caught the bird, tucked it under her arm, and smoothed its feathers. Kylie said they should cut off its head and have it for supper. "Suppress your murderous impulses and get on in that trailer, boy. Can't you see it's startin' to rain?"

An hour later, when they were finishing supper, Hilly lifted her hair, wiped the back of her neck with a paper napkin, and raised her voice against the pelting rain. "I swear you kids eat like fire ants. 'Cept for Kylie having trouble with anything green." She pointed to the salad, which he'd barely touched, and the broccoli he'd picked out from the casserole and pushed to the rim of his plate. "I got peaches and ice cream here, but they're only for kids who eat green stuff."

"Can I eat the salad and leave the broccoli?"

"You been watching too many of them lawyer shows on TV. You can't negotiate with me. Eat all the green stuff. And that cherry tomato too."

Kylie pouted but picked up his fork. Ruth smiled as she collected plates and moved to the sink. It was nice to know someone could get the boy to follow orders. Bending to wipe up a small puddle on the floor, she felt a drop on her head and looked up at a rust stain on the ceiling. "Hilly . . ."

"I know," Hilly said with disgust. "I was planning on having the roof redone, but now . . . " Her voice trailed off.

Ruth said, "No problem," and reached into the cupboard for a pot to catch the leak, but as she straightened, her hand began to tremble. The old adage about "a stitch in time" was surely true. If you didn't fix things, they got worse, and before you knew it, everything was tumbling down around your ears. Nothing, not even a broken heart, frayed your spirit and ground down your self-respect so much as that daily struggle: begging rides because you couldn't afford to get your car fixed, dodging phone calls because you were afraid it would be a collection agency, stretching meals with bread and rice and potatoes, putting up with leaks because you couldn't afford a plumber. Going to a job every day was nothing compared with that grim battle.

Hilly, who'd taken Moo onto her lap, looked over and saw Ruth standing stock-still, hands idle, staring at the linoleum. "Hey, girl-friend, you don't look so good."

"Just tired, bone tired," was all she could get out.

"Then stay the night."

"No. I . . ."

"Let's sleep over. Come on, Grandma, can we sleep over?" Kylie begged, showing his plate and adding, "I ate all the broccoli."

"You don't have your pajamas and—"

"It's raining hard, Ruth. Besides, we can watch the ten o'clock news together."

"At home we mostly sleep in our underwears," Moo put in, so quietly reasonable that Ruth reached over to hug her.

Hilly took charge. "You, Stonewall"—she pointed to Kylie—"into the shower as soon as you've slurped up the ice cream, then straight into bed. My big bed," she added, cutting off the predictable plea for TV. "And you, Ruth"—she spoke in a bossy tone that, when directed at their grandmother, always delighted the kids—"you sit right down, don't clean a thing, an' don't drink any more iced tea or your bladder'll burst."

Ruth ignored the order not to clean up, but twenty minutes later, when Hilly came back in, saying she'd finally gotten the kids into bed, she was sitting at the table stirring sugar into another glass of iced tea. "You're good with them," she said by way of thanks.

"Oh, I'm outstanding. For about an hour. Then my patience gets frazzled, and I want to be with the grown-ups." After opening the cabinet under the sink, Hilly moved a box of detergent, groped be-hind it, and brought out a bottle of tequila. She unscrewed the cap, poured herself a stiff one, and, reaching around Ruth, added a slug to her iced tea.

"Where'd you get that?" Ruth asked, careful to keep reproach out of her voice.

"Stopped by the package store. Some nights plain iced tea just won't cut it." She clinked her glass to Ruth's. "I'd like to say, 'Here's to freedom,' but since we're not goin' to be interviewed for *Lifestyles of the Rich and Famous* . . ."

A wail of "Grandma!" made Ruth get up. "I'll just get them to say their prayers," she said, pouring the glass of water she knew would be the next request, "then we can talk."

"Get 'em to say one for me," Hilly called after her, reaching into her purse to take out the chain mail cutting glove and slapping it against the table.

"I took one of your towels to put under Moo," Ruth said as she reentered the kitchen. "She's been wetting the bed again."

Hilly's head snapped up, and she said, with natural belligerence already fueled by booze, "What fries my ass is that they lied. Stared right in my face and lied. I mean, didn't I go into the office when I was about to buy the car and ask them if our jobs were secure? And didn't they look me right in the eye and say, 'Nothin' to worry about'?"

"Maybe they didn't know."

"Aw, Ruth, how long you gonna be the virgin at the orgy? They don't make these decisions overnight. They knew months ago. Wish we could fight 'em. Prove they lied. But they'd just get lawyers to lie for 'em again."

"We'll find other jobs."

"Oh, sure," Hilly said sarcastically, snapping her fingers. "Just like that! The world's just crying out to hire middle-aged women with no education. 'Bout the only way I could make a dime is to become a lot lizard and hang out at truck stops, but it's too late to wave the red lantern now."

"What about that college program the guy from Atlanta was talking about? If we could get tuition while we're collecting unemployment . . ."

"Go to school? Hell, I dropped out at fifteen to take care of my mama when she had a miscarriage. How'm I gonna fit in now?" She set down her glass with a bang. "Can you imagine walking into a class with kids who're half your age and know more'n you do? That'd make me feel lower than whale manure."

Ruth wanted to say that being a student wasn't about age, it was about wanting to learn, but there was no denying her gut twisted at the prospect of being in a classroom again. "I always loved school," she said softly. "At one time I even thought I'd be a teacher."

"Yeah. I remember. You even did a year of college, didn't you?"

"Uh-huh. I had this teacher, Miss Bradshaw. I guess you could say I was her pet 'cause she was always encouraging me. She used to come to school all dressed up in suits and high heels, and when she'd read poetry, she'd get all emotional. Some kids made fun of her, but I really admired her. She told me it didn't matter if my folks were poor. I could still go to college. I'd never even known there were such things as scholarships till she told me. And she guided me right through and helped me get in. I thought I was going to make it. I thought . . . well, if I hadn't gotten pregnant with Curtis when I came home that summer . . ."

"Yeah," Hilly put in absently, "just when you think life is a bitch, it has puppies." Realizing that it was a clumsy thing to say, she added, flustered, "Hey, I didn't mean . . ."

Ruth laughed. "I know you didn't." It always gave her a mischievous pleasure to see Hilly put her foot in her mouth, which she did with great regularity. "I wonder how Albertine's gonna cope. Henry can't work, so they've only got the one paycheck."

"She'll prob'ly go on welfare."

Ruth was about to ask why Hilly assumed Albertine would go on the dole, but she held back. Hilly would never think herself a racist, but she saw Mexicans as a threat, and when she admired a black person, she was always quick to say that person was an exception.

"I swear I'll slash my wrists 'fore I'll take money from the g.d.

government," Hilly went on. "I've only got myself to look out for, 'cept for the check I send to Aunt Mae so's she can buy little treats. But you're really up the creek, with the kids and all."

By "and all" Ruth knew Hilly meant Roxy. It put a strain on her that Hilly and Roxy had such antipathy toward each other. At least Hilly buttoned her lip about it, but Roxy was always taking potshots at Hilly.

They both fell silent, Hilly drinking steadily, Ruth dispersing the ring her glass had made on the table while they listened to the rain lashing the roof. "It's a damn monsoon out there," Hilly said finally, lifting her hair and wiping the sweat from her neck. "Drench you in the winter; fry you in the summer. 'Member that summer right after Rich went off to Nam and it was so damned hot we went to the movie house every day just 'cause it was air-conditioned? Sat through *Sound of Music* how many times? Kee-rist, I hated that movie."

Ruth muttered, "Uh-huh," but was suddenly wary. If Hilly was talking about Rich, that meant she was far gone. She couldn't handle Hilly's being drunk. Not tonight. "I'm done in," she said.

Hilly checked her watch. "Just a few more minutes till the news." She pulled herself up, cursing as she emptied the pot they'd put down to catch the leak, then walked unsteadily back to the table, where she picked up her cutting glove and slipped it onto her hand. "Know how many years I been wearing this thing?"

"You just took it?"

"Hell, yes. Figured they owed me a memento, so I shoved it in my purse. Would've taken a sewing machine and a couple of sets of fancy underwear if I could've figured out how. Maybe," she said, examining it, "it'll become a new style." Slipping it on, she swaggered out of the kitchenette to the couch, two armchairs, and coffee table that constituted her living room. "You know those fashion shows on TV? Rich people sittin' around clappin' while anorexic baby girls with collagen lips an' silicone titties walk funny down the runway? Sometimes they wear chains an' stuff, so maybe a glove like this'll be the next big thing." Sucking in her cheeks, jutting her hips and waving the glove in the air, she slinked over and switched on the TV.

Ruth burst out laughing. Hilly put her finger to her lips and inclined her head toward the bedroom, then adjusted the sound and felt her way back to sit on the couch as Ruth got up to stand near the armchair. They chattered, nervous as monkeys, through headlines. As the reporter who'd interviewed them came on, they fell dead silent. Ruth gawked, galvanized by her own image. Was that really her? Did she really look so old and raggedy? Why hadn't she had the sense to walk away when the microphone was shoved in front of her instead of freezing like a rabbit caught in the headlights of an oncoming car? Hilly's face, so distorted with anger that it looked like something in a fun house mirror, filled the screen. But she'd no more than started in before the screen went to Celia Lusk, all tears and humility. The reporter nodded with unctuous compassion, then stepped forward for his wrap-up: The plant closing, he seemed to imply, was just one of those things—like a hurricane—beyond human control, but if the victims met the challenge with the right attitude, they could "put it behind them and get on with their lives."

Why, Ruth wondered, were people on TV always talking about putting things behind you and getting on with your life, as though life were no more than a road trip, and smart people forgot the breakdowns and pileups and smashed windshields and just kept on driving to their destination which was what? Death?

Hilly said, "Turn it off before I smash it," and, when Ruth didn't move, bounded up and snapped off the set. Returning to the couch, she drew up her bare feet, wrapped her arms around her legs, and buried her face in her knees. "Oh, shit! Oh, shit," she cursed. "How could I make such a fool of myself! Why do I always flash my tail like a striped-assed baboon?"

"At least you spoke up. It's not your fault they didn't want to hear what you said. I was the one who was pathetic." Ruth sighed, then sat down next to Hilly, putting her arm around her. "Guess we should call it a night," she said finally. "You want me to help you open up the couch?"

"I'm fine." Waving her off and slumping over, she turned her back to the room, fumbled for a throw pillow, cuddled it to her chest, and muttered, "See you in the morning."

Ruth took the afghan from the arm of the couch, unfolded it, decided it was too hot to use it, and folded it back up. She turned off the table lamp, rested her hand on Hilly's head for a moment, hoping the tequila and the sound of the rain would help her sleep, then cut the lights in the kitchen and felt her way down the passage.

The bedroom was close and stuffy with traces of Hilly's jasmine perfume. The bedside lamp threw a dim yellowish light across the bed and up to the velvet painting of a stallion and mare poised on a mountaintop. Kylie, one leg extended, the other drawn up, fists clenched and arms bent as though pumping, looked as though he were running away from something. Moo, her back to him, was curled up like a cashew. She moved Kylie into a more relaxed position, found the sheet he'd kicked onto the floor, covered them both, and snapped off the light. Reaching under her T-shirt, she unhooked her bra, then stepped out of her jeans and felt her way to the other side of the bed. She eased in beside Moo and stroked her head. Lying down felt like a blessing, but she knew she wouldn't be able to sleep.

She hadn't thought about her old high school teacher Miss Bradshaw in years, but now the woman's face came into her mind clear as a photograph. More than her parents, even more than Freddie, Miss Bradshaw had been the person she'd been most eager to see when she came home that summer after her first year in college. Only Miss Bradshaw could fully appreciate what going to college meant to her, because she'd been the one who'd made it possible, not only by her faith in Ruth's abilities but with practical advice. But Miss Bradshaw, she'd learned, was vacationing in Europe. Europe, for heaven's sake! She'd imagined her wandering through castles and museums, riding in gondolas, going to the opera, maybe even meeting a man, though she'd thought Miss Bradshaw (who was then in her thirties) was probably too old to be interested in romance. And that summer, romance had been very much on her mind because she'd fallen, head over heels, in love with Freddie Elkins, who'd come home to Florabama after two years in the navy. "Fallen" and "head over heels" really did describe her first helpless, dizzying experience of sex. By the time Miss Bradshaw came back Ruth'd been married for a month and was three months pregnant. Miss Bradshaw was the last person on earth she wanted to see.

Then one day, months later, she'd run into her at the supermarket where she'd gone to buy Crisco to rub on her stretching belly. Miss Bradshaw had come up behind her in the checkout line. They'd exchanged strained greetings, Miss Bradshaw's gaze staying so resolutely on Ruth's face that Ruth'd defiantly patted her belly and said, "Watermelon season," anticipating, even hoping, to see the disapproval that would allow her to dismiss Miss Bradshaw as an old maid who didn't know anything about love. But Miss Bradshaw had just asked when the baby was due with such a combination of hopelessness and goodwill that by the time Ruth reached the parking lot, where Freddie was waiting in the car, she was in tears. She'd cried so hard that Freddie had gone back into the store and bought her a quart of peach ice cream.

She heard a soft thud, then the clink of glass coming from the kitchen and guessed Hilly had gotten up to pour herself another drink. Moo shifted and snorted. The thing about falling in love, she thought, pulling Moo closer to her and wondering how such powerful snores could come from such a little nose, was that no one could tell you. Hadn't her own mother told her that puppy love could lead you to a dog's life? Hadn't she repeated that to Roxy when Big Kylie had started coming around and she'd seen the power he had over her? Nothing quite as powerful as a handsome young man whose sap was rising. She'd even surprised herself by talking straight out about birth control, which her mother would never have done, even if she'd known about it. But that hadn't helped. Roxy had turned up pregnant same as she had, and there wasn't a thing in the world she could do about it. She'd even hinted that there was a way out, but Roxy wouldn't hear of it. And Ruth understood that too. Didn't every young girl in love think that having her man's baby was the most wonderful thing that could happen to her? She'd got Roxy to the altar before she was showing, bartering for the ceremony by cleaning the church because she couldn't afford to pay the preacher. And she'd never—well, hardly ever—said, "I told you so," when Big Kylie had started to act up.

The rain had stopped. There were no more sounds from the other rooms, so she supposed Hilly had finally gone to sleep. She stretched and consciously tried to relax. If she got a good night's rest, maybe she'd be able to tackle things in the morning. She'd always been able to do what she had to do. She'd find a way. Her life wasn't a complete failure. Her sons had turned out fine. Curtis had made a career in the army and always remembered to call her on her birthday, and Freddie Jr. was a floor supervisor in a California airplane factory, and his wife always sent her a package of jams and jellies at Christmas. But Roxy, and Little Kylie and Moo . . . Tomorrow they'd find a way. What choice did they have? The trouble with experience, she thought as she drifted off, was that you had to do all the wrong things before you got it.

Chapter IV

As the first hints of dawn came through the skylight in Cass's spare room, Bonnie woke with the sickening "Oh, God, I'm conscious again" feeling that comes in times of crisis. The shadowy room was in high disorder. Odd pieces of furniture that Cass, an inveterate fixer-upper, planned to refinish were shoved into corners, along with paint cans, brushes, boxes of tiles, rolls of wallpaper, and curtain fabric. But it was the sight of her own belongings—shoes, rumpled clothes, open suitcase—that made her feel like a bag lady. Today she must definitely find a place of her own.

She'd wanted to start looking yesterday, but after she'd taken a bath to remove the grunge of the motel, Cass had insisted on showing her around town. Fairhope was a surprisingly artsy little enclave situated on the bluff across from Mobile. Normally, nothing would have pleased Bonnie more than seeing the pier and the pleasure boats, strolling around galleries, stopping for espresso, being driven by old houses, and hearing soap opera histories of their occupants, but in her current circumstances these meanderings had only intensified her sense of rootlessness. After stopping at a pet store to buy a leash, bed, case of food, and *How to Train Your Dog* book, they'd gone back to the house to meet Mark, Cass's live-in boyfriend. A pleasant-looking, diffident man about eight years younger and two inches shorter than Cass, he worked as a draftsman in an architectural firm in Mobile. Watching him give Cass a quick kiss before he went off to change out of his work clothes, Bonnie thought how much times had changed. When she and Cass had been in college, only men had mates who were younger, shorter, and less educated. When they came back to the house from the seafood restaurant (where she'd gorged on soft-shell crabs and Cass had grabbed the check), Mark went off to bed while she and Cass sat up, putting away a bottle of Chardonnay and talking, mostly about finances and working at the college.

By one o'clock, slightly tipsy, they were back to their customary who/what/why/when of relationships. "Does Devoe know you've got a job?" Cass asked.

"I s'pose my lawyer told his lawyer."

"Talking through lawyers, now there's an expensive conversation."

"I didn't want it that way, but the finances are in such a tangle it seemed best."

"Bet he's glad you're working now even though he didn't want you to before."

"He didn't really discourage me. I didn't have any particular calling, and I had the kids to raise and—"

"My theory," Cass interrupted, tilting her head and narrowing her eyes, "is that you had a desperate need for a home and family because your mother died when you were so young."

Bonnie laughed. "Cass, you look exactly the way you did when you were taking Psychology 101 and you tried to analyze everyone in the dorm."

"But why else would you stay in a loveless marriage?"

"My marriage wasn't loveless," Bonnie protested. "We just, I don't know how to put it . . . we stopped seeing each other as individuals. We just drifted into being generic wife and husband."

"Sort of like a frog that's put in a pot of cold water and doesn't realize when the heat's turned up and it boils to death?"

Bonnie made a face. "No matter what you think, my life wasn't miserable. I liked being a stay-at-home wife. I enjoyed being a mom," she said lightly, knowing that it would be impossible to convince Cass that normalcy was anything but dull.

"Sure," Cass pressed. "But how long can children be the emotional center of your life?"

"Cass, extolling the joys of marriage and motherhood to you would be like trying to convince someone who doesn't like gardening that it's more than dirt, worms, and manure." Bored with her own defensiveness and feeling a little queasy, she yawned, stroked the puppy, who'd fallen asleep on her lap, and said she thought she was ready for bed. Cass took the hint, saying she'd go let in Bub (short for Beelzebub), who'd been banished to the yard after a hiss-off with the puppy. "And," Bonnie called after her, "*my* theory is that you've never trusted marriage because your daddy walked out on your mother."

"Hey"—Cass shrugged and gave a wicked smile—"I figured that out years ago."

Bonnie carried the puppy into the bathroom and settled him into his new bed, but despite her strokes, he kept struggling out. Cass came to the door, shaking her head. "The reason I prefer cats is that they're like men. Once you understand their nature you don't even think of trying to train them. You're too tenderhearted, Bonnie. You've taken on another burden when you ought to be focusing on yourself." Kneeling unsteadily, Cass put the dog bed in the bathtub and plopped the puppy into it. "You should call him Burden 'cause that's what he is."

The puppy got out of his bed, wobbled to the drain, sniffed it, and turned to Bonnie with a looking-for-love neediness that did, at that moment, feel burdensome. He then tried to crawl out of the tub, scratching valiantly at the slippery porcelain, whimpering as he tumbled back in defeat. He tried again, with the same result. "He's hopeless." Cass laughed as she squeezed toothpaste onto her brush. But wriggling his hindquarters up against the farther side of the tub, he scampered forward with a clumsy leap, gaining purchase on the bath mat, clawing his way up and over the rim to land, stunned, on the tile.

Bonnie laughed, picked him up, and nuzzled him to her chest, saying, "I'm going to call him Ganesha because he can overcome obstacles." She put him back in his bed. Exhausted, he crossed his front paws and rested his head on them.

"You're not gonna brush your teeth?" Cass asked as Bonnie went to the door.

"Too tired to search for my toothbrush," Bonnie said, giving her a good-night hug before they went to their separate rooms.

But Bonnie couldn't sleep, not only because the couch was lumpy and moonlight streamed into the room from the skylight, but because the puppy's struggles reminded her of how she'd knelt, poised and watchful, arms extended, urging, "Come to Mama," when Eugene and Gervaise had taken their first toddling steps. No doubt she had extended her mothering well past the time when they'd actually needed it, driving them places after they had licenses, packing their clothes when they knew how to do it themselves, cooking for them when they preferred to eat out with friends. But habits were hard to break. And even though they'd nicknamed her the Hovercraft, she'd felt they were glad that she'd never become a working mother. She was, she'd believed, the parent on whom they relied. She'd been brought up short by their reactions when soon after Devoe had moved out, she'd asked them to fly home for the weekend so she and Devoe could tell them about the breakup.

Devoe, not to her surprise, had bowed out of the family conference at the last minute, saying he had an unavoidable business meeting and would drop by later to take the kids out to dinner. Secretly she'd felt vindicated by this latest example of emotional avoidance. Surely his absence would shine a bright light on his many past absences; surely the kids would see (though she'd never sink to pointing it out) that she'd been left in the lurch, both emotionally and financially. But Gervaise, after a crying fit, had dried her eyes and gone upstairs to call a friend. And Eugene, after putting his arms around her and saying, "Mom, I'm really, really sorry," and, "You know you can count on me," had asked, almost immediately, what the bankruptcy would mean to his plans for graduate school. She had tried to understand. They couldn't and shouldn't choose sides. They were, after all, in that phase of early adulthood when their own lives and plans had top priority. But she'd been crushed by their seeming indifference. And when Devoe pulled up in the drive—actually honking for the kids to come out because he was too much of a coward to face her—she'd stood alone in her living room, feeling abandoned.

The skylight was now the color of concrete. Her head felt like concrete, too. Well, at least that hadn't changed: She'd been a one-drink girl in college, and apparently she still couldn't have more than two glasses of wine without suffering. She wanted to go to the bathroom and check on Ganesha, but she was afraid of running into Mark. Gervaise had told her that living in coed dorms was "no big deal," but she didn't think she'd ever feel comfortable running into a strange man in Jockey shorts, so she waited until the zesty smells of bacon and coffee pricked her nostrils, then dressed and went to the kitchen.

Mark, in a terry cloth robe that showed well-developed, if surprisingly hairy, legs, said good morning and asked if she wanted wheat or rye toast. "Or maybe," he added, grinning, "just coffee and a coupla aspirins?" Sitting down, she said she'd take the coffee and aspirins first and nodded a wan thanks when he handed them to her and went back to cracking eggs. Cass, wearing tennis shoes and a denim shirt tucked into snug white Bermuda shorts, came in fresh from the shower. Bonnie took it as a rule that no one over fourteen looked good in Bermuda shorts, but Cass was the exception. In fact, Cass's appearance had improved with age. As a young woman she'd been gangly, hunching her shoulders in a misguided effort to disguise the fact that she was almost five feet ten inches, and thick glasses and straggly hair had given her an owlish expression. Now her angular body was fashionable, she'd replaced her glasses with contact lenses, and her hair (thanks to Clairol) was still sable brown but cut close to show off her long neck. Next to her, Bonnie, whose curvy prettiness had been in vogue in their youth, felt like the Pillsbury Doughboy. Weight Watchers frozen dinners didn't help if you ate three at a sitting, and eating alone in front of the TV, she'd been doing just that. Or maybe she just felt unattractive (she occupied herself buttering toast as Mark sniffed Cass's hair and told her he liked the almond shampoo) because the closest she'd come to sex in the past year was a cheeky offer from a snub-nosed carpenter in his twenties who, while repairing the lattice on her porch, told her that if she had "any other needs," he was available day or night.

Cass disengaged herself from Mark and sat down, reaching over to the sideboard for the list of apartments she'd gotten from a real estate agent. "They're all in your price range, and after you called, I crossed out the ones that don't allow pets," she said, munching on a slice of bacon and handing the sheet to Bonnie. So many listings had been crossed out that it looked like a document censored by the CIA.

"Only four, huh? Maybe Burden is an appropriate name after all," Bonnie said, feeling overwhelmed, then excused herself to go take a shower.

The first place they looked at was an ersatz "executives" complex, so spanking new that it had banners (IMMEDIATE OCCUPANCY!) on the pink stucco facade. The place reminded Bonnie of the set for a TV sit-com about swinging singles, and when they saw a lone man and two women (who might as well have had IMMEDIATE OCCUPANCY tattooed on their chests) lolling beside the minuscule pool, she didn't even have to look at the apartment to decide it wasn't for her. The second place was a brick house with dark little rooms that smelled of mildew, located on a street teeming with kids, bikes, buggies, and women in stretch pants. The third was a spacious, light-filled loft— above a bowling alley. The fourth, and last, listing was a carriage house behind a lovely old house with a well-tended garden. Bonnie's hopes were high until the owner, who lived in the big house, complained at length about the loneliness of her widowhood and asked so many personal questions that Bonnie was afraid the woman wanted a companion instead of a tenant. By the time they picked up a Penny-Saver and stopped at a Burger King to read it she felt as cranky as a three-year-old who'd been dragged along on a shopping expedition.

"This one's a possibility," Cass said, her eyes flitting like a speed-reader's over the ads. "'Old country house with garden'—that means it's a shack in the boonies with a scarecrow in the yard—'small but clean'—that means you can't swing a cat in it and they've doused it with a bucket of Pine Sol."

"Go on."

"'Partly furnished' means didn't bother to get their crap out. Wanna give them a call?"

"I guess so." Bonnie fished in her purse for change and started to get up, but Cass said, "Sit," in much the same tone she'd used with the puppy. So Bonnie sat, sipping her watery iced tea, eyeing Cass's chocolate shake, and wondering how she'd fallen into such abject dependency that she had to let someone else make a phone call for her.

Cass stuck out her head from the area where the phones and the bathrooms were located and motioned Bonnie into the ladies'. "It was a neighbor's phone," Cass told her, raising her voice as they went into adjoining stalls. "Old croaker, so country I could barely understand him. Seems the woman who owns the place, a Mrs. Nunnally, had a fall so she went to stay with her daughter in Eufaula. Daughter wants her to move in with her, but the old lady doesn't want to give up her home. You listening?"

Bonnie said yes, her eyes sliding over the usual sexual graffiti to THIS IS JESUS COUNTRY juxtaposed with 666: SATAN RULES FLORABAMA as she wondered what it would be like to live in a county where the natives believed the territory to be hotly contested.

"So"—Cass went to the sink—"they've compromised, and the old woman's going to lease out the house for a year."

Bonnie came out of her stall and winced at her image in the mirror. "Ever wonder why there are more bag ladies than bag men?" she asked, pulling out the tails of the pink silk shirt she'd tucked into her jeans and leaving them loose to camouflage her love handles.

"I suppose it goes back to the cave people. You know, guys out hunting, gals left behind pregnant, taking care of the kids, making sure the fire doesn't go out. Ready to hunt?"

Cass punched the button on the hand dryer and turned back to Bonnie. "Let's check it out."

With the air-conditioning on high, they drove away from town, passing miles of wooded land dotted with the occasional service station, secondhand store, produce stand, or junkyard and an inordinate number of churches, each with a sign out front that listed times of services and offered a biblical quotation.

"The gist of all these biblical quotations seems to be 'You're in trouble, but you deserve it,'" Bonnie observed wryly.

"How else could folks deal with hard times? They were just crawling out from under Reconstruction when the boll weevil destroyed all their crops. Then there was the Depression. You know, my mama was just a little girl when that came along but she's still traumatized by it. Last time I visited her I saw a whole case of Spam and another one of condensed milk in the garage and I said, 'Mama, you gone Egyptian on me? Plan to have food for the afterlife put in your tomb? And if so, can't you do better than dented cans of Spam?' and she comes back with, 'Well, Cass, you never know when hard times are comin' and what with the hurricanes an' all, I'll have food even if there's a power outage.'" Squinting through the windshield at a road sign partially obscured by the summer growth of bushes, Cass asked, "That sign say Sam's Road?" Nodding an affirmative to her own question, she turned onto a recently paved blacktop shimmering in the heat. "This whole area has been rezoned to semi-industrial," she told Bonnie. "There's a cement factory and automobile yard up ahead, and beyond that some trailers—you know, rednecks hanging on to country life. Ol' Marion Hawkins, namesake of our illustrious college, owns most of the land around here. If Mobile keeps growing, I figure he'll subdivide it and sell to young professionals who'll plant arugula on the weekends."

"Hawkins is a friend of Daddy's," Bonnie said defensively. "I remember him coming to supper when I was a kid. He used to do magic tricks, like pulling a nickel out from behind his ear."

"That's about his speed. I expect you knew all of those important guys?"

"Oh, sure, but I didn't really know that they were important. Even Governor Wallace came to our house once. My mama and daddy had a really big fight beforehand. Mama was yelling that she wouldn't have 'that man' as a guest in her house, and Daddy was yelling that it was his house too and 'that man' had done a lot of good."

"So he came?"

"Uh-huh. He came by with three or four of his cronies. Mama stayed in her room. Stayed there for a couple of days, but this must've been around the time she was diagnosed with the cancer, so I don't know if she was sick or just making a point with Daddy." The glamorous studio portrait—arched and penciled brows, glistening lipstick, and controlled curls—that she usually called to mind when thinking about her mother was replaced by a long-suppressed memory of an emaciated face, lank hair, and eyes that asked unanswerable questions.

"So you met him?"

"Uh-huh. He looked right in my eyes and talked to me just like I was a grown-up. He was about a foot shorter than Daddy, but what a little rooster! The kind of man who can strut sitting down. Later, when he was shot, I felt terrible. I guess you'll think I was stupid, but I was almost totally ignorant of what was going on with the civil rights thing."

"Well, we were only kids. What I remember is people saying how the Yankees were going to come down from Washington. I was scared because my grandfather had told me all these stories about Yankees burning his grandfather's farm and killing the cattle. I think ol' George actually wanted them to come down again. See if we couldn't have a replay of the Civil War with a different outcome. But he did do some good for the state—schools, highways, increased teachers' salaries."

"The Duke worked with him to bring in out-of-state business."

"At least he never lied about what he was up to. And before he died, he went to that black church and apologized. How many politicians you know who haven't lied? How many have really apologized, not just cried crocodile tears to bring up their ratings in the polls?"

"We've come a way, and we've got a way to go." Bonnie leaned against the headrest, closing her eyes against the strobelike glare of sun flashing through the trees. "We had a Negro, I mean, black—"

"Go straight to African-American."

"An African-American yardman, but I can't remember his name. And Phoebe came in every day. Usually when I came home from school, I'd find her and Mama sitting in the kitchen smoking cigarettes. I really loved Phoebe 'cause when my parents were gone, she'd let me eat Vienna sausages out of the can. And I saw black employees and their families at the Duke's summer picnic. I knew that black people lived in a certain section of town, and there was this invisible line that I knew I shouldn't cross. What I remember most was that I used to sit with the Duke in his big leather chair and we'd watch Walter Cronkite on the TV news while we were waiting for Phoebe to put supper on the table, but one night he said I couldn't watch the TV news because it would upset me. Then I wasn't allowed to go to school because Mama said there was trouble. Then Phoebe stopped coming in. Actually," she amended, "I never called her Phoebe. Mama said I should call her Mrs. Smalls because she was an adult, which tells me a lot about my mama's attitudes."

"So did she finally come back?"

"No, she never did. Broke my mama's heart. I can't remember . . . Lord, I haven't thought about these things for years. . . . I can't remember how I found out, but I heard about those four little black girls being blown apart at that Baptist church. That really terrified me. Mama told me to pray for them, and—oh, I'd forgotten this part—she drove downtown and bought Phoebe this black suit and a big black hat and had the store send them to her. Phoebe sent Mama a thank-you note, but we never heard from her after that. Years later I ran into our yardman, and he said she'd gone to live in California. I think one of those little girls was related to her, maybe her niece, but I can't remember how I found that out either."

Cass slowed to look at a collection of mailboxes along the side of the road. "Hey, this is it. We're almost there. I go up to a big tree, then when the gravel road stops, turn right." She did just that and said, "Please note that I'm now turning onto a dirt road. Also note that we have a lot of storms, dirt roads become mud after storms, and your car can get stuck and there's nobody around here to help you."

Bonnie took in the fallow field to her right, the virgin woods to her left, the geraniums and marigolds sprouting from tires cut in half to make planters on either side of the road, but her mind was still full of the past, of how her mother, as she'd become bedridden, had started more and more sentences with "If only Phoebe were here," how Geraldine, the younger black woman who replaced her, made toast instead of "brown clouds" (Bonnie's name for Phoebe's fluffy biscuits) and slopped gravy over food instead of putting it in the gravy boat and never scrubbed the ring out of the bathtub the way Phoebe had done. How Geraldine forgot to put a cloth napkin on the tray she took up to Mama's room and told Bonnie to mind her own business when she reminded her. How one night even Daddy, who'd never loved Phoebe the way Mama did, got all watery-eyed and said, "If only Phoebe were here."

A white nurse who wore white stockings, a white uniform, and White Shoulders to cover up the smell of medicines had come to take care of Mama, but Geraldine had stayed on because Daddy said they shouldn't make too many changes. Once, after Bonnie'd refused to eat the dinner Geraldine had fixed, Geraldine had caught her eating Vienna sausages out of the can, told her she was "a spoiled little mess," and complained to the Duke, who'd laid down the law: She would eat what was put on the table or go without. So she'd gone on a hunger strike, defiantly pushing food to the side of her plate until Daddy pleaded and begged her to eat, then lost his temper and sent her to her room, where she'd felt both triumphant and ashamed, thinking maybe she *was* a spoiled little mess. By way of a truce, the Duke let her dog, Rustler, sleep in her room. She always had Rustler to hug and talk to. Until he was hit by that car.

Geraldine had been the one who'd carried Rustler, blood drooling from his mouth, into the house. Bonnie had knelt by him until he'd gone all scary stiff. And even though Geraldine had always complained about his shedding all over the carpets, she'd been the one who'd dug his grave in the backyard. The Duke had told Bonnie that no, dogs didn't go to heaven. Geraldine, who never answered back (though Bonnie had once seen her stick out her tongue when the Duke wasn't looking), told him, "Excuse me, Mr. Duke, but I believes there's a heaven for dogs, leastways the good ones."

They approached the stand of shade trees that sheltered the white farmhouse with the sagging veranda. "Tin roof," Bonnie observed. "I love a tin roof when it rains."

"Unless it leaks," Cass said, turning off the motor. "The neighbor told me the keys are under a brick, which is under the first step of the veranda. How original." After getting out of the car, she walked, hands on hips, to the three wooden steps leading up to the veranda, where she bent, felt, then, cursing, got down on her knees and felt again. Wiping the sweat from her hairline and brushing the dirt from her bare knees, she stood, holding up a single rusted skeleton key. "So much for high-tech security."

Bonnie stepped out into the blazing sun, offering, "Maybe it's so safe it doesn't need high-tech."

"And I am the queen of Romania," Cass muttered, mounting the steps, pulling back the screen door, shoving the key into the lock, and jiggling it.

Bonnie touched the headpiece of a pine rocker sitting next to the door. "This is the genuine article," she said in amazement. "I think you could get at least seven hundred for this. And she's left it on the veranda."

"Wanna steal it and sell it?" Cass grunted as she turned the key and shoved at the rain-swollen front door. They walked into a large, stuffy front room smelling, as Cass had predicted, of Pine Sol. The wallpaper was sun-bleached, showing brighter patches where paintings had hung. A couch upholstered in indestructible brown and yellow tweed fabric, a rocker (twin to the one on the veranda), and a TV stand holding a battered set topped with rabbit ears were the only furniture. Cass, struggling to open a window, said, "Christ, this is depressing."

Looking up at a ceiling fan, Bonnie countered with "Once that fan's turned on, and with those shade trees and these high ceilings, it should stay tolerably cool in the summer."

"Which means it'll be a bitch to heat in the winter."

"The floors are heart pine and in pretty good shape." Having moved to the fireplace, she chipped a fleck of peeling paint from the mantel, leaned closer, and declared, "Solid oak. Can't imagine why anyone would paint over it."

"Shit!" Cass brought her index finger to her mouth, sucked, then examined it. "I got a splinter."

"Don't bother to try to open things," Bonnie said, feeling guilty. "We won't be here that long. Just a quick look-see." She wandered into the passageway on her left and went into the first bedroom. Pale blue flower-sprigged wallpaper, tiny closet, oak chest of drawers almost as tall as she, a double bed with an old but surprisingly clean mattress that creaked as she sat down to test it. A single body had hollowed it out in the center. Mrs. Nunnally must've been a widow for a long time. Not wanting to think about sleeping alone, she moved on to the next room. This must've been where children, now grandparents themselves, had slept. Two sets of bunk beds and high school pennants on the wall. Back in the passageway she saw a rope hanging from a door-size opening in the ceiling, pulled on it, and moved aside quickly as a folding ladder to the attic came crashing down. No time to explore that with Cass calling out for her to come see the dining room.

She answered, "Just a sec," and went into the bathroom. Like most bathrooms built in the 1920s, it was small, with barely enough room for a big claw-footed tub, a washbasin backed with lavender and green tile, and an old-fashioned commode with the water tank and pull chain. Bending down, she turned on the bath faucets. A deep clank and gurgle brought forth a burp of rust-colored effluvium; then water gushed clear and hot, spattering her shirt. "Water pressure's good," she called out, wiping her hands on her pants and moving to the dining room.

"Look at the size of this." Cass drew her finger across a large walnut dining table, exposing a rich shine beneath the coat of dust, then, after stepping to a built-in corner cupboard with an arched top glass door, admitted, "Even I wouldn't mind owning this, though it'd take a forklift to move it. That's probably why they took the chairs and left the table behind. Boy, the furniture was like the marriages in those days: s'posed to last a lifetime." Seeing the look on Bonnie's face, Cass added, "Don't get all nostalgic for ye good old days. A lot of those 'till death do us part' marriages made women long for widowhood." Glancing at her watch, she walked briskly into the kitchen and called out to report, "Stove and fridge look like something from a 1940s Sears catalog, and oh, there's even a potbellied stove in case you want to build up your chest muscles chopping wood."

But the first thing Bonnie saw upon entering the kitchen was the window over the sink that looked out on a screened porch and, beyond that, a flower and vegetable garden withering in the sun. Was there anything sadder than a neglected garden? Leaning against the sink and glancing to her right, she saw a Burpee seed calendar nailed to the cupboard. It was turned to June and had spidery notations "transfer seedlings, fertilize tomatoes," etc. "I wonder what Mrs. Nunnally's first name is. Some old-fashioned name, I bet. Amelia or Grace. And imagine her living out here all by herself in a house that had once been full of people. Carrying on with her garden and—"

"Talking to herself."

"That too." Bonnie laughed and, anticipating objections, said, "I like the place," with more enthusiasm than she actually felt. "It's private."

"You mean isolated."

"It has charm, even though it's rustic."

"It's old and dilapidated. After a couple of days out here you'll start eating frogs and berries and talking to owls."

"You're sure living up to your namesake, Cassandra. Negative. Always predicting disaster."

Cass sucked in her cheeks and raised her eyebrows. "You've forgotten your mythology. Let me remind you that Cassandra had a genuine gift of prophecy, but Apollo cursed her so no one would believe her."

Bonnie sat down at the Formica table. "Money is a factor, you know. For the price . . ."

"Why don't you just move in with me? I know my guest room's a mess, but we can clean it up. At least stay until you've looked around. Something's bound to turn up."

"And if it does, I'd have to move again after school's started."

"That's better than becoming the Girl of the Limberlost." Cass sat opposite and leaned toward her. "I've fixed up old houses, Bonnie. I know what I'm talking about. Not to be negative again, but how handy are you? You've always been able to pick up a phone and pay someone when things needed fixing. To you this looks like a Martha Stewart project, it has 'aesthetic' possibilities; to me it looks like loneliness and a helluva lot of hard labor."

Bonnie tried not to be offended and, noting that Cass had said "live with me" instead of "live with us," ventured, "What about Mark?"

"What about him? He likes you. And after all it is my house. I don't mean that to sound so territorial but—"

"Isn't it ironic that I'm the one who centered her life around a home while you never cared. Now you're the one who owns a house and I'm the bag lady."

"Bag lady?" She reached for Bonnie's hand. "You know Lord Byron said, 'Friendship is Love without his wings.' You don't have the flights of ecstasy, but having had more than a few high-flying romances that ended in a crash, I appreciate friendship. You've been my friend for over twenty years. I've known Mark for six months and don't know if I'll be with him six months from now. He's going through a divorce, you know."

"You seem to get along."

"If you'd had as many affairs as I've had, you'd know that even the rotten ones are usually good for six months. We've lived together for three. Hey, we're still trying out new positions."

"And I don't want to be in the next room while you're trying them."

Cass smiled. "Don't tell me you've gone prudish on me. When we were in college, we necked in the same car."

"It's hardly the same," Bonnie answered quickly, then looked puzzled. "I don't remember necking in any car when you were there."

"Sure. That weekend Riz Mazersky came to visit you. I remember it vividly because I'd never been with anyone who was really rich before. He looked like the Great Gatsby to me. Still in college and he was asking to see the wine list and ordering à la carte at a restaurant where the waiters were better dressed than any of my relatives had ever been at weddings or funerals. And his convertible—straight out of a showroom."

"Riz was always a spoiled kid. And a bit of a show-off."

"To me he was totally intimidating. The guy he brought along for me—I think his name was Bernard—was less impressive. But they both seemed exotic. Maybe because they were Jewish. OK, that dates me, but it was before Woody Allen or Seinfeld and I was from Talladega Springs."

Bonnie scoured her memory and came up with nothing. "I still don't remember necking in any car."

"A white convertible," Cass insisted. "It would be white, wouldn't it? By a lake. The moon was shining, Riz had a hip flask of Grand Marnier—another first for me—then the clutch and grab started. . . ." Puckering her lips, she made smooching sounds. "Oh, the fear and the excitement—maybe the excitement was because of the fear. I don't think kids neck anymore. I think they either do it at fourteen or join some religious group that encourages chastity till marriage. Or both. How did you meet Riz anyway?"

"He was a friend of the family. We'd known each other since we were kids 'cause our fathers did business together. And I still don't remember making out with him."

"That's the trouble with becoming a mother: You developed selective amnesia about your youth so you could give Gervaise lectures with a straight face. Not that you were ever really wild."

"I took Gervaise to Planned Parenthood when she was fifteen," Bonnie said. "But truth to tell, I didn't know if I was doing the right thing."

Cass said, "You were," mopped sweat from her brow, looked at her watch, and got up. "Whew. I need air-conditioning. And we're supposed to go over to the college. I'll cool off in the car while you take a last little look-see."

Alone at the kitchen table Bonnie bowed her head as though waiting for divine guidance. No doubt Cass was right about all the problems of the place; on the other hand . . . weighing the pros and cons made her feel dizzy. Or maybe it was the heat. Getting up, she looked out at the neglected garden again. She'd make a decision tonight. Right now she wanted to get over to the college and get the lay of the land on the job that was going to pay the rent.

Chapter V

"No ivy-covered walls, no chapels or bell towers or statues of famous alumni," Cass said as she drove past the guard shack into the parking lot of Marion Hawkins College. "The architectural style is early seventies institutional; it could be an IRS office, a school, or a minimum security prison. Sometimes I feel like it's all three." Turning off the motor, she gestured toward the sprawl of single-story stucco buildings connected by concrete paths and neat, mostly treeless lawns. "It's strictly a no-frills 'education can help you get a job' operation. Some of the faculty are deadwood, but a few are first-rate—just ended up here because like me, they aren't careerists and it's a tight market. Some of the students can barely read, but every once in a while you find a diamond in the rough."

Bonnie had a hollow feeling in her stomach, and it wasn't just because they'd skipped lunch. Twisting the rearview mirror to get a look at herself she saw that her face was shiny and her hair was limp.

"You look fine, Bonnie. Besides, you already have the job. And officially you don't start till next week. This is just a courtesy call," Cass assured her, getting out. "I'll be in my office. If I get through first, I'll come over to administration."

Bonnie ran a brush through her hair, wiped off a smudge of mascara, put on a slick of lipstick, and opened the door. The heat hit her as though she'd opened an oven. She sucked in her stomach and turned onto the path leading to the administration building. A teenage boy with baggy pants riding dangerously low on his hips, a baseball cap turned backward and a T-shirt that said, YOU CAN LEAD A KID TO COLLEGE BUT YOU CAN'T MAKE HIM THINK, shuffled toward her and, in response to her "good afternoon" gave a listless "yo." A young black woman dressed in an Ashanti print caftan, hair plaited with plastic beads, hurried past, pulling a child behind her. She acknowledged Bonnie's greeting with a quick nod, then yanked the child's hand, saying, "Move, Tanisha! You know I gotta get to work." Bonnie picked up her pace, flung back the door to the administration building, and got a kiss of cool air and a whiff of floor polish.

The hallway was blessedly dim. Sunlight beat through glass doors at either end of the hall, highlighting the floor that was being buffed by a stoop-shouldered black janitor with an electric polisher. She passed a bulletin board and stopped, hoping there might be some For Rent notices. There was none. Nor were there any announcements of sorority meetings, guest lecturers, concerts, or dances, such as she remembered from her college days. Instead, there were official printouts about schedules and financial aid, an invitation to a meeting of the Bible Club, a sheet of lime green paper with a message in calligraphy: ASPIRING POETS, JOURNALISTS & SERIOUS SCRIBBLERS NEEDED TO CONTRIBUTE TO NEW COLLEGE MAGAZINE. CONTACT PROF. CASSANDRA LEDFORTH, ENGLISH DEPARTMENT, three-by-five cards advertising baby-sitting, computer tutoring, and rides to share. She wondered if she should take down the number of a computer tutor. There'd been four computers in the Atlanta house, one for every member of the family. Devoe used his to keep financial accounts (fat lot of good that'd done him), Eugene and Gervaise played with theirs for hours at a time, sending E-mail, visiting chat rooms, and surfing the Net with the same glazed, tongue-protruding absorption they'd given to blocks and Erector sets when they were preschoolers. But except for a file of her favorite recipes, the computer Devoe had given her for Christmas three years ago had remained virtually untouched. They'd all volunteered, even pushed, to teach her, but being fundamentally uninterested, she'd always begged off. Even after she knew she'd need computer skills on the job, even after she'd bought instruction manuals and promised herself to sit down and learn, she'd procrastinated, overwhelmed with lawyers, real estate people, packing, and putting things into storage. She was still, as Devoe had teased, roadkill on the information highway.

"Can I help you, ma'am?" the janitor asked, shutting off his machine.

"No, thanks, I know where I'm going." Straight to hell.

She pushed open the glass doors to the main office and stopped at the receptionist's desk, where a girl with wispy bangs, big eyes, and a prominent overbite said, "Oh, hi!" as though she'd been expecting her, then giggled for no apparent reason and went on, "I'm Norma Jean. I met you when you came in for your interview, remember?"

She didn't. She tried to cover the memory lapse by saying, "Hello, Norma Jean. Were you named after Marilyn Monroe?" The girl looked bewildered. "Norma Jean Baker was Marilyn Monroe's real name. I guess that was before your time."

"My father has a calendar of Marilyn Monroe in his workshop. Maybe that *is* why I'm named Norma Jean," she exclaimed, and, turning to the desk behind her, said, "Did you hear that, Mrs. Snopes? Norma Jean Baker was Marilyn Monroe's real name."

Mrs. Snopes, the office manager, looked up, feigning annoyance at being interrupted though Bonnie had seen her giving her the once-over when she'd walked in. She *did* remember Mrs. Snopes. How could anyone forget those droopy cheeks, penciled eyebrows, and the bouffant hairdo that looked as if it could be lifted off intact? Not to mention the fussy, officious manner. "Good afternoon, Mrs. Snopes," Bonnie said, moving to her desk and extending her hand. "I'm—"

Ignoring Bonnie's offered hand, Mrs. Snopes said, "Yes, I know. You're Bonnie Duke Cullman," as though it were an accusation.

After an embarrassed pause Bonnie said, "I just thought I'd drop by. I'd like to see Mrs. Jackson if she's available."

Mrs. Snopes gave a curt "It's best to make an appointment, but I'll see," got up and walked to the door marked "Director of Admissions," knocked and went in, closing the door behind her. Bonnie remembered that Cass had told her Mrs. Snopes was nicknamed Snoopy, not because of her basset hound cheeks but because she was the campus gossip. Bonnie hadn't even started work, so what gossip could there be about her? Turning back to Norma Jean, she raised her eyebrows, questioning the snub. Norma Jean gave a "what me worry?" smile, followed by another giggle.

Mrs. Snopes called, "Mrs. Cullman?," held open the door to Mrs. Jackson's office, and motioned Bonnie in.

A single pot of ivy stood on the sill of double windows facing the quad. Family photos were displayed on the desk, and an American flag hung in one corner, next to a saintly portrait of Martin Luther King, a diploma from the University of Alabama, and a framed needlepoint that said, "THINK YOU CAN, THINK YOU CAN'T—EITHER WAY YOU'RE RIGHT—Henry Ford." Lena Jackson, a light-skinned black woman in her late thirties, slipped her feet into her pumps and got up from behind her desk, leaning forward to offer her hand. "Mrs. Cullman, it's great to see you." Everything about her—cream blouse underneath a beige cotton Lands' End suit, single strand of pearls, wide wedding band, and hair ironed into a pageboy—said conformity. But her full mouth was painted fire engine red, and her smile was warmly sincere as she said, "Please sit down." Bonnie sat. "Oh, Emily," Mrs. Jackson called to Mrs. Snopes's stiff retreating back, "would you be kind enough to get us a couple of diet Cokes from the little refrigerator? And please close the door behind you." The door closed.

Settling back into her chair and slipping her feet out of her pumps, Lena Jackson said, "I'm so glad you're here," in a voice that sounded not only genuine but positively relieved. "In fact," she continued, "I tried to call you in Atlanta, but the number had been disconnected."

"I've leased my house, and I stayed with family in Birmingham before I drove down to Florabama yesterday. My friend Cass—Professor Ledforth in the English Department?—and I have been out looking for a place for me to live."

"I hope you've found something."

"I think I have."

"Good. Because I'd like you to start ASAP. Of course we'll prorate your salary. But could you start ASAP?"

ASAP was one of Devoe's favorite directives ("Can you get my gray suit cleaned ASAP" or "Let's have dinner ASAP"), to which she'd usually replied, "I'm not one of your employees," but since she now was an employee, she nodded vigorously.

"Let me explain," Mrs. Jackson went on. "Are you familiar with a lingerie company called Cherished Lady?" Bonnie nodded again, wondering where this was going. "They've had a mill here in town since the fifties and they're about to close it down."

"Oh. Yes. I saw something about it on TV the other night," Bonnie said.

"Management at Cherished Lady has been trying to tie into federal and state funds so they can enroll some of the women who were laid off in our displaced homemakers' program. We've had the usual bureaucratic dithering and red tape so we didn't know for sure until last week that their former employees *will* be eligible for the program. We still haven't ironed out all the wrinkles, so I don't know how long it will be before the funds actually arrive."

Bonnie was having trouble keeping up. "But laid-off factory workers aren't displaced homemakers, are they? I mean, they've been employed, bringing home a weekly paycheck, right?"

"Yes. Sure." Mrs. Jackson conceded, making a "here's the church and here's the steeple" configuration with her hands and tapping her chin with her index fingers. "But this program was the only way to get those displaced workers some help." She shook her head. "After you've struggled through hundreds of pages of government guidelines, you'll learn that the only way to get anything done is to figure out a way to get around them."

"I'd thought"—Bonnie tried to sound casual—"that the women I'd be working with would be . . . well"—she opened her hands—"displaced homemakers."

"These gals definitely qualify as displaced. Most of them aren't young and have little formal education. I don't expect many will enroll in the program, and many of those who do will only be enrolling so they can have something to do while they look around for other work. I anticipate a fairly high dropout rate. I'm sure you can imagine some of the difficulties they'll face." Their eyes connected. Mrs. Jackson smiled and nodded. "We'll be administering a battery of tests to help determine appropriate placement in remedial or regular programs. The results will be collated ASAP, and beginning next week, the applicants will meet with you to discuss which programs they're interested in and which classes to take. You'll also be advising them on matters that aren't academic in nature. They may experience adjustment problems with the learning environment, and while their practical problems are not strictly speaking within your job description, it would be beneficial if you could steer them in the right direction. Be an ombudsman of sorts. You should be familiar with both federal and state agencies and programs—DIR, TRA, EDWAA, the unemployment office, et cetera. And you'll probably find it necessary to network with local nongovernmental programs—churches, civic organizations, and the like. Management at Cherished Lady is extremely sensitive to the negative publicity they're getting because of the mill's sudden closing, so they're more than eager to liaise with you. Of course we want to be proactive, so the first step in the process. . . ."

Mrs. Jackson continued to talk. Bonnie assumed a look of interest, nodding to show she was taking it all in. But she couldn't digest it. It was an alphabet soup of abbreviations clotted with management jargon (affillate relationships, targeting, proactive), peppered with psychobabble (empowering, mentoring, and the ever-popular self-esteem), topped with a large dollop of sports' imagery (goals, touchdowns, team effort).

"Any questions?" Mrs. Jackson inquired, unclenching her hands, placing them on the desk, and looking directly at her.

Bonnie swallowed and began, "I think I get the drift, but as you know . . ." As you know what? I haven't had a job in over twenty years? I have only the vaguest idea of what's expected of me? I'm scared shitless? "Well, I'm sure I'll have a lot of questions later."

Mrs. Jackson looked at her watch, slipped her feet back into her pumps, and stood up. "Good. Let me show you your office, Mrs. Cullman."

"Please call me Bonnie."

"All right. Bonnie." Mrs. Jackson smiled but didn't ask to be called by her first name. Office hierarchy, Bonnie thought as she followed her to the reception area, where Norma Jean stood holding two cans of diet Coke. "Mrs. Snopes had to go to the little girls' room, so she asked me to get these," Norma Jean explained, offering the cans with another nervous titter.

That giggle is going to wear thin real fast, Bonnie thought as she took her Coke. Unmotivated laughter was one of her pet peeves. It was, she'd noticed, far more common in women than in men, and even though (or perhaps because) she understood that it came from a desire to please and appear compliant, it drove her up the wall. She also understood that Snoopy's exit to "the little girls' room" was another example of the pecking order: Snoopy thought that fetching Cokes was beneath her, so she'd delegated the task to an underling. Bonnie expected she'd be in line for the same treatment.

Mrs. Jackson said, "Mrs. Snopes worked here way before I came on board." Her eyes met Bonnie's as she opened her can of Coke. After taking a sip, Mrs. Jackson continued, "Come on. Let me introduce you to the rest of the team." Bonnie followed her out of the reception area into a hallway divided into cubicles, where they visited Mrs.

Rusk, Financial Aid; Mrs. Vandom, Student Affairs; Miss Shelton, Student Housing. Bonnie smiled and made small talk with each of her co-workers, trying to recall the tips about how to remember names by association. (Mrs. Rusk was brown and dry-looking, like the baby rusks she'd given to the kids when they were teething; Mrs. Shelton provided shelter). "Now," Mrs. Jackson said when the introductions were finished, "let me show you to your office." Office, not cubicle, Bonnie rejoiced, following as Mrs. Jackson doubled back to reception, opened a door directly in front of Mrs. Snopes's desk, and flipped on the light.

The fluorescent tube sputtered at either end, then blazed into full glare, showing a tiny room with no windows, pea soup–colored walls, two file cabinets crammed into a corner, and two orange plastic bucket chairs backed up to the wall facing a large desk. The desk held plastic in and out trays, a telephone, the dreaded computer, and stacks of papers, folders, and documents. "You may not be familiar with all the new programs"—Mrs. Jackson said, patting the top of the computer monitor (All? Bonnie thought. How about any?)—"but Mrs. Snopes is a real whiz with computers"—(Oh, wouldn't she just be)—"and she'll be more than happy to help you"—(I can see her bouncing with joy at the opportunity)—"so, when do you think you'll be able to start?"

Bonnie's need to comply struggled with her logistical problems and quickly won out. "If I can rent this house I looked at this morning, then I guess I could come in, at least for part of the day, tomorrow."

Mrs. Jackson beamed. "I knew I could count on you. I understand that you'll have to take time off to get things arranged—have your phone and utilities turned on, register your car, set up a bank account and all."

None of which I'd thought of, Bonnie admitted to herself, amending, "But if I don't get the house—"

"We'll fall off that bridge when we come to it," Mrs. Jackson answered amiably. "I have to get back to work. Now, if there's anything you need . . ."

"Yes. Thanks so much. Professor Ledforth is coming by soon to pick me up, so I'll just . . ."

"Yes. Settle in. Familiarize yourself. Good to have you on board."

Bonnie nodded. Mrs. Jackson left but didn't close the door behind her. On board? How about at sea? Bonnie thought, staring out the door at Snoopy, who was now back at her desk, pounding away at her computer keyboard like Van Cliburn playing Tchaikovsky.

She sat down, found the secretary chair too low, got up, and fiddled with the gadget on the side that was supposed to adjust it. As she pulled, pushed, and jiggled, she felt Snoopy looking at her, but when she raised her eyes, the woman immediately looked away. Giving the adjustment gadget one last twist, she pinched her finger, sucked it, stifled a curse, then gave up and sat down, leaning backward because the seat was so low the desk could have provided a shelf for her breasts. She reached for the document on top of the pile of papers, AMENDED EDWAA GUIDELINES, and had to scan two pages before she found out that EDWAA stood for Economic Dislocation and Worker Adjustment Assistance Act. She was totally out of her depth. The job certainly hadn't sounded as though it required this sort of expertise, and she hadn't been foolish or dishonest enough to lie about her qualifications. Perhaps, when she'd been interviewed, her enthusiasm, fueled by desperation, had made her appear too confident. And factory workers! How would she relate to factory workers or learn anything fast enough to be of help to them?

Wanting to look busy, she decided to write a letter to Gervaise. She made the first moves with cautious distaste, as though touching a bug, but when, with an almost undetectable whirring sound, the computer told her that she could proceed, her fingers moved quickly as she typed, "Dear Gervaise, I'm here in my new office. It's ugly as sin and feels more like a prison cell than an office. Not being in the job market for so many years, I'm terribly nervous." She stopped. She had consciously raised her daughter to expect both career and marriage, livelihood and motherhood, but last summer Gervaise had made a few cracks about her being a stay-at-home mother, and one afternoon, when she'd had a rare session with the computer, frustration had made her tearful and Gervaise, with an airy, youthful contempt that didn't even recognize its unkindness, had called her a wuss. She'd have to ask Cass, who studied word derivation, but *wuss* sounded like a combination of *wimp* and *pussy*. Punching DELETE, she started again: "Dear Gervaise, Trip down was fine except for a little rain. I'm now in my office ready to tackle—"

But wasn't it time to drop her "Mother can cope with anything" pose? Hadn't she reached a point where pretense was just plain silly? Besides, Gervaise was probably on her way up to school, a trip that Bonnie'd originally thought she'd be taking with her. She'd even scanned the motor club's brochures, circling points of interest, thinking they'd stop at some quaint inn and admire the autumn foliage. But she wasn't admiring autumn foliage now. And it was probably against the rules for her to be using this computer for personal business. She pressed DELETE and reached for the EDWAA guidelines. Then, feeling so utterly confused and useless that she thought she might cry, she got up and closed the door.

Dammit, get a grip! she told herself as she slumped into one of the plastic chairs. It's not microsurgery; it's office work. You'll get the hang of it. But rage swept through her like a kerosene-soaked rag that had been lit with a match. She hated Devoe as she'd never hated him before. His shady deals, his lies, his emotional cowardice had brought her to this. She was a wage slave in an obscure community college. She'd probably be fired for incompetence. No, she struggled with herself, she couldn't and shouldn't blame Devoe. She was responsible. She'd brought herself to this. By not being prepared, by not being brave enough to test herself in the workplace, by not having the sense to protect herself financially.

Aw, to hell with that "You make your own problems" responsibility crap. It was his fault, and she hated him. As her imagination ran to insane scenarios of revenge, a hullabaloo of voices drifted in through the door. Grabbing a tissue from her purse, she blotted her eyes and moved behind the desk. The sounds drifted off in the direction of Mrs. Jackson's office. She picked up the EDWAA material and began reading: "EDWAA amended Title III of the Job Training Partnership Act provides funds to local substate grantees. . . ." She turned the page, realized that she'd read four paragraphs and hadn't taken in a damned thing, turned back, then heard a male voice she thought she recognized. After a quick tap on her door, Mrs. Jackson opened it and stepped back to usher in Marion Hawkins.

"Bonnie, I think you know Mr. Hawkins, the illustrious namesake of our college." Mrs. Jackson's smile stretched her mouth. "Mr. Hawkins has just dropped by to honor us with his presence and—"

"Drop by whenever I can to check up on things here at the Think Farm," Marion Hawkins boomed, advancing open armed toward Bonnie. He pulled her into a bear hug, then held her at arm's length to say, "Lil' Bonnie Duke. Now ain't you the spit of your mother, God rest her soul. And she was a fine-lookin' woman."

Embarrassed by this display of intimacy, Bonnie glanced at Mrs. Jackson, who was already backing out of the room. "Mrs. Jackson, I—"

"Oh, Bonnie, call me Lena," Mrs. Jackson insisted. "And, Mr. Hawkins, if you need—"

"Not a thing, not a thing," he cut her off. "Be back in your office in a tick." As Mrs. Jackson closed the door, he released Bonnie and stepped back, squeezing himself into one of the bucket chairs. Bonnie took her place behind her desk. He smiled. She smiled back. How could she not be glad to see him? He was a coarser and more folksy version of her father, the previous generation's picture of power and well-being. Tall, with a belly that protruded from his expensive, slightly rumpled suit, he had an alcoholic's mottled skin shaved so close his cheeks were shiny. His thinning hair was wet-combed into a rooster crest, and his eyes behind metal-rimmed glasses were watery blue and sharp as a butcher's knife. Essentially kindhearted, if you didn't cross him. He had grown up saying "ain't" but now used the word consciously, with the same down-home, get-out-the-vote folksiness with which he referred to his real estate empire as his "dirt deals."

"So, Miss Bonnie, think you're gonna like it here?" He leaned back, gave her a wink, and, without waiting for a response, went on. "I was talking to your daddy the other day. What a man he is! One of the last of the true gentlemen. And, Bonnie, tell me, between you and me, how's your daddy's health? I ask him an' he says fine, but that's what I'd expect him to say."

"I saw him just a few days ago, and he was looking good. And I must say you're looking well yourself, Mr. Hawkins."

"I'm maintaining, just maintaining. But that's as much as an ol' coot like me can hope for." He tapped his forehead. "Long as the ol' gray matter's still workin' I can't complain. What you can't cure, you must endure."

They went on with the your-turn-to-curtsy, my-turn-to-bow patter for a time. Then he hunched forward, placing his ham-size fists on the edge of her desk and lowering his voice to say, "Your daddy tolt me about your divorce. I'm real sorry. That Devoe is cruisin' for a bruisin.' Don't understand how he could treat a wonderful woman like you so bad. But you'll be all right, Miss Bonnie. You'll be all right. Got your mama's looks and your daddy's get-up-and-go. You know, your daddy could've been governor of this state, but he always wanted to stay behind the scenes. Used to quote ol' Harry Truman, say it's remarkable how much you can accomplish when you don't care who gets the credit. Yes, your daddy brought a heap of business to this state in the fifties and sixties. I owe him. We all owe him. So if there's anythin' I can do to make you feel at home here, just say the word."

She felt a gush of affection and was about to reach across the desk and take his hand when Cass opened the door. "Sorry," Cass apologized, stepping back. "Mrs. Snopes said you were in here, but I thought you were alone."

"That's OK," Bonnie said. "Mr. Hawkins, this is my friend Cassandra Ledforth. She teaches in the English department."

"Why, sure. I know Professor Ledforth," Marion rumbled, getting up. "Smartest woman in the county and"—he smiled wickedly, about to make a comment on her looks, but thought better of it— "we're proud to have her here. Now I'm going to wander off to see Miz Jackson, and Bonnie, you remember what I told you: Anything you need, give a whistle." He came to her, gave her another crunching hug, and, with a little bow in Cass's direction, closed the door behind him.

"No need to worry about you," Cass said sotto voce, "You've got the Sun King on your welcome wagon."

"Thank God you're here," Bonnie said, gathering up her purse and an armful of files. "I just look at that computer, and I go blank."

"You'll get the hang of it," Cass said encouragingly, then laughed. "Don't know why I say that. *I* never have. But I refuse to be intimidated. Consider this: If all those cyberspace types are so smart, how come they didn't figure out that the year 2000 was going to come after the year 1999? Besides, Mark's good with computers. He'll help you if you get stuck. Come on, let's get out of here."

Cass moved to the hall, but Bonnie made a point of stopping at Norma Jean's desk to say she was leaving. Then she looked past Norma Jean, cleared her throat, and said, "Mrs. Snopes, I'm going to try to make it in tomorrow afternoon, but if I can't, I'll call and let you know."

Mrs. Snopes raised one hand, wiggled her fingers, said, "Toodle-oo. See you tomorrow." A blindingly insincere smile puffed her droopy cheeks. And she kept smiling until Bonnie was out the door.

Knowing Mrs. Snopes had something to say, Norma Jean turned and waited till her cheeks deflated and her smile withered. "You don't fool me, Miss Priss, Miss Bonnie Duke Cullman," Mrs. Snopes finally said, in a low voice Norma Jean knew she was meant to hear, "I've seen your résumé. Only reason you got this job was 'cause HE told Aunt Jemima in there to give it to you."

"You mean Mr. Hawkins got her the job?" Norma Jean blurted.

Mrs. Snopes put her finger to her lips and rolled her eyes in the direction of Mrs. Jackson's office.

"But why?" Norma Jean persisted in a stage whisper.

Mrs. Snopes said, "I can only guess *why,*" in tones rich with innuendo.

"How do you know?" she challenged.

"I know because . . ." Mrs. Snopes said with an air of confidence and mystery, "I know because—"

Norma Jean nodded, quickly and casually, like a detective on a TV show, figuring that Mrs. Snopes had stayed on the line and listened after she'd connected a call to Mrs. Jackson. She'd seen her do that more than once. She'd done it more than once herself. "I know a girl who applied for that job, an' she's not rich, so she really needed the work," Norma Jean said in a spurt of righteousness, "but I guess if you don't have connections . . ."

Mrs. Snopes nodded in sad agreement, gave a quick pull to the sides of her wig, and said, quickly and businesslike, "I'm afraid I've spoken out of turn, Norma Jean. Please just forget it."

"My lips are sealed," Norma Jean promised, and, being of a literal mind, touched her index finger to her lips before turning back to her desk.

As soon as she got back to Cass's place, Bonnie called the neighbor who was in charge of the house to say she wanted to rent it. The neighbor said his name was Jarvis Boggs, and if she wrote a check to Mrs. Nunnally and mailed it to his address, she could move in as soon as she liked. The key was under the front step, and he'd drop by real soon to see if there was anything that needed fixing.

"His name is Jarvis Boggs," she told Cass as she hung up. "I mean, Jarvis Boggs!" She rolled her eyes and laughed, giddy with relief that the transaction had gone so smoothly. "He sounds like something from *God's Little Acre*. And all I have to do to move in is to send him a check made out to Mrs. Nunnally, take the key, and move in."

"That sounds real businesslike. Mark my words, it'll *be* like something from *God's Little Acre*," Cass warned, but when Bonnie mimicked "Mark my words" with deep-voiced seriousness, Cass laughed too.

Feeling she was on a roll, Bonnie called the gas and electric, then the phone company. She refused to let the infuriating and inane telephone menus bother her, though by the time she heard an actual human voice at the Department of Motor Vehicles she was singing "Don't Rain on My Parade" at the top of her lungs.

Early the next morning she drove out to the house, taking Ganesha with her. After missing a turn and ending up at a milking barn, she backtracked and found her way to the house. Once she got there, she moved with the speed of a dervish, scribbling a list of things to be purchased and things to be done, talking to and stumbling over Ganesha, who trailed after her as though he were tied to her shoes. She'd settle for miniblinds even though shutters would be more attractive, but she couldn't live with the blotched wallpaper in the living room. Armed with a shopping list for everything from window air conditioners to toilet paper, she drove back to Cass's, settled Nesha in the guest room, and, after locking the door against the rampaging cat, headed for the nearest Wal-Mart.

Oh, how the mighty are fallen, she thought as she pulled off the highway and saw the store, huge and ugly as an airplane hangar. Some years ago she'd successfully spearheaded a drive to keep a Wal-Mart from being built on the outskirts of her Atlanta neighborhood, and on principle, she'd never been in one. Even as a little girl she'd loved to go shopping, but shopping had been a very different experience then. Women had dressed up, even worn gloves and hats, to make the trip downtown to department stores, many of which were owned by individual families. Goods were displayed in glass cabinets, uniformed elevator operators called out merchandise available on each floor, salesladies came into the curtained dressing rooms to fit your bra or pin your dress for alterations, your packages were wrapped without charge, and the top floor had a little tearoom where customers could refresh themselves. But those bastions of postwar middle-class prosperity were gone. Now it was either Wal-Mart or Neiman-Marcus.

Pulling into the parking lot, she saw people of every age and color, dressed from casual to downright sloppy, streaming toward the doors as though going to a revival meeting. She walked through the swing sets, plants, and power mowers displayed on the sidewalk, passed through a set of glass doors to a lobby, where toddlers galloped on fifty-cent-a-ride horses, older kids punched gum and drink machines, and exhausted seniors slumped on benches, through a second set of glass doors. The air-conditioning was permeated with the smell of popcorn and hot dogs coming from the food stand on her right. On her left, a grandmotherly woman greeted her with "Welcome to Wal-Mart" and pushed a shopping cart in her direction. Steering her cart through the aisles, she dodged discount displays, stray children, hand-holding teenagers, men wearing jeans and buzz cuts shopping for hardware and fishing gear, women in stretch pants (an inordinate number of whom were overweight, pregnant, or both) stuffing their carts with everything from false eyelashes to microwaves. Working-class consumerism at full tilt.

Adding up her purchases as she waited in line, she blanched at the total. "Looks like you're setting up house," the cashier, a black girl with long green fingernails, observed. She said she was and handed over her one remaining credit card. "Better you than me," the cashier said. "Movin's a bitch. Good luck." Bonnie drove to the service area to have the air conditioner loaded, then drove off.

She skipped lunch, went over to the college and put in a few hours at her desk. Ignoring Snoopy's toxic vibes and an unaccountably sullen Norma Jean, she read through government guidelines and "how to" computer books, then called the offices of Cherished Lady. After one disconnect and one long wait she managed to get through to a Miss Ingram, who said she was in charge of the workers' "transition" and promised to call her back.

Saturday morning at daybreak, dressed for serious dirty work, she, Cass, and Mark drove to the house in three separate cars loaded with tools, ladders, and odd bits of furniture from Cass's place. Amazingly, the telephone, gas, and electric had been turned on as promised, and Mark set to work installing the window air conditioner in her bedroom, muttering, "You know this damned air-conditioning is responsible for the greatest influx of Yankees since Reconstruction. They didn't want to come down here when they really had to sweat." Now that he was more relaxed with her, Mark showed a surprising sense of humor, feigning a fall from the ladder and dancing with the rented floor polisher. Cass told him he was simpleminded, but Bonnie could tell from her expression that she was, if not in love, at least deeply fond of him.

They broke for a lunch of beer, ham sandwiches, and cucumber pickles, sitting in the kitchen where Bonnie had scrubbed and put shelving paper in all the cupboards while Cass had cleaned the oven and the windows. "Greater love than this no woman hath: that she clean an oven for a friend," Cass said, mopping the sweat from her forehead with a paper towel.

"I can't tell you how much I appreciate—" Bonnie began.

"Yeah, yeah, yeah," Cass cut her off. "And now the windows are clean we can see how much work that garden needs, but I tells you, Miz Cullman, I don't be doin' no stoop labor."

Bonnie bit into a pickle, wiped the juice from her chin, and said, "I don't know why, but this makes me feel young."

"Your aching muscles will tell you your real age tomorrow morning," Mark warned.

Cass said, "Bonnie, you went from your daddy's house, to a sorority, to living with Devoe. You've never had a place that was just yours. That's why it makes you feel young."

"Only thing I associate with being young is not having any money," Mark said.

"Nuh-uh." Cass shook her head. "Being young is *not minding* that you don't have any money, though I don't think kids feel that way anymore."

Bonnie said, "I can't say I don't mind, 'cause I do. But having friends like you two, I sure don't mind it as much."

Cass raised her hands to the ceiling, shouting, "Thank you, Jesus!" like a TV evangelist, then got up, put her arms around Mark's neck, and whispered so that Bonnie could hear, "Better get back to work 'fore Bonnie goes all soft and mushy on us."

By seven o'clock, when the sun was finally beginning to go down, they called it quits. Mark washed up the paintbrushes in the living room while Cass wet-mopped the floor and Bonnie went out into the garden to pick a handful of daisies. When she came back in, she found them in her bedroom, Cass sitting on the edge of the bed, Mark standing in front of the air conditioner holding his sweaty T-shirt away from his chest. Cass stretched and lay back. "I'm so tired I just want to giggle."

Mark kissed the top of her head, then stretched out next to her. "Give me five minutes; then I'll be able to move again. Then we'll go home and take a long cool shower."

Cass wriggled in discomfort. "After five minutes on this mattress you'll want to move. This should've been your first priority, Bonnie. After all, you spend a quarter of your life in bed. OK"—she laughed, throwing her arm over Mark's chest—"if you're lucky, a third."

Priorities, Bonnie thought, were hard to set when you had many needs and little money. She'd priced mattresses the previous afternoon, but she couldn't afford a good one, and it seemed foolish to settle for a cheap one, so she'd decided to live with it till her first pay-check. "I'll get that second six-pack," she said, heading for the kitchen, "and we'll have one for the road."

Closing the refrigerator door, she heard a car. Six-pack in hand, she went into the living room, looked out the window, and saw a rusty pickup rattling up the drive. An old man wearing a squashed felt hat and coveralls that strained his beer belly got out, slammed the door, and ambled up to the porch. Jarvis Boggs, in the flesh, she thought. Moments later, squinting through the screen door, she heard, "Jarvis Boggs here. Anybody home?" Bonnie opened the screen door and in-troduced herself. Jarvis croaked, "Just come by to see iffen you need any help." Seeing that he was wiping his feet on her new welcome mat and craning to look into the room, Bonnie stepped back and invited him in. He scuffed his boots on the mat again and took off his hat. His hair was black with streaks of gray, and a large pale wart pro-truded from the bushy hairs of one eyebrow, which he raised appre-ciatively as he looked at the sweaty T-shirt clinging to Bonnie's breasts. "Settlin' in all right?"

"Just fine."

His eyes, hooded and sly, darted to the hallway, where Cass and Mark had just appeared. He drawled, "How do," and, without wait-ing for introductions, said, "Damned hot to be workin'. Makes you feel right parched." Fanning himself with his hat, he eyed the six-pack and swallowed deliberately, his Adam's apple riding up and down his sun-ravaged neck.

"Would you like a beer?" Bonnie offered, and, since the answer was a foregone conclusion, handed one over. "Mark? Cass?" she said. Cass said no, but Mark grunted, grabbed a can, popped it open, and chugalugged in such a parody of cracker-macho that Bonnie and Cass looked at each other and grinned. Oblivious, Jarvis drained his beer with lightning speed, handed the empty can back to Bonnie, and croaked, "Well, little lady, you've done right good cleanin' up here."

When he called her "little lady," the women locked eyes again and then looked away, suppressing giggles like seven-year-olds at a church service.

"Yes, indeedy." Jarvis wiped his mouth, focusing on the six-pack. "Grace'd be right proud."

"I thought her name might be Grace!" Bonnie said.

"Yes, indeedy," Jarvis repeated. "You young people have cleaned up real good."

"Would it be all right to use things stored in the attic?" Bonnie asked.

"Grace wouldn't mind a'tall," Jarvis told her, accepting another can with a nod. "Grace'd give you the shirt off her back." Eyeing Bonnie's chest again, he added, "'Course I wouldn't want to see a woman Grace's age without her shirt." Bonnie kept smiling but felt disgusted and uneasy.

Mark took a step forward and, pitching his voice to a deeper register, said, "Phone company came 'round, so Miz Cullman has a number now. I'd 'preciate it if you called 'fore you dropped by."

"All three of you be livin' here?" Jarvis asked with a leer.

"Nope," Mark said. "Lease is in Mrs. Cullman's name, i'n't it? But me an' the missus will be checkin' up on her regular," and in a display of male dominance that might have been seen on the Nature channel, he drained the rest of his beer staring at Boggs over the top of the can, then scrunched the can and tossed it on the floor. After wiping his hands on his jeans, he reached for Jarvis Boggs's hand and shook it so hard Jarvis had to struggle to keep the surprise out of his eyes.

"Well, sure." Jarvis submitted. "Didn't mean to disturb y'all." Backing up to the front door, beer can in hand, he added, with a sniffling grin, "Like I said, just come by to see how yer doin,' Miz Cullman. You call iffen you need anything."

They all stayed silent while Jarvis staggered to his pickup, backed up, and drove off. Then Cass, latching the screen door, whispered,

"Did you see the bumper sticker? It says 'Old truckers never die, they get a new Peterbilt,'" and they all collapsed in laughter. "We've just met the quintessential dirty old man."

Bonnie said, "I'm glad you were here. Especially you, Mark. That was quite an act you put on. Reminded me of *High Noon*."

Mark massaged his wrist. "I think I pulled something crumpling that up," he said, picking up the squashed can from the floor. "Haven't done that since high school, but I think I scared the ol' coot."

Cass put her hands on Bonnie's shoulders. "Don't ever unlock that door without looking out to see who it is."

"I won't," Bonnie promised. The dangers of living alone so far from town flashed through her mind. Her first impulse was to gather up her things and drive back with Cass and Mark as she'd planned, but knowing that she'd have to face the challenge sooner or later, she said, "I want to stay here tonight. I'll come pick up Nesha tomorrow morning."

Cass started to remonstrate but thought better of it. "OK. You're a big girl. Sure you'll be OK?"

Bonnie hugged her and said, "Sure. I'll have to learn to be," and flashing a smile, she added, "I'll come by tomorrow morning so you'll know I haven't been slaughtered in my bed."

The house seemed so quiet after they'd gone that she took the transistor radio into the bathroom with her. She found the National Public Radio station and listened to *The Thistle & Shamrock* as she stripped off her clothes and stood under the spray. She alternated hot and cold water until she felt revived, then stepped out of the shower, saw the pile of dirty clothes on the floor, and realized the rest of her other clothes were still at Cass's. In the bedroom she rummaged through shopping bags, tore the plastic wrapper from the new set of sheets, partially made up the bed with the fitted sheet, then draped the top sheet around her, togalike, and wandered through the house.

The smells of soap and polish and fresh paint pleased her. All the surfaces in the kitchen were clean and smooth to the touch, and her gourmet pots and pans, looking slightly out of place, hung on the walls. Neither the second bedroom nor the dining room had been touched, but the living room restored her sense of accomplishment. Standing on its threshold, seeing the setting sun shining through the new miniblinds and striping the newly painted pale yellow walls and glistening wood floor, she decided it was not just habitable but pretty. The ugly tweed couch had been camouflaged with a yellow, peach, and white print she'd picked up at a fabric discount store and had tucked and pinned into place. Cass, who said it was harder to find bookcases in Florabama than it was to buy a bottle of hooch in Saudi Arabia, had insisted she take two of her pine bookcases, which were positioned on either side of the fireplace. She had also donated an easy chair upholstered in white canvas and a Van Gogh chrysanthemum print. The daisies from the backyard sprouted from a Coke bottle set in the middle of the coffee table.

Suddenly missing Nesha, she went back to her bedroom, turned on the bedside lamp sitting on a cardboard box, then dug through the overnight bag she'd luckily brought along and found the journal and a pen. Sitting Indian style in the middle of the bed, already feeling the ache of rarely used muscles, toga falling from her shoulder, she opened the journal and smoothed its spine. She'd been full to bursting with thoughts she'd wanted to record, but now she felt as blank as the page. She wrote the date and stopped. Was this meditation or was she just starting to fall asleep? She wrote:

Hello Bonnie,

I have just walked through the house. I'm sitting on the bed in a strange bedroom where I'll sleep alone tonight. I wish I'd brought the puppy with me. I feel weird—free, but frightened. Things are stripped to the necessities. I feel stripped too. This sheet I've wrapped around me has fallen off and I see how my breasts sag and I remember standing in front of my mirror examining them just before I got my first bra. Had

*to go shopping with Elice and wouldn't let her come into the dressing
room with me.*

She'd been thirteen then, too self-absorbed to wonder if she was
hurting her stepmother's feelings, though probably she had. It was
around that time that she'd started to keep a diary. She had no idea
what had become of it. She was middle-aged now, and she called it a
journal, but in her heart of hearts she felt much the same. It was as
though her adult life had been no more than an interim, and now
she'd come back to her reflective, questioning, self-conscious nature,
worried about who she was, her place in the world, what the future
would hold.

*I don't know how much I'll miss my old life. It seems I spent so
much of it accumulating, acquiring, and arranging things; maybe I even
acquired Devoe, but I never wanted to arrange him. I always hoped
he'd be stronger than I was, even though I knew pretty early on that he
wasn't. Why did I ignore that? Why did I try to . . .*

She sank back onto the pillows. Exhaustion and self-examination
didn't go well together. She snapped out the light, vowing to write
first thing in the morning.

But she didn't write in the journal again until she'd left
Florabama.

Chapter VI

*B*efore leaving the house on Monday, her first official day of work, Bonnie scrutinized her image in the bedroom mirror. She'd dressed as though she were an actress playing the prototypical professional woman (taupe Ann Taylor suit with cream blouse and matching low-heeled pumps, minimal makeup and jewelry, hair pinned up), but somehow she didn't feel very convincing. She slung her handbag over her shoulder, put on her reading glasses, and arranged her features in an expression of warm attentiveness. Thrusting her hand toward the mirror, she said, "Pleased to meet you. I'm Bonnie Cullman." Talking to mirrors. Another sign of pathological regression. She hadn't talked to mirrors since adolescence, when after making sure her bedroom door was locked, she'd sit at her vanity, take out her retainer, unbutton her nightdress to expose nonexistent cleavage, and play Elizabeth challenging Darcy, Jane pleading with Mr. Rochester, Scarlett flirting with Rhett. "Pleased to meet you. I'm Bonnie Cullman," she tried again and judged her performance to be somewhat improved. It wasn't as though she couldn't act. She'd convincingly played the charming hostess even as she'd ached for her guests to leave; she'd had a long run as devoted wife and always available sex partner, "And," she told Nesha, who sat near the door as if expecting to come along, "I generally got rave reviews as a loving and watchful mother." Nesha barked agreement, trotted into the hallway, then came back, looking up to remind her not to leave him behind.

"No. You have to stay in the house till I come home." She didn't dare look at him. Grabbing up her papers and books from the dressing table, she repeated, "Stay!" and raced to the front door, which she locked behind her.

At seven forty-five she walked briskly across campus, Daily Planner peeking out from the shoulder bag held firmly against her hip, feeling purposeful and confident. She wasn't going to an audition; she'd already been cast. And she was going to be good in her new role. She'd written out a schedule that would make the most efficient use of her time:

8–10: Set up files and computer programs [since Mark had given her several hours of instruction, she felt almost ready to tackle it].
10–12: Familiarize self with details of curriculum and financial programs.
12–3: Visit various community organizations/churches whose services the women in the program might need.
3–4: Meet with Mrs. Jackson.
4–5:30: Clean up unfinished work, and set up next day's schedule.
6:00: Meet at Cass's house for drinks.

Yes, she could pull it off. She was calm. She was loaded for bear.

Entering the building, she saw five or six women seated on folding chairs lined up on either side of the hallway near the doors of the administration offices. One of them had a large black Bible spread on the knees of her purple polyester pants, and as Bonnie approached, she looked up, raised the Bible to the bosom of her lavender T-shirt, and asked, "Are you Mrs. Cullman?" Bonnie stopped midstride and admitted that indeed she was. "Oh, good," the woman said, "'Cause I have an appointment with you for eight o'clock, and I'm s'posed to be at the unemployment office at nine."

"I think there must be some mistake," Bonnie said politely.

"No, ma'am. I don't think so." The woman's face was fleshy, with a button nose. Her eyes were flat as a chicken's. Her long salt and pepper hair had been fixed in a style Bonnie had seen only in old photographs—braided and pinned to the top of her head in a coronet—which was curiously at odds with the frames of her aqua-colored, rhinestone-dotted glasses. "Miz Ingram from Cherished Lady set it up with Miz Snopes."

"Oh." Bonnie stalled. Snoopy hadn't mentioned setting up any appointments. Oversight or subversion? "Mrs. Snopes must've forgotten to tell me."

"I talked with her Thursday," the Bible lady insisted, "Or maybe it was Friday. No, I think Thursday. 'Round three o'clock. No, maybe it was three-thirty. . . ."

Oh, dear, Bonnie thought, nodding to urge her on. As the woman droned on, Bonnie glanced around, her heart rate increasing with each person she saw. First was a black woman with arms like a dockworker's staring straight ahead. Another woman, white-haired, was bent over some needlework. Then Bonnie's attention was caught by a conversation going on between two women sitting across the hall. She heard, "At least think about it, Ruthie," and a whispered reply: "But women just don't do that."

Half-turning, she saw a large-boned, copper-haired Amazon type in a red shirt and jeans in a tête-à-tête with a sweet-faced woman dressed in a blue and white seersucker shirtwaist. The Amazon said, "I never seen you hide behind a petticoat before."

Sweet Face reasoned, "We'd have to pay for the training ourselves."

"Wouldn't take but a month. I saw this show on TV 'bout these two sisters who take turns driving a rig. Haul ass from Maine to Mexico. It's a way to see the world."

"No trucking company would want to hire us. We're too old."

The Amazon was exasperated. "If it ain't sexism, it's ageism with you, Ruthie."

Bonnie turned her attention back to the Bible lady, who was still thrashing around in irrelevancies. ". . . so since I got the appointment at the unemployment office—"

"What's your name, please?" Bonnie asked, struggling to keep the panic out of her voice.

"Celia Lusk. I asked Miz Snopes if she could schedule me early, an' she said—"

"Yes. I see," Bonnie cut her off. "I'll check and be back with you in just a few minutes."

Moving through the office doors, she gave a quick "good morning" to Norma Jean, who responded with a predictable half gasp, half giggle, then walked to Mrs. Snopes's desk.

Snoopy was shaking a packet of Sweet'n Low into a coffee mug decorated with bunnies and daises. Wondering why the real meanies so often had a taste for the cute and cuddly, Bonnie said, "Good morning, Mrs. Snopes." Snoopy glanced up with "What do you want now?" exasperation.

"One of those women waiting out in the hallway seems to think she has an appointment with me," she continued, struggling for calm.

"Yes," Mrs. Snopes told her placidly. "You have preliminary interviews all this morning, this afternoon, and tomorrow."

"But I didn't—"

"You left early the other day, Mrs. Cullman." Her voice had a note of personal injury, as though Bonnie had left her by the side of the road after a car wreck. "Miss Ingram at Cherished Lady called and wanted to set up interviews, so I was obliged to make appointments."

"Was this Thursday or Friday?" No response. "But I told you I was leaving early on Friday because I had to get to the bank and set up an account." Still no response. She could feel the blood rising to her neck. She started to say she was totally unprepared and couldn't possibly see these women now but stopped herself. "And if you set up appointments for me, why didn't you call and tell me?"

"I didn't know the number."

"I told you my phone had been hooked up. You could've called information. Or you could have called Professor Ledforth and left a message for me."

"It's poor office procedure to leave messages with a second party. How would I know if she'd reached you?"

"But you made no attempt to—" Bonnie heard her voice go out of control. And what was the point? Trying to reason with Snoopy was as hopeless as trying to dance the tarantella on quicksand. Folding her arms protectively across her chest, she asked, "Do you have a list of these appointments?"

"It's been on your desk since Friday afternoon," Snoopy said with self-righteousness, and, seeing Bonnie was flustered, added, with saccharine solicitude, "Don't worry, Mrs. Cullman. They're just preliminary interviews. Give you a chance to get to know your 'ladies,'" she said with heavy sarcasm.

Bonnie's anger flared. She wanted to say, "How dare you act superior," but with a curt "thank you" she turned and went into her office, closing the door behind her.

Staring at the door, Norma Jean said, "Miz Cullman sure looks pretty in that suit."

"Are you the cat that looks at the queen? That suit would cost you a week's salary." Mrs. Snopes opened another packet of Sweet'n Low and shook it so violently that it spilled onto the desk. "Hand me a paper towel. Then get back to work."

The list of names and appointments, scheduled at twenty-minute intervals, was on Bonnie's desk. Her hand shook as she picked it up. She thought of going to Mrs. Jackson, but she didn't want to be seen as a complainer. Besides, it was a little early in the game to be upping the ante. She'd just have to ride it out. She checked her watch: eight-nine. She was already behind schedule. Stashing her purse under her desk, she removed her jacket, took a deep breath, and, appointment list in hand, went out to the hallway, calling, "Mrs. Lust?"

The Bible lady looked up in shock. The Amazon laughed.

"Excuse me." Red-faced, Bonnie corrected herself. "I mean, Mrs. *Lusk*. Will you please come in?"

Celia Lusk handed over several forms and sat down, pushing her glasses back onto her button nose, lowering her Bible so Bonnie saw her T-shirt. It showed a dove and the message LOOK-UP! LOOK UP! HE IS COMING! Involuntarily Bonnie looked up, saw the stain near the air-conditioning duct, then turned her eyes back to Mrs. Lusk's application, smoothed it, and put her hands together to stop them from shaking. She read out loud, "You graduated from Florabama High School in 1973, right?" Celia Lusk nodded, then went into a diatribe about public schools no longer teaching moral values and asked Bonnie if she was following the court case about the judge who wanted to have the Ten Commandments posted in his office.

Bonnie said, "Sorry. I'm not familiar with that case," and, after busying herself with a nervous straightening of papers, said, in a firm no-nonsense voice, "So. You graduated high school in '73. And since then?"

Celia Lusk cluttered every answer with such a mishmash of extraneous information and calls to salvation that Bonnie had to keep reminding her, at first gently, then firmly, that she had a 9:00 o'clock appointment at the unemployment office. At 8:45, when Bonnie'd finally wrenched it out of her that she wanted to enroll in the computer training program, she got up, signaling that the interview was over. Still, Celia waxed philosophic: It must be God's will that the mill had closed, and since it was God's will, it must be for the best. Bonnie smiled and nodded, hoping her rambling would relieve her obvious anxiety. But why, she wondered, if the woman truly believed everything was divinely ordained, did she seem so anxious?.

Getting to her feet, Celia paused to enumerate the sterling qualities of her pastor, who, she said, was guiding her through this travail. Bonnie couldn't get a word in edgewise and finally put aside her manners to interrupt, saying, "Thank you, Mrs. Lusk. When we receive your high school transcripts and the results of the various tests you've taken here at the college, we'll be able to make better decisions regarding your placement." To soften the dismissal, she asked, "Any questions?" but was immediately fearful that Celia would question her about something she didn't know or, worse yet, ask if she'd been born again. But Celia Lusk got to her feet, thanked her, and left.

Whom, Bonnie asked herself when Celia Lusk had gone, did the Bible lady remind her of? It was Granny Duke, her daddy's mother, long since dead. Granny D.'s missionary zeal had done nothing to brighten her doom and gloom personality. Granny Duke had brought her Bible whenever she'd come to visit, and she'd never abandoned her attempt to convert Bonnie's mother into a God-fearing woman. "Oh, these Bible thumpers," she remembered her mother saying with a laugh. "Only Sunday is blessed. Otherwise, as Mr. Joyce said, 'All Moanday, Tearsday, Wailsday, Thumpsday, Frightday, Shatterday.'"

Smiling as she went out into the hall, Bonnie called, "Albertine Chisholm, please," and hoped, as the large black woman got to her feet and followed her into her office, that she wouldn't be submitted to another interview–cum–revival meeting. But once Mrs. Chisholm had squeezed her bulk into one of the bucket chairs, she brightened, handed over her application, and answered Bonnie's questions quickly and succinctly. She too wanted to be in the computer training program, but, she explained, her husband, Henry, was disabled so she couldn't sign up for any classes that conflicted with his doctor's appointments. Bonnie made notes, thanked her, followed her out into the hallway, and called for the next appointment. "Mrs. Pruwitt?"

The Amazon who'd been urging her friend to become a trucker stood up. She wasn't really an Amazon—no more than five feet six inches and big-chested rather than big-boned—but her mass of bright, teased hair made her seem taller, and as she tucked her well-ironed red shirt into the bull's head buckle of her jeans and came forward with a chest-out swagger, Bonnie thought she probably *could* handle an eighteen-wheeler. "I'm Bonnie Cullman. Please follow me," Bonnie said. Then, as she turned to walk back into her office it hit her like a ton of bricks: This was the woman she'd seen on TV, the one who'd been in-your-face angry about the mill's closing.

"Please take a seat," Bonnie said as she sat down at her desk. "So. You're Mrs. Pruwitt."

"I don't need no Mrs. tag," she shot back, eyes sharp and wary as she looked around the office.

"All right, I'll call you Hildegard, and you can call me Bonnie."

"Hildegard's my baptized name. Ain't nobody called me anything but Hilly since I was 'bout eleven and started sprouting these." She looked down at her breasts, then crossed her arms over them.

Bonnie couldn't help smiling. "Do you have your application forms, Hilly?"

"When I signed up this mornin,' I handed them over to that young girl who's sittin' out front. She said she'd put 'em on your desk."

"She must've forgotten."

"Wouldn't surprise me. She looks like she's a few sandwiches short of a picnic."

This one's going to be a trip, Bonnie thought as she excused herself, went to Norma Jean's desk, and waited while Norma Jean sorted through a drift of papers before she found Hilly Pruwitt's. After looking them over as she walked back to her desk, closing the door and sitting again, she said, "I see you went to high school in Texas, Hilly."

"Uh-huh. Dropped out 'cause my mama was sick, an' I never much cared to find m' way back in. Can't say as I missed it."

"And I see you've had quite a number of jobs." The list of employment filled up the allotted space and ended with a scrawled "ekkcerata."

"Everything that paid the minimum wage, and a few that didn't. I worked at Cherished Lady for a lotta years. Best money I ever made.

Not to say I didn't earn every nickel of it," she added with barely disguised belligerence.

"I'm sure. So . . ." Bonnie put her elbows on the desk and leaned forward. "I suppose you've looked over the catalog. Is there any particular field of study that interests you?" She herself had been cramming information about programs and curriculum requirements into her head for days and hoped she remembered them.

"Like I said, I never won no prizes in school."

"You can probably get your high school diploma with just a few classes, and after that, perhaps one of the nonacademic certificate programs: Landscape Technology, Culinary Technology?"

"I don't much like messin' with plants." Hilly thought a moment. "I hate it when they give them big-deal names to things, like callin' a janitor a maintenance engineer. I mean, how come they have to call it Culinary Technology 'stead of just cookin'?"

"Perhaps the description is a bit inflated," Bonnie agreed, "but I believe the program covers special methods and techniques that a restaurant chef would use."

"How many four-star restaurants you see in Florabama?"

"Maybe in Mobile, or Birmingham—" Bonnie began.

"Nope. I'm not about to relocate. Got me a good place out in the country, an' animals to care for. Hey, Miz Cullman, can I ask you somethin'?" Bonnie nodded. "When did all this 'lifeboats on the *Titanic*' program for us gals from Cherished Lady get started?"

"This is only my first day, so I'm not sure when the program was set up. But sometime ago, I assume."

"That's what I figured. Management must've known months in advance 'cause when they gave us the boot, they already had this lined up."

"I really don't know anything about that."

"Sure. Sure you don't." Hilly's tone was sarcastic. "Don't nobody know nothin.'"

Bonnie scribbled "needs basic English class" on her notes and thought it was too bad the college didn't offer a class in basic attitude adjustment. She wanted to convince Hilly that she was telling the truth, that she really didn't know when the program had been set up and certainly wasn't part of any conspiracy, but she didn't know how. Vaguely annoyed at having to play saleswoman, she said, "I'm sure there're many programs from which you might benefit."

"I don't have no choice, do I?" Hilly said flatly.

"You're not obliged to enroll."

"Naw, but it's a way to keep busy an' keep some bucks comin' in. They gave us this damn silly book 'bout how to survive a layoff." She held up an eight-by-ten booklet with a slick cover titled *Getting Through Your Layoff* and in apparent demonstration of her disgust, lifted her backside, put it on the chair, and sat on it. "Gripes my ass to think some pickle-hearted suit got more for writin' this crap than I'd make in a year. Woulda done us more good if management had spent the money to buy us all a drink." She snorted in disgust, then looked at the floor. "I already been 'round trying to find work, but work's scarce as hen's teeth, what with a coupla hundred of us laid off."

As she saw a look of dejection flash across Hilly's face, Bonnie's first impulse was to say something comforting but she stopped herself. Who was she, a woman with so much privilege, to try to offer these women advice? Hilly didn't have a husband, and she probably didn't have family or friends who could write her a check that would float her through rough seas. "So"—she stalled—"why don't we meet again next week when your test results are compiled?"

"But school starts in ten days, don't it?"

"We'll meet early next week. You should look through the syllabus—"

"The what?"

"The catalog that lists classes. See what interests you. If you have any difficulty reading—"

There was a tap on the door, and Mrs. Jackson stuck in her head.

"I'm not illiterate." Hilly bristled, ignoring the interruption. "An' if you think I am, I don't see why you're trying to get me to go to college. After all, I'm not black."

Mrs. Jackson, her face so impassive she might not have heard the exchange, said, "Please check with me before you go to lunch, Mrs. Cullman," and closed the door.

"That was the dean of admissions," Bonnie said, making no attempt to keep the disapproval out of her voice.

"I don't care who she is," Hilly shot back. "I'm against affirmative action, and I don't care who knows it. An' maybe she even agrees with me. They're individuals, you know. They don't all think alike. Place like this, you can get in if they can find your pulse, but when good colleges let in kids who aren't qualified, they just take up space; then they flunk out an' feel rotten about it, so who does that help? Color of money is more important than color of skin."

"Perhaps they're interrelated?" Bonnie challenged, then, realizing that she wasn't here to have a political discussion, added, "I think you should be glad for a program like this."

"How come the people who're screwed over are always the ones who're supposed to feel grateful? This program just takes the heat off Cherished Lady and other companies who salute the flag, then turn tail an' bail out of the country. An' it's paid for with taxpayers' money, an' if they hadn't fired me, I'd still be a taxpayer. 'Cause I'm sure as hell no displaced homemaker."

"I take your point." Bonnie forced a smile. "Why don't we talk again next week?"

Hilly got up, looping her thumbs into her belt and straightening her shoulders. "Only if I can't find a job by then. In the meantime, sign me up for anything. I'll be part of the program—leastwise while I'm lookin' for work." She started to leave, then turned, thrusting out her hand, saying, "Hey, thanks for your time. I'm not mad at you. I'm just—"

Mad at the world, Bonnie thought, but said, "No problem. See you next week, Hilly."

As she closed the door, Bonnie's eye fell on the booklet Hilly had left on the chair. She almost started after her but decided she'd spent enough time battling with Hilly Pruwitt. Opening the booklet, she saw charts and diagrams showing life's major stresses. Job loss was right up there, neck and neck with major illness and divorce, but she hardly needed a chart to tell her that. The next pages had questions in bold print—WHY ME? HOW CAN I FACE MY FRIENDS? and HOW CAN I MAKE ENDS MEET?—and fatuous answers in smaller print. She particularly relished DO I HAVE A RIGHT TO FEEL ANGRY? followed by "Yes, you can be angry. Anger is a natural emotion. But you have to learn how to control it. Don't use your spouse, parents, kids, or friends as a sounding board. Seek professional advice. Set up a support group." Seek professional advice when therapists were a hundred bucks an hour? Skimming through HOW TO PACKAGE YOURSELF (with a cutesy sample résumé for "Susie B. Hopeful"), NETWORKING FOR SUCCESS ("We all have friends, relatives, and former classmates . . ."), and HOW TO MAKE A GOOD IMPRESSION ("Be sure to follow up any job interviews with a thank-you note"), she decided that she agreed with Hilly: Cherished Lady's money would have been better spent buying its employees a hell of a good-bye party.

Her stomach grumbled, and she checked her watch. Only 10:05, though she could've sworn it was lunchtime. Rummaging in her purse, she fished out a crumpled stick of cinnamon gum and went to fetch Lyda Jane McCracken.

Lyda Jane's application said she was fifty-nine, but Bonnie, used to her neighbors back in Buckhead who, with the help of plastic surgeons and beauticians, maintained an ageless attractiveness, would have guessed her to be at least in her mid-sixties. Her hair was wispy white. Her eyes behind her bifocals were the color of a frosted pond but had an alert, even twinkly expression. The skin on her face, neck, and hands was soft and as all over wrinkly as a piece of fine cotton that had gone through a wringer. Her feet, in socks and tennis shoes, were splayed and swollen. But it wasn't just her looks that made Bonnie think she was older. She had the self-contained, serene manner of a wise old woman, and when, after the introductions, she took a baby dress out of a plastic bag and started to sew, it didn't seem inattentive or even eccentric, just her quiet way of completing a task she'd set for herself. "That's lovely," Bonnie said, looking at the intricate smocking that gathered the yoke into soft folds.

Lyda Jane smiled up over her glasses, her hands still working. "My granny was real good with her hands, an' after she got the lung problem from workin' at the mills, she stayed home and raised us kids. She taught me smocking, knitting, crochet, tatting. My whole family's been lintheads, far back as they can remember." In answer to Bonnie's questioning expression, she explained, "That's what they called the girls who worked in the mills." And in the same informational tone: "Her second husband was shot to death in that union fight in South Carolina back in the thirties. People don't know nothin' 'bout that now."

Bonnie certainly didn't. She would've liked nothing better than to sit back and hear the entire history, but looking at her watch, she turned the conversation back to enrollment, finishing up with "This layoff must've come at a particularly bad time for you, Mrs. McCracken. I suppose you were looking forward to retirement."

Lyda Jane poked the needle into the baby dress, folded it, put it in a plastic bag, and said, "Miz Cullman, I judge you to be someone I can trust, so I think I should tell you that I'm older than them papers say. I lied about my age when I hired on at Cherished Lady. I'm really sixty-three. You won't tell on me, will you?" She raised her eyes to meet Bonnie's. "No," she assured herself, "I didn't think you would. I know I'm too old for this here program, but I can't get no go'ment health coverage till I'm sixty-five. Mind, I'm not sick, but my heart dances real fast sometimes. I'll do what you think is best."

"Yes. Surely." Bonnie rose, came around the desk, and patted her hand. "I'll give it a good think, Mrs. McCracken. I'll see what I can come up with."

"Thank you kindly. I can walk the line if it ain't too straight," Lyda Jane assured her as she went out.

Bonnie wanted a cigarette, a drink, and a chocolate éclair. Four interviews and she was already undone. She must not, she told herself, let her confidence wane or become emotionally involved. In her first, and last, job with the child protection agency so many years ago, her supervisor had written a less than favorable evaluation of her performance, saying that she overidentified with clients and had not been sufficiently conscientious about enforcing departmental guidelines. That, in plain language, meant that she was a bleeding heart who'd been caught bending the rules. At first, when she came home stewing about her clients' problems, Devoe had comforted her, but then he'd said she was too gullible and softhearted for social work. Why, he'd asked, didn't she just give notice? Which, as soon as she'd become pregnant, she'd done with guilty relief. Clearly she hadn't changed. Maybe she was, and always would be, unfit for social work. Maybe she shouldn't wait to be fired but should just quit.

She sat, palms sweating, eyes closed. Then she took out her compact, saw that she had licked off her lipstick, put on another smear, ran the brush through her hair, and went out to call for Ruth Elkins.

This was Sweet Face and—true to the name Bonnie'd given her—she accepted Bonnie's apology for having kept her waiting, saying, "That's OK. You must be swamped," in a voice so low Bonnie could barely hear it. She was neatly dressed, but her grooming did so little to enhance her natural prettiness that Bonnie thought of those makeover articles that were a permanent feature of the women's magazines. Glancing down at her papers, Bonnie said, "I see that you've already had a year of college."

Ruth got out a soft "Yes, ma'am" and swallowed several times. "Could I get you something to drink?"

"No, thank you, ma'am. I just—" Ruth brought her hand to her throat, and Bonnie saw the sad little engagement ring with the speck-size diamond next to the broad gold wedding band. "I did start college, but then I—"

"Got married?" Bonnie helped her out.

"Yes, ma'am. Got married and had children."

"So did I," Bonnie confided. "Did you have a specific career goal when you went to college?"

"I always wanted to be a teacher."

"I see."

"I tried to go back to school right after my oldest boy, Curtis, was born, but"—she gave a shrug of resignation—"sometimes life interferes with our plans. I've always had a great respect for education."

Bonnie nodded encouragingly. Ruth's eyes showed she had a lot to say, but the strained muscles in her neck also showed she couldn't say it. After another nervous swallow, she went on, "Later, when my youngest, Roxanne, was in grade school an' the money was pretty regular, I thought I might . . . But then Freddie, my husband, died, so I had to get the job at Cherished Lady. You can see I'd worked before that," she put in quickly, as though she didn't want Bonnie to think she was lazy. "But they were just part-time jobs—cleaning work at the hospital, baby-sitting, lunch shift at Jessup's cafeteria, which went out of business when the McDonald's come in—just piddling' lil jobs to help pay the note on the house. Then, when Freddie died . . . Well, I'd always sewed. Made most of my kids' clothes. Made my own wedding dress, an' my daughter's too. I'm sorry." She ducked her head in apology. "I'm getting away from the point. After my husband died, a friend got me the job at Cherished Lady, and I been—I've been—there ever since. Good money," she added. "I'm not in as much trouble as a lot of the girls 'cause I do own my own home."

That's more than I can say, Bonnie thought. "So, Mrs. Elkins, do you still want to be a teacher?"

"Oh, yes," Ruth blurted, surprising both Bonnie and herself. "But I can't. I mean . . . I've got to make a living. I'm willin' to do whatever you advise. Lotta the girls say they're gonna study computers. I don't have a natural . . . oh, what's the word?"

"Proclivity? Inclination?" Bonnie suggested.

"Uh-huh. I don't have that inclination, but if you think that's where I'll get a job. . . ." Her voice trailed off.

"I think you can do whatever you want to do," Bonnie assured her. "Your grades from your first year of college were good, so I'd guess you could pick up at your sophomore year. I'm sure there are scholarships that would allow you to go on to a four-year college for a teaching degree. I'll check into that for you, Mrs. Elkins." She made a note on the scratch pad where she'd written "SNACKS!" and got up.

Ruth, sensitive to the cue, got up too. Bonnie glanced at the paperback she was holding and asked, "What are you reading?" Ruth held up the book. The cover showed a man and woman in period costume, the man hungrily kissing the woman's neck. Ruth tilted her head and smiled. "I know these books are silly, but I've been crazy about reading since I was a little girl. And I like love stories with happy endings."

"So do I," Bonnie said. What had she been expecting? *War and Peace,* which, truth to tell, she'd never finished. "No crying babies or mean divorces or money problems in those stories, right?"

"Nothing like that." Ruth laughed. "Pure escapism." The sparkle in her eyes faded. "Miz Cullman, before I go . . . My daughter, Roxy, that's Roxanne Travis, will be coming in to see you this afternoon. She doesn't really want to enroll, but I've been trying to talk her 'round. I'd appreciate it if you could . . . Well, I know it's not up to you, but sometimes a girl's more likely to listen to someone who isn't her mother."

"I know what you mean. I have a daughter myself. I'll do what I can."

"I was so nervous comin' in here I didn't think I could talk at all," Ruth said softly. "But you've been real easy to talk to, and I do appreciate it."

"It's been a pleasure to meet you, Mrs. Elkins. And don't you worry. You're going to do just fine! I'll see you next week, and if you have any problems, feel free to come and talk to me."

After ushering her out, Bonnie thought about Ruth's situation and had to swallow hard herself. But if there were women like Ruth Elkins, who clearly understood their situation and needed a hand, surely she could help. Couldn't she?

After a desk lunch (a burger and cold fries that gave her heartburn), she continued the interviews.

By late afternoon she'd heard so many stories about family, money, and transportation problems that she felt her job could only be filled by a gynecologist with a Ph.D. in economics and a good notion of auto mechanics. Beneath the women's uniformly good manners, the "yes, ma'am" and "whatever you say," she'd felt the simmer of anger, hurt pride, and fear. The notion of some sort of support group began to form in her mind. Something had to be done to ease the women's sense of alienation from the general student population and address their practical problems of child care, car pooling, tutoring, and the like. She didn't know how to set up such a group, but if she didn't, who would?

Ruth Elkins's daughter had the last appointment of the day at three o'clock. At three-twenty, when she still hadn't shown up, Bonnie walked out into the hall to stretch her legs. She was leaning over the water fountain when the main door opened and she heard the slap of flip-flops and the hammer of heels on the linoleum and, turning her head, saw two young women coming toward her. One had the tiny but muscular body of a gymnast, covered (but barely) with a purple halter top and skimpy black shorts. Her hair, cut close and spiky, was black too. The other one was tall, with long dark hair scrunched around her face. She wore a tight-fitting denim jumpsuit and, despite the heat, high-heeled boots. She had a little girl slung on one hip and was dragging a boy of about six by the hand. And giving him hell. "Whaddid I tell you, Kylie? Whaddid I tell you? You wanna stay in the car? 'Cause I can leave you in the car if you don't straighten up."

As they moved down the hall, the short one asked, "So whosit you're 'sposed to see?"

"Some chick named Cullman," the tall one answered, giving the boy's hand a yank.

"You've found her," Bonnie said, straightening. "I'm Mrs. Cullman. Are you Ruth Elkins's daughter?"

"I'm Roxy Travis. Yeah. Sorry I'm late." She sighed and added, irritably, "My son here wasn't where he was s'posed to be when I went to pick him up from school." The boy hung his head and moved from foot to foot, guilty as charged. "This here's my friend Johnette. She's gonna watch the kids while we talk," Roxy said, passing the little girl into Johnette's arms, one of which had a tattooed snake curled around the biceps.

"Pleased to meet you," Bonnie said.

Johnette bobbed her head but couldn't muster a verbal response, so Bonnie crouched down to talk to the boy, ignoring Johnette's purple flip-flops and black toenails and focusing on the boy's pinched, sullen face. "And what's your name?" she asked.

"He's Kylie," Roxy told her, releasing the boy's hand and giving him a gentle shove in Johnette's direction. "And this here's"—she patted the girl's bottom—"Cheryl, but we call her Moo."

"You know, Moo, like a cow." Kylie got his licks in as Cheryl buried her head in Johnette's neck.

Free of the children, Roxy shook herself and stood tall. She was quite good-looking but bore little resemblance to her mother. Her eyes were dark, widely spaced, and heavily made up; her mouth was sensuous and pouty, affecting the bored, vaguely hostile look popularized in Calvin Klein ads. "You kids better mind Johnette, you hear?" she said in a voice that was both stern and whiny, before she turned to Bonnie, nodded to show she was ready, and followed her into her office.

"I met your mother earlier today," Bonnie began. "She seems to be a very nice woman. Very intelligent."

Roxie said, "Yeah," and leaned back, head tilted to the ceiling, legs stretched in front of her.

Bonnie tried again: "Your friend Johnette, did she work at the factory too?" and got another "Yeah." Maybe, she thought, an inability to speak ran in the family, but where Ruth Elkins's problem seemed to be rooted in shyness or fear, her daughter just seemed rude. As a final conversational prompt she offered a bland "I see" and tapped her pencil on the desk till Roxy said, "Johnette don't have no appointment 'cause she'd got herself a job already."

"That's good."

"She's got a job as a dancer."

Not, Bonnie presumed, in a corps de ballet rehearsing *Swan Lake*. "And where's that?"

"Over to a place called Masquerades. I could prob'ly get work there too, but my mama would croak. She don't understand how much I need money."

"Oh, I expect she does," Bonnie said flatly.

"But it's different for me. I got kids."

"Any chance that your husband . . . ?" Bonnie glanced at the application. None of the boxes under marital status had been checked. Perhaps the children were illegitimate and she'd put her foot in it.

"I was married. Still am, I guess. I didn't mark anything down 'cause there's no box for desertion. Big Kylie run out on me."

"I'm sorry," Bonnie said, and meant it.

"Hey, like the song says, 'I Been in Jail an' I Been in Love, an' I'd Rather Be in Jail.'" Roxy made a sound somewhere between a laugh and a cough, then added, "Don't get me wrong, I never been in jail."

"I didn't think you had." Though it wouldn't have surprised her. Roxy's voice had a whine that didn't inspire sympathy; on the other hand, it would be unfair to expect an abandoned, unemployed mother of two to be bright and cheery. "So," Bonnie tried. "What sort of work are you interested in training for? What sort of job would you want?" She was afraid the answer would echo the standard aspirations of *Playboy* centerfolds ("I'd like to be either a brain surgeon or a bikini model"), but after a pause Roxy said, "I'd like something where I could dress up nice." Bonnie could see how a girl who did factory work wearing jeans and T-shirts might connect her career dreams to a better wardrobe. "So you'd like to work in a bank or an office?" No response. "You're a very attractive young woman," Bonnie added, wanting to tell her that she'd be even more attractive if she'd cut her straggly hair and take the thick makeup off her eyes. "If you developed office skills, you could get a job as a secretary and can make good money." In her youth, being a secretary had been considered a desirable job, but now girls with education and ambition wanted to be administrators, not secretaries, just as they wanted to be doctors instead of nurses, attorneys instead of law clerks, and this had left a gap in the work force. Devoe and his friends were always complaining about the lack of qualified secretaries. "I've heard that good secretaries can pull down good money."

Roxy's jaw tightened. "If I go to school, I'll have to move in with my mama. 'Course she wants me to. But she's got this ol' house with only two bedrooms, an' it don't even have a dishwasher. It'd be like sardines in a can. I got my own place now. I got privacy."

"But you no longer have a job," Bonnie reminded her.

Roxy shot back, "How'd you like to have to move in with your folks?"

Since that had been at least a consideration just a few short months ago, Bonnie felt an easy empathy. "I know that can be rough—I actually am familiar with your situation—" she admitted, "but you've got to consider the big picture. You've got to think about where you want to be ten years from now and make compromises."

Roxy looked at her, long and steadily, for the first time. Then her mouth began to work, lips bunched, chin quivering. She squeezed her eyes shut, wiped her nose, and tilted her head back to rest on the wall behind her. Tears rolled from the corners of her eyes into the hair at her temples. "I've messed up. I've messed up. bad," she sobbed. "Now I'm up shit creek without a paddle. I really am."

Bonnie made ineffectual shushing sounds and thought, I should have a box of tissues on my desk in plain view, like a shrink. She didn't doubt that Roxy was in pain, but there was something—she couldn't put her finger on it—something of a performance about it, like those people who poured out their miseries on talk shows, weeping but acutely aware of the camera. No, Bonnie chided herself as she got up and moved to put her arm around Roxy's shoulder, she was tired and didn't know what to do, and her fatigue and confusion were making her judgmental and hardhearted. Still, she was vastly relieved when the phone rang. After lunging for it, she gave a bright and thankful "Hello?," then remembered to add, "Bonnie Cullman here."

"Yo, girl. It's Cass. How's your walk on the wild side coming along?"

"Yes. Thank you for asking. I'm busy right now, Professor, but I'll meet you, as planned, to discuss it." She hung up, cutting off Cass's laughter, and said, "Sorry for the interruption," to Roxy, though she was so grateful for it that she wanted to laugh. Tucking her blouse into her sweaty skirt band, she watched as Roxy passed the back of her hand under her nose and wiped it on the leg of her jump-suit, her shoulders heaving.

"I've had a long day," Bonnie confessed, trying to sound reasonable instead of frustrated. "And I expect you have too. You're too upset to make any decisions now. Why don't you check out the programs in the brochures, especially the secretarial option? Think it over, discuss it with your mother or your friend Johnette, and we'll talk next week." If procrastination was the thief of time, she could be convicted of grand theft.

Roxy hauled herself up, shaking her head. "I've made a mess of my life. I just don't know what to do," she continued.

Wanting to get her up and out of the office, Bonnie repeated her suggestion as she opened the door, adding, "If your mother's agreeable, moving in with her might be the best option just now. I understand that you're concerned about your personal freedom, but it would ease your financial burden. And I'm sure her help with your kids would give you more flexibility arranging your schedules. Give it some thought."

Roxy nodded, bringing her index fingers up to her eyes and using her long red acrylic nails to scrape the sludged mascara beneath them. "Yeah," she mumbled as she started out. "Yeah, I'll do that."

It wasn't until Bonnie'd closed the door and leaned against it that she thought maybe—at least as far as Ruth Elkins's interests were concerned—it wasn't such a good idea after all.

Chapter VII

*H*illy left Ruth's place madder than a wet hen. It had only been a couple of months since they'd enrolled in school, yet everything had changed. The best thing she could think to do, other than settle in with a quart of tequila, which even *she* didn't want to do on a sunny Sunday morning, was to drive, but even that pleasure was curdled by worries about car payments and the price of gas. What the hell? Pretty soon she'd have to trade in her car for some rust bucket, so she might as well enjoy it while she could.

Stopping at an Exxon station, she filled the tank, handed over fifteen of her last twenty dollars, and headed toward the interstate. Since it was eleven o'clock on a Sunday morning, the knee benders were in church, the sinners were still sleeping it off, and the highway patrolmen were in cafés chowing down on free sausage and eggs, so the highway was blessedly free of traffic. She rolled down the windows, punching up the volume on the CD. When the speedometer hit seventy-five and the wind made her hair fly, she felt like that warrior chick Boadicea she'd seen on the History Channel, racing her chariot into battle against the Romans, with the sun gleaming on her breastplate and a yelping horde bringing up the rear. Suddenly ravenous, she reached into the sack of egg salad sandwiches on the passenger seat, took one out, pulled off the Saran Wrap with her teeth, and bit into it. She'd made the sandwiches expecting to take Ruth and the kids out. All right, maybe she should've called and checked before she'd gone to Ruth's house, but just yesterday Ruth had been saying she had cabin fever, and how many sunny days were there in November? Aw, to hell with it, she thought. She was just as happy to be alone. She only wished Ruth hadn't been so hateful.

When she arrived at Ruth's, she'd been feeling fine, and seeing that Roxy's car wasn't in the drive had made her feel even better. Retrieving a kid's sneaker she spied under a camellia bush, she'd pressed the buzzer long and hard so it could be heard over the blare of the TV, and as she'd looked at the neglected yard, she'd thought maybe she'd offer to pull weeds and mow the lawn when they got back from their outing. Ruth yelled, "Coming," and, "Turn off that TV!" and she called back, "Open up, open up, lil piggy, or I'll blow your house down."

"I wish you would," Ruth said, yanking open the door. She was barefoot, wearing a white slip with a safety pin securing one strap, and her hair was in rollers. "Don't mind the mess," she said distractedly, motioning her in, snapping off the TV as she passed it, and hurried into the kitchen.

No wonder she looks frazzled, Hilly thought, glancing around the living room. Ever since Roxy and the kids had moved in, the place had been a shambles. "Yeah, it does kinda look like a madwoman's breakfast," Hilly called out. Sheets, blankets, and a balled-up package of potato chips were tossed on top of the couch where Roxy slept, and crumbs dusted the couch like dandruff. Nail polish remover, wads of tissue, a hand mirror, and a brush had been left on the coffee table next to a copy of *Cosmopolitan* with "Give Your Man Multiple Orgasms!" on the cover. The carpet was littered with Crayolas, a disorderly company of Power Rangers, a baby doll with a head snatched so bald it looked like a chemo patient. Bending to pick up an up-ended cereal bowl and the milk-soaked paper towel next to it, Hilly saw the mate to the sneaker she'd found in the yard, picked it up, and carried it, along with the bowl and soggy paper towel, into the kitchen, saying, "So let's get out of this mess and take the kids out to the woods. I got a heap of sandwiches an' a gallon of Kool-Aid in the car." But then she'd seen that the ironing board was up and the kids were freshly bathed—Moo still in her panties and undershirt, but Kylie already dressed in his neon blue suit with a snap-on red bow tie—so she'd understood that Ruth was planning to go to church.

Ruth poured her a cup of coffee, told her to help herself to the last doughnut, and said, "Wish you'd called and told me you were comin' over. We're goin' to church."

Hilly said, "I'd think the best way to praise the Lord on a day like this would be to get out and enjoy the weather," but Ruth just kept on pressing the rose-colored dress with the lace collar she'd worn to Roxy's wedding.

"Can't we go drivin' with Miss Hilly?" Moo begged.

"Go, go, go," Kylie chanted. "C'mon, Grandma, let's go."

Ruth shot Hilly a look that said she shouldn't have mentioned anything in front of the kids, then told Kylie to take Moo into the bedroom and help her get dressed. "I need to take the kids to church regularly," she said. "I want them to have *some* moral foundation."

Best foundation for that kid, Hilly thought, as Kylie ignored Ruth's order, grabbed the last doughnut, and raced into the living room to turn on the TV, would be to set his sassy little butt in a tub of cement.

"I'm sorry, Hilly," Ruth went on, "but I'm teaching the Bible class now, so I have to go."

"You're turning into as much of a thumper as Celia Lusk," Hilly said, going to the sink and starting to wash up the dishes.

"You shouldn't be so prejudiced against the Bible. At the very least it's a great book with wonderful stories," Ruth said, hanging up her dress and collapsing the ironing board. "I was talking to Professor Ledforth the other day after class, and she was telling me about a class she took at the University of Chicago called 'The Bible as Literature.' If I go on in school, I'd like to take a class like that."

The way Ruth talked about Professor Ledforth sounded like she thought *she* was the Second Coming. It was Professor Ledforth this, Professor Ledforth that. Ruth had been over the moon when Ledforth had told her she could call her by her first name, Cassandra, which, Ruth'd explained, like it was a big deal, was the name of a prophetess who'd called the score on the Trojan War. Cassandra Ledforth sure acted like she thought she had special powers, always yapping about women's rights and looking down her nose at people who weren't educated. She'd heard that Cassandra Ledforth and Bonnie Cullman were tight friends, but it was hard to figure out why. For that matter, she didn't understand why someone like Bonnie Cullman was working at the college in the first place. Rumor had it that her daddy was a millionaire. Rumor also had it that she'd played hanky-panky with Marion Hawkins to get the job. But those stories, as she'd pointed out to the other gals, canceled each other out. Why would someone as rich and good-looking as Bonnie Cullman mess with an old coot like Marion Hawkins to get a lousy job? More'n likely Bonnie Cullman was going through what women like her called a midlife crisis, which meant they were between husbands and playing at a job.

Actually, Bonnie Cullman seemed all right. She worked hard, she acted like she really cared, and her door was always open. She'd even organized a weekly gab session—which she called a support group—on Friday afternoons. Hilly thought the meetings were silly, but they did give the gals time to work out things like study groups, babysitting, and ride sharing, as well as a chance to bitch, or "vent," as Bonnie called it. Until now Hilly had thought of *vent* as meaning a slit in the back of a garment. At Ruth's urging, she'd gone to all the meetings, but neither she nor Ruth had much to say. She was silent because pride kept her from talking, but Ruth was quiet because . . . well, Ruthie always 'bout gagged if she had to say anything in public.

But the other women talked plenty: Lorraine Phillips complained about her husband watching soap operas and drinking beer instead of looking after their kids; Albertine Chisholm explained more about her husband Henry's health problems than anyone but a medical student would want to know; and Roxy, always quick with a con, blabbed about the stress of single parenthood and the possibility that she might have an attention deficit disorder (this, Hilly was sure, was a hedge against poor grades). Mostly the women talked about how to make ends meet and the problems their being in school created with their menfolk.

"I 'bout fell off my chair Friday when Celia Lusk was raggin' on 'bout her husband being jealous of the time she spends in the computer lab," Hilly said, rinsing the dishes, "but I guess if you were married to Celia, a computer is the only thing you'd have cause to be jealous of. She sure wouldn't strain the zipper on most guys' jeans."

"You know she's really a great teacher," Ruth went on, still talking about Cassandra Ledforth as she put away the milk and orange juice. "Her class is far and away the best one I have. Which one of your classes do you like best?"

"They asked me that question in grade school, and I'd still give the same answer: recess."

"But you're smart," Ruth insisted. "'Member last month when I asked you to read that story I had to write a paper on? That story called 'The Yellow Wallpaper' by Charlotte Perkins Gilman?"

"Yeah. So?"

"You understood what it was about right off. You knew the woman in the story was crazy, and you knew she went crazy because she'd lost a baby and was being persecuted by her husband."

"Yeah. So?" Hilly sponged down the sink and table, then wiped her hands.

"I guessed that too, but I was afraid to say it right out in class. But when Professor Ledforth called on me, I did, and she said I was right. Turns out that story is a feminist classic. It was written in 1899—"

"Geez, Ruthie. Your conversation's startin' to sound like a footnote."

"I only meant"—Ruth persisted—"that you're smart. You understand things right off. Once you get past the remedial stuff and get into some good classes you'll like it better. Right now you're in limbo."

"Limbo? In't that a dance?"

"Come on, Hilly. Stop playing dumb. I'm in it too. It's how I been living for years, I guess in a holding pattern, neither here nor there. Till getting fired shook me up." Ruth glanced at the clock above the sink. "I really have to get dressed. C'mon into the bedroom."

Hilly drained the last of her coffee. "I'll just get those sandwiches from the car so you won't have to fix lunch."

"Don't bother, I've got leftover macaroni and cheese. Speaking of food, I've decided not to cook Thanksgiving dinner this year, and I'm not driving up to my cousin's either," Ruth continued, raising her voice as she moved into the hallway. "They're having a dinner at church. Pastor's wife's doing the turkey, and the ladies are all bringing a covered dish and pies. That'll save me some time and money. Besides, sharing is more in the spirit of the feast. I wish you'd come too."

"I may be in limbo," Hilly muttered to herself as she washed out her cup, "but chompin' on turkey bones with a bunch of Jesus jumpers would really put me in hell." Wandering into the hall, she called out, "OK, Ruthie, I'm gonna hit the road," though she had no idea where she'd go or what she'd do.

Moo, who'd managed to pull on her dress but had left it unbuttoned, came out of the bedroom, socks in hand, and wrapped an arm around Hilly's leg. "Wanna smell me, Miss Hilly?" Hilly turned Moo around, buttoned her dress, then picked her up, wiggling her nose like a rabbit, saying, "Mmm. You smell like a rose."

Moo giggled and shook her head. "No. A labbenda, 'cause Gramma wash me in labenda soap."

"Oh, lavender. Sure. It is lavender. Must have somethin' wrong with my sniffer today."

"Wanna see my new socks? They gots lace on them."

"OK." Hilly carried her into Ruth's bedroom, shifted some books from the bed, and sat down. Ruth had always been queer for books, but now they seemed to be an obsession. There were books on the dressing table, the floor, the windowsill, even books on tape she'd rented from Cracker Barrel. "You got this place looking like a library."

"I wish," Ruth said, taking the rollers from her hair. "In a library the books would be in order." She brushed out her curls and dabbed on face powder while Hilly put on Moo's socks and told her to go get her shoes. "Thanks for helping," Ruth said, slipping her feet into her high heels. "Maybe I can come by your place after Roxy gets home from Johnette's. We could study together. That is, if you promise to really study. No TV, no talking. Just study, 'cause I've got a test tomorrow."

Shit, now she's talking to me like she's my teacher, Hilly thought. What was the point of being with a friend if you weren't supposed to talk? "Wait," she said, picking up the brush, "your hair's all flat in back."

"You know," Ruth confided while Hilly teased and fluffed her hair, "sometimes when I go into the library, I get this sinking feeling because I won't never—I mean, I won't ever"—she corrected herself, as she often did lately—"have time to read everything I want to read. But in a way that's comforting 'cause I figure no matter how old I get, if my eyes stay good, I'll always have an interest, know what I mean?"

"Can't say as I do. Seems to me like you'd have to be pretty dried up 'fore you'd take readin' as a substitute for livin'."

"It's not a substitute," Ruth corrected. "Quite the opposite. It helps you to understand life and people and . . ." She kept talking, saying things like "quite the opposite," that she never would've said before she'd gone back to school. So Hilly tuned her out, concentrating on fixing her hair until she was satisfied with the result, then saying, "You're done."

"Not too much—" Ruth started, but Hilly was already dousing her with hair spray. Well, her hat would flatten it some. "Kylie, you ready?" she yelled. "You better be ready." She moved past Moo, who'd come to the door, shoes in hand.

"I wisht we could go with you," Moo whispered as Hilly took her onto her lap and slipped her feet into her shoes.

"Some other time, sugar." She set Moo down, patting her bottom, and said, "Let's go."

"Spray me too," Moo demanded. Hilly gave Moo's hair a quick brush and even quicker spritz, held her up to the mirror so she could admire herself, then took her hand and walked her to the living room where Kylie slouched in front of the TV staring at a panel of lawyers arguing about campaign financing while wetting his finger to pick up crumbs from between the couch pillows.

"Now hug my neck bye, Moo. And sit quiet so you don't get mussed up," Hilly told her.

Kylie put up his arms, whispering a quick "Can I come feed Garbage soon?" as she embraced him.

Hilly whispered, "Sure can. He's been wanting to see you," then, straightening up, called, "Ruth, I'm leaving."

Ruth came out of the kitchen mashing her hat down on her curls. "Like I told you, Hilly," she said, out of breath, "I can come over soon's Roxy gets here. 'Bout two or three?"

"Or four or five? or maybe not at all?" Hilly reached the front door, then turned back, disgusted. "When you gonna wise up, Ruth? Don't you know Roxy prob'ly won't be home when she says? Don't you know that tryin' to help her is like tryin' to empty the ocean with a spoon?" As soon as the words left her mouth, she was sorry. Ruth's face went hard, then soft, like some damned Christian martyr who'd just got slapped, then decided to turn the other cheek. "Aw, go say your prayers," Hilly said, pulling back the door. "You'll need 'em."

She'd driven for over an hour, the gas gauge was dropping, and she finally felt calm enough to turn back toward home. Maybe she'd study. Fat chance. She didn't mind going to classes, but homework always felt like overtime without pay. Maybe she'd take an afternoon nap or clean up the chicken coop. Maybe she'd call Ruthie and apologize. She was ashamed of herself for saying that about Roxy. Didn't matter that it was true; sometimes telling the truth was just an excuse for meanness. She wouldn't feel right until she'd said she was sorry and Ruth had forgiven her. After taking the off-ramp, but still not wanting to go back to her trailer, she turned south on one of the roads the tourists took to the beaches.

The area had been farmland when she'd first moved here, but now it was pocked with burger joints, auto repair shops, gas stations, convenience stores, and the occasional real estate office or produce stand. A few of the big old farmhouses remained, now occupied by marginal businesses selling homemade rocking chairs, dolls, jams and jellies, and assorted secondhand furniture ambitiously called antiques. She drove past a motel called Sea Breezes, though it was twenty miles from the shore, and, seeing the traffic was getting heavy, wheeled into a wooded lot next to an old two-story house, thinking she would turn around and go home. After pulling up under a large tree, she reached for a sandwich, then glanced over her shoulder, getting ready to back up.

A bare-chested teenage boy wearing a straw hat was up on a ladder, slathering a coat of candy pink paint onto the weather-worn side of the house. Seeing her, he looked around as though poised for flight, then looked again and gave her a broad, relieved smile, calling out, "Chu gona keechin." She had no idea what he was talking about. "Chu gona keechin," he called again, gesturing toward the back of the house with his paintbrush. What the hell did he want? She stuck her head out the window, shading her eyes and calling, "What?" before she saw the WAITRESS WANTED sign near the front door and a larger sign, CASA DEL TORO—AUTHENTIC MEXICAN FOOD, propped next to it. "Row bak," he shouted, still gesturing. Now she got it: "Chu gona keechin" meant "You go to the kitchen," and "row bak" meant it was 'round the back. If that didn't beat all! He thought she was here looking for a waitress job. She snorted, shifted into reverse, then impulsively turned off the motor. What did she have to lose? She already felt lower than a snake's belly. Would slinging hash in a greaser palace be so bad?

Waving the kid back to his work, she got out of the car and walked on a freshly swept pathway to the back of the house. Music was playing—not mariachi or even salsa, but Fats Domino crooning "I found my thr-ill, on Blueberry Hill . . . ," and delicious spicy smells hit her as she reached the porch. She called out, "Hi. Hi there," mounted the steps, and pulled open the screen door. The first thing she saw was a boy of about four, his eyes dark and liquid as chocolate syrup. His hair was shiny as wet black paint and looked as though it had been cut by putting a bowl on the top of his head and hacking around it.

"Don't open the door, stupid! Let Papa open the door!" The voice had the perennial bossiness of a big sister, and as the boy held back the screen and Hilly stepped onto the porch, she saw a girl she judged to be seven or eight kneeling on the floor, shucking corn. The full skirts of a white party dress were bunched around her skinny legs, and a gold cross hung from her neck. She had the same bowl haircut as her little brother with a goofy satin bow pinned on top, but where the boy's expression was sweetly curious, the girl's was tight and suspicious. Poor kid, Hilly thought, these Mexicans have the females down on their knees from the time they're born.

"I guess I want to see—" Hilly began.

The girl turned her head and yelled, "Papa! Papa!" as though Hilly had assaulted her.

Hilly looked around. The porch ran the width of the house but was so crammed with stuff that it seemed small. A few toys, sacks of cornmeal and rice, boxes of canned food with Spanish labels, an iron cot made up with an army blanket, a cardboard box filled with neatly folded clothes next to it, and a rust-pitted freezer wheezing a machine's equivalent of the death rattle. She smiled, but the girl's expression only hardened. The boy watched wide-eyed, more interested in this battle of wills than he'd been by Hilly's initial appearance. Hilly tried again—after all she *was* the adult—bending forward and saying, "Looks like nice sweet corn," but the girl held up her gold cross as though warding off a vampire, then stuck out her tongue.

"Hey, little girl"—Hilly bent closer, locking eyes with her—"playin' with that cross won't help you none if you don't mind your manners. Jesus don't like ugly."

The girl gawped in disbelief. Hilly winked and straightened as the screen door opened and a man in jeans and an open-necked denim shirt with sleeves rolled above his elbows came out, wiping his hands on a chef's apron. He looked to be in his early forties, tall for a Mexican, but so compactly built that he seemed shorter. His chest and arms were muscular and hairless, but the hair on his head was thick and black, with a single white streak near the center that sprang up from his forehead as though electrified. His dark eyes had a wary street fighter toughness that softened as he looked her up and down and asked, "You come about the job?"

"Just drivin' by. I saw the sign," she said casually. She didn't have to feign disinterest. This place was a grass-roots operation if she'd ever seen one. It might never get off the ground, and even if it did, how good would the tips be?

"Come in. Come in, please." He held the screen door back for her to enter. Unlike the chaos of the porch, the kitchen was neat and orderly: A picnic-size table, scoured clean, was in the center of the room; pots and pans hung from an obviously homemade but sturdy rack suspended from the ceiling; and spatulas, spoons, knives of threatening sharpness, bottles of spices and oils were lined up next to a commercial-size gas stove with a double oven. Slatted boards that could be lifted for easy cleaning had been laid on the linoleum.

"Come through to the dining room," he said, holding open the swinging door leading to the front of the house. "Or maybe"—he paused and extended his arm—"you would like a cold drink?"

"Naw, thanks," she said. The rich smell of meat simmering in garlic and herbs made her mouth water.

She followed him into what must've been the dining room in the original house. Old-fashioned pocket doors, leading into what had been the front parlor, had been pushed back to make it one large room. The walls had been painted in bold aqua blue, and obligatory south-of-the-border decorations—straw hats, a couple of serapes, a piñata in the shape of a donkey—were already up. Chairs and tables were still higgledy-piggledy and, to judge from their assorted shapes and sizes, had been purchased from the Goodwill or the Salvation Army. "This musta been a pretty house," she said as he motioned her to a window table.

He pulled up a chair across from her, saying, with obvious pride, "I lease with an option to buy it. We living upstairs. Is a mess still, but you think it will be pretty?" What could she do but nod? "So, Mrs. . . . Please, what is your name?" he asked, leaning forward.

"Hilly Pruwitt," she said, noticing the pale scar that ran from his left ear to his clavicle, "I'm not Mrs. anything."

"Many American woman are proud not to be married," he said, shaking his head at the mystery. "Any children?"

"I said I wasn't married."

"Chur. Sorry. You have been a waitress before?"

She figured he must've been in the country for a long time, was maybe even second generation, because except for the fact that he reversed the regular sequence of words and sometimes pronounced his *s*'s with a soft *ch* sound, his English was good. She said, "Hey, I've been everything before."

He grinned, showing a set of large, white, perfect teeth, and said, "Me too."

He seemed so eager to please that she felt as though she were interviewing him. "I haven't slung hash—" She paused to translate. "I mean—"

"I know what this means."

"OK. So. I haven't worked in a restaurant in years. I was workin' over to Cherished Lady as a lace cutter, but they shut down the mill without telling us."

He nodded, said, "This I read about," then shook his head. "Now so many without work."

His sympathetic expression made her feel defensive. "Yeah. Well. That's the way it goes," she said casually. "So, what do you need here in the way of help, Mr. . . . ?"

"I am Jess Aranda."

"So, Mr. Aranda—"

"Call me Jess."

"OK, Jess," she said, thinking his real name was probably Jesus, Americanized to Jess. "You can call me Hilly."

"OK. Hee-lee." He grinned as though the name pleased him. "I am needing an experienced waitress who know salad prep and polite service. Also, she should be—" He paused, searching for the right words. "You know the saying that people also eat with the eyes, no? So also, she should be pretty."

Hilly wrapped her arms across her chest, searching for a comeback, but when he kept nodding and smiling, she realized that he meant he thought she was pretty. She gave a little laugh. "So when do you plan to open?"

"The dishwashing machine is to come Tuesday. Two weeks maybe. After Thanksgiving."

It was always mañana with these Mexicans. He'd never get it together to open in a week, or even two. She shrugged. "God willin' an' the creek don't rise."

He was momentarily confounded. Then she saw the wheels turn, and he repeated, "'God willin' an' the creek don't rise.' This I like." He leaned across the table, the medal around his neck swinging forward, his hands locked. "I tell you, Hee-lee, if the creek rise, I will paddle faster. The boy you see painting the house—Manuel—he will help. My children will help. For now we open only for the dinners, so I need you only part-time. But when business pick up"—he opened his hands to the possibilities—"then, *comida*—that is lunch—too."

"I'm taking some classes over at Hawkins Community College, so I only want part-time work, in the evenings."

"A college girl," he said, with all the awe of the uneducated.

"I'm not exactly a girl, and it's not like college in the movies. For most it's just a get-in, get-out, get-a-life operation." Or, in her case, simply a holding action. "So, what hours would you need me?"

"To begin, only from six in the evening."

"Till?"

"Till customers go home. Then stay to clean up. I know the law is five dollars forty cents an hour, but I don't have to pay that because you make the tips," he said firmly. "But still I will pay this because I know we be slow in the beginning, but—" His eyes dropped to the table, then came up to hold hers. "There is no paperwork. No Social Security. No benefits. I pay you behind the table, you understand?"

"Under the table," she corrected. "Yeah. I get it. That's more than fine with me. But do I get to keep all the tips?"

"You earn them."

"Yeah, but you know and I know it don't always work like that."

"I know. You keep all the tips. Give Manuel somesing to help you bus tables if you like. And you eat whatever you want. We got a deal?"

The chances of its working out were as good as a snowball's chances in hell, but why not? She extended her hand. He grasped it, placed his other hand over it, gave it a firm shake, and grinned. She wondered how Mexicans, even poor Mexicans, had such beautiful teeth. Must be the beans and rice that made them strong and the contrast with their dark skin that made them look so white. He looked honest; then again, maybe he was just comin' on smooth as a baby's behind so he could con her into working for a week, then not cough up the paycheck. "OK. It's a deal," she agreed, and, aware that his eyes were focused behind her, turned to see the little girl and her brother standing in the kitchen door. And where, she wondered, was Señora Aranda? Where was the wife?

"This is my oldest," Jess told her, holding out his arms as the girl came to him. "This is my moon and my star. My Hermina. Hermina, this is Senorita Pruwitt."

Hermina slipped into the curl of his arm, lowered her head, and bobbed, almost in a curtsy. Jess beamed at her good manners, and Hilly smiled, remembering the rude reception the girl had given her on the porch. "And my son, he is Joseph. We call him JoJo." The boy came into his other arm, squirming as though he wanted to go to the bathroom. "The children are enrolled in St. Elizabeth School. JoJo in kindergarten, Hermina in second grade."

"That's nice," Hilly said, conscious of her lips forming an insipid social smile.

"Papa," Hermina whispered, shooting Hilly a look of pure venom as she twisted in her father's arms. "I'm hungry. And JoJo and Manuel are hungry too."

"Then set the table," Jess said, releasing her. "Hilly, are you hungry?"

"Thanks, but I don't want to intrude on your dinner," she said without much conviction.

"But there is plenty. Please share with us if you have time."

She nodded. Might as well see if the guy could cook.

"You think we should have tablecloths in the restaurant?" Jess asked, getting up. "Would make it more classy, but we don't have no washing machine yet."

Since she'd been asked, Hilly offered, "Why don't you just paint the tables and chairs all different colors, then put a couple of coats of polyurethane on them? That way they'd look bright, but you could just wipe 'em clean. But I think you should have cloth napkins. They make a place look classy, and they're not too much trouble to haul to the Laundromat."

"Good idea," Jess assented. "But I don' know if we have time. I give my word to myself that I open in coupla weeks. Also, I need money comin' in soon's possible."

"You pay me an' I'll come by after school, starting tomorra. I'll help paint chairs and tables. Also, I got a friend with a sewing machine, so I could run up a heap of napkins," she volunteered, thinking that way she'd see if he paid her before she ran out and invested in a pair of arch supports.

"Is a deal." Jess laughed. "I read that entrepreneurs must make split-second decision. So. Split-second decision. You come tomorrow."

She followed him into the kitchen, where the teenage boy who'd been painting the house was pulling bowls down from the shelves next to the stove. "This is my friend Manuel." Jess introduced her. Manuel smiled but ducked his head. "He don't have much English yet," Jess explained, cuffing him affectionately, "but he learn quick. He's a good kid. Works like a Yankee."

Hilly supposed that Jess still used the words *Yankee* and *American* interchangeably. She looked around for the silverware. JoJo sidled up to her, pointing to the widemouthed ceramic vases that held knives, forks, and spoons. Wordlessly she handed them over to him while Hermina filled a water jug and Manuel slipped a pile of warm tortillas into a clean dish towel. Jess heaped rice into a large bowl and handed it to her, then raised the lid of the steaming iron pot, sniffed, and turned his head to tell her, "This is *lomo de cerdo en salsa verde.* Pork in green sauce," and proceeded to stir, taste, add a pinch of salt, taste again, then smile his satisfaction. She moved ahead of him and held open the door as he picked up potholders, lifted the pot, and carried it into the dining room. Manuel had already dished rice onto the plates, and Jess, with the passionate cook's assumption that everyone was interested in recipes, explained, "You take four pounds of lean pork, boneless, cover with cold water, add chopped onion, bay leaf, marjoram, thyme, and salt, and simmer, covered, maybe three hours, until the meat is soft and the flavors—what the chefs say—get married. For the sauce, you puree—" Hermina scooted into the chair next to her father's, giving Hilly evil looks from beneath her perfectly shaped eyebrows, but JoJo climbed into the chair beside Hilly, beaming up at her as though her presence made it a party—"and in the end, stir in cilantro," Jess concluded, adding, "But maybe too spicy for the menu?"

Hilly started to take her first mouthful, then seeing they had all lowered their heads, paused with spoon in midair while Hermina said grace. "You ever been really hungry?" Jess asked lightly. "If you ever be really hungry, you say thanks to God when you eat even if you not religious, hey, Manuel?" Apparently able to understand that much English, or maybe just being agreeable, Manuel nodded, laughed, and spooned in. Jess watched expectantly as Hilly took her first mouthful. "So? Whachu think?"

She chewed, evaluated, chewed some more, then nodded, wiping sauce from her lips. "It's good. Really good. Outstanding."

"We will have tacos an' burritos always too. Cheaper. Also, this is what people think is Mexican food."

"Some folk'll be brave enough to go for the real thing, 'specially if the waitress pushes it," Hilly added.

"You know these things," Jess said happily, raising his glass and clinking it to hers. "It is very lucky that you come."

Manuel and the kids were on their second helping when Hilly took a long drink of water to cool the pleasant fire in her mouth and said she'd leave them to their privacy. Jess got up and walked her to the front door, pointing out the staircase, telling her they'd worked for a long time to strip the paint from the carved banister. "Upstairs is still crazy. We have much to do. So—" He stopped, holding open the door for her and asking, "We still have a deal?" in a voice deep and serious as a Mafia don's in a bad movie.

"Chur," Hilly answered, wondering if he'd pick up on the fact that she was kidding his accent. "See you tomorrow afternoon."

"I don' have your phone number."

"Can't find a pencil," she told him after burrowing in her purse, "but it's listed. Hilly Pruwitt, like I told you. But you'll see me to-morrow 'round five."

"You won' let me down?" He looked into her face, his eyes prob-ing. "No." He decided before she could answer. "I don' think you let people down. See you mañana."

Back at her trailer she hunted through her closet and pulled out a multicolored tiered skirt and an aqua off-the-shoulder blouse she'd been meaning to give to the Goodwill. Sucking in her breath, she hooked herself into the bustier she'd lifted from Cherished Lady, but she still couldn't do up the waist of the skirt, so she clasped it with a silver-dollar belt that bozo she'd played around with last year (she couldn't remember his name, but he always wore a baseball cap to cover his bald spot) had bought her at the county fair. She fished a pair of silver dangle earrings out of her jewel box and fixed her hair to the top of her head with silver combs, turning this way and that in front of the full-length mirror she'd nailed to the bedroom door. Not bad. Not bad a'tall. She'd have to get some good arch support shoes and a can of foot powder, but other than that, she was ready to roll. Flopping on the bed and reaching for the phone, she punched in Ruth's number. As it started to ring, she knew that even before she apologized, she was going to say, "Ruthie, guess what? I just met Je-sus, and he gave me a part-time job."

Chapter VIII

*T*he sun streamed through the bedroom window, glinting off the edge of the mirror and washing the walls in lemony light. Bonnie opened her eyes, closed them, opened them again. There was something so lovely about early-morning sunlight. Its translucent, almost iridescent quality was— She lunged for the clock: 8:45. She'd forgotten to set the alarm! In a state of preemptive panic she was on her feet, pulling her nightdress over her head and lurching for the phone to call the office. She froze in midstride, nightdress above her head as the realization hit her. "It's Sunday." Relief. Reprieve. Hallelujah! Shrugging back into her nightdress, she flopped onto the bed. Nesha, fighting his way out of the comforter she'd tossed over him, gave a yap of approval. "Yes," she told him. "We've got the whole day to ourselves."

Noticing the sorry state of her nails as she scratched his head, she said, "We'll do the laundry, then tackle the garden. Then I'll clean myself up. I'll clean you up too. Want a bath?" She sniffed and turned her head away in mock horror. "You sure need a bath. I'll go grocery shopping and cook a real dinner, so I'll have healthy leftovers. Then I'll read. Do you know how much I've missed having the time to read, Nesha?" Though wallowing in the comfort of her warmth and touch, Nesha still paid attention, looking up with sympathetic eyes. "Imagine what life was like before they invented the alarm clock. It's just not natural to be blasted out of sleep!" All those years when the kids had been growing up she'd been an up-and-at-'em dervish of cereal bowls, shoe tying, hair combing, and lunch packing, cranking up the car in the early-morning hours, sometimes still wearing her robe when she'd driven them to school. Thousands upon thousands of mornings that had seemed natural, even pleasant in a hectic way. But once the kids were grown there'd been the blessed indulgence of waking slowly and naturally, padding down to the kitchen of the big, silent house, going through the ritual of grinding coffee, surfacing into full consciousness when its pungent aroma blossomed, then taking a cup to the sunporch overlooking her garden, thinking through her day or reading until the caffeine stimulated her enough to want a shower. "I never realized what a drag it was to haul your tail to work every morning," she told Nesha, who thumped his tail to signal understanding.

At last count, more than forty women from Cherished Lady had enrolled in the displaced homemakers program. Five had already dropped out, but that was fewer than the dozen both Cass and Mrs. Jackson had predicted. Some had taken her up on her offer to "come by my office anytime," and despite her resolve to be coolly professional, she found herself worrying about their personal problems when she actually had time to stop and think. She'd become more confident with the computer, she could talk the bureaucratic lingo, and she now knew the government and school requirements and guidelines. She'd gotten to know most of the teachers and had at least a telephone acquaintance with various people at the government and service organizations. But no matter how early she went to the office or how late she stayed, even if she went in on Saturdays, she never seemed to catch up. Sometimes she felt so frustrated she wanted to quit, just call the Duke, ask for a check, and take off to . . . where? Sometimes she felt miserably lonely, but sometimes, after a day of Mrs. Snopes, she felt content, even serene, in the solitude of her little house. Though, as Cass had predicted, the house had a lot of problems.

Windows stuck, had to be held open with sticks, and rattled when the wind was high. The bathroom plumbing erupted like Mount Vesuvius. The oven made a sound like a gun shot when she turned it on and had only two temperatures: 250 or broil. The dining room remained a sort of DMZ that she walked through quickly, averting her eyes from stacks of unpacked boxes. She'd gone so far as to make up the beds in the second bedroom, then shut the door on further improvements. Her grand plans for the garden had come to no more than spritzing water on plants that had the strength to cling to life. Her paycheck was so paltry after deductions (she found a new solidarity with people who railed against government spending) that she hadn't even been able to replace the awful lumpy mattress in her bedroom. Had she ever imagined she'd be too broke to buy a good mattress? Still, she was usually so tired when she crawled into bed that she fell asleep in spite of it.

But she often woke during the night. The cry of a bird or a scratch of a branch brushing against a window made her start up, skittery as a virgin in a Gothic novel. Sometimes the very lack of noise, the deep silence of the woods, spooked her, and she'd reach out, her hand sliding across the sheet, searching for Devoe out of habit. Nesha would rouse himself from the foot of the bed and wiggle up to her chest, and doggy breath and hairs up the nose be damned, she was grateful for his company. She loved the way he welcomed her with tail-wagging enthusiasm when she came home, and when she went for walks in the woods, he tumbled along beside her, pausing to nose strange objects and looking up to see what she thought. If she let him off the leash, he trotted ahead like a loyal scout, forgetting her in the wild pursuit of a bird or squirrel, but always coming back as soon as she called him. She was sure her communication with him had gone beyond simple commands. He actually seemed to understand what she was saying, at least he listened with more patience than Devoe had ever shown, and he was definitely more attuned to her moods. Sensing when she was angry, he gave her a wide berth, but when she was melancholy, he'd nudge his head under her hand and make mewing sounds, like a cat, to show he commiserated.

"You're my beautiful baby, aren't you?" she told him, rubbing his silky ears between her thumbs and index fingers and kissing the top of his head. "I wuv you, I wuv you, I wuv you." Oh, Lord, she thought. I'm turning into one of those women who treat their pets like a kid or a lover. Pretty soon I'll start eating as well as sleeping with him and feeling jealous when he lets someone else touch him, and I'll disinherit my kids to leave my money to the ASPCA. But she laughed and told him, "You's my special sweetheart." One of the compensations of living alone was that you didn't have to censor your silliness. You could walk around in the nude, leave dishes in the sink, let your thoughts run on without interruption, bay at the moon at 3:00 A.M. if the spirit moved you. You could also turn into a blithering, antisocial weirdo.

She considered this, gently removing Nesha from her chest and catching sight of her breasts. They still had a mounded resilience that, quite objectively, was lovely. She help up one of her legs. Not bad. Not bad a'tall, if you discounted the dimpled flesh where upper thigh met torso and the fuzz that darkened her shins. Before she went to bed tonight, she'd give herself the full treatment: touch up her hair, shave her armpits and legs, give herself a facial, manicure, and pedicure. But who was there to appreciate her effort to make herself smooth, sweet-smelling, and desirable? Me, that's who, she reminded herself. Her sexual feelings were so dormant she didn't have to bother repressing them. The only remotely attractive man with whom she'd come in contact recently was Mark, and except for a brief moment months ago, when he'd stripped off his shirt while helping to clean up the house, she hadn't had even a shiver of interest in anyone. Who was there to stimulate desire? Her life was spent almost exclusively in the company of women. Apart from a few male students, janitors, campus guards, gas station attendants, and supermarket clerks, the only men she'd met had been at one of those dreadful faculty get-togethers at the home of a professor and his wife the previous night.

Cass had told her she needn't bother to doll up because the pickings would be slim. Slim? They'd been the social equivalent of a crop attacked by locusts. The majority of the men were, as expected, married. Of the remainder, one had reached the doddering stage, another was gay, and the third was a red-socks, pens-in-the-shirt-pocket oddity who seemed to think that a lecture on Microsoft's legal tangles was a form of flirtation. What an awful party it had been. The conversation was desultory, the wine rotgut, the house cluttered and grubby, with the heat turned so high it approached the humidity of a rain forest. The only time she'd laughed was when the gay professor's significant other sidled up to her at the buffet table and whispered, "I never imagined that someone with a Ph.D. in chemistry would serve Velveeta."

A shocking thought came to her: What if she never had sex again? Absurd! She wasn't that old. She was still attractive, or would be if she paid more attention to her grooming. She could pick up a man if she wanted. But she knew she'd never do that. "Get out of bed, you sorry slob," she ordered herself. Hoping a little self-indulgence would keep depression at bay, she made coffee with cream and sugar and curled up on the couch, Nesha on her lap, and read until noon.

Seeing the day was getting away from her, she forced herself up, ate some crackers and cheese, turned on the radio for company, did the laundry, and cleaned the house.

By four o'clock, dressed in tennis shoes, an old pair of cutoffs, and a paint-spattered work shirt, her hair yanked into a ponytail and covered with a cotton scarf she'd found in the spare room, she doused herself with bug spray and went out to tackle the garden. She yanked weeds and cut back vines, cursing the rusty shears and her own stupidity. What had possessed her to think she'd have time for a garden? Nesha, wanting to play, kept getting underfoot. "You know what I had to shell out to take you to the vet? How come you keep getting in my way instead of earning your kibbles?" she asked, pushing him aside more roughly than she'd intended. Suitably chastened, he backed off, ambling over to sit in the shade of the house. She heard the phone ring and, wiping sweat from her forehead, threw down the shears and made a beeline for the kitchen.

She grabbed the phone just as the party at the other end hung up. Thinking it must be the Duke, who usually called on Sundays, she washed her hands, splashed water on her face, and dialed his number. In the middle of the second ring Elice picked up, twittering, "Duke residence. And who might this be?"

"Hi, Elice. It's me, Bonnie."

"Anything wrong, sugar?"

"No. I was out in the garden and the phone rang and I didn't get to it in time. I thought it might be the Duke."

"No, it wasn't."

"Is he around?"

"Daddy's resting. I've put that little boy down for a nap."

"Oh. OK." She reached into the cabinet and took out a box of Triscuits. It always bothered her when Elice called the Duke Daddy, but when she called him a little boy, it annoyed her even more. "Everything OK with you?" she asked without a questioning inflection, wanting to end the call.

Elice sighed so deeply her exhalation of breath seemed to come through the receiver. "Oh, you know. What can't be cured must be endured."

"What needs curing?" Bonnie popped the Triscuit into her mouth.

"Oh, sugar, you know. Not sick, just slowin' down. I don't mean me"—she demonstrated her youthfulness with a trill of girlish laughter—"but the Duke."

Bonnie'd never known Elice's exact age but figured she couldn't be more than six years the Duke's junior. But ever since the Duke's bypass, Elice had talked about him as though he had one foot in the grave and the other on a banana peel. "Has Daddy been having regular checkups an' all?"

"Like I said, he's just slowin' down. He's got that dickey heart. I do what I can to keep him on his diet, but you know how pigheaded he can be. And speaking of diets, how's yours comin' along?"

Bonnie swallowed her second Triscuit. "Just fine."

"You know, I weigh myself first thing every morning, an' if I see that needle on the scale so much as quiver, I cut right back. It's a lot easier to take off one pound than five. And once you let yourself get so out of control you're up to eight . . ." Her voice faded off, indicating the impossibility of Bonnie's task. "'Course, I s'pose, living alone, you don't take care of yourself, and you don't have the incentive. But husband or no, a girl has to keep pride in her appearance."

"Listen, Elice, I've got to—"

"And how is that garden coming along, sugar? You always did have a green thumb. We've still got that clipping from when *Southern Living* came to your Atlanta house, though I guess it's not the same if the property doesn't actually belong to you."

"Garden's fine. Hey, I left the hose running and—"

"We do worry about you so. Down there all by yourself."

Bonnie took another Triscuit. "I'm fine. Really. I'll call back later today."

"And we'll see you real soon, won't we? For Thanksgiving."

"Sure enough."

"Your divorce lawyer spoke to Daddy last week. Daddy's trying to iron it out, but it looks like Devoe's got you in such a tangle you will lose your house." Bonnie shut her eyes and leaned against the sink as Elice went on. "I've always said the woman should be able to hold on to her house. I just can't figure how you could let Devoe—"

"Sorry, Elice, but there's someone at the door, so I have to go. Talk with you later tonight. Bye."

She put down the phone without waiting for Elice's sign-off.

Sometimes you had to put emotional preservation above politeness. After taking one last Triscuit, she shoved the box back into the cabinet, pushed open the creaky back door, and went back into the garden, calling for Nesha. She started raking up leaves and shoving them into trash bags. Stopping to get her breath, she hollered for him again and stood, looking around, expecting to see him bound out from behind a tree. She turned, slowly, in a complete circle, shading her eyes against the low but still intense sun, calling, "Nesha?" A terrible silence overwhelmed her. Dropping the rake, she walked around the house, calling over and over again, her voice going from simple command to annoyance. Dammit, he must've wandered off into the woods, and now she'd have to go find him. "No doggy biscuit for you tonight," she muttered, moving through the garden to the stubble of cornstalks that surrounded it.

Calling and pausing to squint into the woods, she walked all the way to the creek that marked the property line. They'd never gone farther than the creek. It had been a mere trickle when they'd first explored it, but now, owing to recent rains, it had swollen and turned the ground around it boggy. She cursed as her feet sank in, soaking her tennis shoes. Putting one foot on a tree trunk to retie her laces, she got mud on her hands and wiped it on the seat of her pants. Surely he wouldn't just wander off. She'd only nudged him out of the way with her foot, not really a kick. Well, not a mean kick.

The big empty field belonging to Jarvis Boggs, who, blessedly, had not come by since the day she'd moved in, lay before her. So far as she could see nothing was moving in it. Turning, she stumbled back in the direction of the house, pausing to scratch at her bare legs and wipe sweat out of her eyes, mentally talking herself down from a mounting panic while still yelling at the top of her lungs. The fact that the sun was sinking did nothing to improve her mood. What if Nesha didn't come back? How would she hunt for him once it got dark?

Rounding the front steps, she thought she heard a noise under the house and got down on all fours, trying to see through the lattice-work that camouflaged the foundation. She heard a car coming up and swung around, shielding her eyes, wondering who it could be. Please God, not that creep Jarvis, though she was now so desperate she'd ask even him for help. But it wasn't a truck. It was a white Mercedes. Who could possibly . . . ?

The car came to a stop, and a man got out, his tall body outlined by the setting sun. He looked at her and burst out laughing, calling, "Bonnie Duke, can that be you? I swear you've really gone country."

It was Riz Mazersky.

She got to her feet, wiping dirt from her hands and knees and, knowing how she looked, wanting to run in the other direction. "Riz! I can't believe . . ."

"What the hell're you doin', girl?"

"Looking for my dog. He's run away and—" Tears welled in her eyes. She felt about six years old.

"Didn't you ever see *Lassie Come Home?* He'll be back." He walked up to her, still laughing, opening his arms. She hesitated, then moved into them and, as she did so, heard a fearsome growl coming from under the house.

Nesha struggled through a hole in the lattice and ran full tilt toward Riz, barking furiously. "Trying to protect his mistress's honor," Riz said. She bent and swooped Nesha up, scolding and kissing him at the same time. Riz cocked an eyebrow. "Now don't be kissing a dog before you kiss me."

He put his arm around her, touching his lips to her forehead, then licking them. "Mmm. Salty. And I always thought you'd be sweet. Aren't you going to ask me in?"

Chapter IX

*T*wenty minutes later, after one of the quickest repair jobs of her life, she was ready to meet him again. She'd showered and shampooed, brushed her wet hair into a topknot, teased out a few tendrils, and dabbed on foundation and mascara. Her cheeks, flushed from excitement and hot water, didn't need any blusher. Scrounging in the back of the closet, she'd found a hostess dress she'd packed in a hopeful mood but never had occasion to wear. It was one of her favorites and certainly the most "artsy" outfit in her wardrobe, what she called her Isadora Duncan dress, made of whisper-soft mauve cotton with voluminous sleeves, a scoop neck, and tight (now too tight) bodice flowing into a bias-cut full-length skirt (the better to hide hairy legs). She hunted for the sandals that matched it but couldn't find them. She couldn't leave Riz sitting on the front veranda any longer, so barefoot, skirt swirling as she moved quietly through the living room, she reached the screen door, started to push it open but stopped. She'd been too flabbergasted to take him in before and wanted a closer look. Sprawled in one of the rockers, wearing jeans, a tailored shirt, and sports jacket, his long legs stretched out with boots crossed at the ankles, one hand trailing the floor, the other holding an unlit cigar, he looked like an ad from *GQ*. The sun's last rays outlined his prominent nose and jaw and gave his thick dark eyebrows and hair a reddish tinge. Handsome as ever.

Sensing her presence, he turned his head, and she stepped out, feeling like a kid who'd been caught spying. A smile lifted one side of his mouth. He got up, opened his arms wide, and said, "Now this is more like the old Bonnie—or rather, the young Bonnie—I remember."

"At least a passing resemblance." She knew she looked pretty good, maybe even pretty, but she felt the years had changed him far less than they had her. He'd put on a few pounds in the midsection but was tall enough to carry it. His hair had only a few streaks of gray (he wouldn't be vain enough to use that Just for Men dye, would he?), and though his forehead claimed more of his face, that only seemed to emphasize his eyes. The flesh beneath them was softer now, forming little pouches, and two deep creases ran from his nose to the sides of his mouth. More than anything, it was his expression that had changed. His smile was wider but slightly lopsided, more ironic, and disappointment, or maybe just fast living, clouded his eyes; then again, he'd cultivated that world-weary look ever since he'd started chasing girls.

"When was the last time we saw each other?" she asked.

"Four or five years ago. Some fund-raising bash in Atlanta."

"Ah, yes." But the memory was vague. There'd been a huge crush of people, she'd been completely surprised to see him, and her attention had focused not so much on him as on his new wife—his third, but the first one she'd met—a stunning woman in her late twenties whose slicked-back hair and erect posture made her look like a ballerina, though it turned out she was an accountant for Goldman Sachs. "You were on a honeymoon trip, right? Showing your bride the haunts of your youth."

"As a lifelong New Yorker she was under the impression that as soon as you crossed the Hudson, you dropped into the Grand Canyon."

"How is"—a nanosecond before she plunged—"Natalie?" She was reasonably sure of the name, also reasonably sure that they were no longer married.

"I get a canceled alimony check every month, so I guess she's still alive." He shrugged, then smiled again. They continued to stand a few feet apart, eyes locked. "You were wearing a claret-colored cocktail dress."

"What?"

"The last time I saw you. You were wearing a claret-colored décolletage peau de soie dress."

"I'm flattered that you remember. Not many men could describe it that accurately."

"I was brought up in the rag trade, remember? Sol was teaching me the difference between shantung and rayon before I got my first Erector set."

"Wha—" She laughed, because she'd misheard him, at first thinking he'd said "erection" set. Thank God he couldn't read her mind. He asked what was funny and, when she shook her head, asked again, his voice softer, his eyes teasing and appraising. Maybe he *could* read her mind. Maybe he was picking up subliminal messages she wasn't even conscious of sending. She had always loved the idea of flirting, but like dancing the tango, it seemed to require more style and confidence than she possessed, and since she'd married so early, she'd never really honed her skills. She'd known men found her attractive, and she'd enjoyed the compliments and banter, but when attention turned to intention, she'd get flustered. If, at a country club dance, her partner's hand slipped lower than the small of her back, she'd just pretend not to notice, so the man would figure that bedding such a cold fish wouldn't be worth the trouble. In the rare instances when she'd actually been tempted, she'd assume the asexual role of guidance counselor: "Charlie, you've had a lotta bourbon tonight" or "Fred, I know you've been goin' through a lot lately," finishing with a benediction of "Let's just act like this never happened." But now it was different. Maybe the divorce papers hadn't been signed yet, but in her mind and heart she was no longer married. And she'd had fantasies about Riz even *before* she was married. Now here he was, standing close to her in a sunset glow, so charming that she wanted to say yes even before he asked the question.

She turned away, ostensibly to look for Nesha, who was crouched in the corner behind a plant stand, his hind end wiggling as though getting ready to pounce.

Riz said, "Glad you got out here to protect me. I thought that vicious guard dog of yours might attack me."

"Nesha wouldn't do that, would you, Nesha?" She sat, arranging her skirts, holding out her hand. Nesha came over, and she scooped him up, shaking him and looking into his face. "No. You're a good puppy, a perfect little puppy, except when you hide from"—she almost said Mama—"me." She could feel Riz looking at her. Maybe he wasn't coming on to her; maybe she was imagining it.

"I was surprised to hear about your divorce," he said, sitting down.

"I wouldn't think divorce could be a source of surprise for you," she said lightly. "And it's not final yet."

"That's what the Duke told me. I just never thought you'd—"

"Neither did I." Her divorce was the last thing she wanted to talk about. "So, you saw the Duke?"

"No, just called him when I drove through Birmingham. He gave me your number and Cass's number. So when I called you here and there was no answer—"

"I was out in the woods hunting for this runaway," she said, scratching Nesha's head.

"—I called Cass. Didn't I meet her when we were in college?"

"Yes. She was my roommate. You and a friend of yours took us to dinner once."

"I thought so. Anyway, she said she was sure you were here, probably out in the garden, and she gave me directions."

"My God, when I saw you—"

"Uh-huh. I'd always hoped we'd have a dramatic reunion, but I sure wasn't expecting anything like this." He settled back, chuckling.

"You looked like a kid who'd been abandoned in the woods and raised by animals. A real wild child."

Half dismissive, half-embarrassed, she said, "Well, living out here, I don't bother to fix up much."

"When you were a kid, you used to say you wanted to live in the woods with the animals."

"I did?"

He nodded. "Once when we came to visit, you took me down the street to some neighbor kid's tree house. I was surprised to see you climb the tree because you weren't the tomboy type." Eyes half closed, he looked at the cigar, gently rolling it between his fingers as though the memory were wrapped in it. "You had on one of those dresses with puff sleeves and a gathered skirt that little girls used to wear, and I remember standing under the tree trying to get a glimpse of your panties."

"I have no recollection of a neighbor with a tree house." Of course he was coming on to her.

"That's why it's good to have old friends, huh? They remember things about us that we've forgotten. You probably have stories about me that I've forgotten."

Indeed she did. In fact, she could remember the very first time she saw him. She'd been told there'd be company for Sunday dinner, and she was excited because they had funny names, Solomon and Isobel Mazersky. Mr. Mazersky was a business friend of her daddy's, and they lived in a town about two hours out of Birmingham, but they were really from New York, so that meant they'd seen the Statue of Liberty. They also had a son, Robert, who was about her age. She'd heard her mother tell Phoebe that Mrs. Mazersky was "far gone," and when she'd asked what that meant, they'd started spelling, so she guessed that Mrs. Mazersky must be having a baby. She was very curious about where babies came from, so she'd gone out to sit on the steps to wait for them.

They'd come in a big silver car, Mr. Mazersky driving, Mrs. Mazersky near the window, and Robert sandwiched in between. Mr. Mazersky had stopped the car, put on his hat, and gone around to help Mrs. Mazersky, who had black curly hair and lots of pearls and a belly as big as a watermelon! Robert slid out after her. Even then he was a cheeky-faced little rip, looking around and sizing up the situation just like a grown-up. Following his parents to the front door, he saw Bonnie looking at him and put on a show, sticking out his belly and waddling in imitation of his mother, then aping his father by doing a duck walk and playing with an imaginary hat. His disrespect had shocked and delighted her. When Mr. Mazersky looked over his shoulder and caught him in the act, she'd thought, Oh, boy, now he's gonna get it! But Mr. Mazersky just laughed and chased him around the car and, when he finally caught him, wrapped his arms around him and called him "a little *momzer.*"

At dinner he butted into adult conversation as though he'd never heard the "children should be seen and not heard" rule, and his parents, much to her surprise, seemed more proud than angry. He ate neither the squash casserole nor the green beans, but when Phoebe brought in the peach cobbler and homemade ice cream, he asked for a double helping, and got it. Her admiration for him knew no bounds, but Phoebe, who always acted like a deaf-mute when there was company, cut her eyes over to her with a look that said they both knew this was not acceptable behavior.

The Mazerskys stayed a long time. She'd fallen asleep on the sofa and hadn't woken until she'd heard voices saying good-bye, thanks, you're welcome, thanks again and the front door closed. She decided to play possum; that way she could listen and make pictures in her brain about what was happening. Muffled sounds (whispers, maybe kissing?). Then Mama came back into the living room, sat on the other couch, and kicked off her shoes, and Daddy went to the liquor cabinet and asked, "Want a nightcap?" (Why did they call it that?) Clink of Mama's earrings dropping onto coffee table. Clink of glasses. "So, Doctor, give me your postmortem?" (What?) Daddy saying,

"Sugar, you put Dolley Madison to shame." (Who was Dolley Madison, and why should she be ashamed?) "The dinner was first-rate." "You have Phoebe to thank for that." (Boring talk of rib roast and peach cobbler.) "So what did you think of them?" Pause. Sipping. "I liked them both. She's very attractive. He's not much to look at, but he's a live wire."

"He's a fireball. I'm glad I talked him into setting up his factory in Dothan 'stead of going to South Carolina. Any breaks we gave him on taxes and variances are definitely gonna pay off. Bet he'll be employing a hundred people in a coupla years."

"He has a great sense of humor, but that New York accent sure grates on my ears. (She'd forgotten to ask if they'd seen the Statue of Liberty!) But she sounded homegrown."

"Her family came over from Germany way back. Freidkind? Freidnick? Anyhow, her daddy owns that department store called Freddy's in Macon. (She wished her father owned a department store.) Both Sol's parents came from Russia. Can you imagine having parents who lived under the czar?" (She was starting to fall back to sleep.)

"She seemed a little tense, but maybe it's because of the pregnancy. (That woke her up.) She told me the doctor says she might have to have a caesarean. (She'd never heard that word before.) Oh, I do feel weary, Duke."

"And I do feel amorous." (Soft sounds, mama's dress sliding on the couch, a little hiccupy sound—they *must* be kissing now. If only she could peek!) Her mother got up and carried glasses to the sideboard while her father came over to her. He gently worked his arms under her and picked her up. This was the hardest part of playing possum, but she could do it really well. All you had to do was act dead gone, heavy as a sandbag, but every so often you twitched an eyelid or jerked your hand just the teeniest little bit to show you might wake up. He carried her up the stairs, and Mama followed, talking about how she was either tired or tipsy and couldn't tell the difference, then saying, "That Robert! What a brilliant child. So smart, but so sassy. Are Jews generally so indulgent with their children?" Daddy said, "I'm sure I don't know, but they'd better watch out or their little prince will turn into a frog." Mama said, "Or a juvenile delinquent," and she'd thought: Wow! I've met a boy who is so bad he's going to jail!

"Hey," Riz asked, "you still with me?"

"Uh-huh," she replied, shaking herself back to the present. "Riz, what's a *momzer*?"

He turned to her, and even in the gathering darkness she saw the amused expression on his face. "It's Yiddish."

"I know that, but what does it mean?"

"Literally it means bastard, but colloquially it means smart or ingenious. Why do you ask?"

"Because your father called you that the first time I met you."

Riz chuckled. "He's called me a lot worse since then."

"I'll bet he has." Robert Izadore Mazersky, Riz since high school, when a local newspaper reporter had jumbled the letters of his first and middle names to give him a moniker better suited to his athletic prowess ("Riz rhymes with whiz!") had never become a juvenile delinquent. At least he'd never gone to jail. As a teenager he'd gotten into trouble, but it wasn't the alarming, new kind of trouble (antiwar demonstrations, love-ins, drug experimentation that had started in the nation's cities and grew fast as kudzu into the suburbs and beyond); it was the old-fashioned sowing-wild-oats kind of trouble (driving over eighty on deserted roads, bringing a bottle of hooch to a dance, being caught in a state of semiundress in a parked car) that a factory town expected and even secretly admired from a high-spirited boy, especially if his father owned the town's biggest factory. The police who caught him in the act always politely escorted him home, and in the single incident when he'd become so insulting that the officer's pride had forced him to make an arrest, Sol had bailed him out. Riz had known he was the biggest frog in his little pond, and when he'd gone on to Duke University, he'd grown into a real bullfrog. He'd been editor of the college paper, fraternity president, head of student council, and won medals in track and field. And if he spent more time socializing than studying, it didn't matter because everyone knew that once he graduated he would take over his daddy's factory and increase the family's already considerable fortune.

Instead, upon graduation he'd gone off to Europe and stayed until he'd exhausted the trust fund he'd inherited from his grandfather. Then he'd come back with a mustache and a French wife, who'd quickly discovered that life in an Alabama mill town didn't bear much resemblance to life on the Left Bank. After she'd gone back to Paris, divorce pending, it was rumored that he'd gone through a period of heavy drinking. Then he'd seemed to settle in, managing the factory and marrying a local girl. When the second marriage failed (apparently because he too craved a more cosmopolitan lifestyle), he'd accepted an offer to be a public relations spokesman for the garment industry and moved to New York. After that Bonnie had more or less lost touch, except for infrequent reports from the Duke, who still kept in touch with Sol and Isobel.

"We knew each other all those years," she said, shifting position to draw up her numbed feet and tucking them under her. "And now I don't even know where you live."

"I've got an apartment in New York and another one in Washington. I shuttle back and forth."

"Doing what?"

"Whatever pays. Consulting, lobbying, public relations." The light was now too dim to see his face clearly, but his tone wasn't enthusiastic.

"And your parents?" she asked. "How are they? Where are they now?"

"Not wanting to miss a single cliché of the American dream, Sol and Isobel have retired to a condo in Boca Raton. I'm heading down there now."

"Isn't this out of your way?"

"Detours are appealing when you're not anxious to reach your destination." He leaned toward her, talking faster, as though a great idea had just struck him. "Hey, this trip would be a lot more fun if you'd come along. We could make lots of detours, have some real adventures, like those road movies."

"Great idea!" she agreed, joking, before snapping her fingers as though she'd just remembered something. "But damn! I'm booked for Thanksgiving in Birmingham."

"Birmingham? Can't go to Birmingham. That's no fun."

"Naw, that's no fun."

He snapped his fingers. "I've got it! I'll call my folks and say I've come down with some rare disease—"

"—a virulent strain of the Egyptian botch, then—"

"—then you call *your* folks and say—"

"—that the car broke down—"

"—and can't be fixed for a week." They'd joked themselves into rhythmic silliness, kids hatching a plot, laughing as he raised his hand saying, "Gimme a high five, sister!" She slapped at it but missed, thinking, I'm joking, but I'll bet he's still crazy enough to change plans at a minute's notice. She slapped at it again, missed again. He said she was hopeless, pulling his hand away as she tried and failed a third time. She settled back in her chair, her laughter petering out until there was no sound except the whisper of wind rustling through the trees and the steady creak of the rocking chairs. "Ah, Riz." She sighed. "As you told me once, you have to grow old, but you don't have to grow up."

He got up so quickly that the headrest of his chair hit the wall. With a single fluid movement he crossed to the screen door, put his hands high on the frame, and stared out. And what brought that on?

she wondered, but knew better than to ask. No male she'd ever known (teacher, husband, tax accountant, or son) had ever given an answer when directly asked what he was feeling, so she waited, putting her hand on the arm of his chair to still its rocking. After a while he said, without turning, "I gotta tell you, Bonnie, I hate rocking chairs."

"These are . . ." she started, but didn't finish. Riz wouldn't give a damn about the workmanship, history, or value of the chairs. She'd always associated rocking chairs with relaxation, but maybe he associated them with old age. Physically he looked fit, but given what she knew about his psyche, he was probably having a worse time with midlife blues than she was. After a moment she tried to reweave the conversational thread by asking, "And your sister, Julie. How's she doing?"

He didn't move but turned his head to glance over his shoulder, staring at her in the semidarkness, then drawling, "I don't mean to be rude, ma'am, but isn't it past the cocktail hour?"

She got up, tipping Nesha onto the floor, saying, "Where are my manners!" At one time, only a little more than a year ago, if a guest had dropped by unexpectedly, she would have been able to offer everything from pickled okra and imported French pâté to tins of amaretto cookies, not to mention an assortment of wines, liquors, and liqueurs. After Devoe's departure, when she'd let the supplies dwindle down to nothing, she'd fantasized that when she had a life of her own and a place of her own, she'd be like those high-steppin' single women who confessed to *Elle* or *Vogue* that their refrigerators were empty except for a jar of caviar, a bottle of champagne, and the occasional orchid, but now she made a quick and totally unsatisfactory mental inventory of what she had in the larder: several cans of Alpo, a box of Train-&-Treat puppy biscuits, a box of Special K, a bottle of olive oil, a package of linguine, and maybe, hidden way in back, a reserve box of Triscuits or a Snickers bar, pawns in her never-ending diet game. And the refrigerator wouldn't yield more than a package of Folgers coffee, the dregs of a bottle of Chardonnay, some milk, three or four eggs, a hunk of (possibly moldy) Romano cheese, a jar of homemade "Million Dollar Pickles" one of the factory ladies had given her, and a jar of pesto Mark and Cass had made after harvesting their herb garden. "My God, Riz, I don't have a thing to offer you."

"Then let's go out."

"You're in Florabama. The choices are confined to Burger King or Emmy Lou's Family Diner, and Emmy Lou's is probably closed on Sunday nights."

"You have fallen on hard times, Miss Bonnie. But not to worry. I've got a bottle in the car. We'll have a few drinks and take it from there, see if we feel like driving into Mobile or maybe down to some tourist joint on the Gulf."

"I'm a working girl now, Riz, and tomorrow is a workday, so I don't think—"

He opened the screen door, motioning her to come, and, when she stood next to him, wrapped one arm around her shoulder, then took her chin in his hand and turned it up to see the silver circle that had risen in the blue-black sky. "Why, girl," he said softly, "I do believe you've hung the moon." As she turned her face to his, smiling, his lips brushed hers, light as a butterfly wing. Then he was out the door and down the steps, moving to his car. She shivered, wondering why she'd been dumb enough to wear a summer dress in November, knowing damned well it wasn't just the gauzy dress that had raised goose bumps on her arms.

"I'm going to change clothes and put on some shoes," she called after him and, Nesha trotting behind her, went into her bedroom.

Changing into jeans, a baggy blue sweater, and a pair of loafers, which provided not only warmth but a sense of protection (what had she been thinking, running around like a barefoot nymph, showing off her bosom?), she heard him come back in, and when she went to the kitchen, he was already standing at the table opening a large bottle of Rémy Martin.

"What's this?" he asked, nodding to a baby dress wrapped in tissue paper in the middle of the table. "You got a secret?"

She laughed as she reached for some glasses, thinking, That's flattering, but if I were pregnant, it would give new meaning to the term *midlife crisis.* "The dress was made by one of my factory ladies. You don't see workmanship like that anymore, do you? I'm going to drive on up to Atlanta day after Thanksgiving and show it to this woman I know who has a boutique. See if she'll take a few on consignment. My ladies have organized garage sales and set up booths at flea markets, but they're always short of cash."

"Aren't we all?"

"No. I mean *really* short of cash, Riz. Worried that the phone or the gas will be cut off."

"Your ladies?" he asked with a quizzical smile.

"I hope that doesn't sound patronizing, but that's how I think of them."

"Yeah. Cass told me you were the rednecks' Miss Jean Brodie."

"Well, Cass . . . She always acts tough, but really she's just as concerned as I am. More so. I mean, she's been teaching here for years. Hey"—he had already filled one glass to the rim and was pouring a liberal shot into the second—"just a splash for me." She picked up her glass and raised it to his, suggesting, "To old times?"

"How 'bout to new times?"

"That's OK too." They clinked their glasses, sharing another melting look over the rims. She took a sip; he took a swallow. "I'm like Old Mother Hubbard. My cupboard is bare," she apologized. "But if we're drinking eighty proof cognac, I think we ought to eat something. How 'bout if I make us some pasta and pesto?"

"Sure. If that's what you want. It'll be fun to watch you putter around," he agreed, pulling up a chair. She took down the big pot and turned on the faucet to fill it with water, feeling his eyes on her and thinking about those machines that measured fat in relation to body weight. "Are you checking out my middle-aged spread?" she asked, hefting the pot to the stove.

"How come women measure themselves by *Vogue* magazine instead of just looking into a man's eyes?"

But she didn't want to look into his eyes. "About your sister?" she said, retreating to what she thought was neutral ground, though when he started to speak, his tone was more sardonic than neutral.

"Hey, Julie's doing just fine. Julie's a major success, at least by my parents' and the world's standards. She's got a six-figure job with the company that bought out Sol's factory. Now they make everything from corn chips to overcoats, though the corn chips are fried in Mexico and the overcoats are made in South Korea. She has a twelve-room apartment on Central Park West, two lovely children, a devoted husband who shares the chores with their Jamaican nanny when Julie's traveling, which she claims to hate, but I think she secretly enjoys. And she still has time to work out and looks great. I, on the other hand, have even let my membership in the Racquet Club lapse. I have failed to take my place in the projected scheme of things as a second-generation Jewish son."

"I'm not sure I know what you mean."

"Immigrant, businessman, professional, artist. That's the pattern, that's the way it's 'sposed to go. Grandpa Izzie was the striving immigrant, Sol was the successful businessman, and by rights I should've been a doctor or a lawyer and have produced a son who's now playing the fiddle at Carnegie Hall or exhibiting 'film' at Sundance. Woman I was dating last year took me there," he said as an aside, pouring and downing another shot. "I couldn't stand it. All those Hollywood types playing cowboy in their boots and sheepskin jackets. Yeah," he went on, stretching his arms, "we Mazerskys have a story as full of clichés as one of those miniseries about immigrants riding the American dream merry-go-round and catching the gold ring. You know the story: Ol' Grandpa Izadore comin over in steerage, armed with nothing but a sewing machine and twenty dollars. He works fourteen hours a day in a garment factory and in his *spare* time he's hawking rags from a pushcart. Finally he gets enough *gelt* together to set up his own tailoring shop. The cabbage dinners and the six-day weeks are worth it because he knows"—he raised his index finger to the ceiling—"that his son, my father, Sol, will get an education and go on to grand things. But the Depression, then the big WW intervene. Sol figures it's too late to be a college boy, so he makes a move to the sorry South, where unions are either weak or nonexistent, to set up a factory. The irony being that Izzie, in his heyday, helped organize unions."

He finished off his drink. "My parents' first child was stillborn. Then Isobel, my mother, had a miscarriage, so when I came along, they looked at me like I'm really the Messiah. I'm supposed to grow up to discover the cure for cancer or take a case to the Supreme Court."

That explains a lot, she thought, shaking salt into the pot, though high expectations might just as well have led to compulsive achievement instead of helping him turn into a playboy. "Remind me, Riz. I know Sol sold the factory, but I don't remember when."

"'Bout twelve years ago. We had to wrestle him to the ground. For him, retirement was like conceding the game, but even Isobel could see that the business was changing. Multinational corporations were starting to set up shop in the South, and the days of playing king of the mountain in a small town were over. And not to say he didn't make a bundle, but he was good to his employees. Knew 'em all by name, knew their families. Lot of them cried when he told them he was selling out, and they weren't crocodile tears."

"You know," she said, taking the Tupperware container of pesto from the fridge, "you hear about things like factory closings, and businesses moving overseas, but it doesn't register. Now I've seen the faces. I hope Sol gave his workers advance notice before the closing."

"The company that bought him out didn't close the place until six months after he was gone, and I seriously doubt they gave any more than they were required to do by law, and maybe not that if they could get around it."

"Why in God's name? I mean, that's what got the women so angry. Management didn't have the decency to let them know ahead of time, and some of them had been working there for decades."

"If you give workers advance notice, they get pissed off, maybe start stealing things or sabotaging the machinery."

"I don't think any of the women I know would do that."

"Your naïveté has always been part of your charm."

"But it's not fair to treat people that way, especially if they've been there for years and they've been loyal."

"Companies are responsible, first and foremost, to their stockholders."

"It's not right."

"Sweetheart, I didn't say it was right. You're asking me why management does what it does, and I'm telling you what you could have figured out for yourself if you weren't so emotionally attached to your ladies. It's called capitalism, Bonnie. If you can get someone to sew a seam for two bucks a day in Mazatlán, why would you pay eight bucks an hour in Florabama?"

"But what's going to happen to all those people who were making eight bucks an hour?"

He turned his palms upward, and shrugged. "I won't say I don't care, but I don't know. Hey, c'mon, Bonnie. Are we going to talk economics?"

"No. It's a subject about which I'm totally ignorant. During the last few years I've realized I'm ignorant about a lot of things."

"I feel the same way."

"Don't patronize me, Riz."

"I'm not." He poured another shot and stared contemplatively into his glass. "Last year a buddy of mine died. Forty-seven years old.

Heart attack. He left a couple million to the wife and kids he'd separated from. He and I weren't close, but I was asked to clean out his apartment. Twenty suits in the closet, not much furniture, a bunch of file cabinets, a king-size bed, nightstand with a pack of Trojans and an address book. On one of the pages, in the *S*'s, I think, he'd written, 'I've never taken the time to understand my life. I've got to sort things out.'" Riz took a long swallow. "And that's all he wrote."

"I'm sorry." She held a fistful of pasta above the pot, willing the tiny bubbles to burst into a roiling boil. "Food'll be ready soon."

He rallied his wicked smile. "Don't mean to be morose. Don't know why I'm talking about all this."

"After all this time I'd hardly expect us to talk about the weather. Besides, we're old friends." She dumped in the pasta, took a hunk of cheese from the refrigerator and a grater from a drawer, and sat down, looking at him.

She leaned back, and he leaned forward, taking her hand, as though they were a courting couple in a restaurant. "I like looking at you, Bonnie, you know that? You've never lost that expression you had as a kid."

"What expression was that?" she asked, keeping the hand he was holding perfectly still.

"Puzzled but curious, always trying to understand. Compassionate. Blue eyes can look icy, but yours are like cornflowers. Beautiful *shiksa* blue eyes."

"I've always thought brown eyes were the most beautiful because when they go soft, they look like melted chocolate. I mean"—she backed off from the compliment—"brown eyes generally." She slipped her hand out of his and started to grate the cheese, saying, "I don't remember you using Yiddish words before."

"Back to the roots, I guess. Happens to the best of us after a certain age."

"There's this woman in the program. Tough, sexy, big-hair, big-mouth woman by the name of Hilly. She intimidates me, but I sort of like her. She's always coming up with these pithy little sayings. The other day she told me, 'If you don't cling to your roots, you'll be out on a limb.'"

"Isobel didn't know much Yiddish, but Sol used it all the time. I was never told not to use it outside the house. Who'd understand it anyway? When I was a kid, we were the only Jews in town. I used to feel it most on Sundays."

"I guess you would."

"Yeah. On Sundays this special hush would come over the entire town. Sol would drive over to the factory and take me with him while my mother slept in, and we'd go past all the churches and see everyone dressed up and hear the singing. From the white churches it was marching music or dirges, 'Onward Christian Soldiers' or 'Rock of Ages,' but from the black churches I'd hear this sweet wailing or this hallelujah rocking and clapping. I always felt like they were having a party and I wasn't invited. We'd drive on to the factory, and Dad would do his paperwork and I'd rattle around."

"All by yourself?"

"Mostly. Sometimes Sol could persuade Jethro to sneak in and clean up if he gave him time and a half, and Jethro'd bring his son, Thurgood, and Thurgood and I would climb up on the cutting tables and dive into the remnant bins and play horsey up an' down the aisles near the sewing machines. And when Sol'd finished with his paperwork, we'd drive back through town and the churches would be quiet and the smell of fried chicken and biscuits would be coming from all the houses and the kids would be runnin' in the yards and the men would be sitting on the porches or hunkered down smoking and talking 'round the sides of the houses."

"And you never did get into a church?"

"I sure did. When I was about eleven, I asked Thurgood to take me. God, I loved that gospel music. I heard Lucrecia Smalls sing 'I'm on My Way to the Freedom Land' and it knocked my socks off. Know her?" Bonnie shook her head. "She was Thurgood's cousin. Went to

Detroit and became a backup singer with a lot of Motown groups in the early sixties. Last time I heard gospel I paid sixty bucks a ticket at Town Hall in New York."

"What happened to Thurgood?"

"Don't know. We were tight as kids. Shared my first cigarette with ol' Thurgood in the field behind the factory. But by the time we hit adolescence the Giant Invisible Hand divided us."

"What Giant Invisible Hand?"

"The one that separates kids of different races as soon as they start thinking about sex. And the pressure started from Sol and Isobel. They didn't want me to date any non-Jewish girls. Every summer they sent me to this place in North Carolina called Camp Blue Star, so I'd learn about Israel and meet other Jewish kids. I got laid for the first time with a counselor at Blue Star, an older chick from New York who'd lived on a kibbutz." He smiled at the memory. "My folks weren't the only ones who thought I shouldn't date Christian girls. I remember when I asked Ellen Cahill to the prom and she said she couldn't go with me because I'd probably marry Stephanie Kurtz. The Kurtzes moved to town when I was in eight grade, and Stephanie was the only Jewish girl in the school. And how's this for irony?" He chuckled. "I *did* marry Stephanie Kurtz after my first wife went back to France. She was a sweet girl, and I guess I was digging for those roots we talked about. If she'd got pregnant, I'd probably still be there running the factory. But she didn't, and I'm not."

She cocked her head to one side, considering him. "I never knew any of this about you."

"Yeah. I was nuts from the beginning."

She'd finished grating the cheese, and as she got up, looking at her watch and deciding it was time to drain the pasta, he took her hand again. "I bet we'd travel well together. Wouldn't it be fun to just take off?"

"I told you, I work, and I'm going home for Thanksgiving."

"Then how about a nontraditional Christmas? Don't tell me you wouldn't like a break from work and family. Where'd you like to go? New York? New Orleans? Or maybe the Caribbean—Barbados, St. Croix?"

"Riz, you're crazy." She laughed. Slipping her hands into potholders and lifting the pot to the sink, she nodded in the direction of the cabinet and asked, "Could you reach down into that cabinet and find the colander?"

"The what?"

"The bowl-shaped thing with holes in it. Didn't you ever help 'round the kitchen when you were a kid?"

"No more'n my mama did. We had a housekeeper. In fact, we had several housekeepers. They used to quit because they couldn't put up with me."

"You were kind of a brat," she agreed, and, seeing him hold up the colander, told him, "Yes, that's it."

He made his eyes wide with astonishment. "You learn something new every day."

"Just put it in the sink." He did so, and as she tipped out the pasta, it sent up a cloud of steam, and he moved behind her, slipped his arms around her waist, and put his cheek to hers. It had been a long time since she'd been held in a man's arms. She relaxed into it, feeling not so much aroused as nerve alive and comforted, as though she were turning her face to the sun. "I'm enjoying this more than you can know," he said.

"Me too. It's been a long time since I've had a *pleasant* surprise. It's really great to see you." She turned her head to smile, then inclined it to a drawer as she slipped out of his arms. "Utensils and napkins are in there." She gave the colander a final shake, tipped the pasta into a serving bowl, topped it with pesto, and carried it to the table. "I'll fix you a real meal sometime."

"When I'm with you, babe," he said in parody of a seductive growl, "it's always four-star."

The food tasted surprisingly good, and the talk went on, easy as a friendly tennis game, Riz the more active one, verbally bouncing on his toes, serving, volleying, while she, more relaxed, merely waited to return the ball. He'd always been voluble, but the diminished level of the bottle and the flush of his face made her apprehensive. Keeping her tone light as she filled the kettle to make coffee, she said, "Riz, will you be all right to drive?"

"I could race in the Indy 500," he boasted, rising with a graceful vigor that almost convinced her. Then he wobbled enough for her to put out her hands to steady him. He gave in, draping his arms around her shoulders, his cheek roughly grazing hers.

"I don't think so," she said as she straightened up, taking him by the shoulders and looking into his face.

He smiled back with bleary beneficence, saying, "Do you know there are four essential tastes: sweet, sour, bitter, and salty? You, Miss Bonnie, are sweet. You're like a molasses cookie to a ten-year-old boy."

And you're sure acting like a ten-year-old, she thought, but she was more amused than annoyed. "Riz, you've had a lot to drink. What time did you start out today?"

With great effort he remembered, "Six? Six-thirty?"

"You must be exhausted. And frankly, you're drunk, so I guess"—she gave in to the inevitable—"you should stay the night."

"Now that's an offer I can't refuse."

"Good. Then off you go."

"Already?"

"Yes. Already." She guided him into the hallway and through to her bedroom.

Nesha was sitting in the middle of the bed and gave a low growl as Riz sat down, gave his head a swift shake, put his hand to it and muttered, "Hey, you're right. I am drunk," as though the realization surprised him. Bonnie picked up Nesha in one hand and struggled to pull the comforter free as Riz flopped back, oblivious. She set Nesha on the floor, went to the foot of the bed, and began to yank off Riz's boots. He turned on his side, rolled onto his back, and, as she tugged at the second boot, tried to get up, saying, "This mattress is"—he rummaged about, his attention divided between finding the right word and finding a comfortable position—"awful. Why are we sleepin' on this flophouse mattress?"

Not *we,* Bonnie thought, but said, "It was in the house. I hope to replace it soon," and bent to give him a good-night kiss on his forehead.

"Wouldn't notice it if you were in bed with me," he mumbled, making an ineffectual move to pull her down. The warmth of his hands sliding down her arms sent a ripple of desire through her body. She stepped back, catching her breath, acutely aware of the tautness of her breasts and the pulse between her legs. Riz Mazersky in her bed. Even in his present state . . .

Nesha gave a warning bark.

"If you . . ." Riz's voice trailed off, his body stilled.

What was she thinking? She picked up Nesha and tiptoed to the door, looking back at Riz before she closed it.

The spare room seemed unaccountably chilly. Not wanting to go back and get her nightdress, she crawled into one of the twin beds, her clothes still on. Settling Nesha into the crook of her arm, she thought, Here I am again, sleeping with a dog instead of a man.

Chapter X

*T*he next morning, when she got up and crept into her bedroom, Riz was like an inactive but not extinct volcano: no movement, just a quiet rumbling. She collected her clothes, carried them into the bathroom, showered, dressed, and, before leaving, put a note on the kitchen table: "Dear Riz, Great to see you. Please call to let me know you arrived safely in Florida, OK? Lock the door and leave the key under the second brick near the porch door. Regards to your folks, Love, Bonnie."

Despite a less than restful night, she felt buoyant as she drove to work, amazed at how much Riz occupied her thoughts. Not just scraps of their conversation but the look in his eyes, his gestures, his smell, and the shape of his hands came back to her. He'd given her ego a boost it hadn't had in years, and thanks to his imbibing of cognac—she briefly wondered if he drank like that all the time—she had been saved from the sexual showdown for which she was practically and emotionally unprepared. Her desire had taken her by surprise. She couldn't bear to think of herself as a needy divorcée who'd hop into the sack at the first opportunity, but again this morning, when she'd seen him curled up in her rumpled bed, she'd had a powerful urge to crawl in beside him. Then she'd heard that familiar inner voice that said Bonnie Duke Cullman simply didn't do things like that. It would be profoundly, stupidly out of character for her, besides which there were unpleasant but undeniable facts: Riz probably tried to bed every woman he met, he'd lose respect for her, she might be clumsy and inhibited, and she might not see him again.

But, she thought, she wasn't Bonnie Duke Cullman anymore; she was just Bonnie Duke, maybe just Bonnie. Her life had changed in ways she could never have imagined, so who was to say that her personality and character hadn't or wouldn't change too? The possibilities both excited and frightened her, but as she drove through the countryside, the colors seemed brighter, the morning sun warmed her through the windshield, and the New Age tape Cass had given her (saying, "Don't just hear, *listen.* Do you understand the difference?") surrounded her with the susurrating sound of surf, flutes, and temple bells. She was *in* the moment. Going with the flow.

"Oh, and I almost forgot," Snoopy said, handing Bonnie her messages, "Professor Ledforth called not ten minutes ago, but she wouldn't leave a message with me." Her tone was both accusatory and aggrieved. "She wanted your voice mail." Wondering if there was any way Snoopy could tune in on her voice mail, Bonnie said thanks and went into her office. After closing the door, she dropped her things and punched the button to hear the message. Cass's voice was as husky and sexy as Lauren Bacall's. "*Cherchez la femme!* Riz Mazersky called me, so he must've seen you. Didn't call last night 'cause I didn't want to interrupt. So, sweetheart, what's the haps?" Eager to talk, Bonnie called throughout the day, but they didn't connect, so she finally left a voice mail with the message center.

At four o'clock, after working nonstop, she straightened her desk and prepared to leave. All day she'd had the ridiculous notion that Riz might have stayed at her house. She'd called, but there'd been no answer. But that didn't necessarily mean he wasn't there. She wanted to go straight home, but she couldn't because the women's weekly meeting, usually held on Friday afternoon, had been changed to Monday because of the upcoming holiday weekend. Slinging her bag over her shoulder, she stepped into the outer office, where a comic face-off was taking place: Snoopy, sitting at her desk, had her arms crossed over her chest, while Hilly Pruwitt, hands on hips, stood in front of her. "But I gave you those forms last Thursday," Hilly insisted, glancing over her shoulder as Bonnie came out. Their eyes met. Bonnie's expression reminded Hilly of her mama's adage that you could catch more flies with honey than with vinegar. She took the hint, dropping her hands and gentling her voice to say, "I'd appreciate it if you'd look again, ma'am, 'cause if that government form don't go in on time, it could screw up my check."

Knowing Snoopy's sour attitude toward the women in the displaced homemakers program, Bonnie felt embarrassed when Snoopy barked, "I am not responsible for the delivery of papers to government entities."

Hilly bristled. "But you told me to give the damn thing to you 'cause Miz Cullman wasn't here when I came by."

Jowls shaking, pulling at the sides of her wig like an irate British judge threatening a witness with contempt of court, Snoopy growled, "I will not tolerate profanity in this office."

Taking Hilly by the arm, Bonnie said, "I'm sure Mrs. Snopes will find the form, but we'd better go or we'll be late for the meeting." She guided Hilly to the door, stopping at Norma Jean's desk long enough to say, sotto voce, "If you have a minute, I'd sure appreciate it if you could look for Ms. Pruwitt's papers, and if you find them, please just put them on top of my computer."

As soon as they were in the hall, Hilly pulled her arm free and said, "Damn! That Mrs. Snopes is a real pickle heart."

Bonnie smiled. When she'd first met Hilly, she'd seen her as nothing but trouble, but once she saw her bombast for what it was, it was impossible not to warm up to her. Hilly was like a country ham, thick-skinned and crusted on the outside but all tender underneath. "She's like that. Don't take it personally."

"Oh, I don't. I seen her kind. Yankin' on her Zsa Zsa Gabor wig and acting like a big shot. But I'm not gonna let her spoil my mood.

I'm flying high today, Miz Cullman. Found me an off-the-books job workin' at a new restaurant. The boss is a Mexican, but as long as he pays me, I don't care if he's from Mars."

"I hope the job won't interfere with your schoolwork."

"Hey," Hilly reminded her, "I'm not exactly studying brain surgery."

"I know, but they count absences."

"Can't keep my mind on studying if I'm worried 'bout my car being repossessed, and like I said, the money's under the table. No government forms to fill out. Hell, I'd work just for tips alone if I could duck the damned red tape, 'cause you know when you have any intercourse with the gov'ment, it's a one-way screw."

Bonnie laughed. "I know what you mean. I think the same thing every time I see how much they take out of my paycheck."

The campus was all but deserted as they cut across the stubbly lawn to the student union. Pushing open the double doors, they saw the snack bar workers, Essie and Bertha, wiping down the countertop and bagging the trash. Even though the group's weekly meetings took place after their quitting time, they always saved doughnuts that would have been thrown out and prepared a fresh urn of coffee for them. Seeing Bonnie, Essie called, "Coffee'll be ready in five minutes."

Six or seven kids, ranging in age from three to ten, were sitting in a semicircle near the window where Lorraine Phillips, who'd drawn the straw to be this week's baby-sitter, was trying to settle them so she could read them a story while the meeting took place. The women were seated off to the side, plastic chairs pulled into a big circle around a squat Formica table. From the beginning of their weekly meetings each had chosen a particular chair and returned to it as though it had her name printed on it. Approaching, Bonnie saw today's turnout was small, no more than ten or twelve. Albertine Chisholm, always a regular, sat between Sue Ann Shelby and her young cousin Tayisha "Puddin'" Simmons, coaching them through a vocabulary list: "It's not *s;* it's *x* like an X-rated movie. Try again: exten-u-ate." Celia Lusk (whom Bonnie still thought of as the Bible Lady) was trying to convert a bewildered Crystal Jenkins to the joys of the Internet. Lyda Jane, as usual, kept her own counsel while embroidering the yoke of a baby dress. Two other women were thumbing through a copy of *Good Housekeeping*. Ruth Elkins was reading. Her daughter, Roxy, slouched in the chair next to Ruth's, was chipping off her nail polish and looking as though she were under house arrest. But when, Bonnie asked herself as the women acknowledged her and she took her usual chair, had she ever seen Roxy happy? Granted, it couldn't be much fun for someone Roxy's age to spend her time in the company of middle-aged women and children, but it was more a question of personality than age. Puddin' was even younger than Roxy, and she was always in a good mood.

Hilly, none too happy to see that Roxy was sitting in her regular chair next to Ruth, took a plate of doughnuts from Essie and sat down beside Bonnie. Bonnie thanked Bertha for her coffee and, by way of bringing the group to order, said, "Is Judy McCoy here? I have the forms for her to drop a class."

"Got the flu," Sue Ann provided.

"And Cherry Jones?"

"Already left to go visit her husband's family in Kentucky," someone else supplied.

"An' Vernette said to tell you she's not here 'cause her car be broke again," Puddin' told her.

Putting aside notes on various problems she'd tried to solve for absentees, Bonnie took out a clipboard and handed it to Hilly. "Here's the sign-up sheet for next month's baby-sitting. And underneath that there's another sheet to sign up for special tutoring in English. Professor Ledforth met a young man who's practice-teaching at the high school, and he's generously volunteered to tutor."

"What's he like?" Crystal Jenkins, a rail-thin woman with a complexion freckled as a turkey egg, asked.

"I haven't met him," Bonnie told her.

"Hey, Crystal," Hilly teased, "we all know you go for anything that has breath and britches," and raised a laugh from the group.

"And how 'bout Denise Odell?" Bonnie asked. She seemed depressed last time I saw her, and she made a point of saying she was going to come to the meeting."

No one spoke. Then Celia Lusk said, "I heard she was arrested for shoplifting over to the Wal-Mart."

Crystal was indignant. "There's no excuse for that. Her kids are grown. She's only got herself an' her husband to provide for."

Without raising her head, Lyda Jane said, "When men get laid off, they stay away from home and drink a lot. When women get laid off, they mope around the house and eat too much. But both men an' women will be tempted to steal."

"That's sexist," Hilly cut in, bragging, "I promise you I drank as much as any man when they first laid us off." Most of the women chuckled.

"I never did trust Denise," Sue Ann said.

"Yeah," Crystal agreed, "she got a kinda shifty-eyed look."

"I think we might show a little more charity." Even though her voice was low, Ruth Elkins had everyone's attention because she spoke so rarely. "Last week," she said, her hands smoothing the cover of her book, "I was in the store, and I saw some dented cans at half price. I put 'em in my basket. But as I was waiting in the checkout line, I counted my money and realized I didn't have enough. I had my big purse, and for a split second I thought of slippin' those cans into my purse. Just slippin' them in, and walking out with them, 'cause the cashier was real busy an' surely wouldn't've noticed. Standin' in that line, I felt so humiliated. I felt like being broke had an actual smell, and the other shoppers could sniff it on me. So," she finished, almost inaudibly, "I know about the temptation of lifting things."

"So what did you actually *do*?" Crystal asked in a whisper.

"I said excuse me and got out of line and went and put the cans back," Ruth said, hauling Moo, who had wandered over from the children's group, into her lap. Putting her finger to her own lips to warn Moo to be quiet, she swallowed and said, in a louder voice, "We're all different. Don't none—don't *any*—of us know what we might do when we're pushed."

"Jeez, Ruthie, you'd forgive Hitler," Hilly muttered, then, remembering how many times Ruth had forgiven her, added, "I mean you're just naturally tenderhearted."

"The difference is, you didn't shoplift and Denise did," Sue Ann said.

"I do hold people responsible for their actions," Ruth went on, "but I also hold to 'judge not, lest ye shall be judged.' I think we ought to be charitable when someone's in trouble."

"And I still think Denise is trailer trash," Sue Ann declared.

Bonnie tried to shift the focus by saying, "I thought Denise was applying for the night shift at that restaurant—what's it called?"

"The Tailgate," Hilly said. "She tried there, but they turned her down. They want young gals with stacked decks, even if they got rings in their snouts an' snake tattoos crawlin' up their legs."

"That Denise is so stupid," Roxy said, almost to herself. "Everyone knows the big stores put up more cameras and bring in more security guys 'round the holidays."

Ruth shot Roxy a look of disapproval, then quickly transformed her expression into one of bland neutrality. Bonnie, watching, understood a mother's lifelong impulse to correct and protect. As always, she sensed the fear, pain, and anger that lurked just beneath the casual conversation and "business" of these meetings and struggled to think how she might help. "Perhaps . . ." she began.

But Celia Lusk, huffy and self-righteous, interrupted, "I wouldn't hardly call the Tailgate a restaurant."

"They serve food, Celia, so I guess that means it's a restaurant," Hilly countered.

"If you call giving microwaved sausage biscuits to drunks to help 'em sober up serving food," Celia said.

Anxious to break up this familiar logjam of personalities, Bonnie asked, "Celia, what's that 'W.W.J.D?' printed on your T-shirt mean?"

"It means 'What would Jesus do?'" Celia told her solemnly.

Bonnie nodded. "Oh, that explains the question mark. I thought maybe it was a radio station."

"Yeah." Hilly grinned. "Say, like, if your computer crashes? You just look down at it an' ask, 'What would Jesus do?' 'cause surely he'd know about software."

"OK, OK, let's get on to the agenda." Bonnie raised her voice. "Sue Ann, how'd we do at the flea market last weekend?"

"We only took in fifty-three dollars and some change, which I'm turning over to Albertine, our treasurer, after the meeting."

"Good." Bonnie took a note from her purse and read. "Father Quinlan at St. Anne's said that canned food will be given away at the church today and tomorrow from one to five. Brickhouse Baptist invites anyone to their Thanksgiving dinner at three on Thursday."

"We can handle Thanksgiving," Sue Ann said. "Thanksgiving's just food."

"That's why it's my favorite holiday," Puddin' put in.

"Thanksgivin's not just stuffin' your face," Albertine corrected. "It's a feast to *give* thanks. Remember there's people all over this world who don't even have food."

Sue Ann said, "Yeah, but we're Americans. Turkey's a dollar nine a pound. Even we can afford turkey. It's Christmas that's gonna be rough."

"Yeah. Christmas is gonna be a bitch," Crystal grumbled. "My kids are already asking for toys they've seen on TV, and how'm I gonna explain why we can't afford them?"

"Maybe if they didn't watch so much TV . . ." Bonnie ventured to say.

"Hey, TV's my baby-sitter. Rather go without food than cable," Crystal insisted.

Bonnie's mind was wandering back to Riz. "OK. Any more announcements?" she asked.

"I got an A plus on my last computer test 'cause I figured out a problem even the teacher was having trouble with," Celia Lusk said.

"Hey, that's great. Seems like you're a real whiz with computers." Bonnie congratulated her.

Sue Ann laughed. "If Celia hadn't been workin' at Cherished Lady, she coulda outrun Bill Gates."

Hearing a yelp from the play group, Bonnie looked over to see Lorraine Phillips simultaneously stuffing toys into a laundry bag with her right hand as she patted a weeping boy with her left. "Anything else?" Bonnie asked, as the kids scattered and ran into the outstretched arms of mothers or grandmothers. "Any personal problems? Any burning issues?"

Hilly's foot wagged impatiently. Roxy shifted in her chair. Puddin' roused herself from the beginning of an afternoon nap. "Well then . . ." Bonnie started to get up. "Since so many of the gals are absent, let's make it a short meeting. I wish you all a wonderful Thanksgiving and—"

"There is something. A personal problem, I mean," Celia Lusk interrupted. "I'm having trouble with my husband."

Hilly rolled her eyes and opened her mouth but closed it when Ruth shot her a cautioning look.

"Because of school, I mean." Celia bit her lip and looked off into the middistance. "Harvey, he just seems to resent the time I spend in the computer lab. Seems to resent my coming to school at all, even though I don't neglect my household duties."

"They be like that," Puddin' agreed. "Minute I pull out a book, my boyfriend's in my face. Ax like I'm treatin' him mean."

"My husband's the same," Sue Ann said. "I tell him any little thing I learned, and he accuses me of being uppity."

"They're just afraid." Crystal smirked. "'Fraid we're gonna come out of this with more earning power than they have."

"Ain't that," Sue Ann disagreed. "I earned more'n Fred did when I was at Cherished Lady, and he never had no trouble spending it, but he's real pissed off when I go off to school."

Roxy said, "Ah, screw him."

"I do. More'n I want to," Sue Ann admitted, to general laughter. Even Celia couldn't control a smile. "'Cause my mama always told me, 'Men are like linoleum: You lay 'em right you can step on 'em for years.'"

"But, like, he wants me to . . ." Celia's voice trailed off. "It's always when I'm getting ready to go to school and I feel like he's—wadda you call it?—subverting me."

"Not to be crowin', but I feel blessed," Albertine said. "My man, Henry, he's with me all the way. Always telling me he's proud of me."

"I really don't know what to say." Bonnie steered the conversation back to the problem. "I know it must be a real burden when your husband or boyfriend feels threatened by your getting an education."

"An' still expects you to do all the housework," Lorraine interjected.

"Harvey even resents me comin' to these meetings," Celia said, genuinely upset now. "He says we're like a witches' coven—'course he's only teasin'—but he thinks we just get together to put down men."

"Makes me glad I'm livin' alone," Hilly tossed off.

"Celia, I'll find out if there're any counseling services available without charge," Bonnie promised. "I'm sorry you're having to cope with this because you're doing a great job here. You're all doing fine," she added, then looked at her watch. "I promise we'll continue this discussion next time; it's important. Hope you all have a wonderful Thanksgiving."

Driving home in the gathering darkness, she thought about what the women had said at the meeting. Maybe life was less complicated if you weren't involved with a man. Riz hadn't shown much interest in what she was doing. Then again, maybe she was just arming herself against disappointment, which she certainly felt as she pulled off the main road, started toward the house, and saw that the drive was empty.

The house key was where she'd told him to leave it. As she unlocked the door, Nesha jumped from the couch and came up to her to be petted as usual, but she had a strange feeling. Something was different. What was it? A smell she couldn't identify and could only describe as "new." Nesha in her arms, she walked to her bedroom, stopped dead, and exclaimed "Omigod!"

A brand-new box spring and mattress covered in pale blue sateen shimmered like a small swimming pool. She moved slowly to it and sat on the edge, bouncing to feel the gentle give. Her hand slid over the label ("Beauty Rest—Extra Firm Deluxe") at the foot of the mattress, then reached for the note in the middle of it. "What a night! So my Beauty, Rest. Thanks for taking me in. Call you soon, The Prodigal Son."

The phone rang, and she lunged for it.

"Bonnie, it's me. Cass."

"I tried to call you all day. You'll never believe what Riz—"

"I will. 'Cause I already know. He called my office early this morning and asked me what was the best furniture store in town. Said he couldn't bear the thought of your sleeping on a flophouse mattress. Said he was going to have a new one delivered before he left town. So, did he?"

"Yes. I can't believe—"

"I'm going to drive over, OK? I'll pick up a pizza on the way and *you will tell me all.*"

"But a mattress! And top of the line. Must've cost what—six or seven hundred?"

"Who cares? Not only does the man have money, but the man has style. And he sure has plans. You know what a new mattress means? See you in a bit."

Bonnie replaced the receiver and lay back, stretching out spread-eagled. Then, wrapping her arms around her chest, she drew her legs up and rolled from side to side, skittish and delighted as a kid being tickled. Riz had, as Cass had pointed out, not only money but a sense of style. But did he have plans that were focused on her?

Apparently not, she concluded later that evening, when she ushered Cass out the front door. She'd told Cass almost everything about Riz's visit, but didn't mention her note asking him to call when he reached Florida. And since he never called, that seemed just as well.

Chapter XI

*T*he afternoon was sunny with an invigorating nip in the air, and driving under the canopy of trees on the familiar street in Mountain Brook, Bonnie looked out at sprawling lawns, well-tended gardens, and double-car garages of the columned houses and saw the neighborhood as not just "comfortable" but downright luxurious. The Duke's car, a behemoth white Lincoln he refused to part with, was in the circular drive. Pulling up behind it, she passed a statue of a pink-faced jockey and remembered a domestic squabble—it had to be over thirty years ago—between her father and her stepmother. Elice had bought a statue of a little Negro groom. The Duke had asked her to return it. Elice objected, asking how in the world he could disapprove of something she described as (one of her favorite adjectives) "cute." The Duke explained that it might hurt some people's feelings; Elice pointed out that none of "those people" lived in the neighborhood. But the Duke, who usually considered anything to do with the house outside his sphere, stood firm, and Elice had replaced the little Negro groom with the pink-faced jockey.

Recalling the incident, Bonnie felt a wave of affection for her father. He had always been sensitive, not by being touchy-feely or easily hurt, but in his awareness of the feelings of others. And when, several years ago, some of "those people"—a black Harvard-educated doctor and his family—had moved into the corner house on the block, the Duke had been pleased. She couldn't remember many other incidents when he had stood up to Elice. Commanding in the larger world, his style at home had always been one of go along to get along, and since he'd retired, his tolerance had slipped into apathy.

She yanked on the emergency brake and said, "We're here." Nesha, who'd been napping in the passenger seat, came to attention. Bonnie picked up her purse and overnight case and came around to collect him, whispering, "Now be on your best behavior." She was hooking the leash to his collar when the front door opened, and Elice, resplendent in orange silk pantsuit and white-blond curls, trilled, "You're here!" After mincing down the steps on strap heels decorated with red and orange gemstones, she put her hands on Bonnie's shoulders, gave her an air kiss, stepped back to look her up and down, and said, "You've lost weight, haven't you?"

"I've taken off a few pounds," Bonnie said proudly, admitting to herself that a single visit from Riz had done more to strengthen her resolve than months of promises she'd made to herself.

"Well, you know I would never have said anything, but you had been letting yourself go, Bonnie. It's so nice to see you looking better."

Elice had a special knack for giving a compliment that actually made you feel worse, but Bonnie smiled and held up Nesha. "Here's my doggy dog. Hasn't he grown? I've named him Nesha."

"Now where'd you come up with that?" Elice said, barely looking at him before advancing up the steps.

"It's after the Hindu god Ganesha," Bonnie explained, following her. "I met an Indian woman on my trip here, and we got into this strange conversation about—"

Elice turned. "He's housebroken, isn't he?" she asked, looking as though she'd bar the door if Bonnie said no.

"Sure. He hasn't been out in society much," Bonnie said as they stepped inside, "but he'll mind his manners. By the by," she added, setting him on the marble floor, "I hope you won't mind, but he's used to sleeping with me." Congratulating herself for having the courage to get that out of the way, she asked, "Where is everyone?"

"Eugene and his girlfriend got in early this morning, and they've gone with Daddy to pick up Gervaise at the airport. I'm happy to say Eugene's driving. Daddy thinks he's as sharp as ever but . . ." Elice, who had a habit of not completing sentences, or thoughts for that matter, made a sweeping gesture that took in the new outsize mirror and the pair of spotted porcelain dogs with aquamarine eyes and gold chains draped around their necks that had been placed on either side of it and asked, "So what do you think?"

Bonnie said, "It's very nice," though her real reaction was closer to that of Nesha, who backed away, staring at the dogs in a state of appalled curiosity.

"I had the worst time hanging that new chandelier," Elice went on, raising her eyes to the twisted gold branches above them and shaking her head as though she personally had risked life and limb to get the monstrosity in place.

Tilting up her head, Bonnie responded with a soft "Yes, that must've been a lot of trouble."

"Come on through," Elice said, moving into the living room. It had gold and sage brocade drapes, couches and love seats upholstered in sage velvet, and more whatnot stands and bric-a-brac than an antiques store. Chattering and pointing out a new Fabergé-style egg and an ornately framed painting of a shepherdess, Elise made her way through the dining room while Bonnie trailed behind, nodding at the gilt plates arranged on the walls and glancing up at yet another gold chandelier. Elice's fixation with gold rivaled that of King Midas. She could no more leave the house without buying something than an alcoholic could turn down a refill. How did the Duke put up with it?

As though guessing her thoughts, Elice laughed and said, "Daddy says other women shop at Neiman Marcus, but I'm more like a parishioner." Ushering Bonnie into the kitchen, she asked, "Coffee? I've only got decaf. Iced tea? A glass of wine?"

Bonnie said, "No, thanks. I've been drinking bottled water all the way up here. But I am hungry." She spied a cake stand piled with glazed doughnuts sitting in the middle of the table and, having reached for one, was shocked when her fingers touched ceramic lacquer.

"Aren't they lifelike?" Elice said enthusiastically. "Daddy does the same thing—keeps reachin' for them just like they're real."

Wondering how much they'd cost, Bonnie said, "The gals who work in the student union save doughnuts for the meetings of our women's group on Friday afternoons."

"You shouldn't be eating doughnuts. How 'bout a nice tall glass of iced tea?"

"That'd be fine."

"I've got this refrigerator packed with things for tomorrow's feast, but we're going out to dinner tonight, so there's not a thing in the way of snacks."

"That's OK."

While Bonnie sat at the table, Elice fished out cubes from the ice-maker and nattered about Gervaise, saying, "I talked to her on the phone last night. She doesn't seem to want to see her old boyfriend while she's here. Don't you think that's strange?"

"She wrote me a little about that on E-mail. I guess now she's gone to Brown she's met a whole new set of people."

"But he comes from a fine old family. He has good blood in him."

"Even a mosquito can have good blood in him," Bonnie joked.

Elise went on, "But I thought he was serious about her."

"She has plenty of time to think about getting married."

"Sure. But a girl's most attractive when she's young. Older a woman gets, less chance she has. I don't s'pose you've met any men in Florabama, have you? I saw something on TV that said the chances of a woman in her forties marrying, or remarrying, are 'bout the same as her chances of being struck by lightning."

Bonnie ignored that one too and continued, "Gervaise is nineteen. I think we can cut her some slack."

"This lil girlfriend of Eugene's, Fern's her name," Elice rambled on. "She doesn't have much to say for herself, and between you and me, she's no beauty. I just hope Eugene's not going to rush into anything. Never have thought it was good for a man to marry young. And I surely hope she's brought something other than jeans because like I told you, we're going to Botego's for dinner tonight and—" She gave Bonnie a quick glance that said she hoped Bonnie herself had brought something other than jeans, then opened a cabinet. "Where has Pearl put that sugar bowl? I swear when that woman cleans up, she hides things on purpose! So, like I was saying—ah"—she took down the sugar bowl—"this girl Fern said her father's a carpenter, so I don't imagine there's much of a background there, and after my experiences with carpenters—I mean, they're so unreliable—but then again, most workmen these days are. I was telling the Duke. . . ."

Bonnie eyed the ceramic doughnuts, stopped herself from saying, "Please shut up!" and for a moment actually missed Devoe. He'd often acted as a buffer between her and Elice. When he'd see Bonnie getting uptight, he'd give her a look to let her know that she could slip away. Any man, simply by virtue of his sex, had the advantage with Elice, but Devoe had been particularly adept. He'd had the trick of seeming to listen while putting his mind elsewhere—a talent he'd perfected with Bonnie herself—and he'd toss Elice compliments as though he were the king on a Mardi Gras float throwing candy to the crowd. Sure, he'd agree when he and Bonnie were alone, Elice was hard to take, but she had a kind of ditzy charm, and considering how long Elice had been her stepmother, Bonnie should have made the adjustment. It wasn't, she'd explained to him, as though she saw Elice as the evil stepmother in some fairy tale (though sometimes her antipathy did seem almost primal); she quite frankly didn't like Elice as a person. It wasn't just Elice's froufrou style (though style said more about character than most people were willing to admit); it was her need to turn the simplest conversation into a contest, her manipulation, her values, or, from Bonnie's perspective, the lack of them. She simply couldn't understand why her father had ever married her. Devoe's rejoinder had always been that Elice had been—still was—a good-looking woman and that the Duke liked being fussed over.

"So what would you do?" Elice asked, setting a glass of iced tea on the table and sitting down next to her.

Bonnie camouflaged the fact that she'd lost the thread of the conversation by saying, "I honestly don't know."

"I know that these days some people let unmarried couples sleep in the same room, and I don't want Eugene to think I'm old-fashioned—"

Bonnie was glad the issue hadn't come up in her house because she didn't know how she'd handle it either. "Has he asked you to let them sleep in the same room?"

"—but I just don't feel right about it. On the other hand"—Elice held out her right hand, paused to turn a bracelet so that the stone showed, then went on—"that old saying 'Why buy the cow if you can get free milk?' has always made sense to me. I figure if Eugene is already sleepin' with the girl, he'll give it a real think before he asks her to marry him. Then again, he might. Children of divorce sometimes leap into marriage because they lack emotional stability, and I know Eugene is vulnerable because he comes from a broken home."

Bonnie turned very slowly in Elice's direction. She wouldn't try to correct Elice's barnyard characterization of Fern and Eugene as a heifer and a farmer who'd yet to learn the laws of supply and demand, but the suggestion that her divorce had somehow destroyed her son's emotional stability was too much. "What are you talking about? Eugene was full grown before Devoe and I—"

"But children of divorce—"

Bonnie took a swallow to calm herself, then said, in a tone colder than her iced tea. "As to your question, it's your house, Elice. You should put your guests in any room you please. I don't interfere in Eugene's affairs, and I don't think you should either."

"Interfere? I'm his grandmother! I've treasured that little boy since he was in diapers. Just because the kids are off in college and you're living someplace else doesn't mean you can neglect them, Bonnie."

"I'm not neglecting anyone. I just don't happen to have a womb-to-tomb attitude toward my kids." Nesha, sitting in her lap, caught her angry tone and looked up apprehensively. "Nesha's thirsty," she said. "I'm going out to the car to get his bowl."

She made her way to the front door fighting the impulse to knock every damned useless object to the floor. The air outside seem positively cleansing. Opening the car door, she thought how liberating it would be to climb in and drive away, but after a few deep breaths she collected Nesha's food and bowl and the dress she'd spread out in the trunk and went back in.

Elice was at the sink cutting the stems of yellow and bronze chrysanthemums. "These are for tomorrow's centerpiece," she said without looking up.

"Should be pretty." Bonnie filled Nesha's bowl and put it on the floor near the porch door. "Anything I can help with?" she asked, watching him lap up the water. Elice shook her head and continued to arrange the flowers. "Actually," Bonnie said, "I'm feeling a little weary after the drive. I'll think I'll put my feet up for a bit, if you don't mind."

"'Course I don't mind. Go on upstairs."

Bonnie waited until Nesha was finished, wiped up a few drops of water with a paper towel, tucked him under her arm, and said, "I think I'll just go into Daddy's study. See you in twenty minutes."

Having gently closed the door behind her, she set Nesha down and leaned against it. The Duke's study had hardly changed from the way it had been in her girlhood. A TV with an enormous screen had been added, wall-to-wall cranberry-colored carpet had replaced the old Turkish rugs, draperies patterned in browns and reds hung from windows that had once been covered with shutters, but the wood-paneled walls, built-in bookcases, and glass-fronted liquor cabinet remained, along with the big leather couch and easy chairs, and the only painting the Duke had ever bought (Robert E. Lee bidding farewell to his troops) still stood above the mantelpiece. It was the smell of the room that had changed. The mingled scents of cigar and woodsmoke that she'd loved had been banished by the sanitized smell of furniture polish. The old standing ashtray and the brass spittoon the Duke had never used but had treasured because it had come from his grandfather's saloon were gone. The poker, shovel, log fork, and andirons, polished to a high shine, still stood near the fireplace, and the wood bin was filled with logs, but no fire had burned in this hearth for a very long time.

She walked around the big oak desk. Before the Duke's retirement it had always been covered with a mess of papers. Now it was bare except for a gold pen and pencil set and a Daily Planner ("pick up turkey from butchers" and "kids arrive" the only notations for the week). Her wedding picture with Devoe had tactfully been removed, but there was one of her clinging to the birdbath in the backyard, a butterball infant in a bathing suit with a ruffled behind, eyes and mouth wide with delight as someone out of the frame sprayed her with a garden hose, and a high school graduation photo in which she wore a demure black V-necked formal, a single string of pearls, and a sweetly insipid smile. "Yep, that's me," she told Nesha. "You'd be more likely to recognize me from the baby picture. At least I do." She moved to the coffee table, and picked up a biography of Ty Cobb she'd bought for the Duke last Christmas. A bookmark was stuck at the beginning of the third chapter. Slipping off her shoes, she lay back on the couch, settling Nesha on her belly and looking up at the books lining the walls. At one time she'd believed he'd read all of

them. When, she wondered, drifting into a semisnooze, had she begun to understand that he respected the idea of reading more than he
enjoyed the act itself?

Hearing a car coming into the drive, she got up, went to the window, and pulled back the drapery. Eugene's four-year-old Honda, a
high school graduation gift, looking much the worse for wear, pulled
up behind her Volvo. Eugene got out, opened the back door, and offered the Duke his hand, which the Duke waved away, getting out
slowly but under his own steam. Fern opened the trunk and lifted out
Gervaise's suitcase, which Gervaise immediately took from her in a
brisk "I can take care of myself" manner. What a motley crew they
made! The Duke wore his usual gray suit and blue oxford cloth shirt
and a silk tie of geometric design and such hilarious colors that she
could picture Elice picking it out in the men's department. Gervaise
was the epitome of preppy fashion in navy skirt and blazer, beige
sweater, and penny loafers, a Coach bag slung over her shoulder, her
hair subtly streaked and styled in a simple ear-length bob. (Bonnie
could recognize a hundred-dollar hairdo when she saw one and wondered if Elice had been maintaining Gervaise's appearance, not to say
her loyalty, with more than occasional checks.) Eugene looked
scruffier than the last time she'd seen him (travel fatigue or Fern's influence?): His hair was longer, and he was sporting a beard. His torso,
in plaid woolen shirt, showed the general thickening through his
shoulders and chest that made him look like a full-grown man. Fern
was a big girl, almost as tall as Eugene, with a broad, freckle-spattered
face and carrot-colored frizzy hair. As Elice had said, she was no
beauty, and dressed in the same unisex outfit of wool shirt, dunga-
rees, and heavy boots, she and Eugene looked like a couple of lum-
berjacks. "Hey, Mom's here already," she heard Eugene say, and
smiled. Any shadow of the abandonment she'd felt when neither
Eugene nor Gervaise had seemed sufficiently sympathetic during the
breakup vanished, and she felt not just pride but amazement. She'd
managed to produce two remarkably good-looking, intelligent chil-

dren who had a strong sense of values. No, not children, she corrected herself, young adults, and though she knew she'd always feel the umbilical tug, she knew it was too late to lecture or criticize them. Vowing simply to enjoy their company, she almost ran to the door.

The next hour or so was taken up with introductions (Nesha included) hugs, kisses, and catch-up conversation only slightly inhibited by Fern's presence. Eugene announced that he was starving, and since there were no snacks available, the Duke suggested they go out to eat early. Pointedly suggesting that they might want to dress for dinner, Elice ushered them into their respective rooms (Bonnie and Gervaise in Bonnie's old upstairs bedroom, Fern in the big guest room, Eugene in the smaller one down the hall). Gervaise didn't have to change, but Bonnie dutifully put on a beige crepe dress, Fern emerged from her guest room in a sacklike garment of rust-colored nubby cotton that was a minimal improvement over her lumberjack outfit, Eugene obliged by changing his shoes and putting on a corduroy sports jacket, and Elice made an unnecessary switch to another slinky pantsuit, this one in emerald green, and put on more jewelry. The Duke insisted on driving, so they took his behemoth Lincoln, giving one another sidelong glances and suppressing smiles as Elice directed him to speed up, slow down, watch out, turn right . . . no, left.

One of the great things about food was that it supplied a neutral conversational topic while you were ordering and eating it, and Italian food in particular seemed to foster a sense of amiability. Bonnie could tell the Duke was pleased when the waiter greeted him like an old friend and, after being introduced to Bonnie, Gervaise, Fern, and Eugene, suggested that the Duke, as paterfamilias, order for all of them. The Duke willingly accepted the task. A warmth of feeling enveloped them all the way through the antipasto and the pouring of wine, but when the piping hot communal dishes of sausage and peppers, veal piccata, and spinach and cheese ravioli were set on the table, Fern passed up everything but the ravioli, announcing that both she and Eugene were vegetarians. That was news to Bonnie, who'd spent decades urging him to eat his vegetables while he'd gobbled down meat like a jungle cat. When Elice asked why, Fern proceeded with a heartfelt but infelicitous description of animal slaughter, finally turning to the Duke, who was bringing a forkful of veal to his mouth, and asking, "Are you aware of what they do to those little baby calves in order to make what you call veal, Mr. Duke?" The Duke gave her a fleeting look of sympathy—poor girl prob'ly didn't even know she was being rude—said he believed meat eating was related to the survival of *Homo sapiens,* and commenced chewing. Elice, picking at salad, tried her hand at diplomacy by asking Fern what she planned to do after graduation. "We," Fern announced, "are planning to work on an organic garlic farm in Vermont." Bonnie thought: Over two hundred thousand dollars in higher education, and my son wants to dig up garlic? It was difficult to stick to her resolve not to question or criticize, but Gervaise did that for her, asking, with more than a hint of sarcasm, "You two got college degrees so you could be *braceros?*"

"What's *braceros?*" Elice asked.

"Mexican farm workers," Bonnie told her.

"When you're college-educated, you're supposed to be a doctor, or a lawyer, or a businessman or"—Elice waved her fork helplessly—"something."

"Or businesswoman," Gervaise put in. "Which is what I plan to be. After I get my degree, I'm going to go to graduate school at Wharton." News for Bonnie, who wondered how Gervaise planned to finance it, though she felt some relief that Gervaise had a definite sense of direction.

"The biggest challenge for our generation is to protect the environment," Eugene said. "Previous generations have left us in a real mess. They just wanted to take the money and run." Bonnie silently agreed but wished Eugene's assignment of blame hadn't been painted with such a broad brush.

"The real challenge for our generation"—Gervaise corrected her brother—"is to figure out how to maintain our standard of living in a global economy. You're not getting much bang for your buck educationally if you're going to go out and play in the weeds."

"It's not my fault that college costs so much," Eugene countered with sibling swiftness.

"No, son, it isn't," the Duke said. "It's a sorry situation all 'round. But when people, even your parents, lay out a lotta money, they're bound to have expectations."

Elice said, "When Bonnie went to college, it didn't cost much."

"But Mom went to a southern ladies' school. That's not a first-rate college," Gervaise put in.

The Duke was defensive, saying, "She went where she wanted to go."

"Because," Gervaise continued, "she wasn't looking ahead and thinking that one day she might have to earn a living or compete in the real world." True enough, Bonnie thought, though she wished Gervaise didn't sound quite so smug. "And speaking of the real world, Mom, how's your job in Florabama going? Assuming Florabama is part of the real world."

"It's real enough for me and the ladies I deal with," Bonnie said, pushing her plate aside.

"Must be frustrating. I mean, they're factory workers. They can hardly be equipped to go to college."

"I do my best to convince them that they are, and some of them are very bright. Probably as bright as people you go to school with though they haven't had the same advantages," Bonnie countered, not bothering to control the edge in her voice. The hush that fell on their table was exaggerated by whoops of delight as a birthday cake with lighted candles was delivered to an adjoining table.

"Well, it may not be an ideal job, but I think Bonnie was real lucky to get it." Elice, who feared a conversational vacuum as much as a rock concert producer feared a power outage, raised her voice over the "Happy Birthday" chorus. "We were so glad that Daddy was able to put in a word with Marion Hawkins," she went on, "'cause it'd been so long since she'd worked. But when Marion gives them the word at the college, they act like it's the Sermon on the Mount."

Bonnie stared at the tablecloth as though it were a jigsaw puzzle of an abstract painting and Elice had fitted in the last piece: It was still confusing, but it was complete. "You mean Daddy asked Marion to—" She raised her hand to the neck of her dress, which suddenly seemed to be choking her, then recovered and interrupted herself to ask Fern please to pass the bread even though she already had a chunk on her plate.

"This is great bread, isn't it?" Fern said, trying to relieve the tension.

"Yes, and I do have a weakness for bread," Bonnie said, slathering on butter. "I'm not so much susceptible to sweets, but I love crackers and bread and"—so now she understood Snoopy's hostility, Norma Jean's sniggering, Mrs. Jackson's friendly condescension—"pretzels and muffins." Everyone knew she'd gotten the job because her father had connections. Everyone but her. "There was this deli in Atlanta where I used to get the best bagels, though, of course, in Florabama . . ." She heard herself chatter on, foolish as Elice. She stopped. Then: "You know, Daddy, you might have told me."

The Duke looked both aggrieved and sheepish. "Now, Bonnie . . ." It was a tone she'd heard since childhood, the verbal equivalent of a pinch on the arm that told her to hush up.

She knew this was neither the time nor place for confrontation but she couldn't help herself from asking, "How could you do something like that without letting me know?"

Elice's head wobbled as though she had the beginnings of Parkinson's, then slowed to a steady disapproving shake. "I simply don't see how you can object to your daddy trying to—"

"What's wrong with connections?" Gervaise asked. "You can't get anywhere without connections."

"You're your father's daughter, Gervaise," Bonnie said, instantly regretting it.

Fern took Eugene's hand and gave him a sympathetic and meaningful look. The waiter hovered, eyes wary, smile stretching to show a gold molar. Had the meal been satisfactory? Would they like to see the dessert menu? Elice smiled up at him like a street waif, asking, "Would you be sweet enough to bring me a little American coffee? Decaf."

"I'll have some tiramisu," Bonnie said, reasoning that if her mouth was full of cream and chocolate, she'd have to keep it shut.

Lying in bed in her old room, Bonnie scratched Nesha's head, listened to Gervaise take the world's longest shower, and thought perhaps she'd overreacted to the news that the Duke had asked Marion Hawkins to use his influence to get her the job. Given her lack of qualifications, she might not have gotten it otherwise, and on balance, she believed she was doing good work. But it still annoyed her that she hadn't been told. She wondered what her reaction would have been. Only a fool or a saint would turn down special privileges or favors. But what cosmic roll of the dice had blessed her? Devoe's bankruptcy had initially thrown her into panic, but she'd been able to handle it better than she'd ever thought she could. And deep down, she'd always known she had the safety net of the Duke. Having money wasn't just about money; it was about having access to help. The factory ladies put down the "suits" but were terror-stricken when they had to deal with them. She, on the other hand, had always known that help was a phone call away. If she didn't directly know a doctor, lawyer, psychiatrist, banker, real estate agent, or someone in education, she was bound to know someone who did, but people like Ruth Elkins were more than six degrees of separation away from such vital support and information. "It's all about money and sex," she told Nesha. Which made her think about Riz.

She started to imagine them rolling in sweat-slicked passion, but

that seemed strangely impersonal, so she saw herself sitting beside
him in his car, whizzing down a beachfront highway, windows down,
a swift but warm breeze raising the hairs on her exposed arms and
tousling her hair. They'd stop at some cozy out-of-the-way restaurant,
and after they'd had dinner, they'd walk on the beach, soaking in the
moon rays, listening to the surf. The elevator at the hotel would whisk
them to an upper floor. She'd stand at the window looking down on
the twinkling lights. He'd come up behind her, run his hand up her
arm, lift her hair from her neck, and kiss her just where the vein
throbbed in her throat. Thinking about it made her stomach churn
with fear and excitement.

"You're not asleep, are you?" Gervaise asked.

Bonnie startled. "No, I was just, ah, floating."

Gervaise laughed. "You on drugs?"

"You know that floaty feeling you sometimes get just before you
sleep. And thinking."

"'Bout what?"

"Oh"—she stalled—"just about the future and—" Bonnie
yawned. "I'm very sleepy."

"Wouldn't you know I've broken out again?" Gervaise complained, thrusting her chin out for inspection and commiseration.

Bonnie squinted at the tiny blemish near her lower lip and said,
"Nobody's perfect, but you come pretty close." Gervaise got an A on
the current test of good looks. She was blond, leggy, slightly muscular, but with Bonnie's full bosom, and even her de rigueur college girl
sleepwear of baggy T-shirt and men's boxers, which to Bonnie's eyes
looked singularly unattractive, didn't disguise her loveliness. "Do you
know how beautiful you are?" Bonnie asked, reaching out to stroke
her calf. "I hope you appreciate and enjoy it. I remember when I was
young, I was so dissatisfied with my appearance. I wanted to look like
Grace Kelly. Then, when I got older and saw photos of myself at
your age, I thought: Hey, I was really something! How come I didn't
know it?"

"I don't even have any acne medicine with me," Gervaise went on. "And there's no point asking Fern. If she uses anything on her face, it's probably saliva from Guatemalan tree frogs. Is she a pain in the butt, or what?,"

"Are you seeing anyone?" Bonnie asked, breaking her resolve not to pry.

"Seeing? Oh, you mean, like, involved?"

"I guess I mean in love."

"Mo-ther." Gervaise drawled out the word with bored impatience.

"I don't s'pose you'd tell me if you were. It's hard to discuss sex with your mother, beyond the biological aspects."

"Maybe love *is* just biology. I mean, it's mostly hormones. Can't you remember?"

Remember! "I think it's a great deal more than hormones," she said, but as Gervaise walked around to the other side of the bed and got in, she realized Gervaise had no interest in discussing love or sex, even in the abstract, with her.

"Is that mutt sleeping with us?" Gervaise asked as she snapped off the bedside lamp.

"Hey, I love that mutt."

"I'm glad. 'Cause you sure acted martyred when you took him."

"It might be more fitting if you simply said thanks for taking him."

"OK, thanks. It was really nice of you to take him." Gervaise turned her back to her, then rolled over, touching her shoulder. "Mom?" Her voice was both hesitant and urgent. "Mom, I gotta tell you something."

"Go ahead." Bonnie braced herself, mentally flicking through the file of possible crises.

"About Christmas. Oh, I'll talk to you about it tomorrow." She smooched Bonnie's shoulder, then rolled onto her side, fixing a pillow under her head and putting another between her legs. "And

Mom"—Gervaise yawned, throwing back her hand and patting Bonnie's hip—"I'm really proud of you for getting your act together. I love you. Sleep tight."

"You know," Bonnie said, wanting to prolong the conversation, "I always thought *sleep tight* meant 'sleep well,' but Cass told me it's from the old days, when ropes were laced to the bed frame and padding was put on top of them. So *sleep tight* meant the ropes had been tightened so the bed wouldn't sag." Gervaise grunted at that bit of trivia. "What about Christmas, Gervaise?" Bonnie asked after a pause, but Gervaise was already asleep.

When Bonnie was finally drifting off, she heard a cautious padding in the hallway. The door to the large guest room opened—Eugene, she thought, sneaking in to be with Freckled Fern—then closed. A moment later the door to the master bedroom opened—and that will be Elice, checking up—and closed. She shook with silent laughter. It was like being on the set of a French farce.

The next morning, after Gervaise had gone for a run, Bonnie stayed in bed, ignoring the sounds of slamming doors, running water, muffled voices and even the smell of coffee and roasting turkey, but when Nesha danced in agitated circles, demanding to be walked and fed, she hauled herself up, took a quick shower, dressed, and went downstairs.

Eugene, the Duke, and Gervaise were nowhere to be seen, but Fern was sitting at the kitchen table reading aloud from the bread-and-butter gift—*100 Great Broccoli Dishes*—she'd brought to Elice: ". . . and the dark green leafy vegetables are a wonderful source of . . ." Elice, half glasses perched on the end of her nose, a full-length denim apron from Williams-Sonoma tied over yet another silk pantsuit (this one candy pink), peeled sweet potatoes and hummed rather too loudly.

Bonnie said good morning. Elice said, "It's almost noon. I had to get up early to put in the turkey, but there was so much moving about last night I didn't get a wink's sleep."

She slid her eyes in Fern's direction, and Fern, adding insult to injury, said, "I read that when people get older, they don't need as much sleep."

The girl's as dense as butcher block, Bonnie thought, reaching into the cabinet for a cup and pouring herself some coffee.

"I don't know about other people, but I need my rest," Elice complained. "If I don't get my rest, I'm grouchy the whole next day."

So we're forewarned, Bonnie said to herself, hunting in the refrigerator for the half-and-half and wondering if she should risk Elice's annoyance by fixing a piece of toast.

"These look so real," Fern said, obviously hungry, reaching out to touch the glazed china doughnuts, "I'll bet you could buy a truckload of real doughnuts for what these cost."

"More than a truckload I should think," Elice told her. "The difference is that those are permanent. They're a work of art."

"A work of art?" Fern questioned, a smirk of disbelief playing around her mouth, and raised her eyes to meet Bonnie's.

I'm not about to get into this, Bonnie thought, saying, "I'll just take Nesha for a walk. Then I'll be back to help." Escaping through the back door, she wandered to the back of the yard, sipping coffee as she went. When Nesha had relieved himself in the hedges, she sauntered over to the birdbath, where she absently picked a leaf out of the accumulated rainwater. The sky was bright blue with a few scudding clouds, and she removed the plastic cover from one of the lawn chairs and sat down, wanting another cup of coffee, but not enough to reenter the house and give up this moment of peace.

Gervaise jogged up the drive, barely panting, saw her, and walked over. Bonnie said, "Beautiful day, huh?"

Gervaise nodded, bending to touch her toes, then swinging her arms from side to side, saying, "Did five miles." The only evidence of exertion was high color in her cheeks and a mere glisten of sweat around her hairline. She looked toward the house, then sat with her back to it, pulling a pack of cigarettes and a lighter from the pocket of her windbreaker. "I know you don't approve. I know you're going to say how can I do it now that we finally have all the information about the health risks, and when I've just run five miles—"

"Dear, we were calling them cancer sticks when I was a girl."

"But I'm not a kid, and I'm not going to cover up what I do."

"Your honesty is admirable," Bonnie said wryly, watching Gervaise light up and trying not to see those awful pictures of coated lungs. After she had inhaled, Gervaise's expression became calm and serious. Initially Bonnie thought it was just the satisfaction of the first hit of nicotine. Then she realized that Gervaise was getting ready to spring something on her.

"Daddy's gone back to smoking," she said finally.

"Oh, really," Bonnie said in a tone of supreme uninterest, thinking that he'd probably never stopped. They'd pledged to quit at the same time, but she'd still smelled it in his hair and his telltale minty breath. In keeping with the "Don't Ask, Don't Tell" policy of their marriage, she'd never asked and he'd never told. For the first time she considered how burdensome it must have been for him to hide it. That and so many other things. Hypocrisy, and covering up to keep things smooth. She'd played that game too. But it was such a full-time job. She knew she'd never waste her energy on it again.

"You're not going to get on my case?"

"What's the point?"

"Hey, you really have changed." Another drag. "You know I E-mail Daddy as well as you?"

"I guess I supposed you did."

"I don't think he's doing very well."

"I'm sorry to hear that."

"Are you really?"

"Yes, really. I don't have any ill will toward him." That was mostly true. At least she hadn't experienced a full-blown rage for a couple of months. "The sooner he gets on his feet, the sooner we can get our finances straightened out."

"Oh, Mother, it's not just about money."

"Thanks to your grandfather, you haven't seen any appreciable change in your life, but I have. And I'd be lying if I said that at least at this point, it wasn't mostly about money."

"But what's the big deal? Granddaddy and Elice have got it."

"It's not healthy to rely on your relatives for support, Gervaise. The people I've known who live solely on inherited income seem to have trouble keeping any balance. Seems they're either spendthrifts or terribly tight. And the other pitfall—I was thinking about this last night while you were in the shower—is that you start to feel entitled. Not just grateful because you're lucky, but actually deserving of that luck."

Gervaise grunted. "Now you're sounding like your old self again."

"I'll stop lecturing. It's boring. To me as well as you."

"Good. 'Cause I want to be honest. I want to tell you that I miss Daddy."

"Of course you do."

"And I've been hoping—"

"Surely not that we'll get back together. You're too old for that fantasy."

"No, not that." She took another earnest puff. "Just I hope you'll understand when I tell you that Daddy's asked me to spend Christmas with him. I mean, both his parents are dead, and he's not close to any of his relatives."

A situation he brought about, Bonnie thought, because he didn't think they were grand enough for him. "And you want to?"

"Yes, I do." Much fiddling with the cigarette, turning it over, holding it out before the next inhalation. "I may meet this woman he's seeing. He's told me I don't have to if I don't want to."

"And do you want to?" It took great restraint not to ask Gervaise what she knew about the mystery woman.

"Dunno. Yeah, I guess I'm curious. I mean she is part of his life. But I can't believe he loves her. I can't believe—"

"Listen, sugar, most men get married within a year or two of a divorce." Her voice sounded like a box of rocks. "But if you want to spend time with your dad"—she brought her voice back into a more genteel register—"that's all right with me."

"Mom, you're great." Gervaise ground the stub of her cigarette under her running shoe, picked up the butt, wrapped it in the pack's cellophane, secreted it in her pocket, and turned to give Bonnie a hug, whispering, "Will you make it all right with the Duke and Elice? I mean, I'll tell them, but if you say you don't mind, it'll go easier."

"I'll tell them I don't mind." Though of course she did. Not only would she miss her, but the Duke would feel her absence no matter how it was explained, and Elice was bound to take it as a personal rejection. "I love you, darlin' girl," Bonnie said, kissing Gervaise's cheek, pushing back a strand of hair that had escaped from her headband, remembering how she'd finger-waved her baby hair and feeling her eyes get moist. "Let's go in and see what we can do to help get this show on the road."

A little after three o'clock the women carried the food to the dining room table, which had been set with the best china and silver and an impractically large chrysanthemum centerpiece. Elice brought in the turkey and set it in front of the Duke, who, despite her objections, was finishing off his second bourbon. When everyone was seated, the Duke asked them to join hands and pronounced the blessing, then looked over at Bonnie. "'Member when you were just a little girl and I'd say, 'Rolly, rolly 'round the table, fill your tummy while you're able,' and you'd laugh? Oh, you'd laugh till your curls shook, and your mama'd pretend to get mad at me, and that'd make you laugh some more." Bonnie nodded and smiled. The Duke, no doubt wanting to protect Elice's feelings, rarely alluded to anything that had hap-

pened before their marriage, but over the last year or so, Bonnie noticed, he'd started to mention things from her childhood and even his
own. This, she supposed, was the common phenomenon of older
people's developing sharper recollections of distant events even as
their memories of recent incidents became fuzzy. Maybe it was nature's way of helping an individual to sum up his or her entire life. In
any case, it made her feel a special tenderness tinged with sadness for
him. "C'mon, son," the Duke encouraged, turning to Eugene, "you
carve the turkey."

Eugene begged off. "Grandpa, I don't know how."

"Gotta learn sometime. It's the man's responsibility." He handed
over the carving knife and fork, urging Eugene to stand beside him.
"First you stick the prongs of the fork into the joint of the drumstick
and thighbone," he instructed. "C'mon now. Yes. That's it. Now cut
the skin holding the leg to the body and cut down. Uh-huh. Sever the
joint then. . . ."

Despite the clarity and patience with which the Duke delivered
instructions, Eugene had a hard time, hesitantly hacking into the bird
until Elice said, "Daddy, the meal's getting cold. Why don't you
do it?"

"It's not like it's something he needs to know," Fern said, tilting
her head to see around the centerpiece and look at the Duke. "We're
vegetarians, remember?"

The Duke said, "Sure, I remember. But carving is something
every man should know, like how to hunt or rebuild a carburetor."
He almost seemed to be waiting for one of them to say he was old-
fashioned or sexist, but when no one did, he took the utensils back
from Eugene, who looked relieved, and finished carving the bird
while they loaded their plates with green beans, sweet potato casserole, pearl onions in cream sauce, cranberry-orange sauce, mashed
potatoes, chestnut stuffing, and gravy. As each dish was passed, Elice
complained that it hadn't turned out quite right and was reassured
that it was just perfect. It was a good, tasty meal, and since none of

them had been given any breakfast, they ate with relish. They all accepted second helpings, chatting aimlessly and complaining that they'd burst, the Duke beaming at Bonnie and asking, "What'd you used to call it when you made a puddle in your mashed potatoes and filled it with gravy?"

"It's a bird's nest, Daddy."

"I knew it was something like that. I was thinking crow's nest, but that's the lookout on a ship's mast, isn't it?" He laughed, ignoring Elice's warning look and pouring gravy into another helping of mashed potatoes.

"When you kids come back at Christmas, I'll fix more vegetable dishes for you." Elice smiled after blotting her lips with a napkin.

The atmosphere changed so suddenly that if there'd been a gyroscope in the room, it would have gone crazy. Gervaise shot Bonnie a meaningful look, then dropped her glance to her plate. Fern inclined her head so she could see around the chrysanthemums and fixed Eugene with a stare. When Eugene spoke, he sounded as though his voice were still changing. "Actually, Fern's parents have invited us for Christmas. I haven't had a chance to meet them yet, so we're planning to drive up to their place."

Elice, looking crestfallen, glanced from Eugene to Fern, then raised her eyebrows in "I told you he's going to buy the cow" alarm, at Bonnie. The Duke masked his disappointment with an understanding smile, saying, "You know you'll be missed. You'll have to give us Fern's parents' address so we can send your gifts up there."

Apparently deciding that her absence from the Christmas festivities would best be absorbed in the general shock, Gervaise put in, "Grandma and Grandpa, I hate to tell you, but I've made other plans too. It's not that I don't want to be with y'all," she added hurriedly, "but . . . well, I'll explain the situation after dinner."

"So neither of you kids are going to be with your mother over Christmas?" Elice asked.

"I already knew Gervaise had made other plans," Bonnie interjected. "And I'm sorry Eugene and Fern won't be here, but I understand."

After another painful pause, the Duke joked, "Bird's nest, crow's nest, empty nest," and, raising the bottle of Merlot, said, "How's about we all toast to the happiness of being together in the here and now?" The wine was poured, the toast was made, but afterward the food was only picked at.

"I feel plum exhausted!" Elice said, pushing her plate aside.

"What's say we put off dessert?" the Duke suggested. "You can go upstairs and take a little rest, the kids'll clean up, and Bonnie and I will go into the library and have a little chat."

"Sounds like a plan," Eugene agreed, picking up the turkey platter and nodding for Fern to follow him into the kitchen.

"Bonnie's such a pretty name," Fern said out of nowhere. "It's Scottish in origin, isn't it?"

"Sure enough," the Duke confirmed. "We called her that 'cause my grandmother was from Scotland. It means pretty and healthy-lookin'."

"Is that so?" Elice said with a coy burst of surprise. "All these years I thought she'd been named Bonnie after that little girl in *Gone with the Wind* who fell off her pony and broke her neck."

"Well, that was a great dinner, Elice," Bonnie said, raising her eyes to the chandelier. "You certainly deserve a nap." *So why don't you go take one before I'm tempted to knock* you *off your pony?*

Carrying two cups of coffee into the library while the Duke held the door open, Bonnie couldn't help but wonder how she'd be able to get through Christmas. She would miss the kids. And she'd be alone with Elice and the Duke. She set cups on the coffee table while the Duke closed the door and went to his liquor cabinet. "Amaretto? Irish Mist? Crème de menthe?" he asked, rooting around. "Some of these bottles been in here so long they've got dust on 'em. Hey, how 'bout a cognac?"

Remembering her recent evening with same, she declined. "No, thanks. But you go ahead if you want."

"Maybe just a nip of bourbon. Not exactly an after-dinner drink but I never did figure out why you were supposed to drink certain things at certain times." He poured himself a generous portion and came to sit across from her in his old leather chair, settling himself, taking a sip, resettling himself. "So."

"So." Their eyes met and held.

"You're looking good, girl. I hope you're feelin' good too."

"Thanks, Daddy. I am."

"I'm real proud of you for pickin' up and goin' off and takin' on that job an' all."

"The way you say that makes me sound as though I'm disabled."

"Divorce can disable you." He shook his head. "And I know how hard it is to change your life in midstream. I hope you're not mad at me because I didn't tell you I pulled a few strings with Marion Hawkins. He owes me some, and I thought why not. People nowadays might put that down as the ol' boy network, but there's always goin' to be networks; otherwise nothing'd get done."

"I understand."

"Besides, I'd never have done it iffen I didn't think you could handle it. I was real worried about you for a while there, Bonnie."

"Yes, sir."

"You don't have to call me sir."

"It's being in this room alone with you. When I was a kid, we'd only be alone in here when you were telling me to shape up or ship out."

"I hope I wasn't too hard on you. Your mama was the one used to rope you in, and after she went, I didn't know how to handle it. But I know I must've done something right." He looked into his drink. "Your mama'd be proud of you too. No, it's more'n that: Your mama would have liked you."

"You think so?"

"Ah, I know so. You're a lot like her. Damn, she was a pretty woman. Natural pretty. Only woman outa all the women I've known who looked as good in the mornin' as she did at night." He grunted and shifted, embarrassed that he'd admitted to knowing other women. "Oh, she had a warm heart, but Jesus, such a stiff backbone where fairness was concerned. Only arguments we ever had were around issues of principle. She's been on my mind a lot lately." His eyes, once bright blue but now murky with age, were shadowed with sadness.

Surprised that he could be so emotionally open, she was tempted to ask about her mother but knew that was a place he wouldn't, or couldn't, go.

"So," he continued, shifting his weight and resuming his commanding tone, "how you feel about the kids going elsewhere for Christmas?"

"I'm all right with it. Gervaise is going to be with Devoe. She'll tell you about it."

"Don't s'pose we can stop her. She'll come to the right judgment of that scoundrel sooner or later. And speakin' of the devil, I've been talking to his lawyers. Moneywise he's just holding on by his fingernails, so I guess you'll have to sell the Atlanta house."

"Well, I expected that. I just couldn't face it at first. But now I've lived somewhere else it seems easier." She shook her head. "When I think of all the time, money, and energy I put into that house! Like the place itself was the marriage and the family. All the dinners I served, all the parties I gave to impress people I didn't really like and surely don't miss. Well, from now on I'm going to live like a turtle and carry my house on my back."

He looked at her over the rim of his glass. "You're no turtle, Bonnie."

"I know I'm not. Figure of speech. Think I'll get any money out of the house?"

"Damn straight. I'm gonna hold those lawyers' feet to the fire. And speaking about money, I'm gonna change my will. Thought Devoe'd take care of you, so I was going to leave the bulk to Elice and the kids, but now I'll make sure you don't have to worry."

"Daddy, I—"

He raised his hand. "Next time you come up we'll go over the fine points together. Seems," he said, averting his eyes, "that the thing parents and kids can't and don't talk about is death. Not sex, though I never could've talked to you about that, but death." Seeing the look of concern that came over her face, he added, "Don't worry, I'm feeling fine. But there's no point in leaving anyone in the dark. Do you think you'll be staying on at that job? Kinda isolated living down there, isn't it?"

"I don't even know if the job will still be available. Mrs. Jackson—she's my supervisor—says we won't know if the government funding for the program is continuing until around Easter time. Truly, I don't have any idea what I'll be doing, but that doesn't scare me near as much as it used to."

"Want to go back to school? Because if you do—"

"I just don't know. I've been giving all these lectures about the importance of continuing education, but the truth is the thought of being in a classroom again scares me. Besides, I don't know what I'd study. Before I got this job, I really felt desperate. Didn't think I had any marketable skills, but now I don't feel quite so incompetent." She shrugged. "Something will turn up."

Sounds of rattling pots and laughter drifted in from the kitchen. The Duke finished his drink. "You know," he said, wiping his mouth, "Elice has been after me to take one of those Caribbean cruises. Since the kids aren't coming home for Christmas, what's say we do that? You could come along. Give you a nice little break from your routine. And you wouldn't just have to hang around with us old farts. First night out I'll bet some Johnny'll be chasin' you 'round the deck."

Light at the end of the tunnel! "That's sweet of you, Daddy, but

I'd just as soon spend the holidays with Cass and her boyfriend. But I think it's a great idea for you and Elice to go."

"Well, it would be strange to leave home at Christmastime, but it might make Elice happy." Then he raised and dropped his shoulders, admitting that he knew as well as she that Elice's happiness was always a dicey proposition. "The dentist says she's got to have some major work, bone transplants put into her gums, and she's real jittery about it. A trip might help to take her mind off it. You know what you said about giving up your big house?" Bonnie nodded. "Sometimes," he went on, "I feel this place is way too big for us. Almost feel greedy living here. Might start looking into one of these retirement communities in South Carolina or Florida. I don't enjoy goin' 'round as much as I used to. A lot of my friends have already passed on. If we were living in a retirement community, Elice would have all kinds of built-in activities: swimming, golf—"

She couldn't resist: "Shopping?"

"That too. Always that." He chuckled. "Elice ain't about to turn into no turtle. Well, we'll see." She could see him puzzling it through, wondering how to bring his life to a calm and successful conclusion so that he'd never be a burden to either her or Elice.

She couldn't remember a time when either of them had spoken so openly to each other, talking not just as father and daughter, but as adults. She got up to wrap her arms around his shoulders, and she pressed her cheek against his, smelling his after-shave, feeling his characteristic resistance to touch give way. She brought her mouth close to his ear—when had he started growing hair on his ears?—and whispered, as though it were a secret, "Do you know how much I love you?"

"'Bout a hundred bushels?" This answer was part of a game she'd forgotten, a question and answer game they'd play when he carried her up to bed as a child.

"More." She chimed in with her line.

"How much more?"

"A million bushels." She drew back, wiping the tickle from the tip of her nose, opening her arms. "A hundred million bushels. Oh, Daddy, I wish you could talk to me about Grace. About my mother. There are so many things I think I remember, but I'm not sure if I made them up. Just the other day I was thinking about the first time the Mazerskys visited," she began, sitting back down. "It was clear as yesterday. No, actually much clearer."

"I know what you mean. You get to a certain age and the past—"

The door opened, and Gervaise stuck in her head. "Would you like some more coffee? And if not, how about coming out and sharing your illustrious presence with the rest of us? Kitchen's all cleaned up, and we're ready to attack the dessert."

The next morning, driving up to Atlanta to show her friend Nikki Parrish, who owned the boutique, the baby dress Lyda Jane had made, Bonnie couldn't believe her luck. The visit had ended with kisses all around, and now she was free to do as she pleased for Christmas. First thing she was going to do when she got back to Florabama was stretch out on the big new bed and listen to her messages. She didn't have a phone number or address for Riz in Florida, so she hadn't been able to thank him yet for the mattress. But surely he would have called by now.

Chapter XII

*W*anting to make a grand entrance, Bonnie was purposely five minutes late for the weekly women's meeting. Bustling into the student union, pleased to see a good turnout, she called, "Hey, ladies, have I got great tidings for you," as she approached the group. Conversations were cut short, and all faces turned to her, some with a curiously foxy expression she was at a loss to understand since she knew none of them had an inkling of her good news. Taking her seat, she glanced over to where the children usually gathered.

Ruth Elkins answered her questioning look with "The kids were restless, so Crystal took them out for a walk."

Bonnie nodded, barely able to contain her excitement as she put her briefcase on her lap, unzipped it, and asked, "Everyone have a good holiday?"

Sue Ann said, "Guess you sure did," in such an insinuatingly sly tone that Celia Lusk reached over to slap her knee.

"I did," Bonnie assured her, wondering what that interaction was about. "But that's not why I'm so happy." She took a breath, brushed back her hair, folded her hands in her lap, and beamed at them. "I drove up to Atlanta the day after Thanksgiving to visit an old friend of mine. Woman by the name of Nikki Parrish, who owns a fancy boutique specializing in kids' clothes. I showed her a baby dress Lyda Jane made"—she nodded at Lyda Jane—"because I was hoping she'd place an order for some handmade baby dresses. But then we got talking about various styles and what was popular and—" She broke off, so excited that the information came tumbling out willy-nilly. "Any of you know who Jane Austen was?"

"Jane who?" one of the women asked.

"I've read her books," Ruth said.

"Maybe some of you have seen movies based on her books. *Pride and Prejudice? Sense and Sensibility? Emma?*" More blank looks. "Well, somehow Nikki and I got to talking about Jane Austen and dresses of that era. How simple and elegant they were. How popular Jane Austen is now." She reached into her briefcase and pulled out a sheath of papers. "I stopped by the Atlanta library and made photocopies from a costume book." She handed the papers to Hilly, indicating that she should hand them around. "You all know I don't sew, but dresses from that period look to be a fairly simple design. Basically a chemise with an ankle-length skirt gathered into a high bodice with puffed sleeves. The style's called Empire and came into fashion during the Napoleonic Empire. Well, you can see what it looks like. What do you think?"

"Cute, but—" Hilly said, examining a sheet, then turned to Bonnie. "Excuse me, Miz Cullman, but what's the point?"

"The point? Oh, sorry. I'm putting the cart before the horse." What a teacher she'd make! "The *point* is that I thought, and Nikki agreed, that this style would make a great line of party clothes for little girls." The women's expressions ranged from bewildered to mildly interested. "If y'all can make up samples using these designs and Nikki likes them, she's willing to order a bunch. She says she'll pay us forty percent of retail, which is more than generous. She knows about your situation, and she wants to help. But she's also a businesswoman. I mean, she wouldn't do this if she didn't think it was a way to make money."

Sue Ann was dubious. "I can't see kids wearing anything like this."

Vernette Cummings shook her head. "Neither can I."

"Oh, people who shop in boutiques will love these," Bonnie told them. "They'll pay a lot for items that are original and handcrafted, and these dresses would be perfect for birthday or Easter parties. And that's the time frame we should aim for: Easter. We make up the samples now, get them to Nikki before Christmas, and if she likes them, she'll put in an order, probably a big order. You could have money for Easter."

"How much you think they'd sell for?" Roxy asked.

"Nikki thought maybe one fifty. More if they have a matching jacket or bonnet. Little jackets and bonnets were popular then too."

Albertine's eyes bulged in disbelief. "One hundred fifty dollars for a lil kid's dress?"

"You're shittin' us," Roxy said, and with a quick look at Ruth, added, "Scuse my language."

"It's an upscale market," Bonnie explained. "I talked it through with Nikki again this morning, and she says if they're made of high-quality fabric—batiste, fine cotton, or silk—and they have hand embroidery and smocking, she could definitely get one fifty, maybe more."

"'Magine that," Puddin' snorted. "Some people in 'lanta be so rich they'd pay a hundred and fifty dollar to dress up their kid in somethin' people wore a hundred years ago."

"Nowadays rich people like natural fabrics and things that are handcrafted," Bonnie said.

Ruth Elkins shook her head and smiled. "An' to think that when we were kids, homemade shamed us."

"Let's see: Forty percent of two hundred is . . ." Celia calculated. "Eighty dollars apiece! Know what we used to get for piecework at Cherished Lady?"

"Not enough," Hilly bellowed.

"This is a boutique market," Bonnie explained, "and Nikki knows people who have specialty shops in other cities. So the sky's the limit." She opened her arms to the possibilities. "Question is, Can you do it? Do you want to do it?"

"I dunno embroidery or stuff like that," Puddin' said.

"'I don' know nothin' 'bout birthin' babies,'" Albertine teased in a squeaky Butterfly McQueen voice, making everyone laugh. "Don' be playin' stupid so as to get outa work, Puddin'. You can scissor a simple pattern, sew a straight seam, and set in a sleeve, an' that's all gotta be done 'fore we get into fancy details. Both me and Lyda Jane can do embroidery. Any you other gals old enough to know how to really work a needle?"

Sue Ann said, "My grandma taught me, but I haven't done it since I was a kid. Guess I could remember it soon enough."

"This here poke bonnet," Lyda Jane said, peering at the other women over the top of her glasses and tapping the photocopy sheet with her index finger, "looks a lot like the sunbonnets Mama made for us when we were kids. She used to cut the pattern out of newspaper. We used to have to starch an' iron 'em, but we got Pellon to stiffen fabric now. Be easy to make bonnets like these."

"That's the idea," Bonnie put in.

Bertha, who'd been listening from the service counter, raised a doughnut and said, "The whole project is a great idea!" before she dunked it in her coffee.

"But who's gonna put up the money for the materials?" Sue Ann asked.

"Ah, Nikki'll advance that," Bonnie lied. "But we'll need someone to be our accountant. Keep track of our initial investment in materials and keep a log of how many hours each woman works so we can distribute the profits fairly. Any volunteers?"

"I nominate Celia," Sue Ann said, nodding at her. "Celia's best with figures."

Celia, like a child who's been asked to sing for company and wants to milk the request for attention, said, "I guess I could."

"You can set up a program on the computer," Sue Ann suggested, then teased, "'Less you're too busy in the chat room with your new boyfriend." Celia started to object, but Sue Ann rolled right over her with "Hey, I sit next to you in computer lab, remember?" and, turning to the other women, said, "She finishes the classwork lickety-split; then she goes on-line romancin' this dude from Arkansas."

Vernette chimed in with "Bet she's told him she's a twenty-year-old blonde with a thirty-six, twenty-four, thirty-six body," and Sue Ann kept it going with "That'd only be fair 'cause he told her he owns a big ol' farm."

Flustered, Celia said, "He does have a farm. It's near—," then turned beet red.

"A farmer," Hilly said. "Ah, 'A time to plant and a time to pluck up that which is planted.' When you gonna meet this guy and pluck things up?"

Amused by this unlikely bit of gossip about Celia, Bonnie joined in the laughter, but wanting to keep the group's attention, she raised her voice to say, "So, Celia, will you keep track of the money and the hours?"

Glad to be off the hook about more personal matters, Celia gave a businesslike "I'd be happy to."

"Now," Bonnie cautioned, "I don't want this project to interfere with anyone's schoolwork. Keeping up your grades is the most important thing. But if you could get these samples done by Christmas, I'll bet Nikki will put in a big order and we'll have money by Easter."

"I want to help," Hilly said, "but I'll have to work 'round my job at the restaurant."

"And I'm cleanin' the rooms at a motel part-time," Vernette said.

"I'll leave it to you gals to get together after the meeting and arrange things among yourselves," Bonnie said. "And I'll meet with Lyda Jane and see about getting yardage and all. But now—" The doors opened, and Crystal came in, Sue Ann's sobbing infant on one hip and six or seven kids trailing after her while Lil Kylie held open the door, his eyes darting to Roxy for acknowledgment of his good behavior. "Just a lil spill," Crystal explained, moving to the group. "Kimberly fell and skinned her knee."

Reminded of her injury, Kimberly wailed and squirmed, reaching for her mother.

"Kim'ly din't fall," Moo whispered to Ruth as she sidled up to her. "Kylie pushed her."

Sue Ann inspected Kimberly's knee and used the tail of her T-shirt to wipe away her tears, saying, "Baby got a boo-boo? Mama fix it" in a sweet voice while her eyes blazed, first at Kylie, who hovered near the counter, not knowing where to hide, then at Roxy, who stared back with hostile blandness.

Hoping to relieve the tension, Bonnie said, "Perfect timing. I was just about to pass around this week's baby-sitting chart."

"Bring her on over here," Bertha called to Sue Ann. "We got a first-aid kit under the counter." Sue Ann got up, eyes flashing like warning lights at a railroad crossing, and moved to the counter.

Hilly waved Kylie to her side, saying, "C'mon over here, you miscreant," and nodded at Bonnie to proceed. As Bonnie handed the chart to Vernette, she saw Hilly hook her arm around the boy's waist and heard her whisper, "I think you owe someone an apology, young man," while Roxy stared into her cup as though she were reading tea leaves.

The women broke up into smaller groups, and Bonnie motioned for Lyda Jane to come sit next to her. "You done good, Miss Bonnie," Lyda Jane said simply.

Albertine lumbered to her feet and, after lifting her bra straps and jiggling her breasts into a more comfortable position, joined them, saying, "If we be in the military you'd get one o' them 'above and beyond the call of duty' medals, Miz Cullman."

"Thanks. Now tell me, where's the best place around here to find really good fabric?"

"Guess we'd have to go into Mobile," Lyda Jane said.

Afraid that their taste might not appeal to Nikki's clientele, Bonnie said, "Mind if I come shopping with you?"

Lyda Jane was a beat ahead of her. "I was going to ask if you would 'cause you'll have a better notion of what rich people want."

"I'd like to drive along," Albertine said. "Haven't been to Mobile in years, and I could get my neighbor to watch after Henry. When we going?"

"Strike while the iron is hot!" Lyda Jane encouraged.

"Tomorrow afternoon?" Bonnie asked. "I could go right after lunch if that's good for you." They both nodded. She handed Albertine a notebook and pen. "Draw me up a map showing me how to get to your house. You too, Lyda Jane. I'll come by tomorrow between twelve and one. Oh, do either of you have a VCR?"

Albertine said, "We do. I bought one for Henry when I got my Christmas bonus last year."

"Good. I'll swing by the video store and see if they've got any of those movies I was telling you about. It'd be nice for you to get a look at those dresses."

As Bonnie left the building, she buttoned her blazer. The late-afternoon air was nippy, there was a scud of swift-blown clouds in the sky, and she walked quickly, head bowed in thought. When she'd come back to Florabama, she'd expected a letter or at least a phone message from Riz and had been disappointed to find neither. But now the warmth of the women's enthusiasm puffed her up like a biscuit in a high oven. Never having been taken by the entrepreneurial spirit, she was surprised at how thick and fast questions and ideas came. How much would the start-up materials (which she'd decided to put on her credit card) cost? Should they give the project a name, and if so, what? Sense and Sensibility, or maybe just Emma? Where could they find custom labels? Should they get a lawyer and register the trademark? But now she was getting ahead of herself: Enthusiasm was easy; the follow-through would be the test. Sensing someone approaching, she looked up to see Cass striding toward her, hands thrust in the pockets of an eggplant-colored gabardine pantsuit, a mauve mohair scarf circling her neck.

"Don't you know Yankees are the only ones who wear long woolly scarfs?" Bonnie teased.

"Yeah. This is a remnant of my Chicago days. Must've had it for over twenty years. But I have a sore throat. Probably brought on by screeching about the joys of 'lit'ra'cha' to students who only read *TV Guide*." Cass reversed directions and fell in beside her. "I was coming over to get you. Want to come have turkey hash with us?"

"Thanks, but I've got to go home because—"

"Because you've got to check the machine and see if there are any messages from you know who. Are you going to start acting like a teenager with the telephone blues?" Bonnie started to say she wasn't waiting by the phone, but Cass, who knew better, went on. "You ought to invest in one of those machines where you can call up and get your messages when you're away."

"Speaking of investment, the other day I read that in 1929 it took the average worker 44.6 hours of labor to invest in a single share of a blue-chip stock, and now it would take him, or her, 91.6 hours."

"You goin' radical on me? I didn't ask for statistics. I asked if you'd come over for supper."

"I need an early night. I'm coming into the office at the crack of dawn tomorrow 'cause in the afternoon I'm driving into Mobile with Lyda Jane and Albertine to buy fabric and notions."

"So the women were hot for the idea?"

"Very." Bonnie smiled. "Everyone seems really excited."

"They should be. It's a great idea. I can see it now . . ." Cass lifted her hands and made quotation marks with her fingers. "Florabama Cottage Industries. It could happen. Apple Computers started in a garage."

"Know what was funny? Soon as I walked in they all looked at me as though they already knew I had a secret. Foxy, curious looks."

"I'm the only one who knew about it, and I promise I didn't tell a soul. Except Mark." She acknowledged a colleague who walked past them with a quick nod, then kept on nodding. "Hey, Sherlock, I bet I know what those looks were about. Dollars to doughnuts, they heard about Mr. Wonderful buying you the mattress."

"How could they possibly know about that?"

"It's Florabama, sweets. Meant to call you last night and tell you that I heard about it yesterday in the faculty lounge."

Bonnie was incredulous. "You didn't!"

"Not to worry. You've performed a public service. You've made hot, new tittle-tattle all over town."

"But how?"

"You don't have to be a wizard to guess: Someone who works at the college has a friend or relative who works at the furniture store. I mean, how often does the furniture store get an out-of-towner ordering a top-of-the-line mattress and asking for same-day delivery? And Riz was at your house when they delivered, right? So the dirty word was out before you'd even slept on it, and who's gonna believe you slept on it alone?"

"Come to think of it," Bonnie said as they entered the administration building, "Snoopy looked at me funny when I came back from Birmingham, but then, she always looks at me funny."

Reaching the offices, Bonnie pushed open the door. Norma Jean wiggled her fingers in greeting, and Snoopy looked up quickly, eyes glaring, jowls quivering, such a cartoon version of the Grand Inquisitor that Bonnie and Cass had to hurry into Bonnie's office. With the door closed they both sputtered with laughter. Cass eased into one of the bucket chairs while Bonnie moved behind the desk.

"Oh, I know why I wanted to see you—apart from just wanting to see you to invite you over tonight," Cass said when her laughter had subsided. She opened her bag and scrounged in it, brought out her calendar and drew a sheet of paper from it. "Take a look at this." Bonnie took the paper and read:

No temptation of space and sky
in that jail of work,
Neither instinct nor will to lure me to
freedom.

But now, outside this window . . .
Birds fly in a sky blue as a newborn's eyes.

Their wings make m's and w's . . .
Are they spelling *Maybe?*
Are they spelling *Wishes?*

                                    Ruth Elkins

"It's lovely."

"Want to know how it came about?"

Bonnie nodded, reaching into her desk for a package of corn nuts, helping herself and putting the package within Cass's reach.

"I read Vachel Lindsay's 'Factory Windows Are Always Broken' to the class," Cass went on. "Then I asked them to write something about it, and this is what Ruth came up with. Later she told me that there weren't any windows in the room she worked in at Cherished Lady."

"First time I interviewed her I could tell she was intelligent and she really wanted to come back to school."

"I could see it right away. I hate to admit it, but I place my bets the first day of class. Scan the room and look into their eyes to see if anyone's home upstairs. I could see her wheels turning even though she's so tongue-tied it took weeks for her to speak in class. I've made an effort to draw her out, call her in for conferences and all. She's not only motivated but smart, Bonnie." Cass shook out some corn nuts. "Imagine what her life has been like. Working, day after day, year after year, in a place without windows."

"I hardly have to imagine it," Bonnie said, rolling her eyes around her windowless office. "A lot of the women didn't mind the millwork. Some even say they liked it. But for a someone like Ruth it must've been awful."

"She told me that she'd like to go on to a four-year college, get a degree in English, and be a high school teacher. Imagine a more thankless job!—Raging hormones, discipline problems, parents who never come to meetings but threaten to sue when their kid tries to burn down the building. I told her she should get some office training, maybe be a paralegal. But she wants to be a high school teacher."

"Maybe she thinks high school is the last chance to save the kids from bad choices they'll have to live with for the rest of their lives." She ran her tongue around her teeth to dislodge the last of the corn nuts. "Thank God there're always a few people, like you, who have a real calling to teach."

Cass shrugged off the compliment. "I don't have a calling. I was just too screwed up to have a career plan, so I ended up in this cow college. This counts as Ruth's second year, so she'll finish up here in the spring, right?"

Bonnie nodded. "Apparently she had one year of college, then got married and got pregnant. Or, more likely, the reverse."

"So," Cass barreled on, "when you prepare her schedule for next semester, load her up good. Give her the most challenging classes. I'll do whatever I can to push her. We should think about how to get her a full scholarship to the University of Alabama next year. You have any contacts there?"

Bonnie considered. "Back when I was on the lunch circuit, I used to attend the University Women luncheons. Some of those women I met teach at the U of A. But frankly, I don't know if Ruth can make it."

"Why not?"

"It'll be hard for her to leave town. She's got her house and friends and her daughter and grandkids here. It takes a lot of gumption for a woman her age to pick up and leave."

"You did it."

"It's hardly comparable. I needed a job, and this one fell into my lap. I had you here. I didn't have the pull of family. And I desperately wanted a whole new life even though I didn't realize it at the time. Besides, in the back of my mind I knew that if I screwed up, the Duke would bail me out."

"OK. It was easier for you," Cass conceded. "But we've all gotta play the cards we've been dealt. I think Ruth realizes that this is her last chance."

"Yeah. You're right." Bonnie crumpled up the empty corn nuts package, threw it into the wastebasket, punched the SAVE button on her computer and got up. "OK. We'll do what we can."

"Sure you don't want to come home with me? Or would you rather rush home so you can sit by the telephone?" Cass rose with a catlike stretch. "I know Riz Mazersky is a hunk, but by your own account, he turned up unannounced, talked mainly about himself while you fixed him dinner, made a pass, then passed out. By most standards that does not constitute a romantic evening."

"I know, but I—"

"Don't tell me: You felt flattered."

"Well, I did," Bonnie said. "And I expected—"

"Flattered. Expected. When it comes to men, you're still sweet sixteen. Really, Bonnie. Think about this guy's track record: He's a three-times-divorced, self-involved womanizer who lives in another state. I'd say it's probably just as well that he hasn't called."

Who could deny the wisdom of it? "I guess you're right. OK. I'll come over to your place for dinner, but no Scrabble, no wine, and I can't stay overnight because I'm driving into Mobile tomorrow."

"And if you don't come home, Nesha'll punish you, right? First time I stayed out overnight with Mark, Bub peed right in the middle of my bed. Mark said I ought to get a water pistol and squirt Bub whenever he jumped on the bed, but I thought, Hey, I slept with that cat before I slept with you, and I'll probably be sleeping with that cat when you're long gone. Are you ready to make the run past Snoopy?"

"I am." Bonnie made a last-minute check of her desk, picked up her purse, and nodded as Cass opened the door. "I just have to drop by the video store; then I'll drive on over to your place."

The next evening, after their shopping trip to Mobile, Bonnie found herself in Albertine Chisholm's living room, sitting on a plastic-covered couch and eating banana pudding. As part of Atlanta society she'd been a guest in the homes of the city's African-American elite, which, except for presumably genuine and therefore expensive African artifacts, were remarkably similar to those of affluent whites, but this was the first time she'd been in the home of working-class black people. She looked around at the bouquet of silk flowers on top of the twenty-seven-inch TV and cast her eyes up to the "African" hunting shield (probably made in Taiwan) that decked the wall and two prints, one of Martin Luther King, JFK, and Bobby Kennedy in profile, gazing at an American flag, the other a queer version of Da Vinci's *Last Supper*, since Jesus and the apostles were all black. Lyda Jane sat to her right, busy crocheting a baby blanket (did that woman's hands ever stop?), and Albertine's neighbor, aptly nick-named String Bean, was to her left, scraping the remains of her second helping from a Pyrex bowl. Puddin' and her boyfriend, James, snuggled next to each other on a love seat beside an end table crammed with photos of brides, babies, and smiling teenage faces topped with mortarboards. Albertine's husband Henry's wheelchair was pulled up to the dining room table. One of Henry's hands was absently stroking a length of lavender batiste Albertine had pulled from one of the shopping bags; the other was holding the VCR remote. All eyes were fixed on the screen as the video of *Sense and Sensibility* reeled to the nub of the story. A distraught Emma Thompson was being told, "Dear madam, I would not have burdened you had I not believed that, in time, it would lessen your sister of her regrets."

"Anyone want the scrapings 'fore I put 'em in the Tupper bowl?" Albertine shouted from the kitchen.

String Bean yelled, "I do."

Lyda Jane said, "Hush! I don't wanna miss this part," and glued her eyes to the set where the awful truth was finally coming to light, the character confessing, "She was with child. The blackguard who had left her used her abominably ill. During her confinement—"

"Hey, Henry." Puddin' sat up, pulling away from James. "Roll it back, an' play this part again, will you? I don' understand—"

"Ain't hard to understand," String Bean explained. "'Blackguard' means he's a skunk. He done got the girl pregnant; then he run off soon's she start showin.'"

James shook his head. "Now that ain't right," and added, sotto voce, "Y' know when I was a lil boy, I din't think white women could get pregnant if they weren't married."

"Puddin'," Henry said, cutting James a withering glance, "don't be marryin' James even if he ever gets 'round to axing you. He be too dumb to live with in the daylight hours."

Albertine came in carrying another bowl of banana pudding, patted Henry's shoulder, and pecked his cheek as she passed him, then handed the bowl to String Bean and squeezed herself in between String Bean and Bonnie. "Just look at those pretty dresses," she said, gazing at the screen. "But I don' see how these sisters in the movie's s'posed to be poor when they're living in that pretty cottage and wearing dresses like that."

Lyda Jane hissed another "Shussh!" then said, "I'm into this story, Albertine. We can talk 'bout the dresses later."

Except for James, who disappeared into the kitchen for a beer and stayed there, they all watched in silence, punctuated with occasional grunts of disapproval or sighs of relief, until the movie ended.

"Sure did love that last scene where everyone's all happy an' gettin' married," String Bean said as she got up to leave. "Pleased to meet you, Miz Cullman. An' good luck with this sewing deal."

After seeing String Bean out, Albertine came back, asking, "Lyda Jane, Miz Cullman, either of you want to take some fried chicken home with you?"

"Thanks, but no," Bonnie answered. "I'd best be getting along." She looked at the fabrics and notions on the dining room table.

Henry, catching her eye, said, "You gals got you some first-class goods here." Despite the fact that his legs had atrophied, he was a strong-looking man in his mid-fifties. His upper body showed muscle, and his clean-cut face had a chiseled nose and deep-set, playful eyes. As Albertine passed, he caught her hand and said, "Now don't you be messin' up these goods, 'Tine. First year we were married," he confided to Bonnie with a twinkle, "she be makin' me some satin pajamas for our anniversary. Cut 'em so big they swim on me an' she end up wearin' 'em herself. Never will forget how she looked in them satin pajamas—all shine an' sweetness, like the Big Rock Candy Mountain."

"Mountain?" Albertine huffed, pulling away. "I weren't no mountain till you got me pregnant. I was nothin' more'n a bitsy lil hill when I married you, Henry."

Lyda Jane wandered to the table and fingered a cream challis printed with sprigs of green. "You laid out a lotta money, Miz Cullman, but these fabrics are pure gossamer. We gonna make those lil rich girls'll look like princesses."

Albertine asked, "Miz Cullman, you sure you won't carry some of this chicken home?"

Puddin', who'd disappeared into the kitchen to be with James, yelled, "We'll take some."

"You're six ax handles across the rear," Henry called back. "You don' need more fried chicken."

Bonnie said, "And neither do I."

"Oh, you a fine figure of a woman," Henry told her. "Shouldn't lose an inch."

Bonnie kissed Lyda Jane, Albertine, and even Henry on their

cheeks, called out a good-bye to Puddin' and James, and walked to her car.

Driving home, she visualized the fabrics, ribbons, and laces already transformed into beautiful dresses. They'd made the investment. They'd make a bundle. If Riz called, that was fine; if he didn't, that was fine too. She had too much going on in her life to feel needy. Didn't she?

After feeding Nesha, she undressed, got into slippers and a comfortable robe, and, almost as an afterthought, checked the answering machine. The light was flashing, but even before she'd punched the MESSAGE button, she decided she was too weary to answer any calls.

"Hey, Miss Bonnie." His voice was low and seductive with just a hint of urgency. "Sorry you aren't home. I thought we could do a 'you tell me yours, I'll tell you mine' about visits with our folks. Or is that 'you show me yours, I'll show you mine'? Anyhow, I'm at my apartment in D.C. That's area code 202-555-8740. Give me a call. How 'bout a nontraditional yuletide in New Orleans?"

She grabbed the receiver and punched in the number.

Chapter XIII

*T*he plane touched down in New Orleans with a bump that went straight to Bonnie's heart. "I've had better landings, but"— the man sitting next to her said—"I've had worse. Once when I was coming into Mexico City . . ." He'd been trying to engage her in conversation ever since they'd taken off from Mobile, but she'd resisted his overtures to the point of rudeness. It wasn't like her to rebuff chatty friendliness; then again, it wasn't like her to be flying into a strange city to meet for an assignation, and she was nervous. *Assignation* was Cass's word. Bonnie'd said it was pretentious, but Cass'd said it was accurate because it meant an appointment to meet, especially one between lovers. "But we aren't lovers," Bonnie'd protested, then added a sheepish "yet."

When she accepted Riz's invitation to meet him at the home of one of his friends in New Orleans, he'd tactfully mentioned "her room." She knew he wouldn't try to talk her into anything she wasn't ready for, but she'd already made the decision. In fact, she'd imagined being in bed with him so many times she was afraid the reality wouldn't measure up. "It hardly ever does," Cass'd agreed. "At least not at first. And you're nervous 'cause you're out of practice. There've been long stretches in my life when I didn't have a lover, but trust me, Bonnie, you never forget. It's like—"

"Don't say it's like riding a bike. It took me a hell of a long time to learn how to ride a bike. And I can still remember falling off and getting a gash in my forehead that needed four stitches." She'd pulled back her hair to show the evidence.

"Yeah, well," Cass'd said, breaking into a devilish grin as she'd examined the scar, "it's like riding a bike."

The flight attendant warned passengers to remain buckled in their seats until the plane had come to a complete stop, but Bonnie ignored instructions and unlatched her belt. Her feet felt cold as she slipped them back into her shoes, but her hands were sweaty as she lifted her purse into her lap. The man seated next to her squeezed into the aisle, unlocked the overhead compartment and offered to get down her carry-on. She accepted with thanks, thinking about the box of condoms packed in with her navy cocktail dress. The day before, deciding that she shouldn't be coy about taking precautions, she'd found a drugstore she'd never gone to before and would never go to again. After locating the rack of contraceptives, she'd snatched up a box and kept moving, adding a bottle of nail polish and travel-size Woolite to the basket. At the checkout she'd stepped aside to let another customer go ahead of her, then chatted with the salesgirl as she'd rung up her purchases, half expecting the girl to ask, "What's a woman like you doing with a box of Trojans?" The girl was so inattentive that she overcharged her forty cents, but Bonnie wasn't about to quibble. Walking quickly to the parking lot, she recalled how nervous she'd been when shortly after she and Devoe had become engaged, she'd made an appointment with a doctor one of her sorority sisters had whispered was "accommodating." When she'd gone to be fitted for a diaphragm, she'd turned her engagement ring around to look like a wedding band. Things had changed a lot in the last twenty years. Nowadays middle-school teachers dropped by produce stands and bought bananas to facilitate instruction in a co-ed sex education classes.

"Your friend picking you up?" her fellow passenger asked as they walked up the ramp. When she blurted an unthinking no, he offered to give her a ride, but she declined, smiling good-bye as she darted into the crowd. Riz had offered to pick her up, but she'd pointed out that holiday flights were often late, and she didn't want him sitting around the airport after his long drive down from D.C. Her real reason was less practical: Arriving alone and taking a taxi appealed to her sense of adventure.

To calm herself, she stopped at a concession stand and ordered a café au lait and a warm beignet. Her first bite into the beignet showered the front of her peach-colored sweater and the thighs of her beige slacks with confectioners' sugar. As she brushed it off, she felt her nipples harden. The young man behind the counter smiled flirtatiously as she sipped her coffee. It occurred to her that her fellow passenger on the plane had been flirting with her too, but she was so unaccustomed to this sort of attention that she hadn't picked up on it. Maybe she was giving off those unconsciously detectable, powerful hormonal scents call pheromones. In any case, she was feeling sexy and seemed to be sending out vibes.

After stashing her empty cup in a trash can and nodding farewell to the counterman, she went to the rest room. Refreshing her lipstick and brushing her hair, she was pleased to see that even under the cruelly bright light, she looked pretty damned good. Assignation: the poor woman's face-lift, she thought as she shouldered her bags and headed for the exit.

In front of the airport she raised her arm assertively, hailing a taxi. The cab that pulled up was not in mint condition, and as the driver, an old black man with a walnut face, careened away from the airport, she realized it had neither seat belts nor shock absorbers. She gave him the address, leaning on one buttock so her coccyx wouldn't be jarred by the bumps. Rolling down the window, she sniffed the heavy air and tilted her head to see a clear sky with wispy bands of pearly pink and gray clouds. The driver tried the opening conversational gambit about the weather, then, half talking to himself, started telling stories of the city's political and police corruption, chuckling at first, then getting as exercised as an irate citizen at a town hall meeting. By the time they left the highway and started in the direction of the French Quarter he'd turned philosophical, saying, "Naw'lins—they don' call her the Big Easy for nothin'. That the way she always be; that the way she is," then surprised her by quoting, "'Age cannot wither her, nor custom stale / Her infinite variety. . . .'" She couldn't wait to tell Cass she'd had a cabdriver who quoted from *Antony and Cleopatra*.

The image of the city as an ageless but ever-seductive courtesan was a cliché, but apt. Higgledy-piggledy streets were crammed with houses, apartments, hotels, and shops with graceful, if occasionally rusted, ironwork, pretty little balconies, and narrow alleyways that looked cool but promised hot secrets. The air was moist and heavy. Delicious aromas of spicy seafood, roasting meat, coffee, and baking bread mingled with the miasma of liquor and stale smoke that came from the open doors of saloons and the pungent whiff of the Mississippi. Tourists with fanny packs and cameras wandered, goggle-eyed, among hawkers, grifters, street musicians, and regular citizens. The driver turned onto an almost deserted street, pulled to the curb of a narrow sidewalk abutted by a row of flat-fronted houses, then craned his neck out the window to check the number on a two-story pink building with barred windows and announced, "This be your destination."

"Where's the front door?"

"See over to the side? Press that lil button, an' go on through that tall, slim gate." Accepting the fare and tip, he gave a wicked wink and said, "I thank you, sweet lady. An' I know you're gonna have a fine time here."

She pressed the buzzer next to the wrought-iron gate, looking up and down the none-too-sanitary street and feeling as though she were waiting to be admitted to a speakeasy. A low electronic drone, followed by a click, unlocked the gate. She lunged to push it open, afraid that it would lock again, readjusted her bags on her shoulders, then walked through a narrow cobblestone passageway so dark that the slice of sky above looked as though it had been painted. The splash of a fountain reached her ears, and the sweet smell of flowers flared her nostrils before she came into a little garden surrounded by high brick walls. The street side of the house had given no hint of this verdant snuggery, lush even in December. As she paused to look at the statue of a nymph embracing a dolphin whose mouth sent a steady stream of water into a pool, she heard a noise, turned, and saw the sliding glass door open. Riz stepped out. He was barefoot and tousled, wearing jeans and an unbuttoned buff-colored suede shirt. Blinking, he said, "I didn't get here till early afternoon. I was taking a catnap," before his sleep-creased face broke into a grin. "Are you part of my dream or are you really here?"

"I think I'm really here. Pinch me and see," she said. But when he came closer and reached out, she slid the carry-on down her arm, handed it to him, then pinched herself.

"Trip OK?" he asked.

"Fine."

"You OK?"

"Uh-huh." He was giving her that sleepy-sexy look that made her swallow hard.

"C'mon in."

"This'll be the first time in my whole life that I'm not having a tra-ditional Christmas," she said, following him into a room that was any-thing but traditional. It was large, dim except for light spilling from the garden, and smelled of woodsmoke, flowers, and incense (or pos-sibly marijuana). An entire wall was taken up with high-tech record-ing equipment and wall-to-ceiling cabinets containing CDs, tapes, and old records. The other walls were painted deep burgundy and covered with an extraordinary collection of paintings: miniatures, landscapes, primitive portraits of saints, along with an alarming but amusing painting of a large blue dog with two pairs of eyes and a bril-liant Jonathan Green depicting a crew of black farm workers and a putty-colored hound dog in a field of corn. A Steinway grand stood to one side of an eclectic arrangement of couches, one of modern design upholstered in leather, another an antique with stuffing beginning to push through tattered blue brocade, the third low and flat as a bed, covered with zebra skin. Fur and silk pillows were strewn on a Turkish carpet in front of the fireplace. A prancing wooden horse from a turn-of-the-century carousel stood next to the statue of an African fertility goddess and a wind-up Victrola. Riz set her travel bag next to a coffee table constructed from what looked to be an old church door resting on carved marble blocks. "Think I told you," he said. "This place belongs to the son of an old friend of mine. Ever heard of the rapper called Dirty Rice?"

"I don't know much about rap," she admitted. "Maybe 'cause I can't stand it."

"Well, the kid, Josh—he's not really a kid, he's twenty-six, but the time you're allowed to be called a kid has stretched some since we were young—anyway, I've known Josh since he was a babe in arms. Now he's big time. Top of the charts. He's in Europe right now, cashing in on his fifteen minutes of fame, so he told me to use the house. Nice turnaround 'cause ten years ago he didn't want to know from me or his daddy."

"I guess you've told me about this," Bonnie said, "but I don't remember the details."

"His father, Jacob Weinstein—writes under the name of Jay Stein; maybe you've seen his columns—is one of my oldest and best friends. Jay's a New Yorker who came South during the civil rights brouhaha. He went all the way, married a black girl name of Lurline Trask. Ever heard of her?" Bonnie shook her head. "Jesus," Riz said, bunching his fingers and bringing them to his mouth to kiss them, "what a voice Lurline had. She could make you weep. In the long run she sure made Jake weep. Wanna see the house?"

She nodded, and he led the way into a kitchen with a black-tiled floor, white-tiled walls, an industrial-size stove, a brushed steel refrigerator, and a butcher-block table the size of a twin bed overhung with racks of shining pots and pans. The overall effect would have been sterile had it not been for an old-fashioned ice chest, a politically incorrect poster of a beaming Aunt Jemima, and a rack of spices in multicolored glass bottles. "Lurline died of an overdose when Josh was . . . I don't know . . . seven or eight. Jake tried to raise him, but he ended up sending him to boarding school. I would've thought Josh'd be more likely to end up in the Hasty Pudding Club at Harvard than be a rapper, but he went crazy-funky, rented an apartment in Harlem, and started composing, if you can call it that, and changed his name to Dirty Rice. I expect he'd die if the public knew his real name is Joshua Weinstein and he almost got a Ph.D. in art history. Can I get you a drink or a coffee or anything?" When she shook her head, he went to the front room, retrieved her travel bag, then led her through the kitchen down a dimly lit corridor and into a bedroom.

"This room will be yours," he told her, setting her travel bag down on a brass bed made up with fine white sheets and oversize pillows.

The room had darkly stained wood floors and minimal furniture. The shuttered windows, opening on to the street, cast stripes of light on the whitewashed walls and crème chaise longue, glanced off the gold trim and pearl inlays of a Japanese screen painted with water lilies, and picked up the mahogany glow of a large Spanish armoire.

"What's that?" she asked, pointing to a pair of lacquered lavender-colored bell-bottoms fixed to the wall above the bed.

"Those pants belonged to Jimi Hendrix," Riz told her. "They must be worth a bundle 'cause Josh knows how to invest. He sports the heavy gold chains and rings because they're part of the rapper uniform, but they're all fakes. His money is in art and antiques."

"Interesting." She was so acutely conscious that they were standing next to the bed that she couldn't think of anything better to say. Their eyes met. She didn't have to be a mind reader to know they were thinking the same thing. She busied herself unzipping her overnight bag and said she'd like to take a shower.

"Fine. You freshen up. Then we'll sit in the garden and have a drink and talk before we go out to dinner, OK?"

Alone, she found her bag of toiletries and walked into the bathroom. It was almost as large as the bedroom, with a celadon-colored tiled floor, tiled walls with a water lily motif, a sunken tub large enough to accommodate several people with an array of soaps, oils, sponges, and brushes on one of its steps, and an overhead mirror. Next to the double sink were two commodes, one of which she discovered, upon closer inspection, was a bidet. When she and Devoe had gone to Europe on their honeymoon, there'd been a bidet in their hotel room in Rome. She'd never used one before, and she'd thought it was the height of civilization. Devoe'd promised her they'd have one when they struck it rich, but by the time they built the Atlanta house, a bidet had seemed frivolous. Closing the door, she saw a black kimono patterned with red and gold poppies and lined with crimson silk hanging over a full-length mirror. She'd been in the homes of the very rich before, but she'd never seen any that had been furnished with such an eye to playful hedonism. The chaise longue, the dressing screen, the brass bed, and the sunken tub, and now the kimono. This place was enough to make a Carmelite nun want to be a geisha. After shucking off her clothes, she poured a stream of rosemary and sea salt elixir "guaranteed to lift the spirits" into the tub, turned the faucets on full, and sat on the top step of the sunken tub, swirling her hand in the rising blue-green water.

By the time she stepped out of the tub she felt so contentedly sensuous that she was able to admire her full-hipped nakedness in the steamy mirror, but she jumped when she heard Riz tap at the bedroom door. She called, "Coming," in a Lauren Bacall voice and reached for the kimono. Crossing the bedroom, she was conscious that every step brought her closer to him. Never before had she been so aware in both mind and body of the delicious game and drama of sex. She held the kimono tight against her breast, then, as she reached for the doorknob, let it fall from one shoulder. Riz, a glass of fizzing champagne in hand, took a step back and said, "You look reborn."

"I feel reborn."

If he'd made the slightest move, she would have opened the door wide. Instead, sharing the cat-and-mouse fun of it, he slowly lifted the kimono to cover her shoulder, saying, "We've got reservations at Louis Seize in half an hour. You can sip this while you dress," handed her the glass, and closed the door.

Louis XVI was cool, elegantly furnished, and artfully lit. In a nod to the season a Christmas tree decorated with silver and white lights twinkled in the center of the dining room. The waiters, mostly older men, were attentive without being overbearing. The only sounds came from a subdued piano in the bar, muted conversations, tinkling glasses, and heavy silver making a soft thud on linen tablecloths. Riz reached into the champagne bucket, brought out the bottle, refilled her glass, and smiled. Never at a loss for words, he'd been providing most of the conversation. He'd asked what she was thinking, but the thoughts that occupied her (the strangeness of being away from family at Christmas, concerns about how Eugene and Gervaise were doing) didn't seem to fit the mood. "I did tell you that we got the sample dresses to Nikki Parrish and she'd put in a nice order, didn't I?" she asked.

"Yes, you told me," he answered laconically, his eyes never leaving her face.

"We'll deliver the dresses and make some money in time for Easter. I've had so much fun at the sewing sessions. The gals' conversations are funnier than a sit-com."

"What do they talk about?"

"Men, mostly. The stories are so horrific and so trite I just rock with laughter. The other night—" She started to repeat one but stopped. Like Devoe, he didn't seem to be fully engaged in what she was saying; unlike Devoe, his lack of concentration seemed to spring from a preoccupation with her physical presence. How could she be offended when he confessed, looking into her eyes, "I'm sorry. I didn't really hear what you were saying"? They, or rather he, finished the champagne. He asked if he might order for her, and she put aside the menu. He beckoned for the sommelier, who appeared to be impressed with his choice.

After oysters Bienville, salad, and chestnut and carrot soup with crème fraiche and chervil, the salmon entrée with fennel and gooseberry sauce and shrimp croustade with wild rice was set before them. It had been a long time since she'd had magnificent food so beautifully presented, and appetite easily overcame prudence. By the time she rested her fork on her plate, her flesh was straining against the seams of her cocktail dress, and when the dessert cart was wheeled to the table, she shook her head and held up her hands in surrender, telling Riz, "I feel as though I've been at *Babette's Feast.*"

It was sprinkling rain when they got back to the house. As they passed through the garden, the earth smells, champagne, wine, and rich food (not to mention the apprehension of things to come) made her woozy. She collapsed into a garden chair, turning up her face to the dark sky, relishing the mist on her neck and bosom, listening to the splash of the fountain. "Better come on in," he told her, taking her hands and gently lifting her from the chair. "It's about to storm."

Inside, she sat on one of the leather couches while he took off his jacket and went to the bar, asking, "Cognac?"

"Good heavens, no. I've already overindulged." Her voice had an Aunt Pittypat fluster that made her giggle.

"Be right back," he told her, leaving the room.

She listened to the gathering storm while slipping pins and combs from her damp hair. He came back with a towel flung over his shoulder, holding a clear, fizzy drink in one hand and opening the palm of the other to show a red pill and a yellow pill. "Seltzer, antihistamine, and a stress tab," he told her. "You'll thank me in the morning." She hesitated. "Come on," he urged. "Just relax." She hated it when a man, any man, told her to relax. Gynecologists, tax specialists, divorce lawyers, Devoe—they'd all told her to relax. Discomfort, either mental or physical, had invariably followed. "The antihistamine and the vitamins will help you avoid a hangover, and the seltzer will make you burp. I'm just trying to take care of you." She downed the pills, finished the seltzer, and burped. "Good girl," he encouraged, taking the glass from her hand and putting it on the coffee table. "And we don't want you to catch cold, so let me dry your hair." He sat next to her and began to towel her head. Eyes closing like a cat being petted, she gave way to the sensation of his hands massaging her scalp. Now, she thought muzzily, he's going to kiss me. And I'm ready. He smoothed the hair back from her forehead, traced the shape of her eyebrows with his thumbs, then got up and walked over to the wall of electronic equipment. He's certainly not rushing me, she thought, vaguely disappointed. As he turned his back, removing an old record from its sleeve and setting it on the turntable, she opened her eyes and watched. "This is one of my favorites," he told her, carefully setting down the needle.

She slipped off her heels and drew up her legs. "You should've been a record producer."

"Yeah, music's my first love," he drawled, sitting down next to her, "This is Mabel Mercer doing an old Cole Porter number." A clap of thunder preceded the first notes of the song. He loosened his tie and rested his head on the back of the couch as a woman's voice, smoky but sentimental, began to sing:

> Looking at you while—troubles are fleeing
> I'm admiring the view 'cause it's you I'm seeing
> And the sweet honey-dew of well-being
> Settles upon me. . . .

He turned his head to her, saying, "It *is* good to be looking at you."

It had been years since any man had looked at her with that mix of desire and appreciation. She felt late forties going on seventeen, or maybe something in the middle, maybe a hot thirty-two. "It's good to be with you too," she said, raising her arms to the back of the couch, conscious that the movement made her breasts strain against the bodice of her dress.

"You feeling better now?"

"Uh-huh." The wooziness was gone. She felt blissfully relaxed yet concentrated.

The song finished, and another came on, the singer crooning:

> I can be happy, I can be sad,
> I can be good, I can be bad,
> It all depends on you. . . .

He got up to stand in front of her, offering his hand. "Shall we dance?" She nodded, moving into his arms. They were thigh to thigh, belly to belly, her head resting on his chest. They danced slowly, then more slowly, until they were barely moving. She turned her face to his. His kiss was light with a mere exploratory flick of his tongue, making her yearn into him, wanting more. He tensed like a racehorse at the starting gate, reached behind her, unzipped her dress in a single movement, easing it down until it dropped to the floor. With an imperceptible shudder she sloughed off any remaining inhibition; she stepped out of the circle of silk. His voice was husky as he pulled her to him, saying, "This has been a long time coming."

A voice from the street woke her: a deep male voice chanting the same phrase over and over. Her mind struggled up through the watery depths of sleep and finally broke the surface of consciousness. Was it a hawker? No. Hawkers didn't sing out their wares anymore, not even in New Orleans. And she was in New Orleans. In bed with Riz Mazersky. She felt her breasts pressed against his back, licked her lips—Lord, her mouth was dry—and tasted the salt of perspiration, smelled the musk of sex, saw the milky light coming through the shutters. And yes, there *was* a voice coming from the street, though now it was growing fainter, and she judged it to be the "show me the way to go home" dawn wail of a drunk.

As she stretched to touch her feet to his, her body felt deliciously achy. Lifting her hair from her face, she propped herself up and bent to look at him. He was dead to the world, breathing through his slightly open mouth. His eyelids had an oily look, and his lashes were full and dark as a child's. "Poor baby," she whispered, running her hand down his back. "You've knocked yourself out." Deciding to bathe so she'd be fresh when he woke up, she slipped out of bed. He rolled over, pawed the space she'd left, found a substitute in the pillow, and hugged it to his chest.

Closing the bathroom door, she went to the mirror. Her hair was a tangle, she had a smudge of mascara under one eye, her lips were puffy, and the skin around them looked as though she'd been eating raspberries, but she was flush-faced and proud as an amateur who'd broken the ribbon on the finish line at a professional marathon. Turning the bath faucets on full, she looked through the bottles of oils and salts, chose one "guaranteed to soothe tired muscles," poured a generous measure into the tub, and lowered herself into it.

She was blissfully relaxed, soaking up to her chin, shampoo suds on her head and a gray-green clay mask on her face when he gave a knock, then immediately opened the door. He was buck naked, holding what she guessed to be a Bloody Mary, and his sleep-creased face broke into a grin. "Bonjour, madame. Have I interrupted your toilette?"

She grabbed a washcloth and wiped the clay from her face. "Is it a man's prerogative to come into the bathroom without being asked?"

"Only when he's your lover."

Serious, but in a kidding tone, she said, "I think it's bad manners even then. Maybe especially then."

"Tail of the dog?" he asked, holding up the drink.

"Good God, no."

After taking a swallow, he set the drink down, came to the tub, and knelt beside it. "Isn't it bad manners to desert your lover's bed without saying good-bye?"

"I wouldn't know. I'm out of practice."

"You didn't act as though you were out of practice."

"But this morning I have to soak my aching muscles."

"I'll take that as a compliment." He kissed the tip of her nose. "Would you feel crowded if I joined you?"

"Since it's an orgy-size tub, I can hardly object."

She slid forward, and he climbed in behind her, easing her back, saying, "I've never given a woman a shampoo before," as he began to massage her scalp. That's probably the only thing you've never done, she thought. "You know," he went on, "I've wanted to take a bath with you from the time we were kids, but back then my fantasies didn't go any further than dunking you." Hands on her shoulders, he pressed down so suddenly that she had no time to resist. Thrashing and sputtering, she twisted around to grab his shoulders and dunked him. They rotated and splashed like baby seals until he pulled himself up, then lay back, drawing her into his arms and turning her so that her head lolled on his chest.

"You bastard. You got soap in my eye," she said, blinking.

"I'm sorry. Let me kiss it better." He reached for a washcloth and wiped her eye. "Now why don't you rinse your hair, and we'll get going?"

She crawled to the faucets, turned them on, and rinsed out her hair. He helped her out of the tub, toweled her off, then reached for a bottle of oil, uncapped it, and slicked it over her body. "OK." She smiled. "I'm ready. Where are we going for breakfast?"

"When I said let's get going, I didn't mean breakfast," he said, pulling her into his arms.

"Go easy this time," she murmured.

"I'll do the best I can."

They lay flat on their backs, beached, not touching. Half snoozing, she heard his stomach grumble. She blinked, saw that sunlight had invaded the room, and, turning on her side, saw the phone on the night table. The kids! She'd forgotten to call the kids. Sensing her sudden movement, he rolled over, muttering, "Whatsamatter?"

"I said I'd call the kids last night to let them know I'd arrived safely." After reaching for a sheet crumpled at the foot of the bed and wrapping it around her—no man was going to see her naked behind in full sunlight—she stood up and made a beeline for her bag, almost slipping on the slickly polished floor.

"*You've* gotta report in to *them*? That's a role reversal," Riz mumbled, stretching.

"It's not as though I have to report," she explained, glancing back. He was spread-eagled, arms and legs extended, penis coiled against the matted hair of his groin, eyes shut. "I want to talk to them. It's Christmas."

"Not until tomorrow," he croaked.

"The Christmas holiday," she said impatiently, riffling through her bag. "Eugene's gone up to Michigan to meet his girlfriend's folks and—" She fished out her phone book, stumbled back to sit on the edge of the bed, and began to page through it. "Dammit, what is their name? Jurlinski? Janovitch? Something Polish beginning with a *J*."

He squinted against the sunlight. "Looks as though we've missed breakfast. How 'bout a late brunch? Emeril's or the Grill Room?"

"Ah . . . Jawarsky, that's it." She punched in the number, tensing as she waited for it to ring through. A child answered, lisping, "Jawarsky residence. Merry Christmas."

"Merry Christmas to you, too," she said, brightening her voice. "This is Eugene's mama. Is Eugene there?"

"'This is Eugene's mama.'" Riz mimicked her.

She turned, rolling her eyes and shushing him. He pinched her backside, dragged himself out of bed, and ambled toward the bathroom. "Dammit, Riz," she muttered, holding her hand over the receiver, "give me some privacy." She hated to have her bottom pinched, and she was about to tell him so when she heard, "Hi, Mom."

"Eugene. Hi, darlin'." She recovered herself. "Yes, it's me. Merry Christmas. How're you doing? How's Fern?"

Eugene, usually monosyllabic in phone conversations, was perversely talkative. She chatted sotto voce, registering the soft buzz of Riz's electric shaver and, finally, the flush of the toilet. "Yes, I'm fine. Having a good time. So . . ."

Riz came out of the bathroom wearing the black kimono. Tucking his arms into its sleeves and bowing his head, he walked to the bed with mincing steps and bowed. She burst out laughing. "Oh, nothing, Eugene. Just my friend acting silly. I told you I was having a good time, didn't I? . . . uh-uh . . . well, give my regards to Fern and her family . . . I do too . . . Merry Christmas." She hung up, shaking her head. "You bastard! It's hard enough to call my kids while I'm sitting buck naked in an unmade bed and you—"

"Up, up! Gotta eat. Gotta drink. Let's get cracking."

"Not until I call Gervaise."

"God, you're like the old woman who lived in a shoe."

"I have two children, Riz. Two. I promised to call them, and I'm calling them."

"OK." He shrugged and headed to the bedroom door.

She riffled through her address book again, looking for Devoe's number under *D* but not finding it. Then she remembered: When Gervaise called to give her the number, she'd started to write it in pen under *D* but something had spooked her, so she'd changed to pencil, flipped back to *C* and entered it as "Cullman, Devoe." She started to punch in the number and stopped. What if Devoe picked up? Worse yet, what if his girlfriend did? Not that she was jealous. She'd suppressed all those feelings long ago when she'd first suspected Devoe's extramarital activities and, in the interest of preserving the marriage, had chosen to ignore them. Even when they'd separated and she'd guessed he had someone to go to, her concerns about money had smothered her feelings of anger and rejection, so there was some satisfaction in sitting on a love-rumpled bed in a luxurious house in the French Quarter. She punched in the number again and gave a cheery "This is Bonnie Duke. To whom am I speaking?" as the phone was picked up at the other end.

"Mama, it's me," Gervaise answered. "I was worried about you 'cause you said you'd call last night."

"Sorry, darlin'. I just got occupied, and it was too late when we got back to the house."

"I hear New Orleans is a wild place. Hope you and your friend aren't pickin' up sailors."

She laughed. "So far I've restrained myself." When she'd told Gervaise that she was spending the holiday with a friend, Gervaise had just assumed it was a woman friend, and she hadn't bothered to correct her.

"Well, cut loose, Mama. You deserve some fun."

"I'm having a fine time." Gervaise was always telling her that it was a pity she'd "missed" the sixties, and she wondered, glancing upward, what Gervaise's reaction would be if she told her she was sitting under Jimi Hendrix's lavender bell-bottoms. "What about you? You enjoying yourself?"

"I'm OK—just . . . I know I'm too old to feel this way . . . but I miss the family."

"Have you opened the gift I sent you yet?"

"Not yet."

"That shows uncharacteristic restraint. You were always the one who wanted to open gifts on Christmas Eve." She felt tears come to her eyes. "I'm sorry we can't be together. But I'm thinking of you. So tell me how you're doing."

As Gervaise talked, Riz came in dressed in a fresh shirt, Jockey shorts, and socks. He was holding something behind his back. Sitting down beside her, he started to run his hand up and down her leg. She cupped her hand over the mouthpiece and whispered, "Riz, please!," then apologized to Gervaise, saying, "Sorry, I didn't catch the last thing you said." Gervaise kept talking. Riz kept rubbing her leg. "Stop it!" she mouthed, struggling as he pushed her back on to the bed. "Yes," she panted when Gervaise gave her a chance to sign off, "it might be better to talk later. I'll call you soon's I get back to Florabama . . . I miss you too, darlin'. Good-bye. Merry Christmas."

Hanging up, she glared at him, but he put on such a hangdog expression that she couldn't help but smile. "OK, OK," she said, "I'll dress. I'll just run a brush through my hair, and then we'll go eat."

"But first . . ." He brought his hand around and presented her with a small aqua-colored Tiffany box. "I was going to wait until tomorrow, but you've been such a good kid I've decided Santa can come ahead of time."

She slipped off the ribbon, catching her lower lip in her teeth, ashamed that she hadn't thought to get anything for him. It was a gold bracelet with a tiny Christmas tree charm. "So you won't forget this Christmas," he said, taking it from her and hooking it around her wrist.

"I'll never forget this Christmas. It's the biggest surprise I've had since . . . since I got my first bike."

Two days later, firmly buckled into her seat, totally exhausted but wired from three cups of wake-up coffee, Bonnie prayed no last-minute passenger would claim the vacant seats on either side. The flight attendant announced they were preparing for takeoff, but she felt she was returning to earth instead of leaving it. What a weekend.

It had been the honeymoon without the rush and crush of the wedding. They'd dined in the best restaurants, gone to jazz and Dixieland
clubs, walked by the riverfront in the moonlight. But mostly they'd
stayed in bed. Crossing and uncrossing her legs, she could still feel
him.

The plane backed onto the runway. Folding her hands in her lap,
she looked down at the bracelet. It was a sweet and generous gift,
even though he'd annoyed her just before he'd given it to her. It almost seemed as though he couldn't bear to share her attention with
anyone else, even her children. And there was his drinking. Not that
it showed. There was no sloppiness, no ill humor, no slurring of
words. She'd have to count the drinks or check the level of the bottle
to know how much he'd had, which she wasn't about to do. Devoe
had never been much of a drinker, but when he drank, it spoiled his
performance. Riz was consistently vigorous and more than uninhib-
ited, artful. Being a good lover was obviously a point of pride for him.
He always made sure that he satisfied her first. And satisfied she was.
If not in love, then in lust, and how did you tell the difference? "I can
be happy, I can be sad . . ." The words kept going through her mind
like a commercial jingle. "I can be good, I can be bad . . ." She looked
out the window, saw Lake Pontchartrain below, unbuckled herself,
put up the seat dividers, and lay down, putting her purse beneath her
head for a pillow. "It all depends on you."

Chapter XIV

*I*t was almost midnight. The last customers, a thirtysomething couple having a dreary and argumentative conversation about their "relationship," were lingering over their third cup of coffee. Hilly, sitting at a back table, refilling salt and pepper shakers, muttered, "Damn stragglers," under her breath. If they'd been truckers, she would've told them that if they couldn't read the sign that said CLOSING TIME—11 P.M., then they shouldn't be driving. The truckers liked it when she sassed them. One even said he came by regularly because she nagged him so much he felt like he was at home.

The couple wore the jeans and denim shirts that in her girlhood had been authentic working-class gear, but she knew that the closest they'd come to a truck was when their BMW was stalled in traffic. Still, she'd acted friendly when she handed them the menus because she wanted them to order the Red Snapper à la Veracruz. Jess, out of culinary pride, persisted in making one authentic dish every night, though most customers still ordered the enchilada, taco, or burrito combos, which, she'd pointed out to Jess, provided a bigger profit. During the three months she'd worked here she'd gone from dubious ("You're putting chocolate in a chicken sauce?") to curious ("So this stuff is called cilantro?") to smug ("If people were more adventurous, they'd discover all kinds of good things"), and now she wholeheartedly recommended the special dishes, not only because they were delicious but because it gave Jess a lift when the customers ordered them. Not that anything was going to give Jess a lift tonight. Not af-ter what had happened with Manuel.

At her suggestion, the couple had ordered the snapper, but after they'd finished it and she'd removed their plates, refilled their coffee cups, and put down the check, they'd stayed, oblivious of the fact that the place was emptying. Twenty minutes after that, when she'd wiped down all the tables, the man had held up his cup, signaling for another refill. Pouring, she'd thought, I hope your bladder bursts. And now, at eleven-forty, they were still sitting there like a couple of orphans on the steps of a foundling home. She got up and switched off the cassette of Johnny Cash wailing "I Walk the Line." She knew the couple was aware of her but in the way officers were aware of grunts: She was invisible until they wanted to give her an order. And it wasn't as though they'd pay for her time by leaving a big tip. They wouldn't stiff her because it would go against their self-image, but if they sat there till dawn, they'd leave 10 percent right down to the penny. Damn, she hated rich people!

The man pushed back his chair just as Jess walked through the dining room on his way upstairs to check on the kids. The woman fol-lowed Jess with her eyes, hungry-looking as any chick still warming a Tailgate barstool at closing time. If he'd walked any closer, she prob-ably would have reached out and pinched his butt. Funny, Hilly thought, that seeing Jess through other women's eyes had made her realize how attractive he was. She'd never gone for foreign types, but the first time Ruth had come by the restaurant she'd kidded her about working overtime, and when she'd asked if Ruth thought Jess was good-looking, Ruth, borrowing one of her lines, had said, "Only from his hairline to his toes."

She swallowed her pride and made herself smile as she followed the couple to the cash register. The man looked sour when he saw the SORRY, NO CREDIT CARDS sign. "We're gonna get our card machine real soon," she told them. "We're doin' good business now, but we started out as a grass-roots operation." The woman looked amused as she took her hundred-dollar wallet from her three-hundred-dollar purse and said, "It's always a hoot to find a place with a little character." Then, looking up the stairs as though hoping that Jess would reappear, she added, "Tell your chef his snapper was great. We'll be back. And"—she tossed three tens onto the counter—"you can keep the change." The check was for $27.50, so the tip didn't quite come to 10 percent. Hilly didn't bother to pick up the bills but led them to the door, locked it as soon as they'd walked through it, and cut off the outside lights.

Back at the cash register she got out the calculator, toted up the night's receipts, and put the money from the cash drawer into the bank bag. Putting her hands in the small of her back and twisting her head from side to side, she made her way through the dining room, switching off the lights and the overhead fan. She was too pooped even to think about clearing away the couple's coffee cups or sweeping the floor. Manuel usually swept the floors and bused the dishes. But now Manuel was gone.

She'd known he was gone as soon as she'd stepped onto the back porch that afternoon. The air mattress had been deflated and rolled up on the army cot, the blankets and sheet folded, and his possessions (backpack, transistor radio, road atlas, scout knife, a photo of his mother and another of Christie Brinkley in a pink bikini) were nowhere to be seen. As she'd walked into the kitchen, Jess, busy chopping vegetables, said, "Yes, he's gone," without looking up.

Not knowing what to say, she'd taken off her raincoat, stashed her purse, and reached for her apron before asking, "For good?"

Jess stopped, staring down at his hands, and in a voice so soft it sounded threatening, said, "How can it be good to be forced to leave an' don' know where you're going?"

She didn't know how to phrase her next question and didn't really expect him to answer. Though he was completely open about business, when it came to his private life, Jess Aranda was as close-mouthed as those faces carved into Mount Rushmore. At the beginning, when business had been so slow that they'd played dominoes or she'd taught him a few line dancing steps, he'd shied aware from personal questions. But even now that they were friendly, she didn't know much more about him than she'd learned on that first day. Didn't know where the kids' mother was, though she'd conjectured endlessly about that, or what Manuel was doing there, though she thought she'd figured that out. Fluffing the ruffles on the new red blouse she'd made, she'd sat down to change into her work shoes and looked over, watching his hands as she often did. They were too broad to be considered beautiful, but they handled tools with a mesmerizing power and precision. She'd seen him measure and cut wood with the same ease she'd had with the cutting machine at Cherished Lady. He hammered with the speed of a Gatling gun without ever hitting his thumb, cut down the tall grass at the back of the house with rhythmic slices of his machete. He could fix cars, broken pipes, or faulty wiring. But when he played his little squeeze box accordion or put garnish on a dish, his hands had an almost feminine delicacy. Just now they were chopping and slicing with great speed, making celery, carrots, and onions into uniform pieces, a few bits falling to the floor because of the angry thwack of the knife. Wanting to comfort but not knowing how, she blurted, "Did he take anything?"

The minute the words came out of her mouth she was sorry. Why had she said such a dumb thing? There was no reason to suspect Manuel. He was a good kid, and she liked and trusted him. Sure, he was a little shy and tentative, but that only came out of his desire to please. "I just meant . . ." She stumbled on as Jess looked up, his eyes black and expressionless as olives. Oh, shit! she'd insulted him. She'd made everything worse. "I only asked because . . ." She'd heard the front door open, followed by a cacophony of whoops and shouts. "Customers already," she said, shaking her head, shoving her order book into her apron pocket. "An' it sounds like those high school boys who've been comin' in every Friday night. Never order more'n rice and beans and never leave a tip. Last week they used up half a jar of chili peppers. Smeared 'em all over their mouths, saying they wanted to have hot lips for their dates. Woulda gone through the whole jar," she rattled on, "if I hadn't told 'em chilies give you acne." Jess had turned his back on her, pouring oil into a frying pan, tossing in the vegetables. "Well," she'd said, pushing open the door to the dining room, "I'd best get crackin'."

Business had been steady, and without Manuel's help they'd both been run off their feet. Except for hurried exchanges about orders they'd barely spoken, and when he walked through the dining room on his way upstairs to check on the kids, he hadn't even looked at her, so she guessed he was still mad at her.

She looked around the kitchen. The old dishwasher was grunting through the rinse cycle, pots and pans had been scoured and hung up, the stove and prep space were wiped clean, the floor had been swept, the knives sharpened. She didn't think Jess had ever been in the military, but he tackled everything with military exactness, always having an order of battle, always cleaning up as he went along. Reaching into a drawer to get the paper tubes she rolled coins in, she moved to the back door. Jess was sure taking a long time getting Hermina settled down. Then again, the kid was always a problem, a regular little Mata Hari, always spying, never wanting to go to sleep in case she missed something. Way after ten o'clock tonight, when Hilly'd gone to the cash register, she'd glimpsed her sitting at the top of the stairs, her yellow nightdress with the glow-in-the-dark Snoopy on the yoke tucked between her matchstick legs, her eyes bright with curiosity and hostility.

She stepped out, not bothering to turn on the porch light but careful not to let the door slam. The only illumination spilled from the kitchen, but she could see enough to count her tips. Sitting down at the picnic table they'd bought from the Goodwill, she reached into her apron pockets, tossed bills and coins on the table, and eased off her shoes. Oh, Lord, her feet ached! Not to mention her legs, which she knew, even though she wore support hose (at eight bucks a pair), had sprouted enough varicose veins to look like a road map. She emptied her pockets onto the table and took a deep breath of the moist air. The herbs and citronella Jess had planted almost masked the smell of exhaust from the highway and, to her mind, the not unpleasant whiff of cow dung that came from surrounding fields. She felt sure it was going to rain again, so she wanted to hurry, tally up, and say good-night before it started. Pushing crumpled bills to one side, she sorted out the coins, shoving pennies (what kinda jerks left pennies!) to one side for JoJo's piggy bank, making piles of nickels, dimes, and quarters. Her hands felt dirty, so she reached into her pocket, unwrapped a Handi Wipes, and cleaned them, humming "Blue moon, you saw me standing alone . . ." thinking that people who had big money rarely touched or saw it. They used "plastic," transferred it via wire services, had it "laundered" in foreign countries, knowing that the government couldn't or wouldn't catch them.

She heard Jess calling, "Hee-lee?" in that soft way that made her name sound pretty. She called back, "Out here," and listened as he went to the refrigerator. He came onto the porch, put two open bottles of *cervesa* on the table, moved up a wooden box so both of them could use it as a footstool, then sat down. "Good night?" he asked.

"Shush. I'll lose count. Thirty-one, thirty-two"—she could feel him looking at her and was glad the spill of light from the kitchen was dim—"thirty-four, thirty-five dollars. . . . and fifty cents. Yeah. I'll be able to make the car payment and send a little something to my old auntie in Texarkana." She leaned back, asking, "Kids finally off to sleep?"

He nodded and took a swallow of his beer. "Hermina, she don't like to sleep when we're still up. 'Fraid she'll miss somesing."

"Yeah, she's a handful. I can't seem to make any headway with her. It still sets me back when someone doesn't like me."

"Is not you. Hermina is mistrustful by nature. Her mother's nature. Or maybe"—he took another swallow—"she don' like you because you the only woman to come 'round that I like."

She wasn't prepared for that. "Yeah. Well."

"An' tonight she sad because Manuel is gone."

"I'm sorry too. And I know you are. I mean, apart from the fact that we'll have to see about getting more help, you know, I really liked him, and"—she rolled on like a car that had lost its brakes on a downhill slope—"I'm sorry I said that about him stealin' things. I didn't mean no racial, ethnic, wadda you call it, slur. I mean, I liked Manuel. An' if he did take anything—"

"He din't."

"I took my cutting glove from Cherished Lady, and I tucked a bustier into my purse when I picked up my last paycheck. But that was only because I was so mad at them for screwin' us over. Otherwise I never took anything. Not in all the years I was there."

"What's a bustier?"

"It's a corset-type thing. You know. It has stays comin' up the sides and push-up cups that—" She started to demonstrate, squeezing in her waist, running her hands up her rib cage and under her breasts, but when she felt his eyes on her, she dropped her hands into her lap, saying, "About Manuel. He's in trouble 'cause he's illegal, right?" She took a swig of her beer and waited, feeling him weigh how much he would tell her, then encouraged him: "Hey, I'm sorta illegal myself, being paid under the table and all."

"I don' like to break the law. I respect the law. But sometime—"

"The law is for rich people, and hey, you gotta do what you gotta do." She helped him out.

Jess set his bottle on the table and crossed his arms over his chest. "Chur. Manuel, he is illegal. He give all his money to the *coyote* who bring him across the border. He come with no'sing. He work in Texas, then California, then someone we know in, in—" He struggled for the words.

"In common," she provided.

"Yes. Someone we know in common tell him how to find me, say maybe I help him." He paused.

"If you don't help your own, who you gonna help?" She said, stripping the label from the bottle with her thumb nail.

"Hee-lee, don' do that, you spoil your fingernails." Another pause, a breath, a decision. "Yesterday we get a call from someone say *la migra* is making a sweep. I don' want Manuel to go, but I tell him to go. Because I must think of my children. So I give him some money and . . ." He gave a dejected shrug, pulled himself up from his chair, walked to the screen door, and stood staring out. The conversation and the quiet that comes before a storm created a palpable tension.

Hilly stripped the last shreds of the label, wadded them into a ball, and asked, "You're not illegal, are you?"

"No. I am not illegal. I am a naturalized citizen almost eight years. I study the Constitution and the laws. 'We hold these truths to be self-evident, that all men'—now women too—'are created equal.' But like you say, money make things unequal."

"That's the same all over the world," she said in a spurt of patriotic defensiveness.

"Chur. Is worse in most ozer countries."

"And you came here to make money, right?" she challenged him, but then, in a sudden reversal, said: "But I know it's tough here too. There's more money in the hands of a few rich people than there was just before the big crash. We're on our way to havin' us an oligarchy"—she'd learned the word just last week for a vocabulary test— "just like you have in South America."

"Mexico is in Central America."

"Whatever."

"Is to be a global economy now. Very big changes. All people who do not have money or education, not matter where they live, they will be . . ."

"Screwed?" she supplied.

"The girls who will work in your company's factories in Mexico will have it more worse than you did." She considered this glumly as he rallied to say, "I want only to make enough money to give my children an education, enough money to give me dignity."

"And how much would that be?" she asked sarcastically.

He sighed and shook his head, then turned, his tone reverting to its usual politeness, saying, *"Más?"*

She knew *más* meant "more" and asked, "How much more?"

He shook his head at the misunderstanding. "No. I mean, would you like another *cerveza*?"

"I'd like somethin' stronger. You got a bottle of tequila in there, don't you? Maybe you should break that out. Then again, it looks like rain and I gotta drive home, Jesus. Jesus is your real name, i'n't it?"

He laughed, his teeth white in the dim light. "Yes. But is pronounced Hey-sus, an' I don' kept this name because I don' want people to think I have special powers."

"I sure as hell wish you did. Maybe you do. You never tell me anything." Damn! She sounded like a complaining wife.

Returning to his chair and pulling it closer to hers, he asked, "But you, Hee-lee, you don' tell me about yourself either."

"Such as?"

"Such as, where your people are from, where you born."

She studied her feet, which looked inordinately large propped up on the box, and reached down to massage the toe on her right foot that had started to turn sideways, crowding the others into a string of tiny sausages. "I can't separate what's true from what's a story, but I heard my great-great-granddaddy came over from Ireland to work in the coal mines. He was in the Molly Maguires. That was a group of workers who raised hell with the bosses. Seems he got hisself shot an' left his wife with five orphan kids, an' she lit out for Texas. My mama was from Texas, but she moved to West Virginia when she married my daddy. Then she went back to visit her folks in Lubbock when she was 'bout seven months along with me. She went into labor just when a twister was 'bout to touch down, an' they tried to get her to the hos-

pital, but they didn't make it. I was born in the backseat of an automobile, and I've loved cars ever since."

"Your mother, she was a wild woman?"

"Naw. Only hell my mama ever raised was me. My daddy was the
scorcher. An' how about you? How the hell did you land up here?"

"Is a long story."

She wasn't going to let him off the hook. "I got time," she said,
leaning back and lifting the hair from her neck. The wind picked up,
rustling the branches of the lone tree in the yard and making her
shiver. She knew she couldn't prod him, so she waited, feeling him
weigh whether or not to confide in her. He slapped his thighs, got up,
and went to the kitchen. She heard him reaching into the cabinet for
the tequila bottle and a couple of shot glasses. He came out, stopping
the door from slamming with an easy movement of his hip, set the
glasses on the table, filled both, then, touching his to hers, said, "*Viva
la revolución?*" with a sardonic smile. "Your ancestor was the Molly
whatchusay?"

"The Molly Maguires."

"My great-grandfather rode with Zapata."

She'd seen a movie starring Marlon Brando as Zapata when she
was a kid, and she remembered it had made her cry. "But you were
about to tell me about you."

He knocked back the shot as though it were his last before facing
a firing squad and sat down. Resting his elbows on his spread knees,
opening his hands, then bringing them together, fingertips touching,
looking straight ahead, he began, "I come to the United States first
time when I am only sixteen. My uncle Raymundo worked the crops,
an' he bring me over with him. I pick citrus in Arizona and California,
potatoes in Idaho, tomatoes in South Carolina. I would say I see more
of your country than you, but maybe"—he shrugged off his boast—
"maybe I don't see no'sing. Workers' camps are all alike. You ever see
one?" She shook her head. "The camps, the people in the camps,
they all around, but Americans never see, like they—we—invisible."

"Yeah. I know about invisible."

"I am so sad at first. I miss my village very much. Is near Michoacán. I send money to my mother for my brothers and sisters. Sometimes I go back to my home after harvest. Is very hard because everyone expect presents, so money is soon gone. One time I stay because my mother, she is very sick. Not many men are living in my village because there is no work. They go to America, and they leave their wives and children. The wives get lonely. Is only human nature." He took another pull on the bottle, then spoke more softly. "I am shamed to say I put the horns on many men. When I am thinking it is time to marry and plant my seed, I do not do it because I know—because of what I do—that I cannot trust a woman to marry and leave her alone. I think also it is wrong to have children if the man cannot provide."

Hilly grunted agreement, holding out her shot glass. "And then?"

"My mother, she die." He refilled their glasses, then chuckled. "And also I must tell you, at my mother's funeral one husband is threaten to shoot me. So. I come back to the United States. I am maybe twenty-four years then. I pick the crops some more, but I want a better kind of work. I go to the labor exchange in Ventura in California. I find work—illegal, but work. I put up fences and dig trenches; I make houses and paint; I fix cars; I am a gardener in a place for old people. But sometime there is no work. Sometime I work, but there is no pay. Sometime *la migra* is hunting. And then I must go to live in a canyon near San Diego. I don' know for chur where I am. I have only a compass I buy in the store, a compass like children have in school, but Hermina tell me they don' have no compass or geography maps in American schools, maybe because America think it is the center of the world?" He poured himself another shot, then went on. "North, south, east, west. Still in my heart I am lost. Hiding out in the canyon near San Diego was the worst I been. We have only shacks made of tar paper, scraps of tin, a cover stolen from a swimming pool to put over our heads when it rain. We eat only things from cans, and I grow skinny like an old man. *Coyotes* bring people across the border to the camp. These women, they are desperate. A drink of pulque and maybe two dollar they put down cardboard on the ground and let the men . . . And fights, many fights with knives." He shook his head once, violently, as though to rid himself of the memory, then tilted up his chin and leaned back in the chair, eyes on the ceiling.

So that's where he got the scar, she thought. Or maybe it was from one of those irate husbands. "And what happened then?"

"I get out. I go to Los Angeles. Many are dealing drugs. Many in gangs. But very easy to hide. One day—this is true!—I am hitchhiking to a construction job, and who pick me up? My uncle Raymundo. He is working for a restaurant in a place call Silverlake near downtown Los Angeles. He tell me he can get me a job as dishwasher. I think this will be a gringo restaurant, but it is owned by second-generation Mexicans. American citizens. The husband run the restaurant; the wife work in an airplane factory. They have a nice house." A hesitation. "They have a daughter." This last was said with a downward inflection, as though it put an end to the story; then he went on. "I graduate from dishwasher to cook. Men are the best cooks." Having no claim to culinary skills, she let that one go by. "I learn better English. I go always to the supermarket to read labels. I go to the library. I begin to save money. In my village, women make food, but from the time I am small I also learn to season and stir the pot when my mother is sick."

She knew he was rambling so he could avoid the real issue, which clearly had something to do with the restaurant owner's daughter. "But you were still illegal, right?"

"*Sí*, but the family protect me. I live in a bathhouse nex' to their swimming pool. Nobody see me. I don' go nowhere. I work only and save money. I cook, six day a week, not only tacos. I make Pate Cichoacano, Paella Valenciana. The *Los Angeles Times* magazine says the food is good and make more customers come." Another silence.

Still, she knew he really wanted to unburden himself. He'd broken through the barrier, and that meant he wanted to confide, maybe even confess. He was a Catholic after all. Every Sunday morning he put on a suit and tie and dressed Hermina in one of those frilly Kmart party dresses and put JoJo into a little man's suit and drove off to mass at St. Elizabeth's, coming back with a photocopy of "Parish Happenings" that he liked to read aloud. She supposed he also went to confession, but she tried to be broad-minded about it. At least he confessed to a priest in a little booth instead of blabbing his sins on national TV, as everyone from the president of the United States to the trash on the *Jerry Springer Show* did. Jess didn't have a real friend to confide in, like she had Ruthie, and it was cut-your-wrists lonely not to have another human being who knew the worst about you but loved you anyway. "So what about the daughter?"

"Sylvia." He pronounced the name flatly but with unmistakable significance. "She was a kid only when I first work for her parents. I din't much notice her. Then, like overnight, she was sixteen, woman beautiful and wild. I like the wildness in a woman, but in Sylvia it is not a good wildness. She is so"—again his hands groped, trying to find the words—"Americanized. Her parents cannot control her. She wear short skirts and get a tattoo. Like a street puppy, she run with gangs. She flirt with me, but she flirt with all men so she can feel her power. It is not good to love a young woman. You forgive her many things because she is good to look at. You cannot see beyond her beauty to see into her soul."

"Uh-huh," she agreed nonchalantly, thinking about her first husband; she'd been seventeen to J.K.'s forty. She'd been attracted to him because he'd had a car dealership; he'd been attracted to her because she'd had great legs and a bosom so new she couldn't hold a pencil under its droop. She was damned sure J.K. had never wanted to see into her soul. Rich had been the only one who'd ever cared about her in that way.

"I love her," Jess said, his tone simple, deep, and hopeless. He looked at her now, just when she didn't want him to. She didn't know how jealousy affected other women, but it always hit her in the gut. She hadn't experienced sexual jealousy since Rich had gone off to Nam, and the fact that she suddenly felt queasy forced her to admit what she hadn't wanted to: Somehow she'd fallen for a greaser with two kids.

"So?" she asked, thinking Jess was so involved in his story that he wouldn't notice her discomfort.

He asked, "You feelin' OK? You look cold. You want I bring your raincoat?"

"No. I'm OK. Go on."

"She become pregnant." He shook his head. "Not by me. By her boyfriend. One of her boyfriends." He shrugged. "This boyfriend, he say the baby is not his and leave town when Sylvia's father come after him. The mother is angry. She say maybe Sylvia should not have this baby, but Sylvia say she do. So her father say if I will marry her. I think on this for a long time, because I do not think I can be a good father to another man's child. But when Sylvia cry, she make me weak. Also, I tell you the truth, am thinking that if I marry her, I will be part of this family. I will have a beautiful girl who is American citizen. I will become a citizen. I tell myself it is—how you say?—a chance of a lifetime? And I think she will—"

"Settle down?" Hilly supplied, pouring herself another shot.

"Yes. I think Sylvia will settle down. She tell me she love me. She lie to the priest and marry me in a dress white like cake icing. Since I am a small boy, I have never been so happy. I think—I thought—God is going to grant me a good life. Does it matter she make a mistake with a crazy gang boy? With love all things can be good again. So. We marry. I become a citizen." Suddenly he sounded very old, as though the events he was describing had taken place not seven or eight years but an entire lifetime ago. "Even in the beginning," he went on, "I think maybe Sylvia do drugs. But she tell me no. And I must believe her. Love must have trust, so I believe. She get pregnant with JoJo, but she don't want to have him. Maybe you think I am wrong in this, but I tell her she must have him because he is my child. When she is big with him, she seem OK, but after she have him, she is very sad."

"I heard that sometimes women get depressed after birth," Hilly ventured to say. "You know, a natural depression that . . ." Never having had a child herself, she backed off.

"To a girl so young"—Jess went on as though she hadn't spoken—"a baby is a doll. She dress him up; she play with him. But then she get bored with him. She want to go out. She don' want to feed him or change his diapers. She is gone from our home many times. I am a crazy man when she is gone, but I do not tell her mother and father. When she come home"—he shook his head—"many fights. I am holding my hands tight so not to hit her. Then one night I come home. JoJo is standing up holding on to the bars of his crib. He is crying and dirty. Hermina is watching the TV, wearing her underpants only and eating from a cereal box. And Sylvia is gone. Like that"—he snapped his fingers, then raised his hand to cover his eyes—"she is gone."

Hilly whispered, "I'm so sorry."

He shook his head. "When a woman is betrayed, she have the sympathy of her friends; when a man is betrayed, all people secretly think he is a fool."

"Aw, come on," she protested, though she knew there was a grain of truth in what he said. "Besides, when you've been deserted, it don't hardly matter what other people think."

"I know it don' matter, only I tell you to explain . . ."

"How bad you felt. Yeah, I understand."

"Her parents blame me. We get police, detectives, everything to find her. One time we trace her to San Francisco, but when I go there, it is a terrible place. A house where druggies live all together. And she is gone already. Her mother quit her job from the airplane factory to help with the kids, but then she get cancer. I take care of her till she die. Then Sylvia's father right away marry. I see he want to forget all his life before. Soon he will be a papa again. He don' want to be a grandpapa. But I remind him. My children remind him. Also, now, he is not so happy to think I take over the restaurant. So I see it is time for me to go. I must take my children and go. Begin again. I travel, looking for a good place . . ." His hand made circles. "Not many Mexicans here, but still is a good choice, no? An' you come work with me, an' we getting it, how you say? off the ground. But now Manuel." He shook his head again. "I cannot help him. I cannot let him stay."

"That's not your fault. You gave him some money, didn't you?"

"Yes. That I am saving for the new freezer and also to take Hermina to the dentist."

In other words, as she'd suspected, too much. "Damn. I wish I wasn't involved in this fancy dressmaking deal I told you about. If I hadn't reenrolled this semester, I could be here full-time."

"No, Hee-lee. Your education is important."

"Christ, Jess, I never cared about school. I'm too old to care about school."

"But Americans believe, and it is a good belief, that you never too old for education. I would go to college if I could."

Hilly tried to steer him back to business. "We got to find some help. I'll ask around and put up a notice on the bulletin board at the college. But you know there aren't too many kids who wanna bust their tails for minimum, no benefits." But she saw that he was too sad to talk about business.

"It was the drugs," he said quietly.

"I know," she commiserated. "I know about drugs. No matter how much you love someone, you can't fight their addiction."

He didn't say, "How do you know?," only "Who?"

"Rich." His name felt strange as a foreign word, yet familiar as saying "Mama" or "Papa." "He was addicted to heroin when he came back from Nam. He acted crazy, but I thought he was on doctor-type drugs because he was wounded so bad."

Jess turned to her and covered her hand with his. "Tell me, Heelee."

She shook her head. She'd done everything she could to get him to open up, but she didn't know how to talk about Rich. She'd never told anyone except Ruth, who hadn't needed telling because she'd been there. Jess's hand tightened over hers. "Rich was my husband," she began. "I fell in love with him first time I ever saw him." She gave a little laugh. "We got married in a quickie ceremony at the Austin county courthouse." Dressed in jeans, boots, and matching cowboy hats, looking raw and bleary-eyed from nonstop sex in a cheapie motel while waiting for the license to be approved, they'd thought of it as a wonderful joke. They hadn't needed God or the goddamn government to tell them they were joined forever; they were joined forever every time they made love. Strangely, their wedding night had been one of the few nights they hadn't made love. After the ceremony they'd taken their witness (a stranger who'd been at the courthouse to pay a speeding ticket) out to celebrate, and after much beer and barbecue, he hadn't wanted to go home. It'd been two in the morning before they'd pumped him full of coffee and loaded him into his car. Then they'd staggered back to the motel, laughing so hard their guts ached, and fallen asleep as soon as they'd hit the mattress. "Oh, how I loved that man!" she said. The words still cut deep. "He was the only man except my granddaddy that I loved full and true."

"Tell me," he urged again.

Once she started she knew she wouldn't, couldn't censor herself. "His hair was blond-white, like a baby's. An' he wore it long, shaggy like a lion's mane. I cried my eyes out when he came back from basic and it was all shaved off. I never thought you could get everything in one man, but Rich had it all. He was sexy and steady, wild and hardworking. He was quiet with most people, but when we were alone, we talked nonstop. We'd tell about our childhoods, which weren't so great, so mostly we talked 'bout our future. We were both so damned young and ignorant. We believed we could have work *and* fun, kids *and* freedom. We even got us a savings account, and we'd picked out this lil ol' house we wanted to buy an' fix up. Rich was like you in that regard. He could fix anything. But the money started to go once he was drafted. I was so miserable lonely without him! Would've died if Ruthie hadn't been there. And later, after he died, I really wanted to die too. I stockpiled pills an' all, but I was afraid they wouldn't work an' I'd end up like a vegetable. Even tried to drive my car into a tree once, but I was too chicken to do it. See, even when I found out he was an addict, I thought I could turn it 'round because I loved him so much. I thought . . . oh, Christ, I was so dumb." She leaned forward, arms on the table, head bowed, breathing hard.

"When Sylvia leave me, I think of death," he told her. "But I know I cannot do it, because of the children."

Great, wracking sobs came out of her. She couldn't bring herself to say that she'd been pregnant and had decided to have an abortion. No man, however sympathetic, could understand what she'd been through.

He rose to stand behind her and put his arms around her, whispering, "Oh, Hee-lee. I am very much sorry this happen to you." She desperately wanted to give way to the comfort of his embrace, but part of her felt that if she yielded, it would weaken her. Straightening, she pushed him away, wiped the tears from her cheeks, insisted, "Hey, I'm OK," and, looking at the empty bottle, asked, "Don't you have some more booze in the cabinet?"

"Chur, I have it, an' I get it if you want. But it don' do no good. It don' make the pain go away. It only smother it; then you feel sick in the morning."

"I don't give a shit about the morning!" she said angrily.

His voice was soft. "C'mon, Hee-lee. You come sleep in my bed."

"What?" She was instantly stiff-backed and riled. "You think because I—"

"No. When I say sleep in my bed, I don' mean you have to—" He gave a little laugh. "Americans say 'have sex,' but I don' think sex is somesing you have, like an ice cream. Is more than that."

"Hey, I know it's not an ice cream," she snapped, even though she'd sat in bars as though she were at Baskin-Robbins, looking at men and wondering which flavor she'd pick.

"Hee-lee, whassa matter? Hee-lee?"

"It's just that—" Tears streamed down her cheeks, running more freely as she tried to fight them back. "It's just that . . . oh, I dunno. I . . . my feet are so damned tired." She sobbed as though all her misery had concentrated itself there. He moved to kneel in front of her. "Hey, whatcha doing?" she demanded as he slipped off her knee-highs. But as he kneaded her soles with strong thumbs, and pulled on each toe as though he were playing this little piggy, she started to laugh.

"You are tired. You need to sleep," he said in a gentle voice. "You sleep here. Tomorrow is not a school day. An' I don' think you should be driving."

"Yes. I mean no. But I gotta get home. Gotta feed Garbage and the chickens, and I gotta go to this damn sewing session . . . but I guess . . . The rain was heavy; she was tired beyond tired and more than a little drunk. She might as well stay. He seemed to sense the minute she made up her mind, taking her by the elbows and helping her up from the chair.

"I get you up early," he assured her, guiding her through the kitchen and dining room and up the stairs, switching off lights as they went.

As he opened the door to his room, she saw the white expanse of the bed and rain streaming down the pane of the window next to it. He helped her to the bed and threw back the covers before easing her down so that her head nestled in a heap of pillows smelling of Tide and hair tonic. "You sleep now, Hee-lee" he said, pulling blankets up to her chin. The whites of his eyes and his teeth shone in the dark as he bent to smooth back her hair and plant a kiss, innocent as one he might give to JoJo, on her forehead. But when he started to move away, she grabbed at him. He reached for her hand and kissed it, but she pulled it away, flinging back the covers to welcome him, reaching for him again, slithering her hand across his hipbone to seize the bulge in his jeans. His hand covered hers, pressed it to him hard, then pushed it aside. He started to unzip himself. She lifted her blouse over her head, reached to unhook her bra, yanked it free, then lay back ready, more than ready, wet and impatient, scarcely able to believe her eyes when he stepped back, pressed his impressive erection to his belly, and struggled, at first unsuccessfully, to rezip himself.

"Hee-lee—"

She interrupted with an amazed "What are you doing?"

She could feel his body heat and hear his breathing as he tucked his shirt back into his jeans, passed his hand through his hair, then sat on the side of the bed. "Listen to me, Hee-lee"—he reached for her hands—"is not right now."

She threw her arms over her head, her eyes blazing in the dark, quick answers to what she imagined might be his objections bubbling out: She'd had a few drinks?—"I know what I'm doing"—the kids were in the next room?—"Lock the door." She was even ready to say she loved him, but she couldn't get the words out.

He took her by the wrists, holding them above her head, pressing them into the pillows, looming over her, his face inches from hers, the gold cross around his neck swaying. In a barely audible but determined voice he said, "Hee-lee, is not right now."

Her sense of rejection, even shame—that she should offer herself so completely and be turned down—came up like bile and scalded her throat. "Are you some kinda religious nut? How dare you? How dare you!"

He wiped tears she didn't know were there from her eyes. "Sleep, Hee-lee. Sleep now. I see you in the morning." Then he got up and went to the door. He closed it behind him as she swiveled around to the window and drew her knees up to her chest.

Sometime later the rain stopped, and she woke. The moon was hiding behind a bank of clouds. Her skirt and petticoats were bunched around her legs. She tussled and squirmed out of them, tossing them to the floor as she realized where she was. Oh, shit! The underwire from her bra was poking into her armpit, and she tossed that too, trying to reconstruct what had happened. What had he said just before he'd closed the door? Something about dancing? No, that couldn't be right. And before that? She must look pretty damned seedy if a man rejected her when they were that close to it. Why had she made such a fool of herself? She'd never be able to face him again. She should get up right now and sneak out. But her body felt like lead. In just a few minutes she'd get up and leave. In just a few minutes . . .

"How come you slept here?"

Hilly's hands came up reflexively to shield her eyes, then, realizing it was sound she was trying to block out, went to her ears. Oh, Christ! she thought. I'm not ready for this.

"How come you slept here, Miss Hilly?" Hermina asked again. Hilly drew up the covers and squinted at her. She was dressed in her yellow nightdress with Snoopy on the yoke, but her face was as coldly disapproving as a highway patrolman who'd clocked her doing ninety in a forty-five-mile zone.

"She get sleepy," JoJo explained, crawling up onto the bed. "Papa tell her a story, so she go to sleep."

Some story, Hilly thought, blinking against the wickedly bright morning sunlight, croaking, "Where is your papa?"

"Papa sleep in my bed. He make the noise like a pig," JoJo told her, then proceeded to make disgustingly accurate snorting noises. "He wake me up, so I go into Hermina's bed."

"You're the one who grunts like a pig, not Papa." Hermina gave him a push.

Indomitable, JoJo giggled and crawled toward Hilly, telling her, "Papa make coffee for you."

Hermina's eyes went to the mess of clothes on the floor. "How come you don't hang up your clothes like you're s'posed to?"

"You know that goat called Garbage?" JoJo asked. "Papa say maybe you take us to see him."

"And you got chickens too?" Hermina asked, curiosity thawing her expression before she looked back at the heap of clothes, focusing on the bra.

"Yeah, I got chickens." Hilly used the nails of her index fingers to scrape mascara from beneath her eyes, propped herself up, carefully covering her breasts with the sheet, and said, "I got chickens and a goat called Garbage."

"How come you give your goat such a mean name?" Hermina demanded.

"It's not a mean name; it's a true name 'cause he eats everything, even garbage."

JoJo, who'd worked his way into the curl of Hilly's arm and was puddling his fingers in the hollows of her neck, whispered, "Manuel runned away."

"I heard you, JoJo." Hermina was furious. "That's a secret. You're not supposed to tell. I'm going to tell Papa you told!"

Hilly stared her in the eye. "I already know Manuel is gone. I come here 'most every day, so I had to notice, didn't I?" Seeing that Hermina was more confused than mollified, she added, "And I know it's a secret. And I promise I won't tell anyone."

"Swear you won't tell," Hermina insisted. When Hilly raised her hand, crossed her heart, and solemnly swore, Hermina confided, "Is *la migra*. Papa got a phone call. You know about *la migra?*"

"Yes, I know about them."

"But you're an Anglo."

"Yes. But I work here, and I care about you and your papa, and Manuel too, so I know." She decided to take a chance, reaching out, circling Hermina's waist, and pulling her closer. "I know how much you must miss him, but I think he's going to be all right." Hermina nodded. Her lower lip pushed out, but her eyes stayed on Hilly's, sizing her up, loath to give an inch. "You're a smart little girl," Hilly told her. "You're right not to trust everyone, but you can trust me."

Hermina considered this. "You come to our house, but we never come to yours. When you gonna show us your house, Miss Hilly?"

"Sometime. I dunno. Listen, kids, I have to get dressed before your papa—" But he was at the door, holding two steaming cups of coffee.

"I'm sorry," he said, advancing to the bed. "They get up early, an' I cannot keep them out no longer." Hilly raised her hands to smooth the rat's nest tangle of her hair. "It look all right," Jess said. "Is like a sunrise."

"An' that lying Clairol bottle called it Sunset," she mumbled, relieved to see him smile.

"Kids . . ." Jess pointed to the door. "Get downstairs. Your pancakes is getting cold."

"Your pancakes *are* getting cold," Hermina corrected. "In English you say—"

Jess's eyes narrowed. "In English I say go eat. So go eat."

Hermina's glance went from Jess to Hilly, then settled on JoJo, who was still pawing Hilly's neck. If he'd been a kitten, he would have been purring. "He always wastes the syrup," she informed on him. "So you'd better come watch him, Papa."

"You in charge of the syrup, Hermina. Don't waste it. Now go." Jess pointed to the door again. From either parental intimidation or hunger, Hermina inched toward it, and JoJo, after giving Hilly's bare shoulder a resounding kiss, scrambled to the floor and followed. Like Lot's wife, Hermina couldn't resist a single backward glance at Sodom. She looked as though she might turn into a pillar of salt, but

Jess assured her, "We coming soon," and JoJo pulled her into the hallway and slammed the door.

Clutching the sheet to her breast, Hilly started to get out of bed, but Jess came and sat on the edge. "How you feelin'?"

"Like I don' know whether to kill myself or go bowlin'."

He handed her a cup of coffee. "Careful, is hot. If anything burn your lips, I want it to be me."

Smarting from last night's humiliation, she grumbled, "I'n't it a little early in the day for poetry?"

"Hee-lee, you don' understand about las' night."

"No, I don't. Isn't it usually the woman who changes her mind?" Embarrassed, she sipped her coffee, even though it *was* hot enough to burn her lips.

"Las' night we tell each other many things. Please do not be sorry. I am not sorry I tell you." He stared out the window, then went on. "I know many men have courted you." That, she thought, is a polite way of putting it. "But in my whole life I have never courted a woman. Before we—I mean, I like to court you. Maybe I can take you to go out, to go dancing."

"That," she said quietly, "would be very nice."

The Tailgate was the only local place to dance, and Monday was the only night the restaurant was closed, so they settled on the Tailgate for next Monday night. Jess said he'd ask a woman from St. Elizabeth's to baby-sit. He'd pick Hilly up at her place, at seven. Once they'd made the arrangements they acted as though nothing unusual had happened between them. It was the only way they could get through the week.

Chapter XV

*T*he next Monday Hilly managed to get to her morning classes, but knowing that the sewing group was in a crunch to finish up the order and she wouldn't be attending that night, she ditched her afternoon class, drove over to Albertine's, and cut out dresses before she went home. She fed the animals, cleaned the trailer, changed the sheets, and dyed her hair.

By six-thirty she was pacing her spotless living room in her freshly polished boots, surfing channels but barely looking at the TV. In her bedroom she checked herself in the full-length mirror behind the door and hated what she saw. Her makeup was all wrong. She'd used too much conditioner, and it had flattened her hair. She'd thought she looked sexy when she'd tucked her electric blue blouse (top buttons left undone to show cleavage) into jeans that fitted her cheeks like the skin on an apple, but now she decided she just looked trashy. She was wondering if she had time to change when the phone rang.

"Hee-lee, is me. The woman supposed to baby-sit just called to say she can't make it."

Her stomach turned. She swallowed a curse. "Well . . . gee . . . I guess we'll have to make it another night."

"I wonder is it bad manners to call your friend Ruth?"

"She's s'posed to go to the sewing circle tonight, but I'll call her and call you right back." She would plead with her; she would put a gun to her head.

Naturally she only had to ask for Ruth to say yes. She was momentarily relieved, but once she'd started driving to Ruth's house the heebie-jeebies came back with a vengeance. They'd wanted a real date, and this sure wasn't starting out like a real date. Why hadn't she changed her outfit? What if Hermina or JoJo acted up and wouldn't stay at a strange house? What if those rednecks at the Tailgate acted horsey because Jess was a Mexican? Worse yet, what if she ran into some guy she'd been with? Things never worked out the way you wanted. Like her mama always said, "Blessed is she who expecteth nothing, for she shall not encounter disappointment." Seeing Jess's truck parked out front, she jammed on the brakes as though she'd hit a red light. Calm down, she told herself, walking to Ruth's door with her "I could care less" swagger, this is no big deal. But a little voice said, "Liar." Lying to others was bad. Lying to yourself was downright dangerous. And the truth was that she felt her whole life depended on tonight.

She knocked, then opened the door. Kylie, Moo, and Jess's kids were sprawled on a blanket, munching popcorn and watching a video. Even Hermina barely looked up as she stepped in, but Jess, sitting on the couch between Ruth and Roxy, got up immediately, saying, "Hee-lee, you're here!" as though she'd just led the cavalry into a besieged fort. His hair was slicked back, his white shirt starched, his khaki slacks ironed, and the smile on his face could have melted ice.

"Hi, Hilly. Long time no see," Roxy drawled. She was dressed (or, more accurately, undressed) in a T-shirt and short-shorts, and when she uncrossed her legs, you could see all the way to China.

"It's almost eight o'clock, Roxy," Ruth reminded her. "Hadn't you best be changing clothes and getting on to the sewing group?"

"I guess." Roxy stretched, looking at Jess. "Though sittin' 'round workin' a needle with a bunch of old women isn't exactly my idea of a good time."

"Shush!" Kylie hissed without taking his eyes from the screen. "We're watchin' *Babe*."

"It's really good," Ruth said. "I've watched it three times myself." Then she lowered her voice: "Why don't you two make your getaway?"

Hilly hugged her, whispering, "I owe you one," and signaled Jess.

"Is a pleasure to meet you, Roxy," he said, then, making a bow in Ruth's direction, "*Muchas gracias,* Ruth. You are a good friend. Tomorrow a school day so we be back ten-thirty sharp."

"You s'pose you guys could give me a lift to Albertine's?" Roxy asked.

"We're goin' in the opposite direction," Hilly said, moving to the door.

Jess bent to say good-bye to the children, patting Hermina's shoulder, passing his hand over JoJo's head, and telling them to be good before thanking Ruth again.

"Your car or mine?" Hilly asked when they were outside.

Jess drew back, raising his eyebrows. "I theenk you give your heart before you give your car keys, Hee-lee," he said, taking her arm. "I will drive tonight."

As he opened the door of his truck and helped her in, she couldn't stop herself from asking, "So what'd you think of Roxy?"

"She is very pretty, but very *macho*. No, maybe I mean bold."

"She's got the balls of a brass monkey."

He laughed, but suddenly she was afraid that she was the one who sounded too bold. "'Course"—she blathered on—"it ain't Ruth's fault. Her husband, Freddie, was a real loser, an' if a kid's got bad genes, don't matter how you raise them."

"I theenk this is not always true," Jess said quietly, putting the truck into gear and pulling away from the curb.

"Sure it's true. Haven't you seen this stuff about genetic research on TV?"

"I see they make a sheep just like another sheep. Is cloning. But humans . . ." He shrugged. "Humans have a soul."

"Naw. It's like my mama always said: 'Bad blood will out.'" His face went stony. Had she put her foot in her mouth again? Did he think she was saying that Hermina was doomed because her mother had been a druggie? "Well, maybe it's not always true," she conceded, and decided that her only safety was in silence. "Mind if I turn on the radio?"

The Tailgate was big as a barn, with a flashing neon sign of a horse's swishing tail. As Jess pulled into the dirt parking and cut off the motor, she heard the throb of music and, not waiting for him to open her door, bounded out, saying, "Now we'll hear some live music!" But when he opened the door and she stepped in, she saw the bandstand was empty. Apart from the disappointment of canned music, the place was pretty much as she'd expected it to be on a Monday night. The smell was clean but somehow dank. Six or seven couples sat at little Formica tables surrounding the dance floor. Four or five guys hunched over the bar, heels locked on the rungs of the high stools, eyes fixed on the muted TV suspended over the rows of bottles, knocking back booze with joyless concentration. A blackboard proclaiming SOBER-UP SPECIALS! FRESHLY MICROWAVED FOR YOUR DINING PLEASURE with a chalk-written list of the usual offerings hung near a dim passageway with signs pointing left for STALLIONS and right for MARES posted above the arch. How, she wondered, had she ever been dumb and desperate enough to think she could have a good time in this hellhole?

Jimbo, the bartender, acknowledged her with "Yo, it's Mustang Sally. How you doin'? Haven't seen you in a spell."

"This here's my friend Jess Aranda," she said, hoping Jimbo would reach across the bar and shake Jess's hand, which he did.

"Damn musicians is late," Jimbo complained. "What'll you have?"

"Pitcher of beer OK?" she asked Jess, who nodded and felt for his wallet.

She reached over to take a couple of glasses from Jimbo's side of the bar and wandered to a table. Taking several napkins from the dispenser, she wiped it clean, appropriated a candle from another table, then sat, crossing both her arms and her legs.

"What he call you?" Jess asked.

"It's just a nickname 'cause I won a contest dancin' to a song called 'Mustang Sally.'"

"So, no live music." He poured their beers. "Maybe I should bring my squeeze box."

She couldn't even muster a smile. "They'll be here soon. 'Course we'll have to leave before the action gets started."

He took a long swallow, looking around the room over the rim of his glass, his eyes disdainful or maybe just disappointed. Pushing back his chair, he rose and offered his hand. "We come to dance, so we dance."

"The Tennessee Waltz" was playing. They were the only couple on the floor. He held her stiffly, his spine rigid, his fingers barely touching her back. "You ever see one of those big mirrored balls over a dance floor?" he asked. She shook her head. "I see one in the movies," he told her. "In our village we have movies in the school building. The movies is always old, sometime the projector break, but one time I see a movie, very beautiful couples dancing, a big mirror ball over them. It give little flecks of light everywhere, shine on the woman's face and hair to make her look pretty."

"Yeah, I seen those mirrored balls in the movies when I was a kid. Don't think they have 'em anymore." She sighed, glancing up at him. "Seems like all the beautiful things is gone." But he was here and he was beautiful. Maybe that was the wrong word to describe a man, but there seemed no other word for his Indian cheekbones and dark eyes.

"I tell you somesing about yourself maybe you don' know, Hee-lee." He drew into her, looking at her with adoring curiosity. "Everybody's face change when they have different emotion, but your face change more than anybody's. Most time is . . . I wish I could tell you in Spanish—"

"Go on, I'll get the gist of it."

"Like this"—he squeezed her hand so tightly it almost hurt—"sometime, like now"—he relaxed his grip, caressing her fingers and palm—"I see what you like when you a girl."

They danced closer, only peripherally aware when a crowd burst through the door and Jimbo yelled, "Hey, you sorry bastards, you're late!" A man carrying a guitar case cut across the dance floor, jumped up onto the dais, and raised hoots and a smattering of applause when he yelled back, "Little you pay us, you're lucky we come a'tall." The fiddler and banjo player joined the guitarist and began to unpack their instruments. Jess, his eyes never leaving Hilly's, led her back to their table as the gaggle who'd come in with the musicians bellied up to the bar, shouting drink orders, waving to folks at the tables. Jimbo ambled over and tested the sound equipment while the musicians tuned up. The guitar player leaned into the mike, challenging, "Y'all disabled? If y'are, we better find some liberal lawyer to come drag Jimbo into court for not havin' wheelchair access, but if yer not . . . Let's dance! And a one, and a two, and a three . . ."

With a yelp and a whoop, a couple sashayed onto the floor, holding out their arms. Another couple joined them, motioning for others to form a line. "It's fun," Hilly whispered. "Betcha can learn real quick. Want to?"

Jess shook his head. "I want to be alone with you." He got up. She followed him to the door, pretending not to hear when somebody called her name.

It was dark, the face of the full moon covered with clouds. Cool fresh air enveloped them. He breathed deeply, then asked, "We should call Ruth?"

She said, "No. She'll understand. She's probably already put the kids to bed."

Except for giving him directions, they rode in silence, both looking straight ahead.

As they walked to her trailer, the clouds drifted, and the moon shone full. He reached out to stop her, gathering her into his arms, looking up. "Is better than a mirrored ball, yes?" He kissed tenderly, then so hungrily that she staggered. Pulling away, he breathed, "It smell so good."

"Yeah, out here in the country . . ." she muttered stupidly.

"No, your scent."

He followed as she walked, weak-kneed, up the steps and unlocked the door. As soon as they were inside, he was up against her, pressing her into the wall. Almost sinking to the floor, she wrested free, took his hand, guided him through the dark into the bedroom. She felt her way to the bed and lay back, pulling him onto her. "Heelee, I love you," he whispered, and suddenly they were the only two people on the planet.

Chapter XVI

*I*t was a blustery Wednesday night in late March when Bonnie met with some of the women to put the finishing touches on the dresses. Albertine's dining room table became a miniassembly line. Vernette, Sue Ann, and Lorraine sewed on ribbons, hooks and eyes, and Emma & Flora labels. Puddin' (who'd designated herself "Quality Control") cut loose threads and inspected the garments. Ruth pressed them; Lyda Jane and Albertine put them in boxes; Celia tallied up the work sheets.

By the time Ruth gave the last twist of the iron to the last dress, Vernette, Sue Ann, Lorraine, and Puddin' had drifted into the living room to drink Cokes, eat sweet potato pie, and watch *20/20* on Henry's big-screen TV. Ruth looked at the dress for a moment, then handed it to Lyda Jane, who said, "That makes sixty dresses, sized infant to preteen, twenty sunbonnets, and fifteen jackets." Putting it on top of the pile in a box, she fixed tissue paper around it as though she were tucking a newborn into its crib, then nodded. Albertine ripped off a piece of strapping tape, sealed the box, looked up, and said, "Dear Lord, I do believe we done it!"

Celia threw pad and pencil in the air, crowing, "An' a full three weeks before Easter!" while Vernette bounced off the couch, pulled Sue Ann and Lorraine up, and squealed, "Oh, drop-kick me, Jesus, through the goalposts of life!" Puddin' stopped eating long enough to shout, "Whooo-eee! as Henry wheeled himself in from the kitchen, a bottle of supermarket champagne in his lap. They all crowded around the table, laughing and hugging, as Albertine reached into the sideboard for the plastic champagne glasses.

Saying, "I 'spect you've had more experience with champagne than I," Henry handed the bottle to Bonnie.

She popped the cork and poured, toasting, "To the Cherished Ladies!" Even teetotaling Celia downed hers in a gulp and asked for a refill.

"It's too bad all the girls who worked on the project can't be here," Ruth said.

"I'll give a brunch when I get back from Atlanta so everyone can celebrate," Bonnie said.

Since she planned to take a personal day on Friday and drive the goods up to Nikki's, they loaded the boxes into the trunk and back-seat of her Volvo, and after extended good-nights, she started for home. She half listened to the late news and the weather, then switched off the radio, rolled down the window, and started to sing. She began softly with "Here Comes the Sun," bounced into a sassy rendition of "These Boots Are Made for Walkin'," cracked on the high notes of "Don't Rain on My Parade," repeated several choruses (though she couldn't remember all the words) of "I Am Woman," and, finally, pulling off the road and seeing her porch light, gave a full-throated Ethel Merman imitation of "Everything's Comin' Up Roses." She'd come up with a moneymaking project, and they'd pulled it off. The next time she talked to Riz, as she did almost every night, she'd tell him she finally understood what *chutzpha* meant, and she liked having it.

She's seen him only once since New Orleans. Around Valentine's Day he'd managed to fly down for the weekend. Saying he should get some use of his gift mattress, she invited him to stay at her place, but he'd said it was too rustic for his tastes and had booked them into the Adam's Mark Hotel in Mobile. It had been an all too brief encounter of lovemaking and room service, once again making her feel that he

was not so much a part of her life as a vacation from it. But week after next, during Easter vacation, she was flying up to Washington,
and they'd have plenty of time to really be together. Everything *was*
coming up roses, she thought as she made several trips carrying the
dresses into the house.

She still felt like singing Thursday morning as she drove to work.
When she reached the office, Norma Jean, who seemed to have an in-
exhaustible stash of holiday kitsch (she'd put up Halloween witches,
Thanksgiving pumpkins, Christmas Santas, Valentine hearts, and St.
Patrick's Day shamrocks) was Scotch-taping eggs and bunnies to the
door. Bonnie gave her a bright "Good morning" and repeated the
same to Snoopy as she passed her desk. Even Snoopy seemed to be
marginally human. That should have alerted her that something unpleasant was afoot, but she naively supposed her good mood was
contagious. Then, shortly before lunch, Mrs. Jackson called her in.

Lena Jackson, as usual, was neat as a pin. Her lipstick was poppy
red; her hair was ironed into place. She was fond of checks and
stripes (a taste, Bonnie thought, that reflected her need for order),
and today she was wearing a tunic with a black and white geometric
design over a pencil-slim black skirt. Greeting Bonnie with her usual
friendliness, she indicated one of the chairs facing her desk,
smoothed her skirt, and sat down, saying, "I see you've wrestled that
computer to the ground. Your recent reports are detailed and con-
cise. We have a clear picture of how each and every program partici-
pant is progressing." Knowing that Mrs. Jackson's compliments often
preceded a request for extra work, Bonnie smiled and braced herself,
but the praise continued. "You've been such an asset to the college,"
Mrs. Jackson went on. "You've given yourself so completely and tire-
lessly to the program"—this was beginning to sound like a eulogy—
"even though your dressmaking project is outside the parameters of
the program"—Mrs. Jackson exhibited a slight discomfort; college
employees weren't expected to innovate—"you've been such a fine
example to all the women. But—"

"But?"

"But—" She paused again, then went on in a rush. "There's a possibility that your contract won't be renewed."

Bonnie couldn't get out more than a gawky "What?"

"This has nothing to do with your performance."

"That's a comfort," Bonnie said, unable to keep the sarcasm out of her voice.

"You know the complexities of federal, state, and local funding. It seems they haven't been able to strike a deal to continue the program next year. Of course I'll do everything I can to keep you on, but if you do stay, your job description will change. You'll be counseling the general student population. You might go to summer school so you can receive full certification. What do you think about that?"

Bonnie didn't know what she thought. Staring at the circles and triangles in Mrs. Jackson's tunic made her dizzy. "If I've been successful," she said at last, "my success has been based on my concern for this particular group of women. I don't know if I'd fare as well with Gen-Xers. And I don't know if I'd have the time or energy to take classes. And what about the women? Ruth Elkins is the only one who's graduating. The others all have another year to go."

"And you've gotten them off to a grand start." Getting to her feet, Lena Jackson temporized, "Nothing is final yet. They might come up with the money. But in good conscience, I felt I should let you know, so that if any other offers presented themselves . . ."

Any other offers? Why would she have been looking for other offers when she'd assumed she had a job? It wasn't as though potential employers were lined up shouting, "Over here!" Rising from her chair, she thought she might pull a Hilly Pruwitt and start cursing. Instead, she said, "Thank you for letting me know," and moved to the door.

Mrs. Jackson called, "I'll keep you posted," as she closed it.

Seeing the "cat that ate the canary" smirk on Snoopy's face, she quickly went into her own office. Miserable and angry, she reproached herself for not having asked more questions. Was there really a possibility that money would come through so she could stay on, or had Mrs. Jackson just been letting her down easy? Should she start looking? If so, where? She was so anxious that she couldn't concentrate, but by five, when she straightened her desk, she was determined not to let the possibility of future trouble interfere with the current triumph. She was going to stay in the *now,* at least until she'd delivered the dresses to Nikki in Atlanta.

On the way home the Volvo's temperature gauge shot into the danger zone, and the tapping noise she'd been hearing, and assiduously ignoring, for weeks suddenly became a threatening knock. She slowed to a crawl and bumped into the nearest garage. A scrawny middle-aged mechanic, cauliflower ears fairly blossoming as he heard the thump of her motor, came out of the service bay. He grunted as she got out and described the car's symptoms. After rooting around under the hood while she sat behind the wheel turning the motor on and off as ordered, he said laconically, "This here car ain't safe to drive."

"What's wrong with it?" she asked.

Rubbing his hands together, he drawled, "That'll take time to find out, an' even longer to fix," in such a parody of greedy satisfaction that she wanted to yank the straps of his overalls tight enough to squeeze his mean little balls.

"But I have to drive to Atlanta tomorrow," she wailed, hands gripping the wheel.

"Not in this here ve-hicle. We don' keep parts for fer'n auto-mo-beels in stock, an' don't know any other place in Florabama that does. I'll call 'round, but right now you best find a friend to carry you on home."

Flummoxed, she took her purse, slammed the car door, and strode to the phone booth. First she called Cass and got the answering machine. Next she called Lorraine, who lived nearby, and got a recorded message saying the phone was out of order. She tried Albertine. Albertine said she'd be there in fifteen minutes. She drank two cups of machine mud coffee while waiting in the office, averting her eyes from a bikini-clad model astride a Harley-Davidson while Cauliflower Ears tinkered around in the garage. How in the hell was she going to get the goods up to Atlanta?

Albertine drove up in a ten-year-old purple Oldsmobile that sounded only minimally better than the Volvo. Leaning over to open the passenger door for Bonnie, she said, "We got problems, huh? Get on in," in a voice so resigned that it was almost calming.

They drove to Bonnie's house, Bonnie jabbering in frustration, Albertine grunting sympathetically, but warning, "Gonna be hard to find a car on short notice. We best do a telephone tree an' send out the alarm."

While Bonnie fed Nesha, Albertine started calling, reporting, after the first attempt, "Vernette's Ford is outa commission, an' her husband won't let her drive his, but I told her to call Sue Ann." After reaching Lorraine, she sighed and said, "Insurance done lapsed on her Saturn, an' Tiffany's got an ear infection, but she's gonna call around," then: "No point callin' Lyda Jane. Her eyes so bad she give her car to her son, an' I be drivin' her 'round." Swallowing her fifth Triscuit, Bonnie thanked her, walked her to the door, then took over.

She called Celia Lusk, who nattered on about the power of prayer, then, grudgingly, offered the use of her Buick, adding, "But I'll have to get my husband's permission. An' like I say, it's a gas guzzler with bald tires."

Dropping her head in her hand, Bonnie ended the conversation with "I'll call you back if nothing better presents itself."

She was reaching for the Triscuit box when the phone rang. Picking it up, she was surprised to hear Roxy's voice. "Miss Cullman, Sue Ann just called and told me your car's out of commission. I don't have any classes tomorrow, so I could drive up to Atlanta in my minivan."

Bonnie said, "Oh, that's wonderful. That's great," and though the prospect of a long journey in Roxy's company was not appealing, "I'll ride along with you."

"No need, unless you really want to. Fact is, I'd relish some time alone. A long drive without the kids is the closest I'll get to a vacation, and I need time alone to think things out. You know I'm not doing real well at school."

Having little time and less desire to commiserate with Roxy's complaints, Bonnie simply asked, "You wouldn't mind driving up alone?"

"No, ma'am. Like I said, just drivin' alone would be a vacation for me. I'm real sorry I haven't been able to help more with the dress-making project, and I'd like to make up for it by delivering the stuff."

"You've got a deal," Bonnie told her. "When do you want to come by?"

"Guess I should get an early start. Is tomorrow morning 'round six all right with you."

"Anytime you say. The way to get here is . . ." Bonnie gave directions, then confirmed: "So, tomorrow at six. See you then. Roxy, you're an angel." She then called Nikki and left a message to say one of the women would be making the delivery.

It was still dark when Roxy drove up to the house. Pulling a sweater over her nightdress, Bonnie padded to the front door and turned on the porch light. Roxy wore a purple satin blouse, tight black jeans, and a windbreaker. Her hair was rolled around curlers as big as juice cans, but her face was already made up. She followed Bonnie into the kitchen, where Bonnie gave her some cash for gas and a motel and a map to Nikki's shop. Saying she was eager to get going, she turned down Bonnie's offer of toast and coffee, adding that Ruth had fixed her a sack of food and a thermos. After going into her bedroom to pull on some clothes, Bonnie returned to the kitchen and said, "Let's do it." Barely speaking as they worked, they loaded the boxes that Bonnie had put in the living room into the minivan and as the first rays of sun touched the tops of the trees, Roxy took off, waving good-bye with one of Ruth's sausage biscuits in her hand, rock and roll blasting.

Friday night, after Cass had taken her grocery shopping and dropped her off, Bonnie checked her messages: "Bonnie, it's Nikki. They delivered the dresses, and oh, I wish you were here. They're beautiful. I mean precious. I'll be at the shop tonight working on the window display. Tomorrow's going to be crazy, so let's talk Sunday evening. Bet I'll have sold a dozen by then. Thanks to you and your ladies. Are we gonna make some money, or what?" Bonnie punched the REPLAY button and listened to the message a second time, letting out breath she hadn't even been conscious of holding.

Though they'd made no definite arrangement, she assumed Roxy would call Saturday evening, when she was due back. No call came, but she told herself Roxy was probably exhausted from the trip. Roxy would probably call in the morning before she and Ruth went to church or, more accurately, after Ruth had taken the kids to church while she slept in.

Sunday morning, as she stepped out from her wake-up shower, Nesha, who always sat on the mat waiting for her, pricked up his ears and started for the living room. Hearing a car and thinking Roxy had dropped by, she pulled on her robe and hurried after him. He frisked around her feet, making her stumble. Picking him up, she opened the front door and went to the screen door. Much to her surprise, she saw Hilly Pruwitt climbing out of her shiny red car.

After giving the car door a deliberate slam, Hilly straightened and strode toward the house, left arm swinging, right arm akimbo, thumb hooked into the waist of her jeans. She looked so big, bright, and de-termined that Bonnie, holding open the screen door, greeted her the way she'd wanted to when she'd first seen her. "Hello, Ms. Amazon. I sure didn't expect to see you."

"I live right up the road," Hilly told her casually, mounting the steps, "'bout half a mile from the cement factory."

"I hardly ever drive beyond my house, so I had no idea we were neighbors. Come on in. What's up?"

"Ruth called you yet?" Hilly asked, lingering on the porch.

"No. I've been expecting that either she or Roxy—"

"She called me. That's why I thought I'd better come on by."

Hilly's demeanor did not suggest she was the bearer of glad tidings, but Bonnie said, "I guess Roxy's back by now," as she motioned her into the house.

Hilly stepped in, walked a few feet, then stopped, crossing her arms over her chest. "Matter of fact, she ain't. Hasn't come back. Hasn't called."

"She was planning to spend Friday night in Atlanta."

"Yeah. And now it's Sunday. Ruth's frantic. She wants to call the highway patrol, but I told her to wait up."

"Well, if she hasn't heard from her, maybe she—" Bonnie's shoulders lifted in a gesture of helplessness. She put Nesha down, tightened the sash of her robe, and shoved her hands into the pockets, lamely asking, "Do you think she might have had an accident?"

"Roxy's the accident," Hilly said. "Wanna know what I think?" Bonnie wasn't sure she did but nodded. "I think she's taken off."

"Taken off?" Bonnie's stomach churned.

"Maybe I shouldn't say that before I know the facts, but if that friend of yours in Atlanta gave her money—"

"Nikki would've given her a check. How could she cash a check made out to me?"

"I still think she's gone."

"Gone where?"

"Anywhere. *Hasta la vista,* baby!" Hilly's hand flew into the air, made a fist, and punched the palm of her other hand. "Damn, I wish you'd talked to me 'fore you trusted Roxy. From the gutter to her ain't up."

"But I thought . . . I mean, Ruth's so—"

"Ruthie's got nothin' to do with Roxy 'cept she had the misfortune to incubate her. I wouldn't take Roxy to a dogfight, even if I thought she could win. Maybe you should call your friend in Atlanta and find out if she actually got there."

"She did," Bonnie said, starting toward the kitchen and motioning for Hilly to follow. "Here, you can listen to her message." Flustered, she punched RECORD, quickly hit MESSAGE, and said, "Oh, shit, I hope I haven't erased it," as Nikki's voice came on.

Halfway through the message Hilly said, "Rewind that an' play it back, will you?" Bonnie did. "See," Hilly interrupted as they listened again. "She says *they* delivered the goods. I figured Roxy went with somebody. Maybe one of those drifters she picks up at the bar when she tells Ruthie she's goin' to the library. Or maybe that sorry friend of hers, Johnette. Roxy's too gutless to pull anything off alone. Been leanin' on her mama, her whole life." She slid her fingers onto her scalp and pulled her hair out to a full bush. "Why don't you call your friend an' ask her for details?"

Bonnie nodded, pushed aside the discount coupons, bills, newspaper cuttings, and stationery on the counter to find her address book, then sank into a chair, pulling the phone into her lap and dialing Nikki's home number. On the fourth ring Nikki picked up with a sleepy "Uh-huh."

"Nikki, it's Bonnie. Sounds like I woke you, and if so, I apologize."

A halfhearted "It's OK" was followed by a groggy "Didn't you get my message? I'm over the moon. Sold six dresses and two bonnets yesterday. Probably should've ordered more."

"That's great," Bonnie said, then in a desperate need to cut to the chase, asked, "The woman who delivered them . . . was she alone?"

"No, she . . . Roxanne's her name, right? . . . she had a chick with spiky hair helping her unload the car, but I didn't catch her name."

"And they got there when?"

"Friday afternoon 'bout one, I guess. Why?"

"And you gave them the check?"

"I told you I'd pay on delivery." Nikki sounded vaguely insulted. "I had the check made out, but then she showed me your note, so I went with her to my bank and got cash instead."

"Oh, God. What note?"

"The one from you, explaining how some of the women were desperate for cash and you didn't want to wait for a check to clear."

"Oh, God."

"What's the matter?"

"I didn't send any note."

"But it was typed on your stationery. And she showed me how you'd given her your credit card 'cause she didn't have any money, so I figured—oh, shit. You mean—"

"She hasn't come back yet."

"Oh, shit. Oh, shit. I can't believe I did this. I can't—"

"It's OK, it's OK." She didn't want to waste time calming Nikki down. "Did they say anything about where they were going?"

"They said they were going to stay the night and go to Underground Atlanta, but I said since they had so much cash, they should go on back. Or at least have the motel put it in a safe. Oh, shit. I can't believe this! Who is this Roxanne? Have you called the cops?"

"Not yet."

"Oh, Bonnie, you must be frantic."

"No," she lied. "I just need to find out what's happening. I'll call you back later, OK?"

"I can't believe I—"

"I'll call you back later, OK?"

"I gave her over four thousand bucks in cash. Oh, shit. I—"

"Call you later, Nikki. Gotta go. Bye."

Bonnie hung up and looked at Hilly, who said, "Like I thought, huh?"

"Worse. She did turn up with a girl with spiky hair. And she showed Nikki some bogus note she said I'd written, asking her for cash." She felt as though she were watching an action movie where a tiny speck appeared on the horizon, then zoomed forward with rocket speed, ready to explode.

"She gave her cash?"

"Four thousand dollars' worth." She felt as though she were going to vomit. "Could you excuse me for a minute?" she said quietly, and almost ran from the room.

A few minutes later, after she'd heard the toilet flush, Hilly came to the door of Bonnie's bedroom. Bonnie sat on the bed, her purse and its spilled contents beside her, staring down at the open wallet in her lap. "She get your credit cards?" Hilly asked.

"I only had the one. And yes. I guess she did." The shock was quick and sharp as a falling ax. Stunned, she turned to Hilly. "No one's ever stolen from me before. Except for this kid in my Girl Scout troop who stole one of my merit badges."

Hilly laughed. "Ain't you the lucky one. I know some people'd steal a worm off a sick hen."

"I just can't believe—"

"You only had the one card, and you're sure it was in your wallet?"

"Uh-huh. When Devoe, my husband, went bankrupt, I cut up all the others. Just this one. She must've done it while . . ." She tried to piece it together. "I was cold and I had to pee, and I came in here and put on some clothes, and when I walked through the kitchen, she was there. My stationery was on the table 'cause I'd written a letter to my daughter the night before. And my wallet was on the table, but I didn't think anything of it." She hit her forehead with the heel of her hand. "I don't believe it! How could I have been so dumb? But I never imagined . . . and when my car broke down and I couldn't go, I was just so grateful that someone—"

"OK, OK, OK," Hilly said, both calming and impatient. "We've got to haul ass here, Miz Cullman. I'll make a pot of coffee. How 'bout you get dressed an' call the credit card company to tell 'em your card's gone missing? Then we'll ride over to Ruth's." Nesha stood looking from one to the other, sensing trouble. "This here puppy need to be fed?" Hilly asked. Without waiting for an answer, she hoisted him up and left the room, muttering, "You be nice, pooch, else I'll have your guts for garters."

Hilly was already behind the wheel with the motor going when Bonnie slid into the passenger seat. "I was just thinking," Hilly said, "I know where Johnette lives. How 'bout we drop by there and see if we can find out anything 'fore we go on to Ruth's?" Bonnie agreed. If a mark of intelligence was the ability to see the truth of a situation quickly, then Hilly was smarter than she'd ever be. She was furious at Roxy, but more angry at herself. "I can't believe I was stupid enough to trust her like that," she said, "because right from the beginning my intuition told me she wasn't someone to be trusted."

"Yeah, usually we only turn away from what we know when we've got the hots for some man. But don't waste time beating yourself up," Hilly said. "Trust is a damned-if-you-do, damned-if-you-don't proposition. Ruth's the one I'm worried about. If Roxy's taken off with the money . . ." She came to a stop sign, glanced quickly from side to side, shifted gears, and floored the accelerator. Raising her voice over the roar of the motor, she shouted, "I would've driven up m'self, but we're breaking in a new guy at the restaurant, and my boss's little boy has strep throat, so I couldn't leave."

Bonnie yelled, "That's OK," then fell silent, glad that the rushing wind and racing engine made further talk impossible.

By the time they pulled into the oil-stained parking lot between a Burger King and a two-story block of pink stucco apartments with rust stains dribbling from broken drain spouts, the sky had gone dark, and it was spitting rain. Hilly switched off the motor, reached into the glove compartment for her sunglasses, and said, "This is it. I come by here once when Johnette didn't turn up at the mill an' the gals thought she might be sick. She was layin' in the bed all right, but she weren't sick an' she weren't alone." They walked to the entrance and checked out the bank of mailboxes, many of which had no names. Hilly tapped the nail of her index finger on 2B. "J. Rivers" was printed on the tag. "Rick Parton" had been scribbled above it and crossed out; "F. Strobert" had been penciled in. Hilly winked and said, "Rotating roommates." Then, as though they were cops on a stakeout, she moved out, close to the wall, motioning for Bonnie to follow. They crept into the stairwell past scarred metal doors marked "Laundry" and "Trash" and up a flight of stairs that hadn't seen a broom in some time.

"It's awfully quiet," Bonnie whispered as they came on to the second-story walkway.

"This ain't the natural habitat of early risers," Hilly said sotto voce, but as they approached 2B, the sound of a TV and the smell of frying bacon invaded the morning air. Hilly stopped, put her sunglasses on top of her head, slid her eyes over to Bonnie, then rapped on the door. Bonnie shut her eyes. This wasn't reality. This was a TV show.

The door was yanked open, and a man in his early thirties, wearing nothing but sweatpants and clutching a spatula as though it were a weapon stood before them. His shoulders had a Neanderthal slope, his eyes were bleary, and he scratched at his patchy mustache as he uttered a surly "Yeah?"

"You Mr. Strobert?" Hilly asked.

"Whatcha want?"

"I'm a friend of Johnette's. Lookin' for her," Hilly drawled, leaning against the doorjamb.

"She ain't here." Squinting one eye, he dropped his hand to scratch at the crotch of his sweatpants and started to close the door.

"Thing is, I got some money I owe her," Hilly lied.

The mention of money eased the door open enough to show a trashed living room and a TV screen playing a *Road Runner* cartoon. "Hey"—he moved the spatula as though he were flipping pancakes and stretched his lips to show a set of large nicotine-stained teeth— "you could leave it with me. Johnette's s'posed to be back soon."

"She gone to the store?"

Too dense to lie, Strobert said, "Hell, no. She took off with a friend. She was s'posed to be back yesterday. An' she damn well better be back soon 'cause her boss at the club is *beaucoup* pissed."

"Do you know where they went?" Bonnie asked, but got no response.

"'Course he knows," Hilly said, tweaking his male pride. "She's his woman, ain't she?"

He took the bait, growling, "Bitch went to 'lanta. An' she better be back tonight."

"I'm sure she will be," Hilly said. "Maybe we'll come 'round later."

"That money you owe her would be safe with me," he repeated.

"Gotta go, Mr. Strobert." Hilly wiped her nose. "Hey, I think your fat's in the fire. I mean"—she wiggled her fingers in farewell—"I think your bacon's burnin'."

As they clattered down the stairwell, Bonnie said, "Just because she took Johnette with her doesn't necessarily mean—"

"Right. Don't mean a thing," Hilly said sarcastically. "She just wanted a friend to share the sightseeing."

"Maybe she just forgot to tell me that Johnette—"

"OK. Let's just call it a sin of omission," Hilly said, opening the car door.

"A what?" Bonnie asked, getting in.

"I been takin' these instructions at St. Elizabeth's," Hilly explained, jamming the car into reverse, then peeling out of the parking lot. "Sins of commission is when you do something bad; sins of omission is when you *don't* do somethin' you're s'posed to do, like holding back information. Personally, I prefer sins of co-mission 'cause at least evil takes some guts, but sins of omission are chickenshit sins. 'Course I don't call 'em that to Father Genovese's face."

"I guess we should call the highway patrol."

"I think maybe we ought to go direct to the regular cops. Let them contact the highway patrol, 'cause ten to one those lowlifes are on their way out west by now. Hollywood, Vegas, some crappy place they've seen on TV. But we can't find out anything till tomorrow, and you've already warned your credit card people, so—" Approaching a stop sign, Hilly mashed on the brakes. Coming to a full stop, she wrapped her arms over the steering wheel and stared straight ahead. "Y' know Ruthie's been makin' all these big plans, thinkin' she's gonna get to go to U of A and finally get her degree. Now this." She sighed so deeply her chest seemed to cave in. Then, ramming the car into gear, she muttered, "Shit! If today was a fish, I'd throw it back."

Chapter XVII

Ruth's front door was open, exuding smells of Pine Sol, Clorox, and detergent. Hilly yelled, "Ruthie, it's me," adding a warning, "And Miz Cullman's with me," as Bonnie followed her through the neat-as-a-pin living room and into the kitchen. The curtains had been taken down; the countertops were full of sponges, cleansers, and polishes; the washing machine on the back porch was going full tilt. Ruth was down on all fours scrubbing the floor while Moo pushed a toy vacuum cleaner and made "whoosh-whoosh" sounds.

"Scuse the mess." Ruth dropped the brush into the bucket, wiped her forehead with the back of her hand, and got up. "I just couldn't get it together to go to church this morning, so I thought I'd do a real deep clean."

"The woman's nuts," Hilly said, starting to mop up the water. "She always cleans when she's upset. Don't have the sense to pour herself a drink or hide in bed like a normal woman."

"Would y'all care for some coffee? Or would you prefer tea?" Ruth asked, reaching for the kettle. Her eyes were swollen; her face was pale with bright patches on her cheeks. Bonnie couldn't bear to look at her, so she turned to Moo, who let her toy cleaner clatter to the floor and stared back. "You know Miz Cullman," Ruth prompted. "She's the nice lady you see at the college, remember?"

Moo nodded and asked, "Why you's here?"

"Just came to visit," Bonnie said. Moo's thumb found her mouth. The washing machine stopped sloshing, clicked, and went into the spin cycle. Bonnie said, "May I use your bathroom?" Ruth directed her down the hall, first door to her right.

Wanting to give Ruth and Hilly time alone, she sat on the commode and looked around. A worn pink candlewick robe hung on the back of the door next to a black nylon nightdress. The map-of-the-world plastic shower curtain had been yanked back, revealing family-size bottles of generic bubble bath, shampoo, and conditioner set around the edge of a pitted tub with a dolphin-shaped rubber mat stuck to the bottom. A mushy bar of Ivory soap and a soggy washcloth were lodged in the drain. A bath towel had been left on the floor next to a red plastic bucket full of rubber toys and curled copies of *Self* and *Cosmo*. A pile of kids' soiled pajamas, socks, and underclothes gave off a vague whiff of urine. The mess dragged her back to the "I'll never get ahead of it" chaos of early motherhood, but at least the paint hadn't been peeling off her bathroom ceiling, and at least she'd had a husband who came home nights and a part-time housekeeper.

She stood up, looking at the laminated drawing of a mother rabbit instructing two bunnies to "Clean your teeth. Hang up the towels." As she picked up her purse and rooted around for her brush, her eyes moved to the Home Depot storage unit that must've been put up for Roxy. Its clear plastic drawers revealed a jumble of cosmetics, tampons, hair dye, and Musk perfume. Wedged into the side of the medicine cabinet was a sepia-toned postcard of a doleful woman she half recognized. She turned it over, read, "Virginia Woolf, 1882–1941. British novelist and essayist," and, in Cass's handwriting, "Ruth: Your paper on 'A Room of One's Own' was excellent." She shook her head and, deciding that she'd given Hilly enough time to break the news, went back to the kitchen.

Ruth stood in profile, hands clutching the sink, staring out the window.

". . . and that's about the size of it," Hilly was saying. She held Moo on her lap, rocking her and smoothing back her hair. Looking at Bonnie, her eyes begging support, she went on. "So I think we oughta go to the police. They'll contact the highway patrol and whatever else they need to do."

"Miz Cullman," Ruth said without turning around, "I swear I'll make good on the money. No matter how long it takes me."

Bonnie put her arm around Ruth's shoulder. "We don't know anything for sure yet." Ruth stared ahead, seemingly oblivious of her touch. "Where's Kylie?" she asked, wanting to break the tension.

"He's over to a neighbor's. Should I go get him?"

Hilly said, "No. You need to get movin'. Get us a recent picture of Roxy and—"

"I won't turn my daughter's picture over to the police." Ruth's voice was insistent but weak, like a patient saying she wouldn't go through surgery as the anesthesia was setting in.

"But what if she has been in an accident?" Bonnie said.

"Ruth," Hilly urged, "go get a picture. An' papers on the mini-van."

Suddenly clutching Bonnie, and just as suddenly wrenching herself away, Ruth said, "I got the papers somewhere. Insured it a couple months ago. Cleaned out my savings."

"So, go get the papers," Hilly ordered.

Moo took her thumb out of her mouth long enough to say, "Mama gone to 'lanta?"

Ruth rushed from the room, hand over her mouth.

Hilly sighed and said, "Sugar, your mama's done a bad thing," and in response to Bonnie's disapproving look, added: "Hey, you think she don' know that already? Keepin' a kid innocent ain't much of a service. In the end everyone's gotta grow up an' face it."

"Face what?"

"Meanness, evil, the whole nine yards."

"Oh, for chrissake!" Bonnie exploded, reaching for a bottle of detergent, squirting a glob on her hands and turning the faucet on full. "I hardly think it's appropriate to be discussing the nature of evil with a three-year-old child."

"Sorry," Hilly retreated. "I'm just mouthin' off 'cause I don't know what else to do. Just like you're scrubbin' your hands even though they ain't dirty."

At that, Bonnie actually laughed.

"Could you pour me another cup of coffee? I'd do it myself, but I don' wanna move the kid."

Bonnie dried her hands and poured more coffee into Hilly's mug, then sat down and put her head in her hands while Hilly sipped and played this little piggy with Moo's toes.

Ruth came back in and set a paper and pencil, an insurance policy, and a photo on the table. "Here's the State Farm policy. It has all the information about the minivan. And this is the most recent picture I've got." The photo had been torn in half. The part that remained showed Roxy sitting on the living room floor in front of a Christmas tree wearing the black nightdress Bonnie had seen in the bathroom. One of her arms was held to her breast; the other reached out to whoever had been in the rest of the picture.

"Where's me?" Moo asked, wriggling out of Hilly's lap to look at the photo.

"Gramma's kept the part with you in her bedroom," Ruth told her. "Gramma'll give it to you later."

"Now," Moo insisted.

Ruth picked her up and told her to hush, then, indicating that Bonnie should take notes, said, "Roxy's five foot seven. She weighs about a hundred and twenty-five—maybe less 'cause she hasn't been eating right lately. Her hair's naturally light brown, but it's dyed darker—Deep Sable, I think it is. She has greenish brown eyes and a strawberry birthmark on the right cheek of her bottom. I 'member when I first brought her home from the hospital I thought it was a bruise."

"Gramma, I want—"

Ruth snapped, "I said hush!"

Moo puffed out her lower lip and twisted toward Hilly, but Hilly just patted her head, then got up, saying, "OK, we're outa here. We'll be back soon's we talk to the police. You round up Kylie, an' when we come back, I'll take him and Moo over to the restaurant. They can play upstairs with the kids while you get some rest."

"No," Ruth protested. "You've done enough already."

Hilly said, "Shut up, Ruthie," and handed the photo and papers to Bonnie, who stuffed them into her purse.

"We'll be back as soon as we can," Bonnie said, following Hilly to the door. "Then either Hilly'll take the kids or I will."

After mounting the steps of the police station, Hilly pulled open the heavy door, and they entered the lobby. A WPA mural of broad-backed farmers, broad-bosomed women, and broad-faced children, all happily bringing in the harvest, was behind the reception desk. Bonnie stated their business to a sleepy-looking black clerk, who said they should see Detective Bethune and pointed her green Fu Manchu–length fake fingernail down the hall to their right. Searching the nameplates, they found "Randolph W. Bethune, Detective" on the second door, which was open. The man in shirtsleeves who sat behind the desk lifted his feet from it, concluded his phone conversation with "and a pint of heavy cream," added a lower "I love you too, honey," then motioned them in.

He was a ruddy-faced, well-fed man in his mid-fifties, with an affable expression and a walleye. After getting up, putting on his suit jacket, and smoothing a few strands of hair across his dome, he introduced himself with military style, "Randolph W. Bethune here," softened it to "You can call me Rudy," and indicated the chairs in front of his desk. "Now what can I do for you, ladies?"

Bonnie was surprised when Hilly took a backseat, choosing a chair set against the wall, while she took one facing Bethune's desk.

She introduced herself and waited for Hilly to do likewise. Hilly, assiduously studying a file cabinet, finally muttered her name. Seeing that Hilly wanted her to take the lead, Bonnie said, "We're here to report a missing person."

"How long's this person been missing?" Bethune asked.

"She was supposed to be back from Atlanta yesterday."

Bethune smiled. "That's not hardly enough time for you to be worried. Before we file a missing person's report, the party in question has to be gone for—"

"It's more complicated than that," Bonnie said. "Sorry to interrupt, but we're afraid there's been a—" She couldn't get out "theft" or "crime." Bethune rocked back in his chair, thinking, she was sure, of the pie he was going to have with the heavy cream he was supposed to pick up on the way home. "You see," she persisted, "this party picked up a sizable sum of money in Atlanta on Friday, and she was supposed to be back Saturday and nobody's heard from her and—"

Bethune held up his hands. "Wow. Slow down. What's this party's name?"

"Roxanne Elkins. No, not Elkins, that's her maiden name. I guess she's known as Roxy Travis."

"And your relationship to her?"

"We're friends of her mother, Ruth Elkins. Roxy lives with Ruth. I'm a counselor at Marion Hawkins College, and the group of women I—"

"We worked at Cherished Lady till the mill closed down," Hilly put in, adding to the confusion.

"You see," Bonnie tried to explain, "the ladies made dresses on consignment for a boutique in Atlanta. My friend Nikki's boutique. Roxy volunteered to deliver the dresses, and we know she arrived. We also know she was given cash for them." She'd tried to confine herself to facts, but she sounded as hopelessly muddled as Celia Lusk.

"Miz Cullman, why don't you begin from the beginning and go real slow," Bethune advised.

She began again, careful to keep the panic out of her voice. This time she marshaled the facts and sounded almost cogent, but she still felt as though she were describing the final episode of *The Forsyte Saga* to someone who'd never seen the show.

After a good five minutes, during which she'd put the auto insurance policy and photo on his desk, she concluded with "I can't believe . . . I mean, I feel so stupid."

"We all feel stupid when things go wrong," Bethune commiserated, studying Roxy's photo. "I believe my wife, Selma, knows Ruth Elkins from the Ladies' Auxiliary at our church." All business again, he took off his jacket, offered them coffee or a Coke, which they both declined, then leaned forward, asking, "Any problems in the home? Any recent arguments or troubles that might lead her to run away?"

Trying to sound professional, Bonnie said, "I know she's had a less than satisfactory adjustment to her educational program. She seems to have difficulty maintaining a mature attitude toward responsibility, both scholastically and in her personal life."

Hilly cut in with "She shoves her kids off on her mama while she runs 'round with this lowlife, Johnette, Bonnie's been tellin' you about."

There was a glimmer in Bethune's good eye. "I believe I know that young lady and the man with whom she's currently cohabitating."

"Yes, sir. Shacked up with a knuckleface name of Strobert," Hilly answered, feeling more at ease now.

"Why don't you give me your friend—Nikki, is it?—why don't you give me Nikki's number?" Bethune advised. "As I said, it's too early to file a missing person's report, but I'll talk to the highway patrol and contact some folks I know in Atlanta. See what we can find out 'bout motel registrations and all." He got to his feet, hitching up his belt. "I'll just go into the next office and make copies of these," he told them, shuffling out.

"Guess there're some benefits in living in a small town," Bonnie said.

"Oh, sure," Hilly agreed. "His wife an' her whole congregation will know the news 'bout an hour from now."

They were both standing, eager to be dismissed, when he returned, gave the papers back to Bonnie, and offered his hand.

"Try not to worry," he told them by way of good-bye. "Worrying never did help a situation. And give my regards to Miz Elkins."

As soon as they'd left the building, Bonnie said, "Thank God that's over."

Hilly grunted. "It ain't hardly over."

"I guess I should call a special meeting to tell everyone what's happened. Not that I'll know what to say, but I'd like to nip the gossip in the bud."

"Nip it in the bud!" Hilly gave a barking laugh. "It's gonna take over this town like kudzu. When the gals find out Roxy's gone off with their hard-earned cash, they'll prob'ly form a posse to go after her."

"At least Mr. Bethune seemed helpful."

"I guess. Just I hate anyone who works for the government." Hilly turned on the motor, saying, "I'll carry you back to your place."

"Maybe," Bonnie suggested, "I should go back to Ruth's. I can take care of the kids while she gets a nap or a shower."

"No need," Hilly answered, cautiously looking both left and right before she pulled out of the parking lot onto the deserted street. "Jess an' the kids'll be back from mass by now, an' he'll have Sunday dinner goin'. It'll be easier to herd Moo an' Kylie in with them."

"Jess?" Bonnie asked.

"He's my boss, my—"

"Yes, sure." Bonnie interjected, knowing Hilly meant lover because her voice had gone soft as goose down when she'd said his name.

"Jess ain't like other men. I mean, he's got steel balls, but he don't mind watchin' over kids. I won't even have ta go through no long-winded explanation. I'll just say a few words, an' he'll be straight with it. You ever been lucky enough to know a man like that?"

"Maybe my daddy."

"Weren't you the lucky one. Most men I know only got five gears: If they can't eat it, drive it, fix it, or screw it—scuse me, Miz Bonnie—they've gotta kill it. But Jess ain't like that. He's an actual human." Bonnie laughed. "So," Hilly went on, "he won't mind if I go back to sleep the night at Ruthie's."

"I wish you would. I don't think she should be alone."

"Damn straight. 'Cause she's gonna be there waitin' for the phone to ring, and both you and I know that when it does, it's gonna be the cops tellin' her Roxy's long gone. An' no matter how much she's tried to prepare herself, it's gonna hit her like a ton of bricks."

Nesha gave Bonnie a tail-wagging welcome as she came through the front door, but she passed him by, snapping, "Oh, just shut up and sit down," and walked straight through to the kitchen. Her phone machine MESSAGE light was blinking wildly. She punched the button only to hear Vernette asking, "What's up? Please give me a call," then Sue Ann's eager "Is the money here yet?," followed by a barrage of similar calls from the women who had been involved in the sewing project. She thought of calling Cass but remembered that she and Mark had gone into Mobile for a concert. Desperately needing commiseration, she called Riz and got his machine. She was leaving a message when he picked up with a vague "That you, babe? What time is it?"

"A little after one, I think. Riz, you'll never guess what—"

"Hey, sweetheart, can I call you back later?"

"Oh, but it's really hit the fan here. This morning—"

"I'm still in the sack," he croaked. "Took some clients out last night, and I'm really wiped."

"OK. Call me later." She slammed down the phone. *She* would've roused herself to talk to him no matter when he called. True, he was a zombie in the morning, but hadn't he heard the panic in her voice? Maybe, as those "relationship" gurus preached, she should have been more assertive, made her need plain. But she was damned if she was going to shout for attention as though she were at the counter of a crowded deli. She'd done enough of that with Devoe.

After getting out her list of the women's numbers she made several terse calls, cutting off all conversation by saying she was rushed, *absolutely couldn't talk,* but was announcing a special meeting, tomorrow, three o'clock in the student union, where she would give an update on the sewing project. Exhausted, more than confident that the news would spread, she turned off the ringer on the phone, took Nesha into her arms, and went to the bedroom, saying, "Let's take a long, long nap, then see if we can't get up on the other side of the bed."

Hilly met her at the door of the student union. "Ruth's as well as can be expected, but she didn't come to school today."

"I'd guess not."

"This meeting is gonna be about as cheerful as a wake without the whiskey."

"Have you already been inside?"

"Uh-huh."

"Large turnout?"

"What do you think?" Hilly pushed open the door. Feeling like a politician who's been caught with his pants down and was about to face a press conference, Bonnie followed, convinced that she was as ready as she was going to be. She'd told the story twice (once to Riz, when he'd finally called back last night, and again, this morning, to Cass, who'd picked her up and driven her to campus), so she'd had a chance to edit herself mentally. She would make it "just the facts, ma'am" brief (omitting any mention of her stolen credit card or the sleuthing she and Hilly had done at Johnette's) and avoid all accusation and conjecture. Reaching her usual chair, she remained standing. The muttered conversations stopped, chins were raised, and arms crossed over chests. "Good afternoon, everyone. As you all probably know, Roxy drove the dresses up to Atlanta on Friday, and she hasn't come back. I'm going to tell you everything I know, but I won't be able to answer all your questions because I don't know much for certain. But let me begin from the beginning. As you know, I planned to deliver the dresses myself, but my car. . . ." Apart from head shaking, snorts of disgust, and the occasional muttered curse, they listened in stony silence until she concluded with "So the authorities have been notified that Roxy is missing. Let me repeat: We don't know what's happened, so let's not jump to any conclusions. Let's just wait till we hear from them."

Vernette's heartfelt "Goddamn!" set off a cacophony of angry questions, accusations, and imprecations: "I don't understand how—"

"That bitch!"

"Have the cops—"

"Why didn't you—"

Bonnie fielded questions, repeating what she'd already said and struggling to remain calm, but the babble increased in volume.

"Hey." Albertine pleaded for calm. "What's the point in Monday morning quarterbackin'? Miz Cullman told you all she know."

"No point second guessing," Lyda Jane added quietly.

Bonnie lowered her head, smiling at the irony: The two women who'd been most involved and had lost the most were coming to her defense.

"I just don't see," Sue Ann insisted, "how Ruth didn't pick up on the fact that Roxy was runnin' off."

Hilly got up, eyes blazing. "Roxy's gone. Looks like our money's gone. We all feel like manure. But let's not take it out on Ruth. She's so full of shame an' worry she's 'bout out of her mind. Let's just Bob-bitt this conversation 'bout Ruth."

Momentarily chastened, everyone fell silent. Then Lyda Jane raised her hand as though she were in class. "Miz Cullman," she asked, "was your friend Nikki pleased with what we done?"

Bonnie took a moment to breathe. "More than pleased. She'd already sold over a dozen dresses when I talked to her again last night."

"So," Lyda Jane reasoned, "she might order more."

"We didn't get around to discussing that, but I'd think she might."

"I, for one, won't be working without I see the money first," Lorraine said.

"First we're screwed by Cherished Lady; then we're screwed by someone we know. Which is worse?" someone muttered.

"This is worse. This is like someone you know stealin' your man," another woman answered.

"I'd rather have my man than my money stole," Puddin' put in.

"You're learnin' fast," Vernette said bitterly.

Lyda Jane picked up her purse from the floor and put it in her lap. "Not the first time we had disappointment. Won't be the last."

"Oh, Lyda Jane, you make me sick!" Celia, who'd so far been silent, lashed out. "What's with this 'turn the other cheek'?"

"Always thought the preachers read that wrong," Lyda Jane responded without raising her voice. "When Jesus said that, maybe He wasn't tellin' us to take abuse; maybe He was sayin' you should stand firm, not let evil things get to you."

"You're old," Celia retorted. "Nothin' gets to you."

Unruffled, Lyda Jane said, "'Swhy I lived to be old. I may eat a lot of fried chicken, but I don' let resentment clog my arteries." Slowly turning her head, she made eye contact with each of the women, then nodded to Bonnie, rhetorically suggesting, "Shall we adjourn this meeting?" Getting up, she linked arms with Albertine. The two of them moved purposefully to the exit. Singly or in pairs, grumbling and whispering, the other women followed.

"Think we'll ever be that calm and wise?" Bonnie asked Hilly.

"Maybe you. Me—I'll go out kickin' an' screamin'. That Lyda Jane!" Hilly shook her head "Thinks she's a good Christian but she's a damn Zen Buddhist."

Chapter XVIII

*S*tepping into the terminal at the D.C. airport, Bonnie scanned the crowd for Riz, who was supposed to meet her, before she spotted an elderly man in livery holding up a sign with "Bonny Coolman" written on it. Approaching him, she said, "I'm Bonnie Cullman. Did Mr. Mazersky send you?"

"Yes, miss. I'm to drive you to his apartment."

Only mildly disappointed, she nodded and said, "Fine. Let's go."

Riz's apartment was in an older four-story building that looked like a quaint hotel. The doorman gave her an envelope containing a key and a note saying, "Sorry. Be back around five," directed her to the elevator, and said someone would bring up her suitcase directly. Letting herself into Riz's empty apartment, she felt shyly intrusive and devilishly curious. Passing a kitchenette, she went into a spacious room. Shades had been drawn against the light. An oversize leather couch and glass coffee table faced a monster TV; one whole wall was taken up with desk, PC, printer, fax machine, and phones. If it hadn't been for a stereo, stacks of CDs, and a well-loaded drinks cart, it might have been an office. "Sugar, you need feng shui," she muttered, moving to the windows. As she reached to pull open the shades, she brushed against a large potted plant sitting on the floor. Only a woman would give a man a potted plant. Only a man would draw the shades on it. Going into the kitchen to get it some water, she wondered if the woman was giving him anything else.

Wandering into the bedroom, she saw (no surprise) a king-size bed facing another monster TV, an exercise machine, and a walk-in closet the size of a small haberdashery. She paused in front of a chest of drawers, wanting to open it. When Gervaise and Eugene had been teenagers, she'd been tempted to pry into their private things, but she'd exhibited great restraint. She wasn't going to start playing Pandora with Riz.

Coming out of the bathroom, she hurried to answer the knock at the door. After tipping the man who'd brought up her bag, she decided to follow him out. He gave her directions to nearby shops. She had a delicious late lunch in a Vietnamese restaurant, then strolled along the avenue, window shopping. Strange, she thought, admiring the pricey goods, that until last year shopping had been one of her chief entertainments, not to say hobbies. The amount of stuff she'd owned! The amount of stuff she still had to get rid of when she went back to Atlanta! And she hadn't missed any of it. Stopping in a florist shop, she bought a bunch of yellow tulips, found her way back to the apartment, let herself in, and took a bath.

She was just getting out of the tub, wrapping herself in a big, jet black towel when she heard him enter the apartment. He came and stood in the bathroom doorway, arms extended, that charming grin on his face. "This is getting to be a habit," she said.

"And one I don't want to break," he replied, reaching for her.

"You jet-setters aren't the only ones who have things to do," Cass said, tapping her watch and feigning annoyance as Bonnie came off the flight.

After three days in D.C. with Riz and a stopoff in Birmingham to see the Duke and Elice, Bonnie looked travel weary. "I tried to call."

Cass said, "I'm teasing. I phoned ahead, and they told me the flight was late, so I've been here only five minutes."

"I appreciate your picking me up. I hate not having my car."

"Speaking of which, I called the garage and spoke to that

troglodyte mechanic." Cass went on as they joined the crowd streaming from the gate. "Your car's fixed."

"Did you ask how much it was going to cost?"

"Didn't dare. But you got a new credit card in the mail."

"Whoopee. Now all I've got to do is figure out how to make the
payments."

"Yeah. I've always thought the fundamental flaw in the system
was that you can't use American Express to pay off Visa." Cass inclined her head to indicate that they were passing the rest rooms.
"Want to?"

"I thought you'd never ask."

Standing side by side at the sinks, Cass instantly took up the conversation with "Nesha's waiting, none too patiently, in the car. He and
Bub got along fine. I didn't witness the peace conference but they
seem to have reached an interim accord. Wow," she said, noticing, as
Bonnie reached for the paper towels, that a new charm had been
added to her bracelet, "he gave you another bauble."

"Uh-huh." Bonnie extended her wrist to show off the Easter egg
studded with tiny diamonds.

"Not too shabby. But," Cass observed, "not exactly your taste, is
it?"

"Not exactly," Bonnie confessed. When she opened the box,
she'd shown more enthusiasm than she'd actually felt. The gift
seemed strangely impersonal, the sort of thing he'd give—probably
had given—to other women he was sleeping with.

"Well, as my mother would say, it's the thought that counts.
Though, personally, I never believed that. On the other hand, if you'd
gotten more jewelry from Devoe, you would've had something to
hock. You want me to drop Riz an anonymous note suggesting stock
certificates?"

On their trek to the parking lot Cass answered Bonnie's questions: Yes, the whole town, probably the county, was abuzz with
gossip about Roxy's disappearance; no, she hadn't seen or heard

anything about Ruth Elkins; yes, Detective Bethune had left a message on Bonnie's machine; and quite by chance, she'd seen Hilly when she and Mark had gone to a Mexican restaurant friends had recommended. "And there was Hilly in an off-the-shoulder blouse and a three-tiered skirt, slinging hash. Actually, she suggested some spicy fish dish that was absolutely four-star. But how about you? Is love's young dream still thriving? How was Washington?"

"Washington was—" Bonnie dodged a jogging teenager who almost bumped into her.

"And excuse *you*," Cass called after him.

"Washington was," Bonnie went on, thinking how Cass's outbursts had once embarrassed but now amused her, "interesting."

"I tell my students *interesting* is the word people use when they're at a loss to describe something."

"But it was. I'd forgotten the pace of a big city. How everyone's got somewhere to go and something to do. Riz had to work, so I went to the National Gallery and the Freer. And he took me to a movers-and-shakers cocktail party, and we had dinner at this marvelous Argentinean restaurant. Ever had tapas?"

"Forget the menus and the museums. How about Riz?"

Bonnie sighed. "It's a long story."

"Hey, I was the kid who read *War and Peace* when I was twelve."

"Let's wait until we're in the car."

"OK. How was the Duke? Did you tell him you'd been off with big, bad Riz?"

"No, I didn't. Just said I'd been visiting friends. The Duke doesn't really know Riz anymore, and what he knows he disapproves of. And since I'd told him about the fiasco with the dress business *and* the fact that I may not have a job come June, it seemed too much."

"The scuttlebutt around the faculty lounge isn't good. A lot of grant money seems to be in jeopardy."

After reaching the baggage carousel, they waited with other passengers, eyeing the rubber flaps that would spit out the suitcases with all the faith of agnostics waiting for the Second Coming. "Besides," Bonnie went on, "Elice was with us the whole time. God that woman is a southern Joan Rivers—all face-lifts and foolishness."

"Watch what you say," Cass warned, patting herself under the chin. "I'm saving up for a lift. I am not kidding."

"Nothing wrong with maintenance, but she's in total denial. She's pushing Daddy to go on another cruise 'cause she just loved the way all the officers asked her to dance. Oh, Cass"—she shuddered—"if I'm wearing miniskirts and making rouge circles on my cheeks when I'm her age, please bring me to my senses."

Finally her suitcase appeared. She hoisted it from the carousel and followed Cass to the exit. The electronic doors opened, and they were hit by heat and car fumes. Cass stopped dead. "I can't remember where I parked the car." Shading her eyes and swiveling her head, she scanned the lot. "This way, I think. Don't expect me to be your counselor on age-appropriate grooming 'cause as you can see, I'm already losing my mind."

Seeing them approach, Nesha barked frantically, pawing the partially opened window. "My baby, my darlin', my Nesh-nesh, have you missed me? Have you?" Bonnie, almost as excited as Nesha, cooed as she waited for Cass to unlock the door.

"I want you to know that I would find your behavior totally ridiculous if I didn't act like that myself," Cass said as she slid into the driver's seat and punched on the air conditioning.

Once out of the parking lot, she turned, looked over at Bonnie, and said, "OK. So now tell me about Riz."

"Mostly I had a good time. He took me to this cocktail party in Georgetown. Wall-to-wall people, scrumptious hors d'oeuvres. I saw George Will and a bunch of other people I recognized from TV or newspapers. There was a lot of laughter and glad-handing, but everyone seemed to have an agenda. Riz'd introduce me to someone, then wander off, and the person I'd met would immediately determine that I wasn't part of the scene, so they'd cut short the conversation or, worse, keep talking to me while their eyes trawled the room for bigger fish. The next night we went to dinner with this couple. The guy was some Argentinean in the import-export business. The woman, girl really, was introduced as his fiancée, but I wouldn't be surprised if she was from some escort service. She was absolutely monosyllabic. Riz and this guy talked business, and I talked to the waiter. I got a look at the bill, and it was"—she shook her head— "over six hundred dollars. I was flattered that Riz wanted to introduce me to his world, but I mean to say—"

"What do you mean to say?" Cass prompted.

"At twenty I would've found it all very glamorous. At thirty I might still have found it interesting, but now? I don't fit in, and what's more important, I don't want to."

After a pause Cass asked, "When did you first realize that Devoe was a mistake?"

"I think it was on the honeymoon." Bonnie laughed. "Right after we'd checked into the hotel, we made love, but right after that, I mean, *right* after that, he turned on the TV. It hit me as horribly wrong, but—"

"But you said, 'Hey, what's the matter with me? It's a little thing. A petty, unimportant thing,' didn't you? You denied your intuition and looked the other way."

"We were on our *honeymoon,* for godsake. Of course I looked the other way. In fact, it wasn't until we separated that I even remembered it. You know, love is blind."

"Or maybe we blind ourselves in order to love."

Bonnie teased, "Yo, that's heavy, dude." She wasn't sure she could pinpoint her dissatisfactions or even that she wanted to confess them. "Riz is handsome and generous and funny. He knows his way around a mattress, though he might be a tad self-congratulatory about that. But he talks more than he listens."

"Some of the best of us are guilty of that," Cass interrupted, pointing her finger to her chest.

"He's got a lousy track record with women. He's not just liberal with money"—she went on, choosing her words carefully because she didn't want to be disloyal—"he's downright careless." She'd been appalled when he'd said, quite casually, that he was almost a quarter million dollars in debt. "And"—this was a polite understatement—"he knocks back the sauce pretty hard."

"So, lucky you. You don't have to marry him."

Bonnie was silent, loath to admit that the idea of marriage had crossed her mind after the New Orleans trip.

"The great thing about an affair," Cass said, "is that you give what you can give, take what you can, and don't think further than the present."

"He's asked me to go to Rome with him this summer."

"I'd definitely include that in the present," Cass amended.

Nesha licked her hand as Bonnie petted his muzzle. "So, Riz is fine for the present," Bonnie said, "but for continuity, consistency, and affection I should stick with Nesha?"

"You got it." Cass laughed and reached over to scratch Nesha. "Ten years from now you think Riz'd be as happy to see you as that pup was today?"

Chapter XIX

Most of the houses on the street were dark, but as Hilly pulled in behind Ruth's clunker, she saw a faint glow coming through the living room curtains. It was too late for an unannounced visit, but she felt so guilty that she'd decided to drive by after work. Here was Ruth, going through one of the worst times in her life, and she, her oldest and best friend, had shamefully neglected her. But what with Hermina and JoJo being out of school for Easter vacation, increased holiday business, and breaking in a new busboy/dishwasher (not to mention her nights with Jess and the mad dash home the next morning to feed the animals and get fresh clothes), she'd hardly had time to draw breath. She thought she'd see her at school once classes resumed, but today, when Ruth failed to turn up, she'd known she'd have to go by.

After cutting off the motor, she shoved her swollen feet into her shoes, got out of the car, quietly closed the door, and advanced up the steps. She knocked, waited, heard canned laughter, tried the door, and found it unlocked. "Ruthie?" she ventured, stepping in. Ruth, in her robe with a scarf wrapped around her neck, sat on the couch with Moo's sleeping head in her lap, staring straight ahead at the screen. The heat was turned up high, trapping a strange combination of smells (broccoli, Vicks, and singed hair?). "Ruth. Did you know you left the door unlocked?"

"Oh, did I?" She looked up briefly, then turned back to the screen. "I thought you'd still be at work."

"The new boy's cleaning up." Hilly waited for further acknowledgment and, when she didn't get any, said, "He only does round cleaning, but I'm gonna teach him square cleaning." It was a joke they'd made up when they'd been young housewives: "Round cleaning" was when you just tidied the center of a room, "square cleaning" was when you got into the corners. "Why are you wearing that scarf on your neck?"

"Sore throat," Ruth said in a dull voice.

"And what's that smell like burnt hair?"

"I burnt myself while I was cooking dinner." She took her hand from Moo's head. The sleeve of her robe fell back, exposing a makeshift bandage held down with Scotch tape. "I'm all out of Band-Aids."

"Oh, God, Ruthie."

"Don't worry. It's not serious. You know I'm just naturally clumsy."

"No, I didn't know."

The *Late Show* audience whooped and applauded as David Letterman announced the next celebrity guest. Hilly stepped to the TV, hand poised. "Mind if I turn this off?"

Moo snuffled and shifted in her sleep. "Both the kids have colds," Ruth said. "Now Moo's got an earache. I hope it's not an infection; I can't hardly afford an antibiotic."

"Turn on the light, an' I'll carry her in." Ruth reached to turn on a table lamp while Hilly bent, inched her hands under Moo, and lifted her. "How come they seem to weigh more when they're asleep?" she asked, regaining her balance before she started into the darkened kitchen. Switching on the hall light with her elbow, she made her way to the kids' bedroom.

A low-wattage Mickey Mouse lamp was on the stand between the twin beds. Settling Moo into the empty one, she turned to Kylie. His forehead was creased; his pigeon chest heaved; he looked like a little old man. As she pulled up the covers and reached to turn off the lamp, his hand unconsciously searched under the pillow and found a flashlight. Hilly put her hand in the small of her back, stretched, and sighed. A couple of weeks ago, when Kylie and Moo had first spent the night with Jess's kids, Kylie'd announced that he wasn't afraid of the dark and didn't need a night-light. Poor little bastard. Was life always two steps forward, one step back? And if your mother deserted you after stealing from your grandma and her friends, could you ever go forward again? But, she told herself as she left the room, kids were remarkably resilient. Ruthie was the one she was worried about. She'd never seen her this bad before. Not when Freddie had first started acting up. Not even when her mother had died.

Reentering the kitchen, she turned on the light. Dirty dishes were piled so high she had to lift some out of the sink so she could fit the kettle under the faucet. "I'm makin' tea," she yelled, "it'll help your throat," though she doubted there was anything physically wrong with Ruth's throat. Fear had constricted it, closed it right over, as it always had.

"That bottle you left here months ago's still under the sink," Ruth called back.

"Naw. I'm off the sauce. Got any lemon?" she called back, but got no response.

She washed dishes while waiting for the kettle to boil, and as the tea was steeping, she crawled up on a chair to pull a serving tray that probably hadn't been used since Christmas from the top shelf. After setting teapot, cups, sugar bowl, and paper napkins on it, she carried it into the living room and placed it on the coffee table. "Can I cut this off?" she asked again, moving to the TV. "Ruthie," she reminded her as she did so, "you don't like TV. You particularly don't like David Letterman. You always said he was mean-spirited, remember?" It was time to talk turkey. "Called you yesterday and today, but you didn't pick up. And you weren't at school today, were you?" She pulled up an armchair, sat, and poured a cup of tea. Ruth accepted it without thanks. "Miz Cullman an' the gals were askin' after you," she went on, filling her own cup.

Ruth took a sip, brought her hand to her throat, and remained silent.

"You got another call from Detective Bethune, right?" she prompted, dumping a heaping spoonful of sugar into her cup. Ruth nodded. "Miz Cullman told me she got one too. Bethune's such a gentleman." In the scheme of things, Roxy's crime was small potatoes, but Bethune had done all he could do to pursue it. Soon after the disappearance they'd learned that Roxy had run up a couple of thousand dollars on Bonnie's credit card the day she'd hit Atlanta but had the sense to stop using it after that. A week later the minivan had been sold in a used car lot in Oklahoma City. The trail had gone cold until a few days ago, when Johnette had been arrested for soliciting in Las Vegas.

Ruth said, "He said Johnette told him Roxy was fine last time she saw her, but she claims she has no idea where Roxy went after they split up."

"Maybe if the cops lean on her, she'll recover her memory," Hilly said, though she was sure Johnette would have already squealed like a stuck pig if she'd thought it would do her any good.

Ruth covered her eyes with her hand. "I keep seeing her stranded on some highway or passed out and hurt in some alleyway."

"Naw. She's way too smart for that." Her own imagination, closer to the mark, she was sure, pictured Roxy with the best fake ID money and/or sexual favors could buy. She'd be sporting a new hair color and do, wearing tinted contact lenses, answering to Tori or Star, and shacked up with some drugstore cowboy, having the time of her life, saving up for breast implants and hoping for a career in the movies or at least a topless bar. With luck they'd never hear from or about her again.

"And I keep remembering . . ." Ruth said.

"Sure you do." Even Jack the Ripper had a mother.

"I keep going back over things, back to when she was little, wondering where I could've made the difference, wondering where I went wrong."

"You didn't do anything—"

"The morning she left, I should've guessed from the way she was acting that something . . . You know I called her Roxanne after the heroine in a play I'd read in college. I thought it was such a pretty name, but right after she was born, Freddie started calling her Roxy. I always thought that sounded cheap, but after a while I just gave in and started calling her that too."

Hilly set down her cup and leaned forward. "Ruthie, you've gotta snap out of this."

Ruth nodded. "I know. Because the children—"

"Not just for the kids. For yourself. Look at you: moping around here, burning yourself on the stove, watching TV, not answering the phone. Ruthie, you need help. You're real depressed."

"I can't afford—"

"I know someone's got some antidepressants. I could get her to have her prescription filled for you."

"If I'm depressed, it's because of what's actually happened. How's a pill going to change reality?"

"I mean," Hilly argued in a soft voice, "you're not even turning up at school."

"You think I can face Miz Cullman and all those women who worked so hard?"

"Hey, they don't hold you responsible." This was not entirely true. While most of the women felt sympathy and concern for Ruth, there were a few who dredged up incidents from the past and nattered about how Ruth had always let Roxy get away with murder. "Miz Cullman's sure not mad at you. She's got her own problems 'cause they're not renewing her contract. And she's just worried that you aren't coming to school. Hey, even Celia's sympathetic. She's planned some kinda potluck at her church to help raise some money." No point mentioning that Celia'd preceded that announcement with a lecture about family values.

"See what I mean? The whole town knows. Some little boy at Kylie's school told Kylie his mother was a thief."

Hilly threw back her head and ran her fingers through her hair. "Sticks and stones. I've been the main source of gossip in this town since I been here, an' I'm still standin', ain't I?"

"I feel like I should stay at home with the children. I can't abandon them now."

"Nobody says you should. But you can't build your whole life around your grandkids."

"They're not just my responsibility. They're the only reason I have to get up in the morning. I don't know if you can understand, but when I see that Moo's finally learned to dress herself or Kylie's learned to put the toilet seat back down . . . it's the only time I can see that I've actually made a difference in the world."

Hilly took a deep breath and tried again. "I also ran into Professor Ledforth today. She said I was s'posed to remind you that the deadline for your application to the U of A is coming up. An' when Bonnie was in Birmingham, she called this woman she knows who teaches there, and the woman—I think she's a professor too—she wants you to come visit. Seems like she's got a carriage house behind her house or an apartment over her garage or something, and maybe she'd let you live there in exchange for housecleaning. If your scholarship comes through and you've actually got somewhere to live . . . I mean, dammit, Ruth, it's all falling into place! You could graduate from Marion Hawkins in just a couple of months. You can't give up your education now. Not when you've come this far."

Ruth's laugh was more like a whimper. "I never thought I'd hear you beating the drum for education."

"For you! For what you've always wanted!" Hilly was exasper-

ated. "You drop out, you pass up this opportunity you've been waiting for all your life, you raise Moo and Kylie, an' fifteen years from
now they'll be gone, and you'll be the oldest woman flippin' burgers
at McDonald's, and you'll be lucky if they remember to send you a
basket of fruit at Christmas, which is the most your son Curtis ever
does." She could see that hit home.

Ruth's eyes drifted up to the ceiling. "I always figured the boys
would leave without looking back. Once they started fighting with
Freddie, I wanted them to leave without looking back."

"I'm sorry. I know how much you loved—love—them."

"Love them I do, but I've been thinking a lot, and looking back,
I think I fussed over them so because I had to hide a resentment from
myself. I knew getting pregnant was cutting off my life. Roxy was the
only one I planned, the only one I really wanted. I was so happy she
was a girl 'cause I thought girls always stayed, even when they had a
family of their own. I wanted"—she unwrapped the scarf and began
to massage her neck—"to give her all the things I'd never had. I don't
mean pretty dresses or even an education. I wanted to give her a sense
of herself, so she could speak up, like I never could."

Hilly bent forward, elbows on knees, head in her hands, silent for
a long time. Finally she said, "I told Jess I loved him. He asked me to
marry him."

"Oh, Hilly, that's wonderful!"

"I dunno. Right after I told him, I started acting like a horse's ass.
Couldn't sleep. Left his bed and went back to the trailer. Came in late
the next day an' barely spoke to him."

"But why?"

"Why'd you think! 'Cause I know when you really love someone—man or child—it's like putting your head in a noose."

"Not with Jess."

"No." She raised her head and smiled. "Not with Jess. He even
understood why I was acting crazy 'cause he's been burned too. Took
me over twenty-five years to be ready to try again. But you ain't got

that kinda time. This college carousel's not gonna ride by that gold ring another time. Damn, Ruth, I gotta have some air. This place stinks." She strode to the front door, flung it back, and looked out into the night.

"I do understand what you're saying," Ruth said. "It's just that I don't see how I—"

"Jess and I've been talking 'bout the kids. His—I mean ours— and yours. No reason why we can't take Moo and Kylie while you go off to university."

Ruth swallowed. "That's the most ridiculous thing I've ever heard."

"What's so ridiculous?" Hilly demanded, walking back to the couch, hands on hips.

"I couldn't . . . And how could you?"

"I figure it's kinda like keepin' pets: You got to care for a couple, you may as well have a couple more."

"That's crazy."

"Don't see why. We got a whole floor upstairs at the restaurant. We can put Kylie in with JoJo, and Moo in with Hermina. The big ones'll help the little ones. We'll feed four instead of two, we'll put four in the car and drive 'em to school, *no problemo*. And they'd have a foster father. You can't believe how good Jess is with kids. He's real kind, but he don't take no bull."

"People just don't—"

"They sure do. My grandma had six of her own, but she found my uncle Lyman on the steps of her church and raised him up just like one of the family. An' a few weeks ago I saw some couple on *60 Minutes* who'd adopted ten kids. An' those kids were all foreigners, all different shapes, sizes, and colors, some couldn't even speak English, but they got along fine. What's that thing you say about desperate times requiring desperate measures?"

"You couldn't possibly—".

Hilly was firm. "We could if you could. Wouldn't be like you were givin' them up. You could drive down and see them whenever you had the chance. Spend holidays an' all. And it'd only be till you got your degree and got a job." She had a sudden, uncontrollable need to yawn. "Dear God, it must be past midnight," she said, blinking as she closed her mouth and reached for her purse. "Think on it. And think hard," she ordered. "Now get up and lock the door after me."

Ruth trailed her to the door. She touched her arm and turned her around as Hilly stepped out, not being able to say anything.

Hilly shivered and yawned again. "Damn it's chilly out here." She started down the steps, calling over her shoulder, "If you don't pick up that phone tomorrow, I'm callin' the fire department."

Ruth watched Hilly's car until it turned the corner. The street was dark and blessedly quiet. Her feet and hands were chilly but the fresh air was enlivening. She drew in a deep breath and tipped back her head to gaze into the night sky. How long had it been since she'd been alone looking up at the night sky? Even as a child she'd been captivated by the heavens. Sharing a bed with her sister and baby brother, she'd crawled over their sleeping bodies to sit at the window, wondering if God really did live up there and if He really did listen to her prayers. Her daddy'd called her "Mooncalf" and she'd loved the nickname—until she'd found out that it meant she was born a fool. Her aunt Sissy gave her a dollar for her ninth birthday and she bought a glow-in-the-dark map of the constellations at the Salvation Army store. Later still, she used her baby-sitting money to buy astrology magazines. She read them aloud to her mama until one day her mama had said, with unaccountable viciousness, "Your daddy bein' an Aries an' me bein' a Pisces don' hardly explain why I hate him so. This astrology's just hogwash." After that she'd kept the magazines to herself, looking for auspicious dates for romance. But Miss Bradshaw, her high school teacher, had approved her interest, though she guided it in other directions. Astrology, Miss Bradshaw said, was just fun, but, from the beginning of time, thinking people had always looked to the heavens to understand life: Astronomy was a science that had existed for thousands of years. And poets had often found inspiration in the heavens.

Tucking her robe around her legs, Ruth sat down on the steps leading to the front door. Miss Bradshaw was probably long dead. She'd never get to tell her what a wonderful teacher she'd been.

The chilled concrete seeped through her buttocks but she looked up, remembering when, just before they were married, she and Freddie walked through a moonlit, open field. She'd stared up, saying "Looking at the stars makes you feel . . . ," and he'd cut in, saying, "Yeah, makes you feel small" before he'd fixed his mouth to her neck. Even as he'd drawn her down to the ground she'd thought, No, it makes you feel both small and large. It's a mystery. Like love.

Looking up at the full moon and the starry skies, she gave way to the wonder of it. It was a mystery. She wasn't just an unemployed, middle-aged grandmother in a small Alabama town. She was a conscious part of God's universe. Anything was possible.

Chapter XX

"*I* sure wish there was some way to get to Florabama without driving," Elice complained, checking herself in a compact mirror and adjusting her sunglasses before looking out the passenger window. They were only an hour out of Birmingham, but she was already fidgety. If, God forbid, the Duke drove in the fast lane, their lives were at risk; if, as now, he kept to the slow lane, they were never going to get there. And she hadn't wanted to go in the first place.

"If we'd flown down," the Duke said, "it would've meant getting to the airport at our end, landing in Mobile, and either renting a car or having Bonnie pick us up. Right now she's packing up to leave, so she doesn't have time to be driving back and forth to Mobile."

"I still don't see why we have to go."

"We're going," he reminded her, "to see the graduation and meet some of the these ladies Bonnie's been working with. We're also going because our old friend Marion Hawkins is speaking at the commencement and has invited us."

"Bonnie didn't sound very enthusiastic about our coming."

"That's because she didn't want us to go to any trouble."

"Since she didn't ask us to stay with her, I guess *she* didn't want to go to any trouble either."

"She didn't ask us to stay because she's packing up the house she's been renting and she's planning to leave in a few days herself."

"I think it's because she didn't want us to see the place."

"And I think"—he was getting impatient—"it's because she knew we'd be more comfortable at Marion's. Besides, I haven't driven this road in years. It's nice to be able to look around."

"*Don't* look around," Elice warned. "Keep your eyes on the road."

"This patch we're going through was all woods with a rutted two-lane highway when I was a boy. And see that industrial park comin' up on your right?" He inclined his head and pushed his glasses back onto the bridge of his nose. "I helped put together the deal for that way back in the sixties." He squinted at it and sighed. "I think I liked it better when it was virgin land, but people've got to eat."

She reached over to rub his knee. "Never heard you say you preferred anything virgin."

He laughed and patted her hand. "If you're concerned about my driving, you'd best not be squeezin' my leg, girl."

"You know, Daddy, they've got these new cars with cruise control, and if you insist on driving—"

"Nothing wrong with this car, Elice."

"It's not like we don't have the money." She stopped herself from adding that they'd have even more if they weren't supporting Bonnie's kids.

"I like things I'm used to. My car's still fine. And my wife's still fine." He knew better than to think he'd placated her, but she was quiet for a while, no doubt figuring out another line of attack. He'd realized early in the marriage that the vivacity that had initially attracted him to her was no more than chronic restlessness. For a time he'd tried to calm it, as one might try to find toys to amuse a baby, because she was his baby and he did love her, and when he'd vowed for better or for worse, he'd meant it. When he'd had an active life away from the house, things had been fine, but since his retirement he'd felt his energy wane, and her constant discontents had become more burdensome.

"Did you get a chance to look at those cruise brochures I put on your desk?" She started up again. "'Cause if we're going, we should book soon so we can get a good cabin." No response. "The doctor told me they've got seasick pills that are more effective than the ones you were taking when we went at Christmas." Still no response. "I don't see how a man who spent four years in the navy gets seasick."

"I was seasick then too, but since the enemy was firing on us, I didn't notice it so much." He punched on the radio and stared out the windshield, thinking back to the first time he'd seen the ocean and those wild and woolly days when you didn't have to be a poet or a sick person to think of death every damn day of your life, thinking further back to when he'd been a barefoot boy. It had all been farmland and piney woods, and every boy, and more than a few of the girls, knew how to handle guns, but they used them to hunt deer and wild turkey instead of taking them to high school to shoot up their classmates. Who would have believed such a thing could happen in America? Closer to home, who would've thought that he'd have a grandson who believed that eating meat was morally wrong?

"'Course, if you're dead set against another cruise"—Elice was talking again, cutting into his reverie—"we might think about going to Europe. Rita says Rome is worth seeing. This is the time of life when people get up and go."

He thought Rome probably *was* worth seeing but didn't think it was worth traveling there to see it. Why did people want to uproot themselves, trek all over the world, and drop a bundle just to have some of the comforts they enjoyed at home? "Sugar, if you want to get up and go, why don't you get up and go with your friend Rita? You gals could have yourself a good ol' time."

"You know I can't leave you alone."

"On the one hand, you're telling me I should be hauling my tail all over the world; on the other hand, you're telling me I'm so feeble I can't be left alone."

"Watch where you're going!" she said. "You're veerin' into the other lane."

"Then stop talkin' at me, darlin'." He righted the wheel and glanced over at her. "I don't want you to be feeling tied down. I mean it. You and Rita plan a first-class trip anywhere you like. I'll even pick up the tab for both of you."

"Rita's got plenty of money," she said indignantly. "And why would I want to be goin' off with another woman? I want an escort."

He shook his head. "And you've just got an old tired husband."

"Don't be sarcastic."

"I wasn't." Much as she annoyed him, it still pained him when he couldn't satisfy her. Maybe they'd aged at different speeds, or maybe getting older had just made it harder to ignore their essential differences. "Not to change the subject, but I saw a sign for a Cracker Barrel a few miles back. What say we stop off and get us some beans, greens, and corn bread."

"No, thank you." Her mouth bunched like a turtle's. He could see that she was about to bring out the big guns. "I know the real reason you're dragging us down to Florabama: You've got something cooked up with Marion, haven't you?" She didn't have to wait for an answer. She'd been two jumps ahead of him for over thirty years, and when Marion Hawkins had come by a couple of weeks ago with a good-looking younger man by the name of Scott Mallory, she'd known something was up. The three men had closeted themselves in the Duke's library for over an hour, and when they'd come out, the Duke was grinning like a compulsive gambler who was getting the chance to play a final hand. "How big a check you write for Mr. Mallory's campaign? And what's Marion going to do to return the favor?"

"I said I'd endorse Mallory," the Duke conceded, dodging the other questions. "Talked to him, listened to him. He looks like a good man to me." He'd liked the cut of Mallory's jib. And the fact that Mallory was a widower about Bonnie's age had not escaped his attention. "With Marion's support I don't see why he can't win that state senate seat."

"How much?" she pestered.

"Sugar, do I ask you to account for your shopping bills?"

"But you know how much they are."

"OK. Five thousand." More like twenty-five, but a man had to have a few secrets; elsewise he'd consider himself henpecked.

She was dubious, but quiet, waiting for her suspicions to come to a full boil. "You asked him to help Bonnie get another job, didn't you?"

His mouth opened in denial, then closed in a sheepish smile.

"Well, don't think Bonnie's going to thank you for your interference. She didn't like it when you got Marion to mess in her business the first time and—"

"She wouldn't have known if you hadn't told her about it."

"—and she's not going to like it now," she overrode him.

"She didn't like it 'cause she's too honorable to want special favors, but she was glad I did it."

"When she was up at Thanksgiving, she gave me this big lecture 'bout not interfering in your children's lives, and I don't think—"

Now he cut her off, pointing through the windshield to the car driving in front of them. "Elice, see that bumper sticker? Will you let me get one like that?" It said, I NEVER DRIVE FASTER THAN MY GUARDIAN ANGEL CAN FLY. He stepped on the accelerator, passed the car, and, as she put her hand on her chest and closed her eyes, squeezed her leg again. "Sure I can't talk you into some beans and greens?"

Ever since she'd received the invitation to Marion Hawkins's PIG ROAST & FISH FRY—STRICTLY CASUAL to be held the night before graduation, Bonnie'd been thinking of how she could beg off. She'd spent most of the past week getting ready for the move, but things were still topsy-turvy. The prospect of driving hours to attend a party to which half the state had been invited was the last thing she wanted to do. But when the Duke'd called late that afternoon to say that he and Elice had arrived at Marion's and couldn't wait to see her, she knew she'd have to bite the bullet. Not only was she anxious to see him, but her presence would block any further suggestion that they come to visit her. Elice, she knew, was desperate to see where she'd been living, and she wasn't about to give her the chance to feign surprise and sympathy.

A fireball sun was starting to set when she hauled out a white eyelet summer dress she'd already packed, gave it a quick press, and headed to the shower. After putting on her makeup and pulling her hair into a ponytail, she tore out of the house in such a tizzy that she was halfway down the steps before she realized she was barefoot. Going back in, she found a pair of sandals, pulled them on, ran to the kitchen to retrieve the map to Marion's house, told Nesha to behave, and ran out the door.

Be calm, she told herself, as she lead-footed the accelerator until the speedometer hit seventy-five, there'll be so many people there it won't matter if you're late. She put in her New Age CD, but the sound of surf and tinkling bells only fueled her impatience. It was hard to go with the flow when you were swimming against the tide. Moving was a major life stress, right up there next to divorce and losing your job, and here she was, lost again in the Bermuda triangle of all three. Tuning in a local radio station that alternated rockabilly with agricultural reports, she went through her itinerary for the next few weeks: She'd drive to Birmingham and deposit her things at the Duke's, then drive up to Brown to pick up Gervaise. After that she'd go to Atlanta. There'd been a firm, if not impressive, offer on the house. She'd stay with Nikki while she considered that, meet (for the last time, she hoped) with divorce lawyers, and supervise the sale of the truckloads of goods she'd left in storage. After that . . . God only knew.

It wasn't as though she were an orphan of the storm. Both her kids, either because they genuinely wanted to be with her or maybe because they felt sympathetic, had invited her to spend time with them. Eugene had asked her to come to the organic farm where he and Fern would be working and stay as long as she liked. Gervaise, who planned to "squat" with friends in the Fifth Avenue apartment her roommate's parents were vacating for the summer, had made a more circumspect ("maybe for a long weekend") offer, but an offer nonetheless. Riz was still trying to talk her into a trip to Italy. And she could stay with the Duke and Elice as long as she wanted. It wasn't as though she didn't have options. But contemplating them was like surfing cable TV: lots of choices, none of them appealing.

Staying with the Duke and Elice was out of the question.

She did want to spend time with Eugene, even thought she might enjoy hunkering down in a sleeping bag and eating brown rice and steamed carrots in a communal kitchen. But how long could she put up with Fern before she told her she thought she was a prig and then headed for the nearest Burger King?

The visit to Gervaise seemed even less promising. Staying with a group of twentysomethings in an upscale apartment would make her feel like a gofer on that MTV show titled *Real Life* (to her mind anything but) that she'd tuned in to by accident and had assiduously avoided ever since. She probably couldn't get through the weekend without telling them to grow up and hang up their clothes.

And Riz? Flying off to play Wendy to his Peter Pan was tempting, but she was hesitant. They'd never spent more than three days at a stretch together, and she was afraid things would unravel if they were forced to be in one another's company for an entire month. Besides, there was the money question. She couldn't afford to pay her own way, which she wanted to do. A few days ago when they were talking on the phone, Riz, in an earnest but surprisingly gauche attempt to convince her, had said he didn't want to travel alone and always picked up the tab for his companion. She'd winced at the generic "companion," but that was all she wanted to be. Provided she had enough "mad money" to go off by herself if he decided to spend more time in bars than museums, it was bound to be enjoyable. But who would take care of Nesha while she was gone? And more to the point, how could she go traipsing off to Italy when she didn't have a job or a home to come back to?

It was almost dark as she exited the highway near the Tombigbee River. After pulling to the side of the deserted road, she examined the map, then switched on the headlights and headed into thickly forested land dotted with NO TRESPASSING signs. After a couple of miles the paved road ended, and she saw a handmade sign nailed to a tree, directing her to turn right. To judge from the number of cars parked amid the trees, it seemed that Marion had indeed invited half the state. She got out of the car, breathed the humid woodsy air enriched by the aroma of roasting pork, and started up the wide dirt road to the house. It was a sprawling single-story structure so lacking in architectural pretension that it resembled a motel. Marion was standing at the open door on the well-lit veranda, pumping the hand of a stocky man in jeans and a plaid shirt, booming, "Calhoun Waters! Haven't seen you since Jesus had the mumps." After ushering him into the house, he spotted her and called, "Here she come! Rings on her fingers an' bells on her toes. You get lost, Miss Bonnie?" She started to apologize, but he cut her off, planting a kiss on her forehead, then took her by the arm and led her down a long passageway past a gun case that looked as though it belonged in the Smithsonian.

The living room had sliding glass doors opening onto a patio where the majority of guests had assembled. A smaller crowd lingered inside, men clustering around the bar while the women sat on couches. As she looked around for the Duke, Bonnie's attention was taken by the portrait above the stone fireplace. It showed Marion's long-dead wife, Hermione Gladys, a formidable-looking woman corseted into a teal lace evening gown with a matching stole. The artist had been talented enough to capture the steely eyes beneath the Mamie Eisenhower bangs, but commercial enough to give the mouth a sweet, if less convincing, smile. Bonnie doubted Hermione Gladys would be smiling if she could see her living room now. Certainly she would never have allowed Marion to live in the easy, verging on shabby, style with which he was most comfortable. Couches and chairs were swathed in slipcovers that, one guessed, had once been red but were now a bleached-out salmon; the walls were decked with a set of steer's horns and several antique rifles; the coffee table held a large and messy collection of magazines, souvenir ashtrays, and a couple of cans of bug spray.

"Here she is. Here's your lil gal," Marion bellowed to the Duke, who was leaning against the bar, jawing with a couple of cronies.

"You mean my big girl," the Duke corrected, smiling broadly as Bonnie moved toward him. Embracing her, he whispered, "Great to see you, darlin'. Got to talk to you in private later." She accepted a glass of wine before he led her over to the couch where Elice was settled.

Elice pursed her lips in the direction of Bonnie's cheek and greeted her with "Lucky we're here. I like to die drivin' down. You know your daddy's not fit—"

The Duke interrupted with "Let's all go out back where the folks are, shall we?" He offered his hand to her, but Elice demurred with a shake of the head and a tight little smile that said blue jeans, beer, and barbecue were a bit too rustic for her refined tastes. "You and Bonnie go. You know those bugs will eat me alive."

Outside, the Duke was in his element. Vigorous and animated, he knocked back his bourbon with only an occasional glance in the direction of the living room, introducing Bonnie to so many people she gave up on trying to remember their names. "There's someone else I want you to meet," he said, his eyes raking the crowd, "but I don't seem to see him."

"Can we get something to eat while you're looking? I'm starved."

They made their way through the tents, passing tubs of ice and beer, tables laden with corn bread, coleslaw, relishes, and sliced fruit that were set close to the barbecue pit. A crew of black men, wearing chefs' hats and aprons over work shirts and jeans, carved and served the pig and dipped into the deep fryer to bring up sizzling catfish and snapper. Waiting to be served, they started to chat but were interrupted by a cob-nosed man who slapped the Duke on the back and asked, "'Member me?"

"I'd know your hide if it was braided in a whip," the Duke assured him. "Hunley Ward, Mobile Chamber of Commerce, am I right?" The two men smoozed while Bonnie filled her plate.

The Duke tried to disengage himself, but Hunley persisted with "Got any ideas 'bout how we might boost the tourist trade for the Mobile Mardi Gras? You know we had Mardi Gras 'fore they had it in Naw'lins, but they're the ones getting the big bang from the tourist buck."

Knowing the Duke loved to be asked for advice, Bonnie excused herself and wandered away, looking for a place to sit down and eat. The thought of making small talk with strangers didn't appeal, so she passed the tables and went to the periphery of the patio. Standing next to a bug zapper and looking into the woods, she saw a greenhouse maybe fifty feet away and went over to it.

She sat on a wooden bench next to a potting table just inside the door. The hush, the dim light, and a flowery smell so subtle she couldn't identify it were wonderfully relaxing. She forked into the food, relishing every bite. Wiping a smear of sauce from her chin, she heard a rustle and, glancing up, saw some giant ferns move. A man in an open-necked white shirt and khakis walked slowly from the rear of the greenhouse. "'Scuse me," he apologized, as surprised to see her as she was to see him. "I didn't mean to scare you. I just came in for a little peace and quiet. Guess you did too."

"Crowds," she said. "They can get to you."

"I enjoy crowds. I just have to get away from them when I start listening to my own voice." He was about her age, lanky and slouch-shouldered, with big hands and thinning fair hair. "May I?" he asked, indicating the bench. She nodded and moved slightly, though there was plenty of room. Sitting down, he asked, "Have you known Marion long?"

"All my life," she answered, taking in the purposeful jut of his jaw.

"I've known him for some years myself, but I'd never come down to his place before. You learn a lot about someone when you see them on their own turf. I never would've pegged Marion as someone who'd be interested in raising orchids."

"Is that what they are?" she asked, peering into the gloom.

"Ferns and orchids. Mostly orchids. He showed me around this afternoon before the party got going. He was more excited about showing me this hybrid Lady Slipper or Golden Slipper or some such than I've ever seen him before."

"Too bad I can't turn on the lights and see them. I wouldn't have guessed that about Marion." To keep the conversation going, she asked, "Are you interested in horticulture?"

He laughed, shaking his head. "No, ma'am. I was a history major in college. My wife used to say I couldn't tell a lily from a geranium. No, I came to talk to Marion about raising money." Spreading his legs, resting his forearms on his thighs and looping the fingers of his large hands, he bent forward, saying, almost to himself, "I used to think if you were clever enough to get a lot of money, you had to be stupid enough to want it. But now I've changed my tune because I need it to do what I want to do."

She was curious to know what he wanted to do but didn't ask. He didn't seem the type, but maybe he was promoting some hare-brained business scheme. "Well, it's all relative, isn't it? Some people make six figures, and they're still in debt and still chasing more; others get by on unemployment."

"Sure. Money doesn't buy contentment, but it sure as hell puts a down payment on possibility."

"Well, I do sympathize with your efforts to raise money. I used to do a lot of volunteer fund-raising in Atlanta. At first I was shy about asking for it, but I found I could be quite persuasive if it was for a good cause."

"Like?"

"Oh, arts in the schools programs. Things like that."

He looked at her more closely. "And what are you up to now?"

"I'm a special counselor at Marion Hawkins College, working with women who were fired from their jobs at Cherished Lady. That was a mill in Florabama."

"I know," he interjected, nodding for her to go on. "Closed down last year, right?"

He seemed genuinely interested, making little grunts of affirmation as she told him about the program and the women at some length. When she said the program was ending, he surprised her by saying he knew about that too, adding, "And it's a damned shame. So what are you going to do now?"

"Damned if I know. Suffer a crisis?"

Raising the index finger of his right hand, he imitated an Asian accent, saying, "Never forget that the Chinese character for *crisis* is the same as the character for *possibility.*"

She smiled and said, "I'll try to remember that."

He got up, reaching into his back pocket to fish out a card, saying, "Never thought I'd be carrying cards 'round in my pants," and handing it to her.

She read "Scott Mallory, Esq., Jefferson, Mallory and Trask" and a Montgomery address. "I guessed you were in business or maybe an academic."

"No, ma'am. I'm Scott Mallory and"—he extended his arms, cocked his head, smiled broadly, and drawled—"I'm runnin' for the state senate. You know an' I know that the rich are gettin' richer, and the poor—not just the poor, but you workin'men an' women—don't have no ticket to ride that gravy train. I plan to fix that 'cause if we don't fix that, we're gonna end up like some banana republic. Do I have your vote? Do you have a baby I can kiss? Do you have some loose change I can tighten up?" She laughed and applauded. "Thing is," he said in his normal voice, "I do plan to fix it. Irony is, I need to raise lots of money to do it. Hey, someone's boring me, and I think it's me." The sound of a fiddle and banjo tuning up drifted in through the open door. "I'd best get out there and press the flesh. I apologize for interrupting your supper, but it's been a real pleasure to meet you, Ms.—"

"Cullman. Bonnie Cullman. Sorry," she teased, extending her hand, "but I don't have a card."

"I'd appreciate it if you'd give me a call. I'm putting a campaign staff together, and I need someone who's knowledgeable about educational programs and women's issues."

"I'll do that, Mr. Mallory."

"Please call me Scott. It was a pleasure to meet you."

"Likewise. And please call me Bonnie."

He released her hand and started out. "I'll be expecting that call."

She was surprised at the ease and speed with which he'd drawn her into conversation, but being a politician, he'd have to be good at that. Well, she thought, crumpling up her napkin, I should get out more often. Checking her watch, she saw that it was almost ten. Her mood much improved, she left the greenhouse, deposited her plate and crumpled napkin in a trash container, and scanned the crowd. There was a breeze in the smoke-sweet air, and the mood of the party had changed. The musicians were tearing through a lively rendition of "Orange Blossom Special," some guests, sated and subdued, lounged in patio chairs, but the majority, rambunctious with drink, clapped, joked, and talked in loud voices. The Duke was still over near the barbecue pit, talking to one of the men who were clearing the tables. Going up to them, she touched the Duke's arm, excused herself for interrupting, and said, "Daddy, I'm going to leave now."

"Did I give you permission, miss? I did not, and you may not," he kidded, then said, "Don't go, Bonnie. It's the shank of the evening."

"Daddy," she admonished, staring into his bloodshot eyes, "you better go easy on the booze."

"Been drinking," he confessed. "Went off my diet too. Having a great time."

"I really do have to go."

"But there's someone I want you to meet," he persisted. "This fellow by the name of—" Memory failed him. He made a fist of his right hand and thwacked it into the palm of his left. "Dammit, I hate getting old!" he said with sudden vehemence, then, light dawning, added, "Mallory. Fellow's name is Mallory."

"Scott Mallory?"

"That's the one."

"I just met him."

"Scott Mallory?"

"Yes, Scott Mallory." She raised her eyebrows. "Daddy, are we playing who's on first?"

"What did you think of him?"

"First impression, I liked him."

"Marion introduce you?"

"No. I met him in the greenhouse. We talked for quite a while. In fact, he's hiring staff for his senate campaign, and he gave me his card and told me to call him. How's that for good luck?"

"Great good luck." He beamed. "So you told him you were my daughter."

"Uh-uh." She shook her head. "That didn't come up. Why?"

"Well, I'll be damned!" He laughed and swung his head around, shouting, "Marion? Marion, where are you?" above the din.

Viewing the party from the terrace near the sliding glass doors, Hawkins waved and started to weave his way toward them.

"Elice still in the house?" Bonnie asked the Duke.

"Prob'ly already gone to our room. She's not much for the great outdoors."

"I'll just see if I can find her and say good-bye." She hugged him. "See you tomorrow at the graduation."

Reaching them, Marion asked, "Having a good time, Miss Bonnie?"

"Wonderful time, but I do have to go. Thanks for inviting me, Mr. Hawkins," she said, already stepping away.

"But wait, Miss Bonnie. There's someone—"

"Night," she called over her shoulder. Threading through the crowd and up the steps, she glanced back to see the Duke slapping Marion on the back and heard him crowing, "Didn't even need you, you ol' sumbitch! Snagged that fish on her own hook!" Daddy's sure not feeling any pain, she thought. Tomorrow, when Elice is giving him the lecture on overindulgence, I'll have to remind him that he had a great time.

Chapter XXI

Nobody has to convince me about global warming, Bonnie thought as she cut across the sun-baked lawn to the campus auditorium. Late May and it was already in the high eighties. She could only imagine what the summer would be like, but she wouldn't be here to suffer it.

Reaching the shade of the building, she ran her finger around the skirt band of the pale blue suit she'd worn on her first day of work, tucked in her blouse, and smoothed her hair. A group of kids was horsing around in the foyer, smacking one another with commencement programs. Both entrances to the auditorium were clotted with people. Since Hilly had promised to save her a seat, she eeled her way through the crowd, muttering, "Scuse me," then stood near the back row, taking in the scene.

The stage was brightly lit, the Stars and Stripes and the state flag prominently displayed. Large baskets of flowers had been placed near the wings, and double rows of chairs were set in a semicircle behind the podium. The audience was perhaps the most diverse she'd ever seen: black and white, young and old, some dressed in their Sunday best, complete with hats and gloves, others in T-shirts and jeans. Anticipation raised the decibel level to something like a rock concert.

She started down the aisle and heard a woman call her name. Pausing, she located Sue Ann and Vernette sitting over near the wall about a third of the way down, waved, and kept walking, now focusing on the VIP section down front, where she quickly spotted Elice, in dazzling lime green silk. The Duke, sensing her eyes on him, pivoted in his seat and raised his hand in greeting. She smiled, mouthed, "See you later," and turned to the center section. A nimbus of copper hair shone like a beacon from the center of a row just behind the graduates. Hilly, who had Moo on her lap, looked over, removed her purse from the seat next to her, and motioned Bonnie in. Repeating her "Scuse me," careful not to step on toes, she squeezed past a black family, dodging the grandmother's big-brimmed hat and, after patting Moo's head, eased herself into the seat.

Hilly said, "Thought you weren't gonna make it."

"I'm all behind like the cow's tail. Still packing up," she explained, showing a swollen thumb wrapped in a Band-Aid.

"Ouch," Hilly commiserated. Then, touching the arm of the girl in the white ruffled dress who sat on her other side, she said, "Hermina, I'd like you to meet Miz Cullman. Miz Cullman, this is Hermina."

"Pleased to meet you, ma'am," Hermina said sweetly, then, nudging Kylie, who sat next to her, told him, "You're s'posed to say, 'Pleased to see meet you,' dummy."

Kylie, wayward cowlick springing up from his wet-combed hair, wrists peeking out from the sleeves of the bright blue suit he'd outgrown, put Hermina in her place, with "I seen her lotsa times before, dummy."

"And this"—Hilly leaned forward, turning her head to the man sitting next to Kylie—"is my fiancé, Jess Aranda. And his son, JoJo."

Jess shifted the dark-eyed boy on his lap and reached past Kylie and Hermina to touch the tips of his fingers to Bonnie's extended hand, saying, "Is a pleasure, Meez Cullman. You I have heard very much about," before settling back.

"I've never seen you look better," Bonnie said to Hilly, and meant it. It wasn't just her outfit—a white blouse embroidered with Texas bluebells cinched by a silver belt into a full denim skirt—or her subtle makeup. Contentment softened her features and made her eyes shine, and taking a sidelong glance at Jess Aranda, Bonnie could see why.

Hilly whispered, "I'm so damn nervous you'd think I was the one graduating," and looking around at the restive crowd, she added, "Wouldn't you think they'd start these things on time?"

As if on cue, an iron-haired woman in a dark patterned dress and sensible heels stepped out from the curtains that draped the stage. Ignoring the audience, which had hushed at her appearance, she approached the organ with grim determination, sat, adjusted the bench, wrung her hands, poised them like downturned claws, and craned her neck to see into the wings. Apparently getting the signal, she pressed down on the opening bars of the processional march from *Aïda,* and the faculty, wearing their academic robes, filed in as slowly and seriously as pallbearers. Cass, walking behind her department chairman and, Bonnie was sure, wanting to goose him, shot a quick glance in her direction. The dean, a minister, Marion Hawkins, a couple of dignitaries Bonnie couldn't identify, and a stocky black man with a brilliantly colored tie moved to center stage. The dean gave a nod to the organist, who started to pump out "The Star-Spangled Banner." The audience rose, some placing their hands on their hearts, and remained standing until the anthem was concluded. The minister stepped up to the podium and began the invocation: "Dear Lord, look down upon us on this special day . . ." Moo wiggled from Hilly's lap to reach for a gum wrapper on the floor. Hermina restrained her, then pulled her onto her lap as Hilly's eyes stayed fixed on the stage. Kylie made a little fart that sent him into puff-cheeked hilarity, which Jess subdued by firmly putting his hand on the boy's shoulder. "Amen."

The dean gestured for everyone to be seated and, while they were doing so, began, "Graduates, families, friends, and honored guests . . ." His speech was as predictable as death and taxes, and the toneless quality of his voice brought the audience to a state of polite boredom in a matter of minutes. Kylie wiggled with ants-in-the-pants nervousness, twisting his head to Jess and whispering, "Where's Gramma?" Jess slid his hand onto the boy's neck, pulled his head close, whispered, and nodded to his right. Bonnie followed the direction of his eyes and saw Ruth, three rows down, third in from the aisle. Her face, in profile, had a taut but almost girlish look of expectation. Apparently she'd been persuaded to take advantage of Hilly's cosmetic skills because her lips and cheeks were rosy and her hair curled around her mortarboard.

Bonnie forced her attention back to the podium. The dean was introducing the principal speaker. Endlessly. She'd missed the name, but the compulsive and insistent bonhomie with which the dean was stressing their lifelong friendship led her to guess that the speaker was a black man. "Dr. Josiah Washington is a native son. After receiving his M.S.W., he went on to earn his Ph.D. in education. Dr. Washington is the recipient of countless awards and commendations. . . ." The dean listed them all, then, after other reference to their close friendship (by which time Dr. Washington was inching forward on his chair, evidently as eager as the audience to move things along) and a limp attempt at humor, motioned him forward.

After an exchange of "you scratch my back I'll scratch yours" compliments to the dean and an extraneous anecdote that let them know that he'd personally met Bishop Desmond Tutu (Hilly sighed deeply and closed her eyes), Dr. Washington eased into a more relaxed rhythm, leaning forward and making eye contact with the audience. His voice was a powerful well-trained instrument, and once he knew he had their attention, he cut loose. "How is this great nation going to keep being great unless the least of His children are educated to keep pace with those more fortunate? How do you older folk out there expect your Social Security checks to keep coming if we don't have an educated work force? And where will our young people get that much-needed education?" Having asked these and other rhetorical questions, he provided the answers in a thundering preacher cadence punctuated by "Am I right?" and "Do you hear me?" The response first came in single and subdued "Yes, sir" and "Tell it, brother" but soon swelled to spontaneous and passionate assent. The woman on Bonnie's right got to her feet, eyes glistening, hat trembling as she said "Yes!" to the importance and blessing of education.

"Is this a graduation or a revival meetin'?" Hilly muttered as Dr. Washington finished, mopping his brow and bowing to applause that bounced off the walls.

"Aw, come on," Bonnie whispered. "He was good."

Hilly grudgingly admitted that he was, stopped using her program as a fan, and inspected it to see what was next. "Presentation to Marion Hawkins," she groaned.

The dean introduced Marion Hawkins as another "illustrious and dear friend of long standing, without whose generous support this college . . ." and Marion stepped forward. Smart enough to know that Dr. Washington was a tough act to follow but that when the chips were down, speechifying was no match for monetary support, Marion kept his remarks brief but became positively and, Bonnie believed, sincerely moved when he spoke of his pleasure in looking at "all these fine young people who're about to go out into the world from our own local college." There was polite but sustained applause.

Bonnie crossed and recrossed her legs, wishing she hadn't worn panty hose. Hilly eased a bra strap. Kylie wiggled and, in a stage whisper, asked, "When does Gramma come on?," raising a few titters in the immediate vicinity. The dean, glancing in the direction of the disturbance, cleared his throat and announced the presentation of degrees. The organist bore down on the march from *Aïda* yet again. The first row of graduates rose, filed into the aisle, and started up the steps to the stage. Hilly tensed. Kylie craned his neck. Hermina lifted Moo so she could see better. One of the professors lifted the box of diplomas onto the table next to the podium. The dean put on his reading glasses, checked the list of names, announced, "Jamal T. Anderson," and the parade of graduates began. Watching them take that long walk across the stage, Bonnie was struck by how young they were and thought, not for the first time, what courage it had taken for the women from Cherished Lady to be in classes with kids half their age who were convinced they had the world by the tail.

By the time the dean had reached the *E*'s, the stock characters—the big man on campus who raised his fists to shouts of "Yo" and "Go get 'em" when his name was called; the would-be deb, wobbly in her high heels, who almost collided with a basket of carnations; the class clown, who pulled a face and did a dance step that raised guffaws—had already appeared. Ruth, poised on the steps, neck tense, hands crossed in front of her, was so serious she almost looked sad, but when "Ruth Elkins" was called, she stepped bravely forward.

"It's Gramma," Moo squeaked.

"Hey, Gramma!" Kylie yelled. Hilly got to her feet, furiously clapping. Bonnie did the same. "Way to go, Grandma!" someone from the back shouted. "You go, girl!" another voice chimed in. The audience broke into applause that continued until Ruth, scarlet-faced, accepted her diploma. She left the stage head down and weak-kneed as the dean called for Susan B. Elrod.

Kylie asked, "Can we go now?" Jess explained sotto voce that they had to wait until everyone got his or her degree. Fifteen long minutes later, the diplomas having been passed out and the graduates back in their seats, the dean thanked everyone for coming, and the organist struck up the march from *Aïda*. "If she plays that damn thing one more time, I'll go up there and flatten her," Hilly whispered. The graduates filed out of the auditorium, the audience crowding after them.

Ruth, holding her cap and diploma in one hand and running the fingers of the other through her flattened curls, stood in the midst of the milling, noisy crowd. Her face, still flushed, broke into a broad smile as Bonnie, Hilly, Jess, and the kids made their way to her. Shaking her head, she said, "Kylie, didn't I tell you not to—"

"I think is OK." Jess came to Kylie's defense. "He was a good boy mostly."

"You did it!" Hilly cried, wrapping Ruth in a bear hug.

Eyes moist, Ruth said, "I can hardly believe it."

Moo squeezed in between them, capturing Ruth's leg. Ruth picked her up and gave her a kiss, then reached for Kylie and pulled him to her while Jess stepped back, aiming a camera, commanding, "Hold it," and clicking away. "Miz Cullman, you to push in, please," he commanded, clicking again before he told Hermina and JoJo to join the group for the master shot.

"The camera's our graduation present for Ruthie," Hilly said, taking it from Jess and urging him to take her place in the lineup, "but we've been playing with it all morning. Got a complete record of me puttin' on Ruthie's makeup and her gettin' into her gown. OK, everyone, hold it. Hold it . . . JoJo, take your finger away from your nose!" Click. "Now it's yours," she said, handing it over to Ruth.

"It's way too expensive," Ruth remonstrated. "You should hold on to it so's you can send me pictures of the kids."

"No. It's your present," Hilly insisted, forcing it into Ruth's hand.

"Congratulations, Ruth," Jess said, kissing her cheek. "Never have I attended such a ceremony. It was"—his head bobbed in affirmation until he found the right words—"very enjoyable."

"Enjoyable?" Hilly rolled her eyes. "It was about as much fun as changin' a flat tire."

Hermina said, "The best part was when Auntie Ruth was on the stage."

"'Cause she's a graduate," Kylie said proudly.

"She was the oldest one," Hermina observed.

"That makes her even more special," Bonnie told her.

"She's gonna keep going to school. She *likes* goin' to school," Kylie said, making a face at the wonder of it.

Moo cupped Ruth's ear and lisped loudly enough for everyone to hear, "Do we get cake now?"

"Yes, cake now." Ruth laughed and put her down. "Whew, it's hot." She handed her things to Hilly and unhooked her gown to reveal a sky blue cotton shirtwaist, asking, "Where's Professor Ledforth? I really want to see her."

"She said she'll meet us at the reception," Bonnie told her.

Kylie moved from foot to foot, looked up at Jess, then yanked his hand until Jess got the message. "OK, OK, we go to the men's room," Jess agreed. "You, JoJo, come too."

As he took both boys by the hand and moved into the crowd, Ruth said, "Why don't y'all go on over to the student union? I'll go lock my stuff in the car and meet you there." After quick hugs all around, she stepped into the stream of people headed for the parking lot.

"Every place we go," Hilly said, looking back at the auditorium, "Kylie wants to use the facilities. He was getting too old for Ruth to take him into the ladies'. I guess he gets a kick out of going in with a grown-up man."

"Jess is good with the children," Bonnie observed.

"Jess is good with everyone. Even me." Hilly drew in a breath that strained the pearl buttons on her blouse. "I never thought Ruthie'd make it," she confessed. "Never thought she'd get through all that other mess and keep on keepin' on."

"Without you she wouldn't have."

"You an' Miz Ledforth helped a lot." Hilly looked at Hermina, who was all ears. "Hermina, you'll get sunstroke standin' here. Why don't you take Moo and go sit under that tree?"

Hermina gave Hilly a look that let her know she wasn't dumb enough to think Hilly was concerned with the heat, took Moo's hand, said, "They want to talk grown-up secrets," and hauled the younger girl off in the direction of the tree.

"I meant," Bonnie said sotto voce, moving out of the way of another family taking snapshots, "I didn't think Ruth would actually let the kids stay with you and go off to U of A."

"Nor did I. She's always been like a tiger mama with cubs, an' after Roxy took off, she got even worse. Weren't me that finally talked her 'round; it was Jess."

"I imagine he can be pretty persuasive."

"So persuasive he talked me into givin' up my virtue," Hilly said, fluttering her eyelashes and putting a hand to her bosom as Bonnie laughed. "I get a little short with the kids sometimes, but like you say, Jess is good with 'em. Right now Ruthie takes 'em all for a few days so's Jess an' I have some time alone, then we have Kylie an' Moo stay with us a few days. We've told 'em come September, it'll be full-time." She mopped her hairline with the back of her hand and checked to see the girls settling on the grass at the trunk of the tree. "Maybe it's 'cause it's still a novelty, but they seem to be gettin' along fine. And we've talked Ruthie into renting out her house so she'll have the cash to pay for their tuition at St. Elizabeth's. She'll stay with us whenever she comes down. I guess you know I'm quitting school."

"Yes, I know."

"I got my high school equivalency, and that's enough to help the kids with their homework, leastwise till Hermina overtakes me, which I figure will be sometime in the next two weeks. The kids an' the restaurant'll take up all my time."

"And Jess."

"Oh, yeah. Jess comes first. Jess'll always come first." She moved a step closer, lowering her voice. "Did I tell you Ruth got a postcard from you-know-who last week?"

"No."

"Yep. Picture of Grauman's Chinese movie house in Hollywood, but it had a Bakersfield postmark. And the message—wait'll you hear this—the message said: 'Don't worry, I'm fine. Sorry I had to leave like that. Give my love to the kids.' Can you feature it? 'Sorry' for ripping everyone off? And 'Give my love to the kids'!" Hilly's mouth bunched as though she were about to spit.

"How did Ruth take it?"

"Relieved at first. Got all weepy. Then she got mad. I've always told her it's better to be pissed off when you're pissed on, but getting mad don't come natural to Ruth. She thought 'bout callin' the cops, but I talked her out of it. Just close the book on it, I said. 'Course you know and I know she'll never be able to do that, but she did rip up the postcard and throw it in the trash. Her mail's gonna be forwarded to our place, an' you can bet that if I get any more messages from Miss Pond Scum, I'm gonna to do the same and never tell her about it. Hey"—Hilly wriggled her shoulders as though shaking off a burden—"let's not ruin a great day by talkin' 'bout that sorry piece of work. You wanna come over to the restaurant after the reception?"

"I'd love to, but I can't," Bonnie said. "My folks are in town. In fact, I'm waiting to meet up with them now. I don't know what's taking them so long." Shading her eyes against the sun, she glanced back to the auditorium and saw the Duke holding open the door as Elice stepped out. "There they are," she said, waving.

"Your daddy's sure a fine-lookin' man," Hilly noted as they approached. "An' your mama—"

"My stepmother."

"—your stepmother, say, she's sure rigged out. Looks like one of them spokeswomen on the shopping channel."

Bonnie enjoyed a full-throated laugh. "You hit the nail on the head every time."

Joining them, the Duke apologized for keeping her waiting. Bonnie made the introductions, and the Duke, obviously impressed, said, "Miss Pruwitt, you surely were blessed with a fine head of hair," to which Hilly, mindful of Elice's envious glance, tossed off "Don't know 'bout blessed. I drink a tablespoon of cod-liver oil every night, wash it in Mane and Tail, dye it every four weeks, an' use a big ol' tease comb."

"Mane and Tail?" Elice asked, eyebrows arching.

Hilly could've played nasty with that one, but decided to be lady-like, saying, "I'd like you to meet the munchkins," and motioning the girls over.

Elice greeted them in the fluting, singsong voice people use to show they're fond of children. "Why, hello, you pretty little things. And who are you?"

Resting her hand on Hermina's shoulder, Hilly said, "This is Hermina, my fiancé's daughter."

Elice gushed, "What an unusual name!" If Elice's conversation were written out, Bonnie thought, it would be like an adolescent's letter: minimal content and maximum exclamations. "You know, Hermina," Elice went on, "I love to see a little girl with a bow in her hair. We wore bows in our hair when I was a girl."

"Hilly says it's old-fashioned, but my daddy likes it 'cause he's a foreigner," Hermina said.

"He's an American citizen," Hilly put in.

"Oh, that's nice," Elice enthused, and turned back to the girl, who was obviously going to be the best source of information. "And that little white dress makes you look sweet as divinity."

"You mean like God?" Hermina asked.

"No, no, no," Elice trilled. "Divinity is a kind of soft candy."

"My daddy makes candy. My daddy can make anything, but Hilly don't know how to cook." Remembering her manners, Hermina nudged Moo. "This is Moo. She's kinda like my sister."

"Kind of like your sister?" Elice asked with the wheedling friendliness of the Grand Inquisitor.

"Yeah, 'cause you see, Miss Hilly come to live with us, and Auntie Ruth, well, she's not really my auntie"—Hermina began, warming to her story like a reporter who'd just been released from a gag order—"but she's Hilly's friend so—"

Ever the diplomat, the Duke cut short the explanation by bending down, taking Moo's chin in his hand, and saying, "Hello to y-o-u, M-o-o," stretching the vowels till he made her giggle.

"My fiancé's gone off with the boys and—" Hilly looked behind her. "Oh, here he comes."

As Jess and the boys approached, Bonnie could see Elice struggling to figure out the tangled relationships but made no attempt to enlighten her. Moo, knowing she'd won the Duke's heart, imprisoned his leg and whined, "I'm thirsty."

After another round of introductions, they all started off in the direction of the student union. The men led the way, Kylie between them, taking exaggerated strides and looking from one to the other as though they were elder tribesmen taking him on his first hunt. Elice and Hermina followed, Hermina much taken with Elice's jewelry and, in answer to her questions, getting a "diamonds are a girl's best friend" crash course in the relative value of clear versus semiprecious stones. Hilly, Bonnie, and the younger children brought up the rear, JoJo making a play for his share of attention by slipping his hand into Bonnie's and confiding, "Garbage has come to live with us."

"Garbage is my pet goat," Hilly explained after telling Moo to pick up her feet.

"An' he stepped on Papa's garden an' Papa got real mad," JoJo informed.

"Uh-huh." Hilly said. "He does it again, an' we'll be having goat stew."

"No-o-o," JoJo wailed.

"Just kiddin'," Hilly assured him. "I had to"—she spelled it out—"k-i-l-l my chickens when I moved in with Jess. An' I'm gettin' ready to sell off my trailer 'cause once we get enough for a down payment an' Jess cleans up some legal business in California we're gonna buy the restaurant property. God"—she shook her head—"selling off my trailer hurts. But the house where we have the restaurant is real big an' Jess says he's gonna fix up this lil back room used to be a trunk room for me. He says we'll call it my sulking room, an' I can go there when I need privacy. But it's scary. Minglin' body fluids ain't near as scary as minglin' money to buy a house, know what I mean?"

"Oh, I surely do," Bonnie agreed.

"I just hope I can adjust to living with people as well as these kids have done."

"You will," Bonnie said, giving her a sidelong glance. "I'd never lived alone until this year, and I got used to it. In fact, I like it."

Hilly was contemplative. "At our age I think it's easier goin' in that direction, but hey, no one drafted me. I'll manage."

"You'll do more than manage. You'll be happy. Think you can stand it?"

They fell silent, listening to the snippets of conversation that floated back from the others. The Duke and Jess seemed to be discussing business loans. Hermina, adoringly staring up at Elice, was saying, "If I look like divinity, you look like a lime sherbet. With sprinkles."

Bonnie and Hilly locked eyes. Bonnie said, "Flattery won't hurt you."

"Not unless you inhale," Hilly added, which sent them into such giggles that the others turned around.

"I just can't believe the college didn't hire you back. Just like a damn government institution: They get someone real good so they go an' fire her."

"I didn't take it personally. It's just about funding."

"So you're gonna settle in Birmingham?"

"I don't know about settle. For now it'll be home base." On the long drive home last night she'd started thinking about the possibility of working for Mallory. Not only did she need a job, but this one sounded as though it were something she'd be good at; she'd liked Mallory; Montgomery was closer to Birmingham so she could keep an eye on the Duke. By the time she got into bed, she had been so fired up she found it hard to sleep. Not only did she want the job, but she'd decided with a confidence she couldn't have imagined a year ago that she was going to get it.

"You have a gentleman friend, don't you? Any long-term possibilities?" Hilly asked.

"He's great to be with, but I don't think we're a long-term fit."

"You mean you'd rather go to bed with him than wake up with him."

Bonnie laughed. "You hit the nail on the head again."

"Too bad it takes us so long to learn the difference. An' some women never do. Life sure do be strange, don't it?"

"It sure do," Bonnie agreed, stopping to pick up JoJo, who had been uncomplaining but was starting to drag behind.

"You two coming along?" the Duke called back.

"Comin' right along," Bonnie answered, though by now there was a good forty feet between them.

"Hey, there's the student union," Kylie yelled, racing ahead. "This here is where they have food."

"And an even better surprise," Hilly said, smiling at Bonnie. "So don't you go runnin' off."

Chapter XXII

*C*rowds of people were clustered outside the building, chatting, embracing, taking pictures, chasing children, sitting at tresseled tables or on the grass, eating from plastic plates. Just inside the doors, a reception line of school officials waited: Mrs. Jackson, in a trim black-and-white sheath; the dean; the financial aid officer; and a leggy teenage girl wearing a rhinestone tiara and a very short, very tight black dress with a ribbon draped from shoulder to hip proclaiming her "Miss Marion Hawkins." Hilly and Jess skirted the line, shepherding the children to the food table while Bonnie introduced the Duke and Elice to Mrs. Jackson, waiting until they were engaged in pleasantries before excusing herself to move into the room.

She'd been hearing about plans for the reception for weeks. Norma Jean was in charge, which probably accounted for the fact that it looked like a cross between a wedding reception and a country picnic. Pink and white balloons dangled from the ceiling, pink and white ribbons were looped at the sides of the long tables, and a swan carved out of ice, sitting in a pool jetting pink punch and surrounded by camellias from Snoopy's garden, provided the centerpiece.

The catered food—crustless white bread sandwiches, cheese, sliced fruit, raw vegetables, dip, bowls of cashews, and a large white sheet cake (already severely hacked) with "Congrats Grads" scrolled in anemic pink frosting—had been supplemented with homemade (and surely more tasty) macaroni salad, ham biscuits, lemon squares, and little pecan tarts. Norma Jean, a tiny blob of dip on the lace bib of her dress and clearly in a state of agitation, came up as Bonnie was ladling punch into a plastic champagne glass. "I tried to keep it Martha Stewart," she complained, "but people kept bringing in food, and I couldn't—"

"Of course you couldn't; that would have been rude," Bonnie commiserated. "Everything's lovely, Norma Jean. Just lovely."

"Do you really think so? 'Cause Snoopy, I mean Mrs. Snopes, said—"

"Snoopy," Bonnie told her, "would complain if angels lifted her to heaven and sat her at the right hand of God." Instead of laughing, Norma Jean looked mournful. "And where is dear Snoopy?" Bonnie asked, looking around. "Because I really don't think I can leave without thanking her for all the encouragement she's given me during my brief tenure."

"She came in to deliver the flowers, and then she started sneezing and scratching an' had to go home to get her allergy pills."

Bonnie shook her head. "Too bad I missed her."

Norma Jean turned all warm and runny, sniffing, "Miz Cullman, I'm sure going to miss you."

"We all are," Sue Ann, who'd sidled up to them, said. "Hey, Miz Cullman," she went on as Norma Jean drifted off, "the gals—at least the ones who wanted to see Ruth graduate—are over there." She motioned to a corner where Albertine, Lyda Jane, Vernette, Lorraine, and Puddin' were sitting in a circle, munching and gossiping.

"Where's Celia?" Bonnie asked.

"Well"—Sue Ann lowered her voice—"she told her husband an' everyone else she was going' off to visit her cousin in Talladega. But I know better."

Bonnie took the bait. "So where did she really go?"

Sue Ann drew closer and, in a conspiratorial whisper, asked, "'Member that guy she was always talkin' to in the chat room?" Bonnie nodded. "I happen to know"—Sue Ann paused to draw out the suspense—"that she's gone off to meet him. Yes, ma'am. They got to writing each other every day. Can you imagine fallin' in love on the Internet?"

"No," Bonnie said, "I really can't."

"Well, seems like they did. He sent her money to come meet him. Now what do you think's gonna happen?"

Bonnie said, again truthfully, "I have no idea. I can't wrap my mind around it."

"Could be she's long gone. Just like Roxy."

"What about her husband?"

"It'd serve him right. You know he's been on her case ever since she come back to school, tellin' her she was too big for her breeches, an' shouldn't be wearin' breeches in the first place 'cause she's supposed to be a Christian woman." Sue Ann's features melted into a wicked grin. "Boy, I'd love to be there when her congregation finds out."

"I guess I would too." Bonnie smiled and moved aside as the grandmother in the big hat, who'd been sitting next to her at the commencement ceremony shouldered in. "Oh, there's Albertine's husband," she said. Henry had parked his wheelchair near the window and was looking out at the more restful scene of treetops and sky. "I want to go say hello, I mean good-bye."

"Don't you dare leave 'fore you talk to me again," Sue Ann warned.

"Wouldn't think of it."

"'Cause the gals have got somethin' for you."

"I'll be right there," Bonnie called over her shoulder.

Crouching next to Henry's wheelchair, she said, "Glad you're here, Henry. Didn't see you at the ceremony."

"Too much trouble messin' with my chariot in that crowd, so we just come over here."

"Would you like me to get you anything?"

"No, ma'am. We brought those ham biscuits and ate 'bout a dozen while we were fixin' 'em. Go on and get yourself one." Since she'd had nothing since breakfast, she said she would, but as she stood up, he seized her hand and pulled her back down. "You know Albertine and Lyda Jane just sent off some more dresses to your friend in 'Lanta?"

"I do, and I'm proud of them."

"They wisht the other gals hadn't give up, but"—he sighed—"some people don't have what it takes for the long haul. We still believe we can make a business of it, but we're not doin' it as a cooperative. Albertine and Lyda Jane done formed a partnership. They're the chief executive officers, an' they're just gonna hire helpers as they need 'em. Pay 'em by the piece."

"I believe you can make a go of it," Bonnie said, the image of Lyda Jane and Albertine as "management" making her smile.

"I'll be helpin' out too. I've got my heart set on havin' a camcorder come Christmas. 'Stead of watching TV, I plan to become a documentarian of the en-tire neighborhood." He chuckled. "An' how 'bout you? You headin' out soon?"

"Tomorrow. Driving up to Birmingham."

"Then?"

She shrugged and leaned closer. "Then? Damned if I know."

Henry patted her hand. "No matter what you do, you'll do fine. You've got the mojo."

Feeling she'd been blessed, she whispered, "Thank you, Henry," squeezed his hand, got up, and headed back to the table. It looked as though it had been invaded by a plague of locusts. She managed to get the last ham biscuit but had trouble swallowing. Glancing around, she saw Cass, alone behind the service counter, reading a book. Going over to her, Bonnie said, "News flash: The ice swan's beak is starting to drip. Think we should wind this up?"

"You bet. Mark's getting off work early, so we'll be by this afternoon to help you load up."

"And claim your beautiful new-to-you mattress."

"And anything else I can get my hands on while you're not looking. That nasty Jarvis Boggs been by yet?"

"Came by yesterday to give back my cleaning deposit."

"Damn straight. Place is in a lot better shape than when you moved in. Remember when he came by when we were cleaning it up?"

"I'll never forget that day. I was so damned nervous, and you and Mark were so—" She was stuck for words.

"Stalwart, fond, and true?" Cass offered.

"Cass, I'm going to miss you so much."

"Spare me the maudlin sentiment. It's not as though I won't be seeing you again. I mean, you can get your mattress back when you find a place."

"No, thanks. I'm going to travel light for the rest of my life."

"Uh-huh. You and the Dalai Lama."

The crowd had thinned, the conversation softening to rainlike patter as people touched one another's hands and shoulders, promising to meet or call. The grandma in the big hat yanked a boy, cheeks bulging with food, eyes filling with tears, toward the door. Most of the VIPs, having put in their obligatory thirty minutes, were long gone, but Marion Hawkins, the Duke and Elice at his side, was still glad-handing stragglers as they exited. Bonnie pictured the old reprobate alone in his greenhouse, tending orchids, and felt a deep fondness for him.

Mrs. Jackson was urging two girls to start clearing the table. Ruth, ever helpful, had joined Norma Jean in picking up plates and glasses that had been left on chairs and windowsills. The Cherished Ladies were still there, sitting in a semicircle as though waiting for the weekly meeting to start. "Miz Cullman," Albertine called, "come on over, will you please?"

Dreading the good-byes, Bonnie stopped by the table to fill her glass with fruit fly punch, then walked to them. Henry, motorizing his wheelchair, followed. Marion Hawkins, the Duke, and Elice ambled over, and Ruth joined them. Guessing that she was about to be ambushed into some kind of farewell ceremony, Bonnie took a swallow of punch.

Albertine pulled a large gift-wrapped package from underneath her chair. "Where's Hilly?" Ruth asked.

"She be outside with those kids," Puddin' said. "Just hold on." She galumphed to the doors, stuck out her head, and yelled, "Yo, Hilly! Come on in!" with all the gentility of a hog caller while the others waited, smiling so insistently in Bonnie's direction that she turned her eyes back to the ravaged table.

"Sorry, sorry," Hilly gasped, rushing in, followed by Jess and the kids. "We're all here now."

Jess pulled up a chair and motioned for Bonnie to sit.

Albertine patted the package, then handed it to Hilly.

"No," Hilly remonstrated. "I'm not makin' the presentation."

"You're the one with the gift of gab," Lyda Jane said.

"No. It was Ruthie's idea, so Ruthie should present it," Hilly insisted, shoving the package into Ruth's hands and moving to stand beside Bonnie.

"Well, someone do it," Puddin' said impatiently. "We be the last ones here an' the cleanup people be wantin' us out."

"C'mon, Ruthie. You said you would." Hilly's voice was both encouraging and impatient.

Ruth sank into a chair, put the package in her lap, and smoothed the paper. Her hands were caressingly gentle, but the muscles in her throat were tight, and her mouth worked silently, forming words before she was able to speak. "This gift," she began softly, "is for Miz Cullman. It's a small token of our esteem and—" She stopped, knowing the words were so clichéd that she must sound insincere. Glancing from Cass to Hilly, she began again. "When Cherished Lady fired us"—the day came back to her in its full shock and horror—"Hilly was so mad she wanted to burn the place down; Celia was crying and praying; Albertine was real upset but trying not to show it. Lyda Jane just folded up her knitting, but her face went all ashy. It was a terrible day. I thought I'd crack. But now"—she brought her head up—"I think it was the best thing that ever happened. Not that there weren't casualties. You know and I know there were." She squeezed her eyes shut and closed her lips tight, unwilling either to visualize or to talk about them. "But"—she went on in a stronger voice—"we all know that if we hadn't been booted out of the mill, we'd have been there for the rest of our lives. I'm not so optimistic that I'd say everything happens for the best, but I do know that what seemed like the end became an opportunity." Now she was confident enough to look into their faces as she continued. "Miz Cullman, Bonnie, never saw us as sorry or treated us like names on a computer sheet." But that is how I did see them at first, Bonnie thought, lowering her head. "She always treated us as individuals who had dreams and potential. She helped us over the hump, and"—her voice cracking with emotion, Ruth swallowed again, then finished with a toastmaster's confidence—"in token of our deep respect and appreciation, we'd like to give her this small gift to remember us by." There was silence as she placed the package in Bonnie's lap. Bonnie, who couldn't do more than mutter, "Thank you so much," began to pull gently at the ribbons.

"Aw, rip it open," Hilly encouraged, making everyone laugh.

Grinning like a naughty kid, Bonnie did just that, tossing the ribbons on the floor and tearing away at the wrapping as Kylie squawked, "I know what it is. I saw 'em makin' it." As Bonnie had already guessed, it was a quilt.

"We were workin' on it same time we were makin' the dresses," Lyda Jane told her, inching forward so their knees touched. "It's an original pattern. We're callin' it Florabama. It's made from our own stuff." Albertine got up, took it from Bonnie's lap, and proudly shook it out. Sue Ann grabbed one end, Puddin' took another, Vernette the third and spread it to show its multicolored glory.

"That patch of denim is from a pair of m' ol' jeans," Albertine explained, pointing, "and this piece is from one of Lyda Jane's tablecloths. That piece over there, that bright red Lycra, that's from a Scarlet Lady bustier Hilly snitched from the factory, this lavender

batiste and green cotton's scraps from the dresses we made for Atlanta, and. . . ."

"It is truly extraordinary," Bonnie said when Albertine had finished explaining and the women had folded up the quilt and given it
back to her. "I'll cherish it. Always."

While Moo and JoJo scrambled to pick up the ribbons and wrapping, she hugged each of the women. Starting to leave, she felt arms
close tight around her and turned to see Hilly. There were tears in her
eyes, and the corners of her mouth trembled. "Don't be sad," Bonnie
comforted. "I'll come back to visit."

"It's not you," Hilly, honest to the last, told her. "It's Ruthie. She
talked. Right out in public. She made a speech to strangers. She's
never been able to talk out like that in her whole life."

"Come on now, don't be acting like that," Bonnie coaxed. Nesha,
who knew something was happening, had been mooning around and
hiding under what was left of the furniture since yesterday. Now he
was sniffing the spot on the kitchen floor where his food bowl had
been. "I've got it in the backseat of the car. You're going to be all
right." She picked him up and carried him in her arms as she walked
slowly through the house, doing a last-minute check, turning off
lights as she went because the morning sun was starting to come
through the windows.

After closing the front door behind them and depositing the key
under the front steps, she paused again. Surely she'd forgotten something, but whatever it was, it couldn't be important. "You lucky
pup," she told him, settling him into the seat beside her and starting
the motor. "You are now going to hear my entire repertoire of songs."
He growled and hid his head in the folds of the quilt. "Ganesha.
Ganesha the Great. Everything will be OK," she said, taking one last
look at the house before she pulled away. "After all, we know how to
overcome obstacles."